P9-DWS-430

ALSO BY ELIZABETH CROOK

*The Raven's Bride*
*Promised Lands: A Novel of the Texas Rebellion*
*The Night Journal*

# MONDAY,
# MONDAY

# MONDAY, MONDAY

## ELIZABETH CROOK

SARAH CRICHTON BOOKS
FARRAR, STRAUS AND GIROUX
NEW YORK

Sarah Crichton Books
Farrar, Straus and Giroux
18 West 18th Street, New York 10011

Grateful acknowledgment is made for permission to reprint lyrics from "Monday, Monday,"
written by John Edmund Andrew Phillips, performed by the Mamas and the Papas.

Library of Congress Cataloging-in-Publication Data
Crook, Elizabeth.
     Monday, Monday / Elizabeth Crook. — First edition.
         pages   cm
     ISBN 978-0-374-22882-8 (hardcover) — ISBN 978-0-374-71137-5 (ebook)
     1. College students—Fiction.   2. Campus violence—Fiction.   3. School
shootings—Fiction.   4. Psychological fiction.   I.  Title.

PS3553.R545 M77 2014
813'.54—dc23

                                                                    2013038734


Designed by Jonathan D. Lippincott

Farrar, Straus and Giroux books may be purchased for educational, business, or promotional
use. For information on bulk purchases, please contact the Macmillan Corporate and
Premium Sales Department at 1-800-221-7945, extension 5442, or write to
specialmarkets@macmillan.com.

www.fsgbooks.com
www.twitter.com/fsgbooks • www.facebook.com/fsgbooks

10   9   8   7   6   5   4   3   2   1

FOR MARC

# CONTENTS

# MONDAY,
# MONDAY

# I

# THE TOWER

Shelly stared at the graph of imaginary numbers on the chalkboard, confounding figures represented by the letter $i$ and less relevant to her life than fairies from her childhood or the vanishing rabbit in the magic show at the Student Union last week. The professor had the face of a cherub and arms too long for his squattish body, and was marking on the chalkboard as he spoke. "The square root of minus four," he said, slashing the numbers onto the board, a ring of sweat under his arm, "is two $i$. Two $i$ squared is negative four. That's two times two is four—times $i$ times $i$, which is negative one . . ."

The room was uncomfortably hot, air only slightly cooled rattling insufficiently from the vents. From her seat beside the window Shelly could see out over the trees and walkways of the South Mall. At the nearest end of the mall a gaudy fountain of bronze horsemen reared from a pond of turbid water into a shower of sunlight, towing a chariot with a winged rider. Far away at the opposite end, beyond the branches burdened with ball moss and summer foliage and large flocks of grackles, the massive stone main building, with its pillars and terraces and the tower rising nearly thirty stories, imposed itself against a hot, pale, cloudless sky.

The professor turned to the class and repeated the concept. Few of the students gave any appearance of understanding. "So we've been looking at the real numbers up to now," he said. "Numbers that fall on a number line. They include both rational and irrational numbers. Now we are talking about imaginary numbers. These fall on a different kind of number line—one that is perpendicular . . ."

Shelly began to think the cramping in her stomach might be caused by her period about to start, and she calculated the weeks. She had been home to visit her parents in Lockhart the last period. She remembered buying a box of tampons at the grocery store there, on the same day she had argued with her father about the Peace Corps. And yes, it was a month ago—two math exams back. Maybe when class was over, she would walk across the plaza to the Rexall on the Drag and buy another box of tampons and a bottle of Midol, and have a Coke and a sandwich at the soda fountain. She had agreed to a blind date with an upperclassman in the International Club who intended to go to El Salvador with the Peace Corps, and she wasn't about to miss the chance to hear about José Napoléon Duarte because of monthly cramping.

"Does everybody follow what I'm saying?" His cherubic face was tilted. He was young for a professor. "Does anybody follow? Marvin?"

"No sir."

"Raise your hand if you follow."

Half the students raised their hands. Shelly kept hers on her desk, drooping a pencil over the ugly construction of lines and numbers she had copied into her notebook from the drawing on the board.

She wondered what El Salvador might look like. What kind of trees, what kind of towns. They didn't teach you anything about El Salvador in Lockhart, which was just as well since she might end up going to Honduras or Venezuela or maybe Ecuador. Or Bolivia. She had heard there were herds of llamas in Bolivia, and maybe she could see them. Not that this decision about where she would go could be made anytime soon, since she had finished only one year here at UT. Even if she took classes every summer as she was doing now, she would still have two or three more years before she could apply to the Peace Corps. And she would have to master Spanish.

The professor turned to the window and surveyed the tower clock. "Imaginary numbers *will* be on the test," he said. "We'll call it a day at this point—for those of you who understand. For those who don't, we'll take fifteen minutes and go over it again. And I'll be in my office from seven to eight tonight if anyone wants to come by."

Most of the students were already closing their books and rising from their desks. He spoke his daily benediction of mathematical quotations as they filed out of the room, lifting his voice over the noise of their departure. "'Go forth with great numbers to solve the world's problems,'" he told them. "'Keep in mind that you achieve perfection not when there is nothing left to add, but when there is nothing left to take away.'"

Shelly closed her notebook and stood up—and hesitated, one of those small, seemingly inconsequential actions that she would recall for the rest of her life. She should stay, but fifteen minutes would hardly be enough to address her confusion about imaginary numbers. The room was oppressively hot, and her cramps were uncomfortable. And today was only Monday; she had the rest of the week to study. Still, she didn't want the professor to think she was cavalier about the math. She had managed to make a perfect grade point average her freshman year and wasn't about to spoil it in a summer math class.

"Are you going?" the girl seated behind her asked.

"I'm not sure. I guess I shouldn't."

Sitting back down indecisively, she noted dampness between her legs, the tacky feeling of blood. She rose and, turning as if to glance casually out the window, wiped a hand across the back of her skirt to see if blood had shown through. It hadn't, for now, but she would have to take care of the matter.

"No, I think I'll go," she told the girl, and stuffed her belongings into her bag. "I'll come back tonight," she told the professor. She was the last to exit and tried to walk quietly to the ladies' room. Classes were still in session. Doors had been left open to ensnare improbable drafts of air. But her sandals were wooden-soled and impossible to silence. Clomping past the doorways, she saw envious glances from students still captive in classrooms.

The tower bells were chiming a quarter to noon when she walked back down the hall and down the flights of stairs, the melodious notes overlaying the clop of her sandals. She recalled that the Spanish word for tower was *torre* and pictured the map of Central America, with tiny El Salvador pressed up against Honduras and Guatemala.

Outside, belligerent grackles greeted her with loud squawking. The August heat was thick. She started along the shaded path toward the main building and the tower, squinting even before she left the shade of the trees. Crossing a narrow street, she walked under the statue of Woodrow Wilson and mounted the steps to the upper part of the plaza as a boy carrying a transistor radio, blaring "Monday, Monday," passed her on his way down. *Monday, Monday*—Shelly hummed along with the Mamas and the Papas as she climbed the steps—*can't trust that day / Monday, Monday, sometimes it just turns out that way.*

On the plaza, the sunlight was unnerving. It whitewashed the massive stone arches and the carved pillars of the main building before her, making the tower look as flat against the sky as if it had been pasted on blue poster board. The song sounded tinny now, reduced to a mere ditty behind her: *Every other day, every other day / Every other day of the week is fine, yeah / But whenever Monday comes, but whenever Monday comes / You can find me crying all of the time . . .*

Perhaps she should have a Sego diet drink at the Rexall and skip the Coke and sandwich, she thought, starting across the plaza. She had put on five unwanted pounds during her freshman year, and the pencil skirt she wore felt tight around her waist. She was heading toward a grassy square around a flagpole, intending to cut across, when she noticed a boy from her biology class coming down the steps of the main building. He fumbled through the pages of a book as he walked, and she tried to remember his name in case he noticed her. Chad, she thought it was. Or Chet. When he started across the plaza, he lifted his eyes and saw her. He closed the book, tucked it under his arm, and raised his hand to wave. But something puzzled her: instead of a smile, a sudden grimace. The raised hand flung itself back at the wrist, and one leg cocked forward. It was a clownish gesture, and she wondered how to respond to it. In the same second she heard a sharp noise like a car backfiring, or maybe it was the jostling of construction equipment on the Drag, where the theater was being renovated.

He fell facedown, the book tumbling open beside him and a splotch of red spreading on the back of his plaid shirt. An ungainly lurching movement seized his legs and then stopped.

She stood looking at him, trying to understand, and was taking a step toward him when something struck her, slinging one of her arms outward and spinning her toward the small hedge that bordered the grassy square. She tried to break the fall, but the side of her head struck the ground and she lay for a second, stunned and embarrassed to have fallen in public. She tried to get to her knees and get her balance so she wouldn't topple over. But her arm was coming apart. It seemed almost detached. The bone above the elbow jutted jaggedly out of the flesh, and the lower part was weirdly twisted. Blood poured from her breast. She tried lifting her hands to stop the blood, but her arm wouldn't comply. It hung at her side. The pain was electric. She pressed the other hand against her breast but the blood ran between her fingers and spurted down her side, soaking the tattered bits of her bra and the pattern of yellow flowers on her blouse. She reached to get her book bag and gather what was scattered—her books, her math notes. But her arm hung like a puppet's.

Clarity took hold slowly. The boy lay dead before her. She heard the sound again ring down from the sky, plunking itself into the clear heat of the day. Someone began, horribly, to scream, and a man yelled something about the tower. A woman fell to the ground not far from Shelly. Birds flew from the trees and cement exploded upward. Shelly tried to stand again, but her legs wouldn't support her and she sat back on her knees. She had suffered dreams like this—her limbs refusing to move, the atmosphere as thick as water and weighting her down.

*Crawl*, she told herself. *To the hedge.*

She tried to look at the tower, but the sun was too intense. She pawed at the ground, breathing hard and coughing with nausea, but her wounded arm just hung there. She heard herself wail. The hedge was only knee-high and wouldn't protect her even if she could reach it, yet it was the only vertical shape the world offered. Everything else was flat ground. Things flew about her. There was the thud of impact on flesh and bone. Not hers, she thought. *Not me this time.* A whimper and cry. The hot concrete seared her palm when she tried to pull herself forward, dragging her mangled arm. Blood seeped into the porous stone beneath her. The frayed bra held her breast to her body and kept the lump of flesh from dropping like Jell-O. She whispered for someone to help her and methodically lifted her palm, then methodically set it down, pulling her knees forward, watching her blood bubble into the ground.

———

The sound instantly struck Wyatt Calvert as out of place, blasting over the stentorian voice of his professor and bouncing through the plaza outside. "Destruction of Kiev," he was writing in his notebook, "—Mongols, 1240." He looked up as the sound repeated. It reminded him of deer hunting and the concussion of rifle shots in a canyon. A student with a crew cut who was near the window stood up and looked out over the crown of an oak tree, and the professor paused from his lecture.

"There's something happening on the mall," the student said.

A girl got up and looked out. "I think it's something to do with the Drama Department."

Wyatt made his way through the rows of desks to the windows. The panes were dirty, the view partly cluttered by a tangle of branches. Fumbling with a lock, he shoved a window open and pulled hard at the frame until it jerked upward, creating an open rectangle of raw heat and admitting the buzz of insects and the sudden flutter of wings, and then the blast again, louder now, and its echo. Stone gargoyles in the overhang a few feet above blocked the noon sun. Below, a dozen people in the bright square of the plaza had an odd disruption in their movements, a hesitation. Some had come to a standstill and were looking around. A boy with a laundry bag ran diagonally across, shouting over his shoulder. At the steps to the lower part of the mall a plump girl in red pedal pushers lay on her back, her hands clutching her stomach, her legs lifting and sinking at the knees in a languid gesture as if to escape the scalding concrete. In the center of the plaza a guy in a plaid shirt and black trousers lay motionless, half on his side, his arm thrown out and a book on the ground beside him. Close to him a girl in a skirt dragged herself laboriously toward the hedgerow with the use of one arm, leaving a trail of gore and moving like a wounded beetle.

"Christ," Wyatt said. "Somebody's shooting people."

He didn't move for a second or two, his eyes fixed on the spectacle. A man climbing the steps from the lower part of the plaza toppled backward, followed by the blast of sound again. Thick in the shoulders and heavy, he lay faceup on the steps, as if tobogganing on his back, headfirst, down, the soles of his shoes pointing upward near the girl in the pedal pushers.

Wyatt swung his gaze to the tower and searched the rows of windows up to the top. The gold hands of the tower clock marked the time at 11:51. On the high, walled deck below it, a figure appeared and then eerily vanished. A second later it popped into view again, aiming a glinting rifle down at the East Mall. Smoke puffed out of the barrel as the sound blasted. From below came a muted noise and a muffled, lingering shout. The figure on the deck disappeared again and then reappeared a second later. Wyatt saw the white bloom, but didn't hear the blast this time. The window beside him exploded.

"Get down!" the professor yelled. "Away from the windows! Down!"

Only a few of the students complied at first; then everyone moved at once, crouching beside their desks and crowding against the wall.

"They're shooting at you, Calvert!" someone yelled at Wyatt. "Get out of the way!"

For a second, he squatted under the windows in the shattered glass scattered over the floor. Then he started crawling.

"Stay down, Calvert!" the professor ordered, but Wyatt kept moving. When he reached the door, he stood up and ran through the hallway, shouting for students to stay in the building and away from the windows. "Someone's shooting from the tower!" he shouted. Students turned and stared at him, not believing. He knocked into an underclassman, who snapped, "Hey, watch it!" In a room at the end of the hall he found a group of students gathered around a map that hung from the chalkboard. "Has Jack Stone left already?" he asked them, breathing hard.

"I think he's in Wood's office," a lanky girl in a brown jumper replied.

"Someone in the tower's shooting people on the plaza," Wyatt called over his shoulder as he started for the professor's office.

"Is this the experiment in psychology?" the girl called after him. "The one where they see if we'll go help?"

"Don't go outside!" he shouted back.

He passed the underclassman he had knocked into a moment ago, and the guy cleared out of his way now, backing against the wall and joking, "Shooter in the tower! I bet! Everyone run hide!" A scatter of laughter followed. But as Wyatt rounded the corner, word was spreading and a sense of alarm rising, voices escalating.

The office he was headed to was on the far side of the building. Rushing in, out of breath, he found his cousin Jack talking with the professor.

"Where's Delia?" Wyatt said. "Where were you going to meet her?"

"On the plaza. Why?"

"There's somebody in the tower shooting people on the plaza. Where was she coming from?"

Jack was already on his feet. "She would have parked on the Drag."

The professor picked up the phone. "What do I tell the police?"

"At least four people shot on the plaza, at least one guy with a rifle up in the tower."

Jack started down the hall, now crowded with students. Wyatt was close on his heels. "Go outside the other way or you'll walk right into it!" Wyatt shouted over the noise.

"I'm going the way she would come," Jack said.

But at that moment Delia appeared before them, wide-eyed, running up the stairs, her black hair clinging to her damp forehead. Jack swept her into his arms. "Thank God," he said. "Go to Wood's office. He's calling the police. Stay in the office with him. And stay there if he leaves."

"Where are you going? Jack?"

Jack had already started down. "Go to Wood's office and wait for me."

"And call Elaine at work at Sears," Wyatt told her as he passed her. "Tell her not to come near campus."

Two boys pushed by, heading down, yelling about a "shoot-out." Wyatt warned them to go back up, but they shoved past him. Running a step behind Jack, almost on top of him, Wyatt thought of the bodies on the plaza—how easily the man had dropped backward on the stone steps without even trying to break his fall.

A group of new freshmen touring the campus had crowded into the lobby, and a woman was trying to corral them into a classroom. Wyatt and Jack pressed through and exited to a covered area that adjoined the plaza. Half a dozen underclassmen stood there guessing about how many gunmen were up in the tower. One of the girls said this must be the start of a revolution or a student uprising. A stout boy in Bermuda shorts said Cubans were attacking. A thinner one with limp blond hair peered up at the tower from under an archway. "I think it's only one guy, and he's gone around to the other side of the tower."

"Move back from there," Jack told him. "Whoever's up there can see you. Have you heard more than one shot at a time?"

"Nope," the limp-haired boy said.

"It's hard to tell, because of the echoes," one of the others said.

The sky, Wyatt saw, was clear blue. A low wall with stone balusters ran the length of the plaza, broken midway by the steps that led to the lower walkways. At the top of the steps the black shoes of the dead man jutted upward. A girl with a halo of blond curls bent over the girl in red pedal pushers, who was lying on her back. The blond girl called for help, her voice carrying the flat, repetitive tone of diminishing expectations: "Can somebody help us? She's been shot. Can somebody help us?" A receptionist from the dean's office hid behind an oak tree near the wall, her face against the trunk.

"I swear my dad could shoot that guy from right here," the limp-haired boy announced. "He's shot wild turkey that far."

Wyatt had been in the tower many times; he knew the view. It was open, clear to the horizon. Austin spread like a puddle. Pedestrians were the size of bugs. To the south, the capitol dome looked small; to the west, storefronts lined the Drag. To the east and north were dormitories, classroom buildings. "What's his range?" he asked.

"Five hundred yards with a high-powered rifle from up there," Jack said, squatting to tighten the laces on his sneakers. His hair was cropped short; he had lost part of an ear in Vietnam, and the flesh that remained was flanked by a patch of bald scarring. "I'm going out there to get that girl off the steps." He stood up.

"I'm going with you," Wyatt said.

"Keep moving in a zigzag," Jack told him. "Hug the wall. Don't stop and think; just move. We'll carry her down the steps. Be careful; those shoes won't have traction."

"There's another girl," Wyatt said. "In the center. You can't see her from here; I saw her from the window. She was trying to crawl to the hedge."

The tower bells had begun to chime, and the limp-haired boy in the archway leaned out to look up. Wyatt saw him drop and thought he had slipped. But it wasn't a usual way to fall—on his back, with his legs turned under. There was a hole in his forehead, just over his eye.

"God!" the boy in Bermuda shorts screamed, pressing his hands over his ears and staring down at the body. "Oh God! Gary's been shot!"

Jack and Wyatt gripped the lifeless body under the arms and dragged it toward the door. A lump of bloody skull and silky hair lay on the ground. The girl tried to help; the boy in shorts bent over and vomited, then raised his head and screamed, "He shot Gary! He shot Gary!"

Looking at the plaza, Wyatt saw that the blond girl who'd been calling for help was gone. The girl in the pedal pushers still lay at the top of the steps, near the dead man tobogganing backward. A tall man wearing a coat and tie strolled into the open from the far side of the plaza, and Wyatt waved his arms at him and shouted, pointing toward the tower. But the bells drowned out his voice. The man's face splintered. Part of it flew away. His arms rose in the air.

———

Shelly heard the gunshot whistling through the melodic notes, followed instantly by a boom as loud as a cannon. The man in the black suit entered the edge of her vision, and she saw his face explode. Empty sky hung where his jaw had been. He stayed upright and teetered there. A guy climbed over the wall and pulled him to safety, shoving him over the balusters into someone's reaching hands.

She lay still, breathing shallow wisps of air. The spectacle of her arm grilling on the hot cement was grotesque, so she tried to keep her eyes closed. Occasionally she opened them to a slit, admitting a view of a thin, bright, topsy-turvy rectangular world partly obscured by her shattered arm. She was lying in a puddle of blood. With the hand that was operable, she tried to hold her breast in place while still appearing lifeless. She was barely shy of the hedge and could force herself to crawl the last few feet, but the shooter in the tower might be looking at her through his scope, searching for movement or breath. For the blink of an eye, even. She had forgotten what it was like to lie so still, but a fragment of a childhood memory came flapping haphazardly into the horror of the present. She had played dead with a neighbor boy in a field in back of his home, a trick to attract the buzzards so that the boy, lying flat on his back beside her with his BB gun pointed into the air, could shoot at them when they circled. "Don't move," he had told her. "They have good eyesight. Don't blink. Close your eyes."

The shots were coming now from a different side of the tower and sounded slight and harmless. Shelly's jaw was beginning to pump, rattling her teeth together. She remembered one of her high school teachers talking about the symptoms of shock but couldn't remember what they were. Rapid breathing or slowed breathing—she had forgotten which. Rapid pulse or slow. The only obvious thing about her pulse was that it was pumping the blood out of her arm. She had stopped her frenzied panting. Afraid of passing out and bleeding to death without knowing, she thought she would stop playing dead if she felt any sense of darkness, and would try, once more, to drag herself toward the hedge. She wouldn't be able to wedge herself beneath it; she would need to get through the opening and crawl across the grassy square to the stone base of the flagpole to find protection.

If she had to, she would try to stand up and run.

The concrete baked her side and her ruined arm, and she wanted to cradle her face and protect her cheek from the heat, but she had locked her hand around her breast to stop the bleeding. From her awkward vantage she saw two men run toward the girl at the top of the steps; they leaned and scooped her up and carried her down, out of sight, her legs, in bright red pedal pushers, dangling over their arms. They left behind her textbooks and her sandal. On the steps, the soles of a man's shoes pointed up, like the ears of a curious rabbit.

Shelly summoned the voice of her childhood neighbor demanding that she close her eyes. She imagined the piercing, weightless gaze of buzzards circling, and heard the popping of guns, and realized some of the firing now was coming from ground level. Moving her head just slightly and peering from half-closed eyes, she saw someone shove a barrel out of a window of the history building and fire up at the tower.

The smell of blood baking into the ground sickened her. She was aware of the dead boy lying behind her, and heard moaning and cries. The tower clock struck fifteen minutes after the hour. She wondered if she would live to the half hour. When the gunfire blasted down again, she felt it through the ground. Fragments flew over the wall. Thoughts arose in pieces: her mother spreading jelly over a slice of buttered toast, a dog in the distance barking, her father changing a flat tire—his shoulders moving as he pumped the jack.

*Count the seconds*, she thought. *Count the seconds that I can stand this.* She was waiting for the bells.

————

Wyatt knew the girl in the pedal pushers was dead the moment they lifted her from the ground, but there was no time to reconsider the effort to save her. They carried her down the steps, skirting the dead man. Wyatt lost his footing once and lost his grip on the girl's legs, but dragged them up again.

They laid her close to the wall. She was soaked in blood from her chest to her thighs and smelled of feces. A blue clip tacked her bobbed hair to her temple. She was stocky and muscular—stout through the middle and short-legged. Her pretty face stared blindly upward, past the face of Woodrow Wilson and through the limbs of an oak tree.

People had started firing up at the tower; gunshots came from the

English and history buildings and peppered the air from the football stadium. An ambulance from a funeral home backed hurriedly toward Wyatt and Jack on the narrow street that ran between the steps and the tree-covered parts of the mall. Then a bullet pierced the rear window, and the driver pulled forward again. Wyatt felt the girl's wrist for a pulse. But he knew she was dead.

"The girl by the hedge," Jack said. "Did you see if she was alive?"

"I only got a glimpse. She wasn't moving. I saw somebody moving on the ground up closer to the main building, but he'd be hard to get to." He wasn't sure he could bring himself to go back out on the plaza, but pulled his shoes off anyway.

A policeman with a shotgun came running from the direction of the fountain, darting through the trees and then across the street to where Wyatt and Jack crouched over the girl's body. He positioned himself beside them and was surveying the plaza from between the balusters that topped the wall, when a series of rapid shots chipped at the balusters and he pulled his head down and squatted between Jack and Wyatt, nearly stepping on one of the girl's hands.

"Mother of God. That was a carbine. An M1," he said.

"That's the first I've heard it; it's been bolt-action," Jack told him.

"You think there's more than one asshole up there?" Sweat streamed from under his cap.

"I think he's got more than one gun. He's pinned down by return fire and shooting from the rainspouts. What's the plan?"

"My plan is to get up there and kill the son of a bitch." He raised himself cautiously for another look and then, after a glance, lowered himself again and settled his back against the wall, his boots planted in bird droppings beside the dead girl's head. Pulling his hat off, he wiped an arm across his face.

A volley of gunfire came from the business and economics building, and the bells chimed the half hour. The rapid, flat, cracking sound of the carbine moved to the west side of the tower. The officer shoved his hat on and tugged at his sweaty uniform. Struggling up from his crouched position, he leaned to look cautiously up the steps, his gaze lingering only a second on the dead man. "You boys stay here," he said, and mounted the steps at a run.

Wyatt raised his head high enough to look between the balusters and see the top of the tower. Bullets fired from the ground had struck the clock face and freckled the stone. But the shooter up there was invisible. The officer moved rapidly across the bright plaza in a loping stride, bullets striking the ground around him and flinging up dust at his heels.

"At least now we have police here," Wyatt said.

But how many police were there? He had seen only the one, who didn't have much of a plan for storming the tower and whose shotgun would be useless from the ground against a high-powered rifle and an automatic carbine.

"If the other police aren't armed any better, they might as well throw rocks up at the fucker," Jack said.

A bullet nicked the baluster. Ducking his head, Wyatt noticed a movement on the plaza. The corpse of the girl lying beside the hedge opened her mouth and lifted her head from the ground.

———

Shelly called to the policeman running past her, a spray of bullets nicking the ground at his heels. When he was gone, she pulled her legs in closer to make herself smaller, and lay motionless, watching a fly move about in the blood on her arm. The arm was becoming numb. She was unbearably thirsty. She heard shouting, sirens in the distance, and continual gunfire, and thought she still heard the song playing—*Every other day, every other day / Every other day of the week is fine, yeah*—but then realized this was only in her mind. The ground started to rumble and her field of vision was invaded by a large vehicle—an armored car of the type she had seen transporting money on the highways—lumbering heavily across the plaza. She thought it was coming to rescue her, but then she began to fear it, it looked so sightless and enormous. It blocked her view. The sound of the motor drowned her thoughts, and the exhaust made her cough, jolting her injured body. She felt an eerie rising up of the ground, and opened her eyes again and saw the monstrous creature leaving, making its way slowly across the terrace. The bells chimed again, sounding heavy and ominous in the upside-down world. A second policeman followed the path of the first, passing her by. She had stopped hoping for rescue. Her legs had started to shake and to jerk at the knees. She thought of the gap in the hedge. The gap would open to grass, and grass would offer—if not refuge—relief from the scalding heat.

She was thinking of trying to crawl again, when two men came running rapidly up the steps in her direction. They were the same two guys who had carried away the girl in the pedal pushers. The shorter one was quick and athletic. His white shirt was smeared with blood. The other was tall and barefoot with a colorful madras shirt that was coming untucked from his trousers. He wore glasses with black frames. They came to her quickly, and she braced herself for the pain. The shorter one took hold of her twisted arm and laid it over her chest. "Don't!" she screamed, trying to kick him away.

But they did what they had come to do. "Take this, take her arm, take her *arm, goddamn it*—" "She's bleeding from the chest—" "Support her head—" "We're going to get you out of here. It's okay, it's okay."

The pain was unimaginable. "It's not okay!" She turned her head and vomited as the ground receded and she was lifted. She couldn't see, couldn't breathe, and her screeching and squealing seemed to come from someone other than herself. The blue sky turned white. The guys steadied her arm. Her blood-soaked fingers grasped the madras shirt.

Concrete burst around her, and the deafening boom of the rifle emptied the world of air. "Ah, God, he's shooting at us!" one of the guys was saying. "Don't drop her—" "We can't make it to the steps— This way, *this way, fuck*—" "Support her arm—" "The flagpole's closer—" "It's not enough—" "Go to the flagpole—" They pressed her arm so tightly she heard the bones grating. The tall boy's eyeglasses were askew. The world jostled from red to blue; the faces blocked the light for parts of seconds. The slanted flagpole sliced the sky in two.

———

The last thing Wyatt saw before his glasses fell to the ground was a face in the large center window on the third floor of the English building, just under the red tile roof. It seemed to be looking at him. From a window next to it, someone fired up at the tower and retreated.

But the face in the center window never moved, as if frozen in a sudden awareness that the sky could drop, life could stop, the world could instantly explode into pieces. It looked weirdly disembodied—pale and blanched—the clarity of the features, at such a distance, abnormal, as if the face were not exactly human but instead an artist's rendering of how a human face reacts to horror. Like the primal face of fear. For half a second, an inexplicable wintry sharpness invaded the hot August air, and then the face dissolved with the rest of the world when Wyatt's glasses fell. He reached out but couldn't find them. He snagged a bare foot in the grass and stumbled. The girl sagged in his arms.

"Goddamn it!" Jack cried.

They threw themselves to the ground behind the circular block of concrete that was the base of the flagpole. In the grass nearby, a boy in shorts and a surfer shirt lay writhing, bleeding from the neck. Wyatt folded the girl into his lap as Jack tried to move in closer. But the space couldn't shield all three of them. A bullet hissed in the air; the grass kicked up. "He's aiming at us!" Jack shouted, "The fucker's aiming at us!"

Wyatt locked his knees around the girl to hold her steady, her back against his chest. Planting his feet on either side of her body, he placed her mangled arm against her stomach and tried to make more room for Jack, who pushed himself in sideways. "Pull your knees up," Wyatt told him, inching back. "Get your back against her stomach."

"I'm too far out." Jack said. He paused to catch his breath. A bullet hit the ground beside his foot, another beside his knee. "Fuck, I'm getting out of here. There's no room." He got to his feet and ran. Wyatt held the girl more tightly.

Jack was running when the bullet hit him. Wyatt saw him fall. He saw it indistinctly without his glasses. Drawing his knees to his chest, Jack rolled from side to side, yelling to Wyatt, "Stay where you are! I can get up!" But he didn't get up. He clutched his thighs. "Wyatt?" he yelled, more plaintively.

"God, Jack—"

"Wyatt?"

"Can you get up?"

"It's bad—"

"I'm coming to get you—"

"No . . . stay there."

"Where are you hit?"

"Shit. Ah, God—"

"Where are you hit?"

"Don't come."

"Can you walk?"

His knees were tucked to his chest.

"Is he up there?" Wyatt yelled. "Can you see him up there?"

"No. Don't come for me. You hear me? Fuck you if you come for me!"

"I'm coming for you, Jack—"

He tried to think of a way to let go of the girl and still protect her. A bullet hit the flagpole over their heads, and the vicious vibration made him think he had been shot. He looked at the girl and saw that she was screaming, but he couldn't hear her. "Can you stay upright, on your own?" he shouted. But he couldn't hear his words, and he wasn't sure he had said them. He had no sense of what he needed to do.

Only gradually, as he held her, did the whimpering of the girl break through.

———

Shelly's mouth was dry, her voice trapped by her clattering teeth. The blood still flowed out of her arm. She harbored herself between Wyatt's knees, her back against his chest. His sweat had soaked her. He was holding her arm too tightly against her body. But if he let go, it would drop. He maneuvered himself slightly away; she felt his knuckles against her spine as he unbuttoned his shirt. She felt him peeling the shirt away. He swept it around the front of her and knotted the sleeves at her chest. "What's your name? What's your blood type?" he asked her.

"Shelly Maddox."

"Your blood type?"

"A-positive. I think. I don't know."

"How does my cousin look? How bad is he? I can't see without my glasses."

"He's on his side. I think he's shot in the legs. The thighs."

"The other guy—is he moving?"

"I can't tell." She tried to focus her eyes. The world was heaving from side to side. Every breath was painful. She noticed a man's face staring down from the center window on the third floor of the English building, and for an instant saw herself through those distant eyes: how small she looked, bundled into the arms of the stranger.

A small plane in the sky started to circle inward. "Could they shoot him from up there?" she whispered.

"From up where?"

"The airplane—is it coming to help us?"

"I don't see a plane."

She tried to nod in that direction to show him where it was. The airplane looked as flimsy and weightless as a bird. She watched it drop, and thought it was falling, but then it bounced back up again, the canvas sides rippling in the wind. Gradually it started circling inward. But after a rapid firing of gunshots from the tower, it turned away and disappeared behind her line of vision.

Jack was getting up. Wyatt shouted to him over Shelly's head. Jack yelled back, but Shelly couldn't understand what it was he said. He pivoted onto a knee, as awkward as an inchworm. His hands clawed at the grass. Wyatt leaned out, trying to see the tower. "Don't," Shelly murmured, her mouth so dry the word sounded inhuman, and then, in a whisper: "Don't go." She intended to mean it for his sake. But then she said, "Don't leave me." She said it several times, and tightened her hold on his arm, sinking herself into the heat of his body.

Jack struggled toward the wall, hunched in the middle and dragging a leg. When he had nearly reached it, someone climbed over the balustrade from the other side and helped him over and out of view.

Wyatt rested his face against Shelly's head. He seemed to be melting into her. But his weight stayed solid against her back. His knees on either side of her walled out the world. His naked arms, locked tightly around her, kept her from falling sideways. His shirt secured her arm; his bare feet were like the feet of stone pillars in the grass beside her. She felt he wouldn't allow her to die, as if he breathed for them both. She allowed herself to drift, her mind to wander.

Her fear began to drain away. Closing her eyes to the bright light, she was aware she was whispering and he was whispering back. Vibrations of his voice rose and fell like the notes of a song, though she couldn't make sense of his words. She felt he was trying to keep her awake, and begged him not to stop talking.

But then she grew tired, and after a while stopped listening. The clock was chiming the hour.

It chimed the quarter hour. She wondered if several hours had passed. The firing continued and seemed to grow more distant. Less consistent. A mere pattering of raindrops. Eventually, it stopped.

# 2

# TRIAGE

Wyatt knew the shooting was over when the sirens grew suddenly louder and drowned out the sound of his own muttered whispers to the girl. Like children emerging from a game of hide-and-seek, people rose up from beneath ledges and stepped from behind trees silently, cautiously, as if unsure the game was over.

His glasses lay somewhere out in the grass. The weight of the girl in his arms kept him pinned where he was. His shirt, tied around her, secured her arm across her stomach. He was bare-chested, covered in her blood, burned by the sun and scalded by the concrete base of the flagpole at his back. In the grass before him the boy in the surfer shirt had stopped moving.

He waited. Setting the girl aside was out of the question. She had turned her face sideways; her cheek was against his throat. He saw the brush of her lashes when he lowered his eyes. He had cupped his hand around her breast to stanch the blood, and he could feel her heartbeat and the slow rise of her breathing. He had devoted so much effort to keeping her awake, and now he was reluctant to disrupt her peaceful sleep.

But she was bleeding to death.

"We need help!" he yelled, and again louder, "We need help!"

People approached like sleepwalkers, spilling cautiously out of buildings and ascending the steps from the lower part of the mall. "Over here!" a girl shouted when she saw Wyatt. "We need an ambulance over here!" A siren grew closer, the high-pitched scream separating from the endless scream of other sirens, and then abruptly fell silent. A man arrived for the girl, but he was alone and had no stretcher. He told Wyatt the stretchers were all in use and the ambulances filled.

One of the drivers had been shot, he said. He searched the grass for Wyatt's glasses and gave them to him. A fat girl came with a bottle of Pepsi. Someone brought a glass of water and patted it onto the wounded girl's face. Shirtless and sticky with blood, Wyatt withdrew his stiffened arms from around the girl and helped the ambulance driver carry her down the steps and arrange her body into the back of the station wagon. She groaned, and tried to roll to her side, but did not wake. Students and a policeman loaded a dead man, shot in the chest, beside her. His arm flopped over her face, and Wyatt moved it away. He took a long look at the girl's face, having not yet seen it clearly. It had the disturbing, colorless look of something unfinished—a painting in progress, the flesh colors left out, her skin transparent and pale under the smeared blood, the blue veins on her throat showing through. Her hair was shoulder-length, reddish-brown, soaked with sweat.

A student with a gaping shoulder wound and a janitor with a bloody towel tied around his hand got in the front with the driver. Wyatt fumbled around in the glove compartment and found a pen and scrap of paper and wrote the girl's name: "Shelly Maddox." He considered writing her blood type, but she had been uncertain, so he decided against it. "Which hospital?" he asked the driver.

"Brackenridge—we're taking almost everyone to Brackenridge."

"My cousin was shot in the leg and taken from here a while ago. Is that where he'd be?"

"There's no way to know," the driver said hurriedly. "I think a few people were taken to Seton and St. David's. Get in if you want a ride." But he was already pulling the door closed, and Wyatt urgently wanted to find Delia and be sure she was all right. They could search for Jack together.

He retrieved his shoes from the base of the steps and put them on. The dead man on the steps and the dead girl in the pedal pushers were both gone. Police and medical personnel brought bodies out of the tower, rolling the gurneys across the plaza and lifting them down the steps. Highway Patrol cars and more ambulances arrived. A Texas Ranger came running with a rifle over his shoulder.

"Did they get the shooter?" a girl asked him as he ran.

"They got him; he's dead," the Ranger answered.

Wyatt walked to the history building, his naked arms feeling empty without the weight of the girl. Her blood was smeared on his chest. A guy who had been in the history class with him two hours before pulled a shirt from a gym bag and tossed it to him, and he put it on and buttoned it as he walked.

Roaming the halls of the history building, he could not find Delia. From a phone in an empty office, he tried to call Elaine at her job in the women's department at Sears, but the lines were tied up. In the restroom, he washed off as much of the girl's blood as he could and drank from the faucet. The shirt he'd been given was small for him, and the blood had soaked through as if it were his blood. An underclassman came in, stared at him, and asked if he had been shot.

When he returned to the office to try the phone again, he found students and a professor gathered around, unable to get a connection, so he started back across the plaza in the blazing sunlight, heading toward the undergraduate library and the bank of phones in the lobby. Crossing the plaza, he had the feeling of being watched and kept looking up at the tower. He skirted the smear of blood on the pavement where Shelly Maddox had tried to drag herself to the hedge.

People had crowded into the service driveway outside the tower to see the sniper's body brought out, some holding the deer rifles they had fired, and everyone oddly silent, as if part of some sweltering vigil. Wyatt made his way through the crowd and into the undergraduate library, where he found long lines waiting to use the phones. He was considering whether to leave, when cheering erupted outside and a girl flung open the door and shouted for everyone to come out and look at the sniper. People left their places in line to go out, and those who stayed behind tried to place their calls repeatedly, coins jangling in the useless phones.

He should go to Brackenridge, even without Delia, and look for Jack. Police had blocked off most of the streets, and his car was parked on the north edge of the campus. So he started on foot, jogging southward on the Drag in the draining heat, through the deafening swirl of sirens, past store windows punctured by bullets. Through the open doors of the co-op, he saw people clustered around a blaring radio at the register and heard a newscaster announcing the sniper's name: Charles Whitman. In the window of a jewelry store the crazed light of bullet holes looked like shattered gems. A trail of blood snaked from the sidewalk to the carpet inside. An empty Studebaker idled at the curb, the driver's door open, the radio announcing, "Nine people are currently known to be dead, and many more thought to be critically injured."

He pushed himself to jog faster, breathing hard, passing others headed in the same direction. When he neared the hospital, police were putting up barricades to control the traffic. Ambulances had parked in the center of the street, their sirens blaring, and people in street clothes unloaded the wounded on stretchers and hauled them into the building.

Wyatt saw a reporter who was toting a heavy camera with LIFE MAGAZINE printed on its side, and followed him around to a back entrance, where a guard admitted the reporter and directed Wyatt to triage, assuming from the bloody shirt that he was wounded.

Passing the switchboard room, Wyatt heard fragments of urgent speech, the operators all talking at once as they tried to connect calls. He found his way to the emergency waiting area and encountered dozens of wounded on stretchers and gurneys, their legs drawn up, their arms sprawled out, their heads cocked weirdly sideways. The smell of blood was overpowering. A boy dry-heaved over a bucket. Nurses inserted catheters, and cinched tourniquets, and packed gauze into bullet wounds, calling for supplies over the din of voices. Their white shoes were soaked red. The nurse in charge directed Wyatt to the corridor of green tile at the center of triage, where he looked into the rooms for Jack. A girl he knew from a class lay bleeding on a gurney from which dangled bottles of intravenous fluids. In one room, emptied of beds, a priest stood over bodies laid out on the floor.

Finally Wyatt returned to the lobby and climbed the stairs, two at a time, to the surgery unit. A nurse stopped him from entering, and he pressed her for information until he saw Delia standing in front of a window among the throng of people waiting, the tower rising in the distance through the window behind her.

"I don't know anything yet," she told him as he came to her. "He was in surgery when I got here. They don't have enough surgeons, so I don't know if they've operated—they're taking the most serious first."

"Are you all right?"

"I'm okay."

"You're sure?"

"I'm sure."

"Did you talk to Elaine?"

"Yes. She already knew what was going on; they were all watching it on TVs on the sales floor. I didn't tell her you had gone out on the plaza. I didn't know you had, at that point."

"But she was staying at Sears? You're certain?"

"I'm certain."

"And you stayed in the office, with the professor?"

She shook her head. "I had to go where I could see."

"Could see what?"

"What was going on."

"You saw—"

"Everything on the plaza. From a window."

"God, Delia. You saw—"

"Everything that happened on the plaza." She flashed him a challenging look. "And I'm not sorry. It was better than having to guess. I did enough of that when he was in Vietnam."

"I need to call his parents," Wyatt said. "If I can find a phone that works."

She sat down and looked at the floor and bobbed her foot. Her sandals were green, her toenails painted red.

"You're sure you're okay?" He sat down beside her. "I guess you know the guy who did this was killed."

"Don't tell me a thing about him. Not his name. Nothing."

"How bad do you think Jack's hurt?" Wyatt asked. "I couldn't tell. My glasses came off."

"I saw them come off."

"You really saw—"

"Everything. Did the girl live?"

"I don't know. She was alive in the ambulance, but I didn't see her downstairs."

A doctor in scrubs came out of the ICU and asked if there was anyone there for Jack Stone. Wyatt got up to talk to him with Delia, but she waved him back, so he sat and watched the two of them in conversation. The doctor looked illogically young; his mouth turned down at the corners as he spoke. Delia backed against the wall, a look of concern on her face, her hands pressed to her stomach. Behind Wyatt, a man slammed a phone into the cradle, shouting about the lines being tied up.

The doctor spoke with Delia only briefly before he left her, and then Wyatt went to her. "He's all right," she told him, but she didn't look like she thought so. "The bullet went all the way through. They didn't have to remove it. It didn't hit the bone. They're short of rooms, and we're supposed to get him out of ICU and look for an empty bed on the third floor."

They found Jack lying on a gurney in a curtained corner, his bandages forming a lump under the blanket. He muttered, trying to emerge from the stupor of ether, his face pasty and swollen. Delia kissed him and stroked his face. While she steadied the IV bottles, Wyatt figured out how to unlock the wheels of the gurney, and together they maneuvered it through ICU and into the hallway. Though several elevators arrived, they had to wait for one with room enough for the gurney.

On the third floor, nurses were moving patients out to make space for trauma victims, and by the time Wyatt secured a vacant room, Jack was waking up. He was subdued and didn't say much as they helped him into the bed. Delia stayed with him while Wyatt went to look for a phone.

He found one in the cafeteria, but it was out of order. The place was chaotic, food and drinks set out for the taking. People wept and tried to console each other. They discussed what they knew of the sniper. "Who would raise such a boy?" they asked. The lab was out of blood, and people asked where they could donate. The blood bank down the street had too long a line, someone said, and none of the blood given now could be processed in time.

Wyatt helped himself to a sandwich and ate it on his way up the stairs to the fifth floor, where he found a phone and got a connection to Sears. But the store operator didn't answer, and the phone just rang and rang. He tried to call his parents in San Antonio and couldn't get through, but managed to reach Jack's parents, who lived next door. Jack's mother, his aunt Jenny, answered. "We've been watching the television," she told him apprehensively. "We've been trying to call. Your parents are over here. Are you and Jack okay?"

He told her what had happened. "Delia's with him now." The connection had gone silent, and Wyatt thought he had lost it. But then his uncle's voice came on the line, and Wyatt had to start over again.

"We're on our way," his uncle told him. "Here's your mother."

He reassured his mother that he was all right, and then returned to Jack's room and found him sitting up in the bed, a wild, watery look in his eyes. He half-expected him to make a joke about coming home from Vietnam to get shot, but in a glance saw how stupid that thought had been.

"Can I bring you a Coke?" he asked him.

Jack only looked at him.

Delia followed him out to the hall. "His parents are on their way," he told her.

He was still talking with Delia when Elaine came hurrying down the hall toward them, her dark hair streaming. Seeing her in the same dress she had worn to work that morning, Wyatt was struck by the fact that it was only hours since he had dropped her off in front of Sears.

She didn't say much, but was grave and serious and held him tightly. The three of them stood talking quietly, and then Delia went in to sit with Jack, while Wyatt and Elaine sat against the wall outside the door, Elaine's long legs, tanned from the summer, stretched out in front of her. Wyatt tried to talk about what had happened but couldn't remember it all correctly. Only after he finished did he realize how much he had left out. How could he put into words what it was like to hold someone who was bleeding to death, and all but breathe for her? He was still sitting in the hallway with his arm around Elaine when the elevator door slid open and an orderly pushed a gurney out, and he recognized the girl on the gurney. She was motionless and covered in blankets, but her eyes were open.

He got to his feet. "Shelly?"

A man in a sheriff's uniform walked alongside the gurney, and on the opposite side a freckled woman with hair in a flip the color of cherrywood had her hand on the rail.

Shelly's arm lay cocked in a cast over her chest. The side of her face that had rested on the cement was red and slick with salve. Dried blood matted her hair. Her eyes rolled back and forth, but she reached for Wyatt as she passed him, took hold of his hand, and held on until the orderly pulled to a stop.

"You know my daughter?" the sheriff asked. "Was it you that helped her?"

"Yes sir, along with my cousin," Wyatt told him.

"God bless you, young man," he whispered, offering his hand. "I'm Adrian Maddox, and this is my wife, Janie." He was stout and handsome, in his forties, with muscular shoulders.

The woman said, "How can we ever thank you?"

The orderly was impatient. "I need to move on," he said. Rather than pull his hand from Shelly's grip, Wyatt walked alongside. He glanced back at Elaine, but she waved at him to go on.

Shelly was having trouble focusing her eyes. When the gurney was wheeled into a room, she loosened her hold on Wyatt's hand. He thought for an anxious second that she had stopped breathing, and he put his face to her mouth to feel her breath.

Her mother settled her in the bed, and Wyatt went out in the hall with the sheriff. "Is there anything we can do for your cousin?" the sheriff asked him. "I understand he was hurt trying to help my daughter."

"No sir, but thank you. His parents are on their way."

Wyatt did his best to answer the sheriff's questions, but the man broke down in tears. "Her mama is going to want to talk to you later," he said when he got hold of himself. "Could you give me your phone number?"

They dug around in their pockets for pen and paper, but Wyatt found only a receipt from a hardware store in Abilene, where he had never been, and remembered that the shirt didn't belong to him. "My number's in the phone book," Wyatt told the sheriff. "I live in the housing for married students on Town Lake."

Returning to Jack's room, he found Elaine and Delia sitting on the bed with Jack, who was sleeping. A nurse was replacing the IV fluids. A slant of evening sunlight came through the window.

"I think you should go home for a while and come back later," Elaine urged him. "I'll stay here with Delia."

The lingering heat settled over him as he walked back to the campus. It was past six. The light was a rosy yellow and the shadows were stretched out long. Overcome with sadness, he stepped into an alleyway so no one would see him crying, his face pressed against a stone wall. Then he took the shortcut to the South Mall, past the shimmering fountain of winged riders and along the pathway under the oak trees up to the open plaza. Birds had resumed their noisy racket in the branches.

People were gathered about in small groups on the plaza. It had been hosed down; a steamy, earthy smell rose from the hot cement. The flags had been lowered and taken away. Two maintenance men emptied bags of sand onto the remnants of blood. Students drinking beer sat on a stone bench, looking up at the tower.

Wyatt stood among the people and the heaps of sand in the open part of the plaza and gazed up at the clock face shattered by bullets fired up at the sniper. He studied the base of the flagpole, where

Shelly's blood still darkened the ground, and walked to the place in the grass where Jack had fallen. For a while, he stood at that place, staring down at the grass as if he were looking for something, though he wasn't sure what it would be. A disconcerting feeling that someone was watching him began to settle over him, and he realized gradually that the impression didn't come from the tower, but instead from the English building behind him. Remembering the face he had seen looking down, he turned and looked up at that window. It was the center window on the third floor, just under the roofline, larger than the other windows, wider than tall, six panes across and four down. He found it empty now, and yet the face, with its pale expression of anguish, still seemed strangely present there, cloaked in darkness, as chilling and disturbing to Wyatt as if it were the physical embodiment of every emotion he had felt that day.

He walked on, skirting the main building and cutting across the northern edge of the campus to where his car was parked. The evening was turning the same ripe purple hue that he had created that morning from vermilion and cobalt blue.

# 3

# JACK

Driving west to his apartment, Wyatt listened to the KTBC report on the day, the information continually updated by the police department. The sniper's name was Charles Whitman, and he was a UT student, an ex-marine, and a former Eagle Scout. Police had broken into his tidy little house in south Austin and discovered his wife slaughtered in the bed. They had found his mother bludgeoned to death in her apartment not far from the campus. His mother had worked at the cafeteria at Hancock Shopping Center. This last bit of news struck Wyatt, since the Sears where Elaine worked was at Hancock Center and she often had lunch at that cafeteria. She had probably crossed paths with the poor woman.

Apparently Whitman had killed his wife first, and then his mother, before disguising himself as a janitor and hauling a footlocker of guns up into the tower. No one knew why he had wanted to murder so many people.

It was only twilight now, but it seemed darker. The warmth in the car thickened the smell of souring blood on Wyatt's shirt. He drove with the windows down, in hopes of escaping the smell, but a feeling of doom followed him and grew stronger the farther he was from campus and from Jack. He reminded himself the day was over. But he couldn't forget the look of the bodies. How they lay. How they moved and then didn't. The plastic hair clip in the soft brown hair of the dead girl in the pedal pushers. The way she smelled of feces. Now that he was alone, his mind reeled uncontrollably through the memories.

Stripping the shirt off, he climbed the steps to his apartment and went inside and got in the shower. For a long time, he stood there, running the water hot and then cold, but nothing stopped the memories.

He couldn't recall what he had thought at the time it was all happening, and now he felt as if he were watching it over again, but this time from the outside, like someone watching a movie. Only when he remembered lifting Shelly into his arms did he feel like part of the picture. The slippery feel of the blood. How her breast had melted into his hands. The sound of the bullet when it hit the flagpole. Jack falling, trying to stand, falling, standing, a puppet—up, down, up, down.

Wyatt scoured his hands with the soap and dug remnants of blood from under his nails.

"Don't come for me!" Jack had yelled.

He had been so quiet in the hospital, his bandages hidden under the blanket. Certainly he must have seen worse bloodshed in Vietnam, but there had been a troubling look of detachment in his eyes today in the hospital that Wyatt hadn't seen before—and he knew Jack better than almost anyone did. Having grown up next door to each other in San Antonio, they were more like brothers than cousins. Jack was two years older. He had a moralistic streak so strong that even as a child he wouldn't so much as sneak a grape from the grocery store that Wyatt's father managed unless he paid for it. Wyatt had sometimes found these standards intimidating and irritating, but he had secretly admired them, too.

Arvin Street, where they'd grown up and where their parents still lived, practically backed up to Fort Sam Houston, and when they were grade school age, Jack would hang around the gates and watch the soldiers, and Wyatt would often tag along. The two of them would stand on the cemetery wall at attention during burials, or play army among the tombstones. Jack could name all the Buffalo Soldiers buried together in one section, and in junior high he won a ribbon for a paper on Geronimo's imprisonment at the fort. He was so entranced by Geronimo that he talked his parents into driving him out to Arizona to look for the caves in the mountains where the warrior had hidden out when the army was looking for him.

Wyatt wasn't much interested in Geronimo; he preferred card games and board games—Careers, Life, Four Square, and six-card poker—which he and Jack played with the rest of the boys on the street. He was the neighborhood poker champion by the time he was thirteen, and when there weren't enough kids to play, he would make up games with different hands that didn't exist in the real game. They played croquet with Wiffle balls and nine irons, and Jack was the only

person he was never able to beat. He could beat Jack in backyard basketball, though, playing Horse with tipping, and could beat him at
Monopoly, since Jack only stockpiled the money and wouldn't take any
risks. Chess was the only game in which they were equally matched,
both having a natural patience with the process of attrition.

Jack was a senior in high school, working for his father in the parts
department of the Chevrolet dealership, when he walked into a Mexican restaurant in a barrio of San Antonio one day and met Delia, who
was waiting tables. Her family owned the restaurant.

Wyatt met her a week later when Jack took her to the movies. She
was slender, with small breasts and straight black hair that fell to her
shoulders. Jack was already in love with her, but waited several months
before he told his parents about her, knowing they would disapprove,
since she was a Mexican and a Catholic.

When he finally did tell them about her, their reaction was so heated
that Wyatt and his parents heard the yelling from next door. Jack
hauled his belongings over and moved into Wyatt's bedroom, where
the two of them bunked like brothers until Jack graduated from high
school.

"White people should date white people," Jack's father declared
whenever his sister, who was Wyatt's mother, tried to talk him into
changing his mind. "That girl should find a Mexican boy." He was a
card-carrying Democrat who refused to vote for Kennedy on the
grounds that Kennedy was a Catholic.

When Jack left San Antonio for Austin and UT, Delia stayed behind and worked at the restaurant and took classes at a local Catholic
university. Jack came home to see her almost every weekend until he
graduated, and enlisted in the army, and was sent immediately to
Vietnam.

Wyatt was at UT himself by that time, and when he was home to
see his parents he would go by the Mexican restaurant to see Delia.
They would sit together in one of the booths and she'd let him read
parts of Jack's letters—mostly love letters that didn't say much about
anything Jack was doing, except that he was clearing the area around
an air force base called Bien Hoa. It was early in the war, before major
protests had started, and no one knew much about what was going on,
or cared much about it.

By then, Wyatt was getting involved with Elaine, a grave, tall, sexy
girl from the East Coast, with long hair that tumbled about her when

they made love. He didn't think about the war any more than he had to.

When Jack returned home after nine months away, minus part of an ear and half his hearing, his parents welcomed him, with the hope that he might have forgotten Delia—as if the explosion that took his ear might have blown her out of his mind.

Instead, he became a Catholic in order to marry her. The wedding was an elaborate Catholic ceremony, and, since then, Jack had seen his parents only a couple of times. Remembering how disoriented and helpless Jack had looked in the hospital bed today, Wyatt wished they weren't coming.

After showering, he dressed quickly and drove to the hospital, where he found the parking lot filled and the hallways crowded. He stopped at Shelly Maddox's door, wondering how she was doing. He could not quite empty his mind of her. But her door was shut, and he didn't want to disturb her.

Elaine and Delia were still in Jack's room, awaiting his parents' arrival. The air was close and stuffy. Jack looked unnatural in the fluorescent lighting, his eyelids partly closed. A box of Camels lay on the bed beside him. He asked if he could have a minute alone with Wyatt, and the women quietly left. Wyatt pulled a chair beside the bed, and Jack shifted under the blanket, his face sweaty against the stiff pillow, and said, "Guess what happened to me today."

Wyatt studied him, trying to guess what he wanted. "You got shot in the leg by a crazy fucker."

"Try again."

"Not a crazy fucker?"

"Not shot in the leg."

"What do you mean?"

"I mean I got shot in the balls." He made a noise that was supposed to sound like laughter, then waited for Wyatt to take in what he had said. "For whatever it's worth, I'll still be able to have sex."

"Then there's no problem," Wyatt said with relief.

"The minor one of fertility. No kids for Delia."

"The doctor told you that? You're sure?"

"It's what he told me."

"And he's sure about it?"

"You want me to give you the details?"

"Does Delia know?"

"He told her."

"I bet there's something someone can do."

"Nope, nothing to be done." He stared up at the ceiling. "I'm a goddamn freak. I've got one ear. I can't give her kids. This morning I was her husband, and now I'm this . . . *thing* she's stuck with."

"She doesn't see it that way."

"No. Do me a favor, will you? Don't tell anyone."

"Of course."

"Not ever."

The sudden oppressive weight that Wyatt felt was worse than pity—it was guilt. He thought of the moment when Jack had fallen, and wondered if it should have been him instead. He was the one who had looked through the balusters and seen Shelly Maddox moving after he thought she was dead.

He remembered how Delia had looked standing in front of the doors to the ICU and talking with the doctor. How she had backed against the wall and put her hands to her stomach.

# DAY FROM NIGHT

Shelly came awake in the hospital at intervals, her thoughts fogged by Demerol, time lurching from moment to moment as jerkily as pictures in a View-Master. She blinked and people appeared and vanished. Her mother stood at the foot of the bed, hair flattened against her head as if she had slept in the chair. Then her father stood in the same place with cards and flowers. Then no one was there. Her roommate, Becky, sat beside her, offering pea soup and cookies. Daylight spread in sloping squares, disappearing and reappearing abruptly. It shrugged itself into corners. Shelly knew day from night, but dawn and dusk confused her. Voices drifted from the hall. Nurses inserted needles into the veins in her hands, and helped her urinate into a pan. She asked about the guy named Jack who was injured because he'd helped her, and she was told he was down the hall. But she was too weak to go see him. She asked about the shooter in the tower, but later couldn't remember what she'd been told. She remembered his name made a whirring sound that reminded her of a bird. A nurse said that policemen had shot him.

Memories of that day snapped at her at unpredictable moments: the awkward gesture of the boy as he fell in front of her, the flies wading in her blood. The worst were seared in her mind by the bright sunlight that day, and her only trick to dispel them was to haul the rescuing image of Wyatt and Jack into their midst. Once, she opened her eyes and saw Wyatt watching her from the chair. Later he was gone.

She knew so little about him: that he had worn a madras shirt. That his feet had been bare. That he wore glasses. Jack was short and muscular and had run low to the ground in her direction as she lay on the plaza. Wyatt was taller; he had come straight at her. At the flagpole he had shielded her and wrapped her twisted arm in his shirt. He had embraced her and cocked his knees around her, making a cave of protection. She recalled his feet on either side of her in the grass.

She heard her mother talking to him in the hall. "God bless your parents for raising such a good young man like yourself."

Drowsy from medication, Shelly composed a note to Jack: "I feel so guilty that you were hurt. I won't ever forget how you saved my life. When they let me get up, I will come to thank you in person."

Her mother took the letter to Jack's room, and returned and said Jack was sleeping but that she had left the note with his wife. "She's a Mexican," she said, "—real pretty."

Later, Shelly continued to ask about the person in the tower. "Who was he?"

"He was a son of a bitch," her father answered angrily. "He was a goddamn son of a bitch." She had never heard him swear.

Her mother said, "He had a brain tumor. They found it when they did the autopsy."

"Plenty of people have brain tumors," her father said. "And they don't go kill a bunch of innocent people."

"How many people did he kill?"

"Sixteen," her mother told her.

"And gunned down nearly forty," her father added. "The son of a bitch. Ex-marine. Boy Scout. Of all the goddamn things. He stabbed his wife to death. Murdered his mother. Then went up in the tower and shot people. Hell of a psychopath."

"He was a student," her mother said.

Later, Shelly's father offered to walk her down the hall to see Jack Stone, but she wanted to go alone.

"It's room three fifteen," her father said. "His wife's name is Delia. She's a nice young Mexican lady."

Shelly's arm throbbed in the cast and her legs were weak, but walking felt good. She knocked on Jack's door, and when no one answered, she said, "It's Shelly Maddox." She was about to give up waiting, when Jack said, "Come in," and she pushed the door open and saw him sitting in a chair with a blanket over his lap. The sight of him sent her mind whirling back to that day.

"How are you doing?" he asked her.

"Better. What about you?"

"I want to get out of this place," he said. "But I'm glad to see you.

I've been trying to get hold of a wheelchair so I could come see you." He gestured toward the foot of the bed. "Sorry there's not another chair. Sit down."

Her legs dangled over the edge. "When do you think you'll go home?"

"I'm hoping tomorrow. What about you?"

"I don't know when. I was worried you'd leave before I could get out of bed and come thank you. I can't help feeling responsible for what happened, since you were out there because of me."

"I was out there because of a schmuck up in the tower."

She hadn't remembered the problem with Jack's ear, and wasn't sure she had noticed, that day. She tried not to stare. He lit a cigarette and offered her one, but she shook her head. "No thanks. You know what I wonder? It's pointless, but I can't quit wondering why he chose us—what made him choose the people he did."

Jack tapped the ash from the cigarette onto a saucer. "I've got a hunch there wasn't a lot of thought involved in it," he said.

"Probably not," she agreed. "And I shouldn't be dwelling on it. But I am. And I can't seem to sleep. It may be the medicines. Do you have stitches in your leg?"

He nodded. "I guess you've got plenty of stitches."

"That, and screws to hold the bone in my arm together. I thought they'd take the screws out at some point, but the doctor says they're going to leave them in. Your wife's not here?"

"She went out to get cigarettes." He held up the nearly empty pack.

"I hope I can meet her," Shelly said. "And of course I want to meet Wyatt. He came to my room, but I'd had a lot of medicine and wasn't able to talk to him much. Or at least I don't remember it if I did."

"He was checking on you."

She looked toward the window. Craning her neck, she could see the tower. "It's still hard to believe what happened," she said. "Not that I don't have proof." She lifted her cast. Of course Jack knew about proof, she thought, with another glance at his ear.

He saw her. "Vietnam," he explained.

"Oh."

"Just an accident on the base. I was the lucky survivor."

He didn't look lucky, sitting stiffly in the chair with the blanket over his lap and half his ear missing. He looked tired. She guessed he wasn't as cheerful as he tried to seem.

"I should get back to my room," she said. "My parents are there. Has your family been here?"

"Come and gone," he told her. "Listen, if you get bored, come back and see me."

"I might come back tomorrow, and maybe I'll meet your wife. And if Wyatt comes back, will you tell him I'd like to meet him?"

"I believe the feeling is mutual," Jack said.

Back in her room, she continued to think about Jack, and hoped he didn't regret going out to help her on the plaza. It would be easy for him to regret what he'd done, and it mattered to her that he didn't.

When she finally fell asleep that night, a sinister impression that something was fundamentally wrong crept into her dreams—that a disturbance, not just in her mind but in the world in general, had made something vital go suddenly missing. She tried to struggle awake, but felt pinned to the bed. Lifting herself onto her elbow, she felt a crushing pain through her arm and remembered the cast. Her eyes opened to darkness, and the room seemed to be turning in circles around her. She tried to reason that this was from the medication, but still could not shake the feeling that something had gone terribly wrong. She lay sweating and listening, searching the dark, her heart pounding. The bandages on her breast squeezed at her breath as if a snake had tightened around her. "Mom?" she whispered, even knowing her mother was not there. "Mom? I need you." Gathering courage, she forced herself up and out of the bed and groped her way to the door and pulled it open, facing the dim and deserted hallway. "Is there a nurse? Please?" she called, and started toward the nurses' station, but there was no one there. The door to Jack's room was ajar. She stumbled toward it, pushed it open, and saw Jack asleep in the bed and someone else in the chair. "Can I come in?" she asked in a desperate whisper.

It was Wyatt who got up out of the chair. "Shelly?"

"I'm sorry. I'm dizzy. Maybe it's the medicine. I just feel . . . awful. I feel scared."

He put a hand on her forehead. "You're sweating. You're hot. I'll get the nurse."

He settled her into the chair and then left to get the nurse. She curled her legs up under herself and tucked her gown around her feet. Tears ran down her cheeks. Wiping the sweat from her forehead, she watched Jack as he slept, his arm cocked over his head.

Wyatt returned with a nurse, who flipped the lights on, and Jack sat up in the bed. The nurse put a thermometer into Shelly's mouth. "A hundred and two," she said when she checked it. "You probably have an infection. I'm going to talk to the doctor."

When the nurse had gone, Wyatt sat on the foot of the bed and looked at Shelly in the chair. He took off his glasses and cleaned them on his shirttail and put them back on.

"I'm okay," she told him.

"You're sweating pretty bad."

"I feel horrible."

"I can take you back to your room and stay with you, if you want. Or you can stay here."

"I don't know. I don't know what's wrong. I had this terrible feeling someone was in the room. Like someone was watching me. I've never felt that before."

"You've felt it," Jack said from the bed. "That day. Stay here."

"Do you want the lights on, or off?" Wyatt asked her.

"Off," she said. She had started to shiver.

"Take my blanket," Jack told her, pushing it toward the foot of the bed.

Wyatt covered her up, and switched the light off. "Try to sleep," he said. She drifted, aware of the nurse returning and placing pills in her hand and giving her sips of water, and aware of Wyatt standing nearby, and Jack's cigarette glowing.

Before daylight Wyatt and the nurse walked her back to her room and tucked her into the bed. Later, she woke to the sun shining brightly through the windows and her parents standing over her. Wyatt had left his phone number scribbled on a napkin with a note that said "Call anytime."

During the day, the fever left her. She hoped Wyatt would stop by the room, or that Jack would come down in a wheelchair, but neither of them did. The following morning she returned to Jack's room and found he had left the hospital.

# 5

# LONG-DISTANCE

When Shelly was allowed to leave after a week in the hospital, her parents took her home to Lockhart and settled her into the squat little frame bungalow where she had lived all her life until college. Neighbors and friends from childhood brought cards and flowers.

At first Shelly liked having visitors, but after a couple of weeks she became impatient with so much small talk. Friends asked her a lot of questions about what happened that day. Other friends avoided the topic, as if the shooting had never occurred and Shelly had come back home on vacation.

One day a girl she had played volleyball with in high school brought her a *Time* magazine with a cover picture of a stocky young guy in black-rimmed glasses. Shelly thought it was just a magazine until she saw the heading MADMAN IN THE TOWER. She felt as if something had grabbed her by the throat. He was sitting with a dog on a bench and reading a newspaper. "I'll read it later," she told the girl, and put it away.

After her parents had gone to bed that night, she got the magazine out and sat among old sneakers in her closet to read by flashlight, flipping past pictures of Luci Johnson's wedding and an article on race riots before she found the story. In one photograph, he was seated at someone's breakfast table beside a potted plant. There was a diagram of the UT campus littered with red and black stick figures, the red ones spread out flat, with their names written beside them. These were the dead people. The females were drawn in triangular dresses to distinguish them from the males. The figures in black were hunched as if they were crawling. Shelly stared at the one near the hedge, who was supposed to be her. Inside the square made by the hedge, not far away from the flagpole, was the stick figure supposed to be Jack. In real life, he'd been shot later than she was, but here he was on the same flat, timeless plane, hunched over the same way. Beside him, the boy in the grass was drawn in red.

So, she thought. That boy is dead. She remembered his surfer shirt and how he had bled from the throat, and recalled the sounds he had made. Closing the magazine, she looked at the picture of Charles Whitman on the bench with his dog, and studied his hands and how he held the newspaper, and imagined his finger pulling a trigger.

One morning her mother drove her back to Austin to see the orthopedist who had operated on her arm. The tower seemed to grow taller as they drove closer to town. When they were close enough to see the clock face, her mother said, and not for the first time, "You know we don't have to come here. We could go to a doctor in San Antonio."

Shelly told her she wasn't afraid of coming to Austin. But this wasn't exactly true. And she kept her eye on the tower.

When they were back in Lockhart, her mother went to the grocery store, and Shelly attempted to fold laundry. The cast was heavy and made her clumsy, and her arm sweated into the gauzy interior, intensifying the swollen, claustrophobic feeling. Stitches under compression bandages tugged at her breast. She spread the blouse flat on the bedspread and worked to smooth it out and fold the sleeves, but it puckered at the shoulders and she couldn't anchor it. She got on her knees and tried to pin it down with her chin, then yanked it up and flapped it around and threw it onto the floor, where it lay in a wrinkled heap on the carpet. Eventually she picked it up and sat on the bed awhile, holding the wadded shirt and staring down at the laces dangling from her tennis shoes. She had not been able to tie them. The window unit made grinding noises.

She wanted to cry, but had done enough of that. She was dizzy from the medication. Her mother was still at the grocery store, her father at work. She sat on her bed with a *National Geographic* from two years ago, leafing through the story about the Peace Corps.

Bolivia. Tanganyika. Gabon. Turkey. Sarawak. Ecuador.

There were lots of pictures. She had looked at them so often the pages were wrinkled: Volunteers in Bolivia vaccinating a little girl against smallpox. Trainees on an obstacle course—rappelling, rock climbing. It would be a long time before her arm would be healed enough to manage something like that. Eventually, though, it would, and she would make sure she was ready. Only one person in four who applied was accepted for training, and not all the people who trained would be chosen to go abroad. But if anything stopped her from going, it would not be her arm. It would not be a crazy guy up in a tower.

One series of pictures had the caption "Softhearted city girls learn to kill chickens for their dinner." She wasn't thrilled by the look of the knife whacking the head off or the picture of the volunteer nursing a man with leprosy by coating his arm in hot wax. But she could do those things. She could do all of that.

She studied all the pictures. Two guys were herding sheep in Bolivia, and she liked the way they looked. In Gabon, volunteers stood talking with Albert Schweitzer at his jungle hospital. Schweitzer wore a white safari hat and a bow tie. In Sarawak, a volunteer wore a headdress and loincloth, and his leg was painted to look like a tattoo. His glasses reminded Shelly of Wyatt Calvert's. He was tall like Wyatt, too. In another picture a girl sailed a canoe in the Indian Ocean. The sail was made of patchwork, and the sun shone through it romantically.

Shelly turned back to the guys and the sheep in Bolivia. She wondered if guys like that would have any interest in her now, with her arm and her breast as they were. She would look better with time. But how much better? The doctor had been vague about that.

She was still looking at the guys herding the sheep when the phone rang in the kitchen, and she found herself talking to an old boyfriend from junior high, who was calling from Texas Tech. "I just found out that you were one of the people that got shot," he said. "My mom told me."

"I'm okay," she told him. She was tired of talking to people who couldn't really understand. "What about you? How's Tech?"

They talked awhile, but even before she hung up, she felt lonely. No one she knew had any idea what it was like to have a bullet through your breast and your arm, and she didn't want to explain. Wyatt Calvert and Jack Stone were the only people who could ever understand what it was like out there on the plaza.

She got Wyatt's number out of a drawer and stood looking at it, wondering what he would say if she called him. She wasn't sure what his wife would feel about that. At last she dialed the operator and asked to make a person-to-person call to Wyatt Calvert in Austin. His phone rang and rang, and Shelly waited, wrapping the phone cord around the puffy fingers ballooning from the cast. Finally, a woman answered. "Hello?" She sounded distracted. Her voice was muffled by the hissing long-distance, and Shelly heard music and voices in the background. "I have a call for Wyatt Calvert from Shelly Maddox in Lockhart," the operator said.

Shelly noticed a pause, and then the woman dropped her voice and whispered to someone, "It's Shelly Maddox from Lockhart."

Wyatt's voice came on the line. "This is Wyatt."

When the operator connected them, Wyatt said, "Hey, I'm glad you called. How are you? How's your arm?"

"It's all right. Is this a bad time? It sounds like you have people there."

"It's not a bad time at all; it's just hard for me to hear. My wife's having a party for some girls from her sorority, so it's pretty loud. Are you feeling any better?"

"Much better."

"And I guess you're still in the cast?"

"For a couple more weeks," Shelly told him. "Unless I chew my arm off first."

The background chatter grew louder above "Wooly Bully" by Sam the Sham and the Pharaohs. "What did you say?" Wyatt asked. "I'm sorry, I couldn't hear you. They're in the other room, but they've got the radio turned way up."

"I have to wear the cast for a couple more weeks," she said.

"Will you be coming back to school?"

"I plan to, but I don't know when. The doctor told my mom I shouldn't go back this year. I will if I can, but my dad doesn't think it's a good idea."

"Well, he's the sheriff," Wyatt said.

"Of Lockhart. Not of me."

"But maybe you should take it easy and just rest up for a year."

"In Lockhart? Maybe you've never been here."

"I have. For barbecue."

"Really? At Black's, or Kreuz Market?"

"Both. Jack and I used to drive over from San Antonio sometimes on Saturdays. He liked Kreuz and I liked Black's, so he'd drop me off at Black's and eat at Kreuz and then pick me up and we'd go home."

"How's he doing?"

"Really well. Glad to be home."

"I never got to meet his wife," Shelly said. "Or yours. What's your wife's name?"

"Elaine."

"Is she from Texas?"

"From Hartford, Connecticut."

"How did she end up in Texas?"

"I'm afraid I'm responsible for that. She was in school in Vermont and came down here to visit a friend, and we met at a party. And later she transferred here for her last year—she was a year ahead of me. We've only been married a few months. How about you? How come you were in summer classes?"

"I wanted to hurry and finish so I could join the Peace Corps. Which is why I don't like falling behind. I guess I shouldn't complain, though. A lot of people lost a lot more than a few months."

"It's fine with me if you complain," he said. "I'm happy to have a reason not to deal with the sorority sisters."

Shelly looked at the clock over the stove to see how long she'd been talking. The call would be charged to her parents' bill. It was almost five-thirty, and her parents would be home any minute for supper and to watch the *Dick Van Dyke Show*; the final episode was being re-aired tonight.

"How did you get interested in the Peace Corps?" Wyatt asked her.

"I heard a speech Kennedy made on the radio, and it sounded interesting. Like a good thing to do. Also . . . honestly, it sounded like a way to get out of Lockhart."

"You don't have to go to Borneo to get out of Lockhart."

"No, but the Peace Corps would be an adventure. Of course I have to get through school first, and learn a language, and that's going to take time. If I don't go back this year, I'll probably stay here in Lockhart and learn Spanish. What about you? What are you studying?"

"I just started a graduate program in art."

"Art? That's fantastic."

"Or a fool's errand." He laughed—a nice, soft laugh, she thought. "Kind of a sissy profession, according to my wife."

"It's not. What kind of art?"

"Painting. I've been using old-style tempera paint. Do you know what that is?"

"You're forgetting I'm from Lockhart. I barely know about crayons."

He laughed at that. "It's made with egg yolk. The oldest paint there is. You can't blend it like oil paints or watercolors. You have to put the layers on top of one another. Very thin layers. It takes a lot of patience."

In the background, a woman was calling him. "Sorry," he said. "It's crazy here."

"You should go back to your party," she said.

"It's not mine. But you're probably right. Can I call you back later?"

She almost said yes. But it didn't seem right. He was married. "I'll look for you when I'm back at school," she told him.

"All right. And meanwhile, you have my number if you need anything."

"This is going to sound ridiculous, but thank you for saving me."

"My pleasure."

Afterward she stood thinking about the conversation, and tried to picture him brushing layers of thin paint one on top of another. She had forgotten to ask what he painted. Landscapes? People? Maybe abstracts.

Her arm, trapped in the cast, had started itching again. It was time for the daily changing of the bandage on her breast, so she went to her bedroom and worked her T-shirt off over the cast, looking at herself in the long mirror that hung on the closet door. The air from the window unit made a breeze at her back. She had lost weight and was thin, and her blue jeans were loose. Her breast—the one that was whole—was pale. The other was taped with gauze, which she carefully peeled away. The bullet had gone through sideways at a downward angle, tearing away part of the breast and then blasting through her arm. She stared at the bruises checkered with stitches that ran in several directions. The nipple had not been injured, but a section of flesh the size of her palm was missing, leaving a crater that puckered into the stitching.

Pulling her hair over her shoulder, she tried to cover her breast. If only her hair would grow faster. It had some red like her mother's, and she tried to imagine it down to her waist and covering all the problems. Frustrated, she tugged at the ragged tips, but they reached only down to the nipple. The air played softly at her back. The plaster cast kept her elbow bent at a right angle. Sweat dampened her forehead, and her shoelaces trailed on the carpet.

# 6

# TEMPERA

Shelly didn't return to school that year. Her arm had not healed correctly and required a second surgery, and afterward the scars still tugged and pulled it in a way that made Shelly hate it. She couldn't stretch it out properly, and the elbow didn't bend right. She thought the whole mess of it was incredibly ugly, and she grew her hair longer so she wouldn't have to look at her breast when she didn't have any clothes on. But the new hairstyles were short, so she cut it again. She wore long sleeves, but when spring and summer arrived, she felt bound up, sweating in long sleeves. She was too tied to her parents and the house, and her only friends were the ones who hadn't gone off to college, but had stayed to work at the local creamery or the poultry-processing plant or the peanut factory. A former boyfriend named Billy worked on the oil rigs sixteen miles down the road in Luling, and on weekends he took Shelly to the drive-in movie in San Marcos in his rusty pickup truck.

In the dead of night, when the trains rattled through Lockhart, Shelly lay awake in her little room and wished she were traveling in one of them. It wouldn't matter where she was going, as long as the train was moving.

Sometimes during the weekdays she borrowed her mother's station wagon and drove to the roller-skating rink in Fentress and skated around in circles. It was the closest she came to freedom.

The most useful thing she did was to teach herself Spanish and read books from the library about the countries she hoped to go to if the Peace Corps would accept her. She figured she could take things one step at a time: learn the language, study the countries, then go back to school. She would have to remain patient. She sat at the kitchen table, speaking Spanish to herself, saying sentences like "*¿No quieres* *pasear por unos minutos, Pedro?*" It came to her one day that she was asking a phantom Pedro to go on a walk with her, but she wasn't asking any real people.

It was September of '67, a year and a month after the shootings, when she finally returned to UT. Relieved though she was to move back into the dorm with college friends and resume a normal life, she soon realized how disruptive her memories of the shooting were going to be. They dogged her around campus, and she avoided the South Mall plaza. She intended to walk across it someday, but the tower was threatening and the clock still looked like an eye. Sometimes she tried to stare the eye into retreat or submission—as if she could make the tower uproot itself and go away by the sheer force of her contempt. She glared at it from classroom windows or from the distance of the street, and the scariest thing about it was how little it seemed to care. The bells continued to ring on schedule, hammering fear into her heart all day long, every quarter hour. The song "Monday, Monday" could stop her in her tracks wherever she was, and sometimes she would wake in the night with the lyrics soaring disturbingly through her dreams.

Always she kept her eyes open for Wyatt or Jack. But when six weeks passed and she hadn't seen them, she decided they were no longer there. She was surprised at noon one day in the Student Union, on her way to the Commons for lunch, when she saw Wyatt walking in her direction in the crowded corridor near the Chuckwagon cafeteria. He didn't appear to notice her. He looked slightly different now from how she remembered him. His hair and sideburns were longer and the frames of his glasses were bigger. He wore a blue work shirt and carried a navy surplus pea jacket and a green book bag. She paused to think about how to greet him, and someone jostled against her and caused her to drop her books.

What Wyatt saw was a girl in a yellow cardigan and a skirt the color of ball moss, scrabbling on the floor and shoving her rescued books into the bend of an arm that was strangely immobile. She had secured the books before he realized who she was.

"Shelly?"

"Hi," she said.

"Hey there." He stood grinning at her. "How long have you been back?"

"Just this semester—a couple of months."

She was thinner than he remembered, and prettier than he had thought. "Were you headed to lunch?"

"Yes, at the Commons."

"The Chuckwagon's better," he told her. "Come on. Come with me."

It was filled with longhairs, who were smoking around the tables, and the din of clattering trays and utensils was deafening. Wyatt took trays from the stack and ushered Shelly into line in front of him.

Two bearded guys behind Wyatt joked with him. "Hey, Earp. You're in art. You know Farrah Fawcett?"

"Everybody knows Farrah, Kyle."

"Can you get me a date with her?"

"I couldn't even get you a date without her."

He introduced the guys to Shelly while she studied the food selection. They wrote for the student paper and were complaining to Wyatt about the increasing amount of censorship. "It's the fucking administration," one of them said.

Shelly chose a bowl of watery green beans and a square of orange Jell-O pebbled with miniature marshmallows.

"That's all you're planning to eat?" Wyatt asked her.

He ordered the chicken-fried steak platter, helped himself to a slice of chocolate pie, and insisted on paying for Shelly's meal at the register. She claimed a table in the corner while he carried the trays one by one. "How do you usually do this?" he asked, setting her tray on the table.

"I've never been in here," she said.

He sat across from her. "Not your kind of people?"

"No. The kind my father would arrest."

He laughed.

"A bunch of hippies running down LBJ and the war," she said, and took a bite of the Jell-O. "How is Jack? Is he around?"

"He's around. About to get his Ph.D. in history, and also working as a night watchman at Frost Bank."

"So he's all right?'

"He is."

"It feels strange talking to you."

"It's kind of a weird connection," he agreed, starting on his chicken-fried steak while she ate her wobbly Jell-O. "Are you eating the green beans last?"

"Why?"

"It just seems like Jell-O would be dessert."

"In my family, Jell-O's a salad."

He studied her. Her hair was styled in a loose flip the color of polished bronze, and she had an open, friendly look, with eyes that were an interesting shade of green and tilted slightly upward at the outer corners when she smiled. Her skin was light and smooth. A speck of orange Jell-O clung to the downy hairs on her upper lip. He wondered about her injured breast. He had never been sure if she was struck by one bullet or two.

Watching him stir the puddle of white gravy into his mashed potatoes, she decided she didn't especially like the stylish look of his glasses. Black at the top, the frames faded to clear at the bottom. And she wasn't sure she approved of his sideburns, either. And his hair was unkempt. But he was great-looking, somehow. His face had a nice lean structure. He watched her with an attentive, unhurried expression.

Putting her fork down, she said, "What do you remember about that day?"

"Are you sure you want to talk about it?"

"When you first decided to help me. How did that happen? It looked to me like you came out of nowhere."

"We came out of the history building, initially," he said.

"Is Jack sorry he came to help me?"

"No, he's not sorry."

"How do you know?"

"I know."

She didn't see how he could, for sure. She looked at his plate. "Do you like the chicken-fried steak?"

"Not really. Do you want some?"

"I don't really like that kind of gravy. So how are you and Jack cousins—through your moms or your dads, or what?"

"His father and my mother are brother and sister. You've got some Jell-O over your mouth."

She wiped it off with her napkin.

"Are you in a dorm?" he asked.

"Yes. Kinsolving,"

"Oh, so you're one of those lucky ones with the air conditioning. It gets pretty hot in student housing where I live. And Elaine and I had a baby in August."

Shelly tried not to react to this. She shouldn't care if he had a baby. She should be happy for him. But her mood dropped. Somehow, fatherhood made her connection to him seem tawdry and incidental. "A boy or a girl?"

"A boy—Nathan. Nate."

"So your wife's at home with him?"

"Until I get the car to her in a little while." He didn't actually want to discuss Elaine, having argued with her before leaving for campus. They were behind on rent and needed a second car besides the '61 Cutlass he had purchased used, and he couldn't afford to buy one as long as he was in school. Either he or Elaine had to stay home with the baby, and the other needed to earn a decent paycheck, and it was obvious to both of them that Wyatt—even working part-time painting houses—was currently doing neither.

"Were those guys calling you Earp because of Wyatt Earp?"

"It's the never-ending joke."

"That's not who you're named after?"

"I'm named after my grandfather. We're from a long line of Wyatts." He looked at her arm in the sleeve of the yellow cardigan. It lay crookedly on the table. "It's all right?"

"I can bend it, but I can't straighten it out the whole way. It feels like there are rubber bands around the elbow, keeping it like this. It looks pretty bad."

"Can I see it?"

"See it?"

"Look at it."

"Now?"

"If that's okay."

"If you're up for it. I don't usually show it to anyone. It's ugly. Beware."

He watched her pull the cardigan off her shoulder, push her shirt-sleeve up, and reveal a thin, misshapen arm webbed with inflamed scars. Above the elbow, the arm turned oddly. "The bullet went all the way through," she said. "Right here. There's a piece of metal in there, holding the bone together. Or I guess the bone has grown back, but the metal's still in there. If you press here, you can feel some of the screws."

He put his fingers where she indicated. The scars felt smooth and oddly erotic to his touch. A girl from his design class paused to talk, but when she saw his hand on Shelly's arm, she was flummoxed and walked on past with her tray.

"Feels creepy, doesn't it," Shelly said about her arm.

The ropy, sensual feel of the scars unsettled Wyatt, the pulse of the blue veins in Shelly's wrist reminding him of how he had felt her heartbeat while he was trying to stop her from bleeding. He turned her arm over, noting the high school ring on her middle finger and the blunt cut of her unpainted nails, then turned it back again and looked at the scars. "Not creepy at all. It looks nearly perfect."

She dragged the cardigan off the opposite shoulder and stretched her right arm out beside the left. "It used to look like this."

But he felt somehow more entitled to look at the injured arm.

"Is it horrible?" she asked, rolling the shirtsleeves down and buttoning up the cuffs.

"It's wonderful. They put it back together. Are you going to finish your beans?"

She pushed the bowl toward him, and he ate the green beans and started into his chocolate pie while she tugged her sweater back on. "Is that paint under your nails?" she asked him.

He looked at his nails. They were cut to the quick, but no matter how short he cut them, he couldn't prevent the blue paint stains from collecting under the edges.

"I'm just getting you back for the Jell-O I had on my mouth," she said. He noticed a fleeting smile. "So I take it you're still painting?"

"When I can."

"Landscapes? Portraits?"

"Objects," he said. "Rocks. Chairs. Windows. For practice. If you'll walk over to the art building with me I'll show you. A couple of my students are using tempera."

"You're teaching?"

"Just a freshman foundation course."

He carried their trays and returned to the table for his jacket and book bag and Shelly's books. Shelly was still seated.

"Can we go down Twenty-fourth Street instead of across the plaza?" she asked him.

He pulled his jacket on. "You don't ever cross the plaza?"

"Twenty-fourth Street is just as close," she said.

"No it isn't." He sat back down. "Are you planning to avoid the plaza forever?"

"For three more years."

"Very funny."

"Actually, I've been trying to get up the nerve to walk across it."

"How about now?"

She frowned.

"Come on."

"Do you cross it a lot?"

"A couple of times a week," he said.

"Does Jack?"

"He does. Look, I bet it won't be as hard as you think."

Finally, she agreed. But in the corridor, her feet dragged. "I don't want to be out there when the bells ring."

He checked his watch. "We've got ten minutes before they ring. And we can get across in a few seconds. We'll walk a straight line along the front of the building and over to the East Mall."

They exited into mottled sunlight and an autumn breeze tumbling leaves through the courtyard. Bevo, the Longhorn mascot, was tethered to an orange livestock trailer parked at the curb on the Drag, next to a Peace Corps booth, his student handlers, in orange shirts, allowing people to pet him. Nearby, a girl with a placard for SDS sat in an open plywood shack that was covered with antiwar slogans and paintings of bombs falling on villages, and an old man plucked a banjo, shouting obscenities at people who stopped to listen. He shook his banjo at a dog chasing a Frisbee. A banner tugged in the trees like a sail, announcing that *In Cold Blood* author Truman Capote would be reading at the Student Union.

The tower was obscured at first by the roof of the undergraduate library, but it emerged into view as they stepped away from the Student Union. Shelly's heart started to knock in her chest, and she was glad for the canopy of branches partially blocking the view. Still, she could see the tower rising above her, and she couldn't shake off the ominous sense that it could see her as well.

A student wearing a Colonel Sanders mask and a Mae West inflatable vest approached and handed Wyatt a pamphlet, then moved on, swinging his satchel.

"What's the pamphlet?" Shelly asked.

He opened it. "It says 'Join the Shadebourne Twink.' "

"What's the Shadebourne Twink?" She didn't want to keep walking.

"I don't have a clue."

Everything about the day was different from that day over a year ago when she had started across the plaza. She reminded herself of this. The weather was different. The air was chilly now, not hot. Clouds that looked like mounded scoops of ice cream traveled across the cold blue sky, shoved along by the breeze. And she would be walking from west to east, very close to the building, not diagonally across the center of the plaza from the opposite direction.

"You're sure your watch is right?"

"I promise."

When she started walking, her legs felt heavy. Off to the right, the flagpole rose from the concrete base. She didn't look at it. She looked at her shoes and made herself keep walking. A scatter of grackles out of the trees startled her, and she drew to a sudden stop but then continued, concentrating on her shoes hitting the pavement and the wind pushing her along. The air gusted, and the light shifted. Time didn't slow as it had on that day; everything moved. The flag tossed in the wind, clanging the chain against the pole. Shelly narrowed her focus. She kept aware of Wyatt beside her, and fixed her eyes on the black blur of her shoes scudding across the ground. She intended not to glance toward the place where she had fallen, but then gave in to the impulse, and looking at the spot pictured herself lying there in a lopsided circle of blood. She wanted to run, but willed herself to keep walking at the same steady pace, and then stopped and asked Wyatt to wait for her. She walked over and planted her feet on the square of pebbled cement where she had fallen, and made herself look up at the tower.

It was huge. Its height created the illusion that it was leaning toward her. She studied the deck and the enormous clock face and thought of Whitman's eyes from the cover of *Time* magazine. She pictured his finger on the trigger. *He's not up there now*, she told herself. But in her mind, he would always be up there. *It's cold today, not hot. I'm walking from a different direction.*

Her reassurances were empty whispers. Her heart pounded. But she didn't run. She glanced around and saw the students going about their business: a girl in a blue coat and black Mary Janes, a boy tossing his arm around his girlfriend, people moving with purpose across the plaza, energized by the cold.

Wyatt was waiting for her, holding her books, but she decided not to leave this spot until she no longer wanted so badly to run from it. She kept her feet planted exactly where her face had been seared against the hot cement that day, as if she were standing on her own crippled body. And she eyed the tower, the rows of windows and the observation deck at the top.

Finally she turned and looked at Wyatt. He was watching her. She lifted her palms, as if to say, See what I'm doing? and make light of it.

She thought he might smile, but he didn't. She walked to him and they continued across the plaza together, down the steps to the East Mall. She made herself walk slowly, but at the base of the steps her knees began to feel weak again, and her heart wouldn't stop pounding. Tears rolled down her cheeks.

"What is it?" Wyatt asked her, leaning his head down so he could see her eyes.

She kept walking, but couldn't stop crying. "I'll stop this in a minute."

When they had reached the art building, she splashed her face in the water fountain and drank more than she wanted, hoping the cold water would wash away the anxiety. But the pulse in her temples didn't slow down.

"I'm fine," she insisted. "I'm fine. I want to look at the paintings."

On the second floor he took her to a studio where one of his students, bent over a desk, was sanding a square board that was coated in what looked to Shelly like plaster. The student was a thin girl with a high forehead and sloping chin, and she smiled shyly when she saw Wyatt.

"Just like you warned me," she said, showing him the board. "The gesso bubbled."

He introduced her to Shelly as he adjusted the heat under a double boiler filled with pale brown glue, then ran his fingers over the plaster coating on the board, inspecting the surface and edges. "You'll need at least four coats on the back, and you should use a finer-grit sandpaper for this," he told the girl. He showed her how to make firm and efficient strokes, the sanded plaster covering his hands in white dust.

"Can Shelly see your geraniums?" he asked, and the girl took Shelly to a table on which a painting, about eight inches square, was lying. It was an amateurish work—Shelly could see that—but Wyatt pointed out colors and the interesting composition, and the girl was obviously pleased with the praise.

Afterward, he led Shelly down the hall to a boxlike corner office that he explained a professor had loaned him for the semester, and pulled from a bottom drawer in the desk three of his own paintings, laying them side by side on the desktop.

They were even smaller than the girl's painting, about as big as Wyatt's hand spread open, and at first Shelly thought they were photographs. When she looked closely, she was astonished.

One of the three was a long-stemmed white rose pictured against a black background, the petals so precise that Shelly had the impression she could touch them and feel the velvet texture of real petals. Another was of a half-submerged sand dollar with rippling water washing over it, every speck of sand distinct and the image of the sand dollar, exquisite, with its starlike shape in the center, slightly distorted by the movement of the shallow water.

The third painting, and the one she looked at longest, was of a red apple on a sunny windowsill. The apple was bruised and scarred, and the windowsill old, with cracking paint that gave the sense it could be peeled off in curling rectangular slivers. The bruises of the apple were painted so convincingly that Shelly could imagine the sweet, fermented flavor.

Pulling a book about tempera from the crowded shelves, Wyatt laid it open on the desk. He turned to illustrations showing how the paint was made, and explained that Andrew Wyeth was the contemporary master of tempera. "A lot of people dismiss him as too representational," Wyatt said. "But I think he's brilliant. Usually painting with tempera is about being precise, and for the artist there can be something nice and private about that, because people looking at the painting don't have to consider the artist or what he intended; they're just drawn to the subject. In my opinion Wyeth takes it beyond that, because his paintings aren't just about the subject. They're almost as much about what you don't see, as what you do. And I'm not talking about the configuration—like in this one, where you're looking through a doorway and can only see part of the room. I'm talking about an ethereal quality that's hard to describe. As if he's using a kind of paint the rest of us don't have. I'm not explaining it well."

"No, you are." Turning the page, she stopped on a painting by Wyeth titled *Wind from the Sea,* which revealed a view through a half-open window to the bright landscape beyond. Airy, transparent curtains with embroidered birds along the edges fluttered inward on the wind, and down below, outside the window, a curve of tire tracks crossed the flat land toward the water.

"One problem with tempera," Wyatt said, "is that roaches like to nibble the paint because of the egg yolk."

She put the book back on the shelf. Looking out the window, she didn't respond to anything he had just said. He wondered what she was thinking. Finally, with her back to him, she said, "I want you to see it."

"To see what?"

"Where he shot me."

He didn't know what she meant at first, but when she glanced at him, he did.

"Is it . . . because I was out there with you?"

"I don't know."

He waited.

"I don't know."

He hesitated, watching her, and then reached over and closed the door.

She pulled her sweater off and felt as if she were ridding herself of something oppressive. Unbuttoning her shirt and shifting the cup of her bra, turning her face to the window, she exposed the scarred breast, aware of how ugly it was.

He wondered if she was testing him to see if he, also, would look away. But he couldn't have done so. The light from the window lay across her, showing the purplish scars and creating a shadow in the indentation where the flesh was missing.

"There it is," she said. "That's what it looks like." She repositioned the bra, buttoned her shirt, and pulled her sweater back on. "Let's talk about something else."

In that moment, Wyatt's concern for Shelly's emotions partially obscured what he was feeling. But he knew that his life was changed. By revealing herself to him, she had declared the absence of rules. She hadn't seduced him in any way that either of them recognized, but she had laid herself bare, and the effect on him was immediate. Her trust bewitched him. He was confounded and bemused. Aroused and embarrassed.

Nothing he felt for Shelly at that moment was like anything he had ever felt for Elaine. He had never felt called on like this. Elaine was at home, unhappy with him for a number of reasons. He wasn't a good provider; he was barely supporting his family. She didn't like that he was in graduate school instead of out making a living. She didn't believe he could make a decent living as an artist.

And here was Shelly Maddox, implying that just looking at her was enough, and would heal her somehow.

# 7

# A PERFECT LIKENESS

They were drawn to each other, imprinted on each other. They had survived Charles Whitman, and the intensity of the experience had lingered in both of them. And the future was written the moment Shelly pulled her sweater off and averted her eyes.

They were not clueless or blameless. They were not their best selves in each other's presence either. A certain helplessness and weakness settled in, and self-deception. Shelly knew her feelings sooner than Wyatt knew his, because she couldn't escape them: when she thought of Wyatt, her heart pounded and her stomach knotted. Now when she walked with him across the plaza, she was unable to separate her anxiety about the tower from the anxious feeling of falling in love. She became keyed up and sleepless, nervous all the time. She knew she was trespassing. He was married. She was fretful every time she planned to see him. But when she was alone with him, in his car or in his office, she felt suddenly restful, as if nothing in her life could ever go wrong again. He had looked at her ruined breast and her twisted arm and hadn't been bothered by them. Other guys might have turned away, but Wyatt was different. She had nothing to hide from him.

Wyatt, on the other hand, lied to himself, refusing to think he was falling in love. He believed he was in control of his feelings right up to the moment he suddenly knew he wasn't.

The moment happened in November. Elaine had gone to Houston with a friend for the weekend and taken Nate with her, leaving Wyatt in Austin on his own with the car. He meant to spend the time on campus catching up on work, but Saturday morning he walked by Shelly's dormitory, thinking he might see her. When he didn't, he hung around the entrance and then walked around the dormitory and stood on the sidewalk under her window. He was about to ask himself what, exactly, he was doing here, when Shelly looked out and saw him. He waved at her, and she came down, and they sat in his car to talk. He mentioned that overcast days like this reminded him of days in high school when he and Jack would drive from San Antonio to Port Aransas during Christmas break and nearly freeze on the beach.

"I've never been to Port A in winter," Shelly told him.

He pictured how she would look walking on the beach in the wind and the cold, and thought of the churning water, the cawing gulls and scampering sandpipers. The shells and seaweed tumbling in with the foam. And suddenly he wanted nothing more than to drive Shelly to Port Aransas. They could be back that same night.

She balked at the suggestion. "I don't know. It doesn't seem right."

"We're friends," he said. "It's okay."

The drive took three and a half hours. When they passed through San Antonio, he turned off the highway into his old neighborhood and pointed out the old haunts—the stone wall of the cemetery at Fort Sam Houston that he and Jack used to climb over, and the street where they had grown up and where their parents still lived. He didn't drive down the street, in case his parents or Jack's parents might recognize the Cutlass, but he was happy talking about his childhood with Shelly.

On the ferry crossing from the mainland to Port Aransas, they got out of the car and stood at the rail, tossing bits of bread and crumbled crackers to seagulls flapping in the cold sky, and watching dolphins surface alongside in the gray water. Wyatt put his arms around Shelly, and that was the moment he knew. The wind and the salt air carried away the last of any pretense about what they felt for each other. Looking at the tugboats and shrimp boats moving slowly along the Lidia Ann Channel, Wyatt understood that his life, as he had known it, was slipping away at the same methodical speed.

On the cold beach they collected shells and sand dollars, and studied, up close, blue men-of-war that had washed ashore. They huddled against a sand dune watching the whitecaps gain speed and stretch outward and disintegrate into froth.

"It isn't fair to you," he said. "And Elaine doesn't deserve this. I have to think about Nate." But he didn't let go of Shelly. He bundled her in his arms.

"Should we not see each other at all?" she asked. The wind drowned out the question, and she didn't repeat it. She already knew the answer. "We should go home."

Driving back to Austin, he held the wheel and stared through the windshield at the flat road under the darkening sky, the sinewy rows of dried cornstalks running along either side. He wanted to pull to a stop and make love to Shelly. Her hair was tangled from the wind. She had taken her coat and sweater off, and underneath was a peasant blouse, cobalt blue and smocked in a way that revealed the slope of her shoulders and the clarity of her skin.

"What are you thinking?" he asked her.

"That we shouldn't see each other again."

But her conviction was as doomed as the waves they had watched rolling in.

A month later, most of the students and faculty had gone home for Christmas break when Shelly met Wyatt in the art building and he took her to the studio to show her one of his paintings. They puttered around for a while, looking at projects in the room—clay sculptures, charcoal sketches, half-painted canvases sitting upright on easels. Shelly kept returning to a tempera painting Wyatt had done of a rocking chair beside a shuttered window. The painting lay flat on a table, and they were standing over it when they felt the absolute stillness of the building and realized how alone they were.

He resisted touching her. He had never kissed her. He watched the sweep of her lashes as she studied the painting, and looked at the pink tint to her lips, and said, "Let me paint you."

She didn't look up, and didn't respond for a long time. He wondered if she had heard. She kept looking at the painting.

What she actually saw was his hand resting beside it. The shape of his knuckles, and the blue paint under his nails. "How do you mean?" she asked.

"A portrait."

"What kind?"

"Without your clothes on."

That was when she looked at him.

"I won't touch you," he told her.

She could see the specks in the irises of his hazel eyes, and pictured what he would see if she stood in front of him naked—the ugly breast and the twisted arm.

"You would only have to pose for a few minutes," he told her. "I would make sketches and take pictures, and paint from those."

"And what would you do with the painting?"

"The painting isn't the point."

"What is the point?"

"Just that I could look at you."

"What would be the point for me?" She said this with a half smile. "I look at myself all the time."

"Not through my eyes. You would love yourself through my eyes."

Eventually she took off her blouse and bra, and he locked the door, and she stood in front of a wooden screen that was painted a chalkboard green, in the cold, moderate light from a bank of windows. She left her scarred breast visible—"You've seen that one already"—but covered the other with her hand.

Wyatt studied her, mesmerized by the softness of her face, and the breast, and the cold light pooling in the hollow of her shoulder. There were goose bumps on her arms. He loved the way she was made. The curve of her hip. "The blue jeans?" he asked.

"I'm scared to." But she leaned over and unlaced her shoes, and pulled them off, and took her jeans off and hung them over a chair.

"The underwear?"

She pulled them down and sat in the chair to pull them off, and then sat looking at him, her legs pressed together and her hands clutching her knees. "You're sure you locked the door?"

He walked backward to test it, unable to take his eyes off her as she got up and stood in front of the screen, wearing nothing but the ribbon in her hair.

"This is impossible," he told her. "I want to make love with you." He walked around her and looked at her from different places, and admitted to himself solemnly that he was in love with her to the point that he was no longer in love with Elaine. Every second he looked at Shelly was a danger to his marriage. And he was betraying Shelly as well as Elaine. He knew he was wrong to do this. But the light shimmering in over the treetops turned her skin opalescent.

He sketched her in pencil, and photographed her, asking her to turn, and to move her hand, and reposition her arm, and relax her fingers. Half-joking and half-hoping, he said, "Now sit down in the chair again and open your legs."

It frightened her how close she came to doing what he said. She was ashamed of herself, and tried to quiet her conscience. She was only a model for his painting, she told herself. He had seen women do this before. She wasn't the first. And there would be others. He was an artist, and she was the object. She was the bruised apple.

Half an hour later they heard voices in the hall, and Wyatt put his camera and his sketches away.

And the following day, when Shelly's parents had come to take her home for Christmas break, Wyatt began a week of feverish painting. He smoothed the gesso with a wooden block and painted at odd hours, alone, in secret, stoned sometimes, creating what for him was almost a spiritual icon. Stroke by stroke of the brush, Shelly became visible as he layered colors one on top of the other. Setting her image onto the Masonite board was the closest he could come to taking hold of her. He made his paint from dry pigments and water and combined the colors—cadmium and earth reds, yellow ocher and terre verte— with yolk from eggs he'd plucked from under the warm bellies of chickens on a hippie farm east of town. He stared at Shelly's photographs until her face was so familiar that the face of his own wife, when he looked at her across the kitchen table or in their bed at night, began to seem foreign to him. He ground his own malachite from chunks of raw mineral, washing and grading it himself, and formed the blossoms of her cheeks with cadmium red, modeling the shadows in the dark green of verdaccio and applying the pink flesh colors, working from midtones up into the highlights with titanium white, and down into shadows again. His brushstrokes were gently possessive, the paint diluted and thin. Shelly appeared in the soft tones of the early layers like a ghost. His fingertips made her breathe. At times he painted through the night. He wanted to go on painting her for the rest of his life.

The portrait was on an easel covered by a sheet when Shelly returned to Austin and Wyatt brought her into the studio early one morning. It was small for a portrait but large for a tempera painting— eighteen by twenty-four inches. He apologized for the lingering odor of souring eggs in the paint, and pulled the sheet away.

And Shelly confronted herself. The image extended down below her waist. She was posed in front of the green board, facing the viewer directly, her ribbon dangling over her shoulder, her skin smooth. The scars wove back and forth across her arm and her breast. Her elbow was bent, and her hand lay on her upper chest, the fingers resting in the crevice at the base of her neck.

"Do you like it?" Wyatt asked her.

Even the fingernails were hers. She blinked. Nodded. She didn't approach the painting or touch it. Her posture, as she stood surveying herself, was the same as it was in the portrait—her forearm lying upward between her breasts.

"You're beautiful," he said.

She loved the painting so much, she was speechless. Wyatt thought he had failed her. "It's all right, Shelly, if you don't like it."

"I love it too much," she whispered, turning to look at him. "And everything I feel for you is wrong. And I can't make it right, and I can't keep any of it." She waved her hand at the painting, a look of heartbreak on her face. "I wish I had left my clothes on. I wish you could paint them on."

But he couldn't reduce the portrait to something less than it was, dress it up in clothing—even if Shelly asked him to. Her body was exquisite. He loved the scars. They made her unique: herself. He loved how her arm was bent at the elbow, dividing the breasts—one of them perfectly shaped and whole, the other marred with imperfections that were dignified by the way she bore them. He couldn't just cover her up with paint.

"But could it be done?" she asked him.

"It could, but that would ruin it. The paint would be too thick. And see how the hair spills over your shoulder? I'd have to paint over that part, and start over on the hair. It wouldn't look right."

"But what can we do with it now?"

He didn't have any answers. "I can store it for now."

Later, when she had gone, he wrapped the portrait in paper and tape and carried it up to a storage room on the fourth floor of the building. He shoved it upright among students' abandoned paintings, removing from sight what he could not remove from his mind.

# 8

# WHAT THEY COULDN'T HAVE

How he wanted her. He might have talked himself into thinking he deserved to love her—this was the sixties, after all. He knew couples who were divorcing just to live together in sin. But Wyatt's moral preferences, like his artistic taste, tended toward the outmoded, and he was already perilously bending the rules. He had told Elaine about his chance encounter with Shelly at the Student Union but not about any encounters since then. Certainly he had not told her about the portrait.

And he did love Elaine. If only he hadn't needed to remind himself of it so often. And he adored his little boy. Nate was five months old now.

So he spent a lot of time fantasizing about events he never believed would happen. He went about his daily life, working on his paintings, caring for Nate, and making love with Elaine. On weekends he painted houses for extra income. But every few moments his mind would wander to Shelly. He would think about some plan he had made to see her. From the corner of his eye he would glimpse a shimmering place that seemed to belong to a different world from the one where he was living.

And on a cold morning in January, it took only a small windstorm to shatter the partition that had kept him out of that world.

He was driving to his friends' farm for fresh eggs to use in his tempera paint, and he had invited Shelly to come along. His friends were out of town, and Wyatt was to help himself to the eggs in the henhouse and feed the dog.

Later he wouldn't be able to say at what point he began to know what would actually happen. It might have been as early as when he invited Shelly to go with him, or when he caught sight of her, bundled in her coat, waiting for him on the corner of Twenty-fourth and Lamar, leaves skittering around her feet. Or maybe it was at some point on the drive, while she practiced Spanish by reading to him from her text-book, and he couldn't keep his eyes on the road and kept looking at her lips moving.

It could also have been when he pulled to the shoulder and they sat in the car and talked, and he couldn't suppress his imagination long enough to care what she was saying.

She was in a chipper mood that morning and had a radiant smile. "You're being awfully serious," she said. "And it's a gorgeous day. Look at the sunshine." She gave him a moment to say something. "Is this a problem with me? Or something else?"

"With you." Because there she sat, and he was unable even to touch her.

She didn't have to ask what he meant—she knew. And she wanted him desperately. But there was nothing to do but make light of it.

He wasn't sure what depressed him more—thinking he couldn't have her, or knowing that somebody else eventually would.

He started the car and drove on, approaching the farm along a dirt road with grassy pasture on either side. It was a ramshackle group of structures: a dilapidated old house, a shed, a two-stall barn empty of horses, and a walk-in henhouse. Wyatt had come here many times to collect the fresh, warm eggs, and had once been here with Elaine for a summer solstice party. The party had turned strange, with people on hallucinogens wandering around naked, swatting at swarms of gnats and waiting for the sun to set so they could look at the stars. He had thought Elaine would be eager to leave, but she hadn't been. She had smoked a hash pipe and discussed Tolstoy and Nabokov and the Ber-lin Wall with a longhaired guy who was stoking the campfire.

A black mutt with a coat full of cockleburs came loping from the back of the house when Shelly and Wyatt got out of the car. The wind was so fierce the dog squinted. They went around back, where Wyatt scooped dog chow out of a metal trash can and filled the water bowl from the garden hose. He used the lid of the trash can as a shield against the wind while he filled the bowl. Shelly liked watching him do these domestic chores. She had grown to like even his untidy hair and the modern look of his glasses, and wished she could lie in a patch of sun in the tall yellow grass of the pasture with him and make love. She had never, completely, made love before, having come close only with her high school boyfriend, Billy, and now she wished Wyatt could be the first and the only. Through the screen door to the back porch, she saw an old couch draped with a Mexican blanket, and wished they could go inside and lie down on it together.

Of course, then there would be that afterward moment, when she would realize what she had done and would suffer the sinking knowledge that the act was irretrievable.

The dog was eating hungrily when they left him. They went to the henhouse and found it dank and cold, filled with the musty smell of the hens and their droppings. Three small windows, closed and dirty and high on the walls, admitted dusty sunlight. The hens dropped down from their perches and gathered around Shelly and Wyatt, clucking and pecking for food. Shelly got handfuls of corn from a barrel and littered the ground with kernels, while Wyatt selected eggs from the nests and put them into a carton. Light through chinks in the walls striped the floor and the cubbyholes of the nests, and Shelly looked around the place and listened to the rush of the wind and thought she would be happy to live on a farm like this with Wyatt. They would have children, and feed the chickens and dogs, and Wyatt would build a studio and paint beautiful works of art.

They closed the henhouse and got in the car, and were driving away when Shelly noticed the door to the shed had blown open and was flapping in the wind.

Wyatt pulled up close and got out to examine the door latch. The screws had worked their way out of the rotting wood. He went inside and searched the shelves, lined with old cans and rusted tools, for twine or rope, or anything else he could use for a makeshift latch. Finally he decided to haul an old lawn mower out and prop the door shut from the outside, and had extracted it from a pile of rat-eaten storage boxes when he turned and saw Shelly. She stood in the doorway, clutching her coat tightly around herself, bouncing on her toes for warmth. The light lay on her hair.

And he didn't think to resist any longer. After weeks of holding himself in check, the effort simply vanished as if the wind carried it off. He walked to her, and took her into his arms, and kissed her.

In the backseat of the car, he made love with her, the car door open, the shed door swinging open and shut in the wind, a strip of winter light sliding back and forth over Shelly's body. He traced her scars with his fingers and kissed her wounded breast, and together they entered the dangerous love affair, feeling as if they were safe in each other's arms.

And then the winter light seemed to go pale. The cold contained a leaden sense of doom. Shelly wept inconsolably for what she had been given and could not keep, and Wyatt tried to comfort her, but was too remorseful and too burdened with his own guilt to say anything useful.

"I wish it hadn't happened," Shelly said on the way home, wiping at her tears, "that we could undo it. I have this terrible, dark feeling I can't get rid of."

It was only just past noon when he let her off on the street corner. Driving away, he turned to see if she looked at him, but her head was down and she was already walking toward campus.

He went to the studio in the art building and mixed his paints and tried to create something. But Shelly was all he could think of. How she moved, and how she had tipped her head back and fastened her arms around his neck. Several times he walked outside and around the building, hoping to get her out of his mind. For hours, he tried to push the pictures out of his mind. And then for hours he gathered them back up.

# 9

# BEFORE LONG

He shuffled his marriage, even his son, to the back of his thoughts. Everything not related to Shelly was as pale as the first thin layer of paint on gesso. He arranged his days to see her and missed classes to be with her. Elaine chided him for being obsessed with his work. He neglected his friends. Shelly remained in Austin over that summer and he saw her repeatedly, even despite his intentions, as if he had no say in the matter. And she clung to him as if she had no willpower. She felt as if she didn't even belong to herself.

Jack suspected a love affair, and challenged Wyatt about it. "Who is she?"

"You don't know what you're talking about—there's no one," Wyatt told him.

"You're a fool if you screw things up with Elaine."

He would have left Elaine if not for Nate. He lied to her almost every day about where he was going or where he had been. At times, when he was coming home to her, or when he was trotting through the apartment with Nate on his shoulders, his duplicity filled him with self-loathing.

Then later in a parking lot on campus, Shelly would slide into his car and look at him with her soft eyes and slip her hand into his, and he would sweep her into his arms. His intimate knowledge of the tragedy that had helped to form her made him feel as if he had been with her at the moment of her conception. It gave him the sense she belonged to him—that they belonged together. The exceptional origins of the affair seemed almost to justify it.

Shelly knew the risks. And yet she allowed Wyatt, who was the greatest threat to her future, to become her touchstone. In the fall, she thought of leaving Austin—taking a bus and going somewhere and staying away long enough to forget Wyatt. She could get a job and support herself. Or go back home to Lockhart. But she didn't have the resolve. She told herself that in two years she would do it. She would join the Peace Corps and leave Wyatt with his family, and distract herself in a foreign country from a broken heart. Now was only the meantime.

Spring came, and on a cloudy April afternoon, Shelly walked out of a shop on the Drag, carrying a birthday gift for her mother in a box under her arm, and saw Wyatt standing at the curb with a beautiful woman she knew must be Elaine, who held a baby. Elaine looked like Cher, her dark hair parted and swinging around her as she cradled the baby and leaned to retrieve something out of Wyatt's car. Wyatt lifted the baby out of her arms, and when he turned, Shelly saw the child's face—the round eyes and toothless grin as he looked up at his father and his father looked at him.

She walked in a daze back to her dorm and sat for a long time on her bed, wondering how she had let herself become this person. Until that day, Elaine and Nate had been faceless to Shelly, but now she couldn't dispel the awful feeling of seeing Wyatt in his other life, and couldn't deny how well that life seemed to fit him. She couldn't forget the look of happiness on the child's face when he was in his father's arms, and she tried to summon the strength to stop seeing Wyatt.

# 10

# HOW AFRAID SHE WAS

Hoping distance would break the spell, Shelly went home to Lockhart for the summer and got a part-time job keeping the books at the local feed and hardware store. She was at a desk piled with accounting ledgers in a back room crowded with boxes of plumbing supplies when she realized that her period was three days late.

For two weeks she waited, sleepless and worried, praying at night on her knees as she had not done since she was a child. Afraid to go to her family doctor, she asked her high school boyfriend, Billy, to take her to Austin on his day off from the oil rigs.

"I need to sign up for fall courses," she told Billy as an excuse.

They drove in his rattling Ford pickup. It smelled like oil from the rigs, and the cabin smelled of exhaust fumes. Shelly bounced around on the uncomfortable bench seat, feeling sick to her stomach. But she chatted with Billy. He was nice-looking, with dark curly hair, and he wore a black ball cap with a John Deere logo. One of his eyes was brown and one was a cloudy blue and had what looked like a bubble on it from an accident with a firecracker when he was in second grade.

He let her out near the campus and drove off to Barton Springs to meet a friend and go swimming. When he was gone, Shelly put on a ring she had inherited from her great-aunt, then walked to Sabine Street, to the Planned Parenthood clinic that a girl from her dorm had once been to and talked about. It was a stucco house with a portico, and she climbed the steps and went inside and registered in the front room under a made-up name, pretending she was married.

The doctor was kind to her. He examined her, took a urine sample, and told her to come back on Thursday or Friday for the results.

"But do you think I'm pregnant?" She tried to sound happy about it.

He didn't appear to be fooled. "Let's wait and see," he told her. "We'll know in a few days."

"But we used a condom. Aren't they effective?"

"Usually they are. Not always."

She walked back to campus, unsure what to do next. She wanted to go to the art building and see if Wyatt was there, but couldn't think of what she would tell him. His life would be ruined if her fears were true. Over and over, she recalled the details of making love with him six weeks ago. It was one of the only times they had been in a motel room. A fan had turned slowly over the bed. *I Dream of Jeannie* was playing on television.

They had been so careful. Surely she couldn't be pregnant.

On the Drag, she sat in a booth at the Rexall and drank a Coke in the air conditioning and waited for Billy to pick her up at the corner.

Later, when she was back in Lockhart, the wait became terrible. She felt nauseated and feverish and tried to tell herself this was only due to her emotions. But every passing day confirmed her anxieties. She worked on the books at the hardware store and went home exhausted to fall on the sofa and watch TV with her parents, fearing that the ease and contentment of everyone around her was only based on their ignorance of a secret she wouldn't be able to keep for long. Already she felt like a moral outcast. Her mother was helping to plan a neighborhood party for later in the summer, and Shelly promised she would go to Luling and pick out the watermelons herself. But she had no idea what her life would be by that time. The people who loved her now might not love her as much then.

She called Billy and asked him to take her back to Austin on Thursday. He was working that day, he said, but he could take her on Friday.

This time he parked on the Drag, and said he would meet her back at the truck in an hour. She walked to Sabine Street in a hurry, and was ushered into the doctor's office.

He told her to take a seat and looked at her curiously. He was a balding man with a nice manner. "You don't have to answer this, but I have a suspicion that you're not married."

"The test came back positive?" She knew by the look on his face.

"Yes, my dear. It did."

He asked if she wanted to talk. She sat in the chair and looked at him and tried to manage her thoughts. But everything had gone side-ways. She tried to stand up and the room became dim.

"Sit for a minute," he told her. "Take some deep breaths."

She stayed for nearly an hour, and cried, and admitted she wasn't married, and that she didn't know what to do. He offered to put her in touch with the sisters at the Home of the Holy Infancy, a Catholic home for unwed mothers on Nueces and Twenty-sixth Street. She could live there until she had the baby. The sisters would arrange an adoption.

But Shelly had seen the home—an imposing brick building—and had seen the pregnant girls out for walks and the sisters pushing baby strollers. She had felt sorry for the girls, and now could not imagine being one of them. And she wasn't interested in giving the baby up for adoption.

After a while she dried her tears, paid the bill, walked to the art building on campus, and climbed the stairs to the studio. When she didn't find Wyatt there, she left him a note in his mailbox. "Can you meet me on Sunday in the parking lot of the Nighthawk on South Congress? I'll be in my mom's station wagon. I need to talk to you about something."

She didn't attempt to hide her swollen face from Billy. He had been waiting a while when she climbed back into the truck. "I'm expecting," she told him flatly.

"Expecting what?"

"A baby."

The truck sat idling.

"Just drive," she said.

"God, Shelly." After a minute he said, "Can I ask who the father is?"

When they were on the highway, she said, "He's married."

"Oh. Man."

"And I love him. And I don't know what to tell him. He has a baby already."

"He doesn't know you're expecting?"

"I have to come back on Sunday and tell him."

"Oh God, Shelly. Is he going to leave his wife?"

"No."

"But what about you?" He waited. "Do you think you could . . . you know. Have an abortion?"

"No."

"I mean, I know it's against the law," he said. "What about giving the baby up for adoption? A lot of people want kids."

"I couldn't give it to strangers."

"What is your father going to say?" Billy had always liked her father. His own father was drunk all the time.

"I don't know. And my mom. I don't know who to worry about most." She was most worried about Wyatt.

"Worry about yourself," he said.

"And the baby," she said.

"What about Spain, or wherever it was you were going?"

She stared at the road.

# II

# IN THE RAIN

Friday night she lay awake staring at the darkness. Storms threatened on Saturday. Thunder rumbled in the distance, the skies grew dark in the afternoon, and the evening came without any change in the color of the sky. The night stretched out forever. On Sunday Shelly awoke to the sound of a heavy downpour. Over bowls of oatmeal, her parents invited her to an afternoon social at the church. But she asked instead to borrow the station wagon. "I'd like to go to Fentress and skate this afternoon, since I'm cooped up working all week." From the doorstep, she watched her parents drive off in the rain in her father's patrol car.

At noon, she left for Austin. Rain beat hard on the windshield for an hour as she drove. In the parking lot of the Nighthawk restaurant she waited nearly an hour for Wyatt, fearing he wouldn't come. He finally drove up and parked beside her, the rain pummeling him as he got in the station wagon. "I had Nate with me," he told her. "I couldn't leave until Elaine got home. What's the matter?"

"I'm . . . you know." The words wouldn't come out.

He waited.

"I'm going to have a baby. I'm sorry," she said.

At first he thought she wasn't serious, and he continued to think this for a few seconds even after he knew she was. His thoughts went back to the motel room. "How could that be?"

"I don't know—it just is. I had the test on Friday."

"Oh, Shelly . . ."

"Don't say anything yet. First of all, this can't ruin your life or your family. I won't let it. Second of all, you have Nate already. So that's enough said about that. You can't leave him. I wouldn't love you if you could do that. And I wouldn't be able to live with myself. So don't even think about that."

He was already shaking his head. "I'm not going to leave you alone in this."

"It's the only way I can do it. I'm not giving you any choice."

"But the test could be wrong. Did the doctor say—"

"I threw up this morning. My breasts are sore. I wish I didn't believe it, but it's true. It won't help for you to say otherwise."

She had started to cry, in spite of having promised herself she wouldn't. He pulled her toward him and held her. His jacket smelled of damp wool. "We were so careful," he kept insisting. "I don't see how it could have happened. I'm going to figure out what to do."

"It can't be *fixed*. The baby isn't going *away*. And I won't have an abortion."

"You can't raise a baby on your own."

"Of course I can. I'll quit school. I'll get a job in Lockhart. They'll hire me full-time at the feed store."

"But you can't stay in Lockhart for the rest of your life."

"I'm not talking about the rest of my life. I'm talking about getting on my feet."

He couldn't stand the thought of himself. "Look what I've done," he said. "You trusted me, and look what I've done." He had come to her aid, and then he had wrecked her life. And now he wanted her more than he could ever remember wanting anyone. And the world was melting in the rain around him. His little boy was waiting at home. His wife, his future, and what was left of his self-respect required that he open the car door and go back to where he belonged.

Finally she told him to go. "You have to," she said.

But he couldn't leave her. He kept thinking there was a way to reverse what had happened. He had been telling himself every day that at some point he was going to do the right thing about Shelly—that at some point he would be sure what the right thing was. And now that chance would never come. "I'm not going to leave it like this," he said.

"I love you," she told him. "But we're not in this together. I can't keep seeing you. Not if I have the baby. Please. Just go." But even as she said this she clung to him. The rain against the windows formed a gray curtain between them and the world. He kissed her face while she cried.

In the end he stood in the rain watching the taillights disappear from the parking lot, then got in his car and pounded the seat beside him and shouted against the noise of the rain. Absently, mechanically, he willed himself home to Elaine.

Shelly drove back toward Lockhart, blinded by the deluge. The swipe of the windshield wipers made her dizzy. She wanted Wyatt more than ever before. She felt there was nowhere left in her life to go, and pulled to the side of the road. Pushing the door open, she stumbled out, as if the rain could wash something away. She buried her face against the hood of the station wagon and let the downpour soak her.

When she was driving again, she began to talk to herself because she felt so lonely, and after a while she realized she was talking to the baby as well. "We're going to get through this," she said, clutching the steering wheel with dripping hands. "First I'll talk to my mom tomorrow. We'll see what she says. She has a weakness for babies."

Meanwhile Wyatt was home. He ate what he could of his dinner and bathed his son, and thought about telling Elaine the truth, and vacillated between two worlds: one here, in his home, with his family, and one out in the rain with Shelly. He was twenty-five years old. He had married too young, and married the wrong woman. He was trapped in his life.

# 12

# THE MINNOW BABY

Shelly suffered through the night, tossing sleeplessly and crying in her pillow because she loved Wyatt so deeply and could not be with him, and because everything she had ever wanted would be out of reach now and maybe forever. Her only solace throughout the night was also her torment: the baby, the tiny, tiny thing, cozy inside her, protected and nourished, that no one could take away.

In the morning when her father left for work, Shelly made a cup of hot chocolate and wandered, as if casually, still in her pajamas, into her parents' bedroom, where her mother was searching for something inside the closet, her freckled back exposed by an open zipper.

Shelly sat on the bed and watched her. The window beside the bed revealed a rusty swing set from her childhood in the rainy backyard.

"Mom?" she finally said, sipping her hot chocolate while gathering courage. "I've done something. It's not as bad as you're going to think. I've worked out what to do, so please be calm. I'm going to have a baby. I don't want to say who the father is, because I'm not going to marry him."

Her mother turned to look at her, the back of her dress hanging open, her hand on the doorframe. She came over and sat on the bed. She was a slender woman, but she sat down heavily and stared at the dresser against the wall.

"I know you think it's terrible news," Shelly said. "I promise you that it's not. I know exactly what I'm going to do about it. I'm going to quit school, and work full-time. If I can stay here with you and Dad for a while, then I'll get on my feet, and later be on my own."

Her mother's face had started to crumple.

"Please, Mom. Don't cry."

Her mother rocked forward and back. She opened her mouth but didn't say anything. She patted Shelly's leg without looking at her, and Shelly only felt frightened by such a hopeless gesture. Finally her mother spoke in a shaking voice, "Oh, honey . . . I don't believe this could happen."

"There's no point saying that, Mom."

"After all your hard work to get over the accident . . ."

"Yes, after that."

"I can't believe you would do this."

"Getting shot wasn't an *accident*. And it has nothing to do with this. I know you're disappointed in me—I'm disappointed in myself. But I can't think about that right now. I have to do what's right for the baby."

"Adoption is what's right—"

"No it's not."

"Of course it is. How can you question that?"

"I don't think it is!"

"Who is the father?"

"I told you I don't want to say."

"But you're not even dating anyone. Not that I knew of. He won't marry you?"

"I don't want him to marry me."

"Is he not a good person?"

"He's a good person. He's the best person I know. I don't want to talk about it."

"But why wouldn't you want him to marry you? Is he . . . Is he already married?"

"Stop, please?"

"Oh, Shelly."

"Don't say that. You're acting as if I've destroyed my life. And it isn't destroyed."

"Tell me he's not married."

She flung the lie at her mother. "He isn't married!"

"Thank goodness for that. Thank goodness. I didn't think you would do that. But you can't raise a baby without a father."

"Why not? Widows do. Nobody tries to make widows give up their children."

The conversation went nowhere. Words seemed to evaporate even before they were spoken. Nothing could be decided. Shelly got up and left the room while her mother was still talking, and she stayed away from her the rest of the morning. Before noon, she left without saying goodbye, and walked through town to the hardware store. She left it up to her mother to tell her father what had happened. He would be home for lunch. Already the story no longer belonged to her. Her parents could say whatever they wanted about it. The only thing that still belonged to Shelly was the baby.

She worked all afternoon at the store, nauseated from the syrupy smell of sweet feed, and wished for Wyatt magically to appear. She pictured the baby swimming inside her like a minnow. Sorrow made it hard for her to breathe. She dreaded the conversation she would have to have with her father.

At five o'clock, she walked home and found her father at the kitchen table, waiting, his face flushed and sad. "Do you want my opinion?" he asked Shelly as she sat down. "It would be a mistake to keep the baby, honey. Your mother and I can look for a good family. You owe it to the child to give it a mother and father who have a livelihood and a home."

A scared part of her began to fear she would come to see it that way.

"You're not going to say who the father is?"

"I really can't. No."

"Well, he's a coward," her father said. "That much we know. What kind of a man would do this and not show up?"

"He's not hiding, if that's what you're saying."

He looked around. "Where is he?"

"I'm not going to listen to that," she said. "You can say whatever else you want, but don't talk about him like that."

He studied her, weighing the fact of her loyalty. "It's his loss not to marry you. But the baby needs a father. We can find a good home. And you have plans, Shelly. You didn't survive that shooting for nothing. You need to do what's right, and then go on with your life."

She looked him in the eye. She wasn't interested in her life. She would just as soon it was over.

# 13

# WHAT JACK SAID

Wyatt struggled for days about what to do. In the studio where he had painted Shelly, he pored over the photographs he had taken of her for the portrait. He spoiled his work in progress: a painting of a steep cliff, an oak tree with massive roots clinging to layers of sedimentary rock. Reckless with emotion, he brushed pigments that were too bright over his subtle colors until the ochers turned orange and the shimmering celadons were buried under a garish green.

Outside, the rain kept falling. The ground was saturated and the bark on the trees turned black. Leaves bounced and thrashed, pounded by the deluge. Wyatt drove toward Lockhart, intending to go to Shelly's house and find a way to see her. He was halfway there when he saw Nate's small shoes on the floorboard and turned the car around.

He arrived home after dark and found Elaine in bed smoking a cigarette. The light was on, and Nate was sleeping in the crib. Elaine smiled. "Guess what happened. My parents called. They have a three-year lease on a house in Provincetown that they're not going to be using most of the year. So if we want to move there, rent-free for a while, we can. If you ask me, it's perfect. So many artists live there." She tapped the cigarette into an ashtray nestled in the covers. "It might be a big break for you. And I'd be closer to home. Mom and Dad could spend time with Nate."

He tried not to reveal his shock with any gesture or change in expression. He could think of nothing to say. This had come from nowhere. He couldn't imagine being so far from Shelly. And yet Elaine looked so hopeful—so pleased.

"It's a remarkable offer," he stammered. "But a big imposition on your parents."

"They want us to take them up on it."

"I think we're better off here," he said. "We have more independence."

"We don't even have an extra car. How independent is that?"

"There's a good chance they'll hire me on the faculty here—"

She was shaking her head. "Think about it—a town full of artists and a house for free. You can't tell me you'd rather be here. Do you know how many galleries there are in Provincetown? I've only been there a couple of times, but that's what I remember—the art galleries. And we'd only be three hours from my parents. We'd be crazy not to do this." Putting out the cigarette, she waited.

She was right about one thing: Moving to Provincetown could be the turning point in his career. He could build a reputation and make some money. And send money to Shelly, to help her with the baby. He could get his footing, and then the options would widen. But he couldn't imagine making this move.

"It wouldn't have to be forever," Elaine said.

He sat on the bed and pulled his shoes off.

"And it's beautiful, with the water." She said this softly, enticingly. "Wyatt, don't you think we should go?"

She spoke so seriously that he almost wondered if she might know about Shelly. He almost wished that she did, that she would release him from the smothering burden of lies he had heaped on their marriage.

"It would be a cool place for Nate," she said.

He knew he should pull her into his arms and keep her there as long as it might take to forget about Shelly. She was a smart and beautiful woman and deserved to have a husband who was in love with her.

He got up and looked at Nate asleep in the crib. The wispy brown hair of babyhood had grown long enough to make soft curls at the nape of his neck. He had fallen asleep holding on to a rung of the crib, and Wyatt studied his face and stroked the little knuckles. Finally he said, "Do you mind if I take a drive? And think about this?" He started putting his shoes on.

"Now?"

"Yeah."

"Okay." But she didn't sound as if it was.

He drove to Jack and Delia's garage apartment and sloshed his way heedlessly through oily puddles in the gravel driveway. The rain had stopped and the night was muggy. He climbed the steps and knocked. Jack answered the door.

"Can you come out and talk?"

They sat on the wet wooden steps. Wyatt dropped his head and stared down between his knees. "You were right about what you thought," he said. "I'm in love with someone."

On the radio in the apartment, Johnny Cash was singing "A Boy Named Sue." Delia appeared at the top of the steps and invited Wyatt in for cherry pie. He looked up at her, and when she saw his anguished face, she went back inside.

"Who?" Jack said in a toneless voice.

"Shelly Maddox. And she's pregnant. I found out a few days ago."

Jack said nothing.

"Elaine doesn't know anything," Wyatt said. "And Shelly says she's going to raise the baby alone. She doesn't want me to leave Elaine. I've been trying to figure out what to do. And now Elaine just told me we have an offer to move to Provincetown. To a house her parents would let us use. But I don't see how I can go and leave Shelly here with a baby. Quit looking at me like that."

"I guess Shelly's parents must appreciate the hell out of you now."

"Fuck you," Wyatt said, and sank his head onto his arms and stared at his muddy feet in buffalo sandals on the wet, rickety step. "I feel like such a cheat and a liar."

"You are a cheat and a liar."

Wyatt raised his head and looked at him. "Goddamn it, I came to you and—"

"And what? What do you want? You've fucked up."

"I want you to hear me out."

"Well what else do you have to say?"

Wyatt stared at him, then got up and started down the steps. He was almost to the bottom when Jack spoke from behind him. "If Shelly was willing, maybe Delia and I could take the baby."

Wyatt drew in a breath of sodden air before he turned to look at Jack.

It was nearly an hour later when they climbed the steps and went inside to talk to Delia. Jack went into the bedroom to get her, and she came out wearing her jeans under her gown. The room was filled with the scent of freshly baked pie. The windows were open into the summer night. Jack turned the radio off, and they sat around a coffee table. Delia waited, puzzled, looking from one to the other.

"You should do the talking," Jack told Wyatt.

He did it the best he could.

# 14

# A KNOCK AT THE DOOR

Shelly was at her parents' house the next day, watching *The Edge of Night,* when she heard the knock. She didn't get up from the couch because there was no one she wanted to see. She was sick from the pregnancy and relieved to have solitude while her mother was at the beauty parlor.

But the knocking continued.

Finally she got up and stood in the narrow hall of the little house and stared at the door. "Who is it?"

"Shelly, it's me."

She pulled the door open and there was Wyatt, standing where she had never thought he would be.

"Where can we talk?" he asked her.

He shouldn't be here, and yet she loved him for coming. She threw herself into his arms and led him into the front room, where they stood in the corner and held each other until Shelly pulled away.

"I told my parents, and they want me to give the baby up for adoption, but I'm not going to," she said. "I haven't told them you're the father."

"Oh God, Shelly. You can't do this on your own."

"I have to. There's not any other way."

"There might be another way."

"Of course there's not. What do you mean?"

"I mean . . ." He couldn't seem to say it.

"What?"

"Jack and Delia could take the baby."

"Take the baby? What are you talking about?"

"If you're willing, they want to adopt the baby."

"You asked them to do that, without talking to me?"

"When I told Jack you were expecting—"

"You told Jack?"

"Yes. And then . . . he offered . . ."

"To take the baby?"

"Yes."

"To take it off my hands? Like a favor? I can't believe you're saying this. It's not a favor."

"That's not what I meant."

"They can have their own babies."

"Actually, Shelly, they can't."

"What do you mean?"

"They can't. They've been talking about adopting. I told Jack what had happened, and then we talked to Delia. She thought about it for a day, and then . . . then she said she would love to do this. It could be the right thing, Shelly. They would be the perfect parents. I know you don't want to give the baby up, and I'm not going to try to talk you into that if it's not right. But please think about it; it could be the best choice for you as well as the baby."

He put his arms around her, and she felt his heart thumping, and felt his chest heave. He whispered, "But if you don't want to do this, I'll come up with something else."

"You don't have any money for anything else." She thought of the motel room. The fan revolving over the bed. Wyatt making love with her. She remembered the ferry crossing to Port Aransas, how the flocks of gulls had hovered in the wind and lifted bread from his fingers.

"And there's something else I need to tell you," he said, drawing back to look at her. "I might need to move to Massachusetts—to Provincetown—not forever, just for a while. Elaine's parents have a house they've offered to let us stay in, and she wants to go, and I don't have a reason to tell her I won't. You're my only reason. And if I go, I might be able to get things started with my work and send some money for the baby."

"What are you saying? That you're going to move?" She waited for him to deny this, but he didn't. "For how long?"

"I don't know. I don't want to go. But if we can't see each other—"

"We can't." She heard a car turn into the drive, and pulled the curtains back to see who it was. "My Dad's here. Go out the door in the kitchen."

"No—I'm not leaving like that."

"You need to go. He doesn't know it's you."

"I'm not going to."

They listened to the car door close, and then her father walked in. He was carrying mail from the mailbox. He paused when he saw Wyatt, and then he shut the door behind him, set the mail on the hall table, and stood looking at the two of them. Shelly could see that he understood exactly who Wyatt was.

Wyatt said, "Hello, sir."

When her father finally spoke, his voice was less harsh than she expected. "She didn't tell me it was you."

"I'm sorry, sir." Wyatt took a deep breath, looked at Shelly and then at her father again. "I just came to give her a phone number."

"Your phone number?"

"Not mine—"

"Whose, then?"

Wyatt hesitated, and Shelly said, "He's here because Jack Stone and his wife offered to adopt the baby. Not that I'm going to do that, but—"

"I wouldn't want her to do it unless that's what she wanted," Wyatt added. "But I needed to tell her they had asked. I won't defend what I've done, but Jack and Delia are good people. He's my cousin; I've known him all my life. I've never known a better person. And his wife would be an excellent mother. Sir, I love your daughter. I want you to know that, and to let your wife know how sorry I am for what I've done. I would marry Shelly if I could."

Her father looked at Wyatt in silence for a long time, and Shelly couldn't tell what he was thinking. "Yes, I believe that," he finally said. "I believe you would."

"Thank you, sir."

"But you should go now."

"I was wondering if I could talk to her in private for a minute."

"I don't think that's a good idea."

"Dad, I want to talk to him," Shelly said. "I need to."

Finally he nodded at Wyatt. "My best to you, son." He turned and walked down the hall and into the kitchen.

"Can we talk in my car?" Wyatt asked Shelly.

She wanted to say yes, to get in his car and drive away with him and never look back. But she shook her head. "That would just make it harder. We can talk here. There's nothing we need to say. I don't want to give the baby up. I just don't. You seem to think that keeping it would ruin my future. What future? It's not like I can go on with my life as if this didn't happen. All I want to think about is what's best for the baby."

"Can I at least give you Jack's number?" He didn't take his eyes from hers. "In case you change your mind?"

Reluctantly, she took the scrap of paper on which he had written the number.

"I know it's your decision. I want you to think about yourself as well as the baby," he said.

If she thought about herself, she would still keep the child. It was the only thing to tie her to Wyatt in any way that was possible—even if she never saw Wyatt again. It was the only thing she had left.

She had started to cry.

"Oh, Shelly, God. I can't stand myself."

"Don't feel that way because of me. I love you so much."

"Please, can't we talk in the car?"

She closed her eyes so she wouldn't have to see him standing in front of her. "I wish you would just walk out."

"Look at me, Shelly."

"No. I mean it. I want you to go."

"I won't go like this."

"I'm asking you to."

"I'm going to come back for you. I'm going to find some way to do that."

She opened her eyes. "Don't say that to me. I don't want to be waiting. If I start waiting, I'll never stop. I want you to say you won't come back. Because both of us know you can't—"

"Shelly—"

"I want you to say it and mean it. We both know it's true. I don't want false hope—you can have it if you want it, but for me it would only make things harder. I would be waiting for you to write, or call me—"

He took her in his arms, and she buried her face against him as her tears streamed down. "Please," she begged him, "be honest with me that it's over."

He whispered, "If that's what you want me to say . . ."

"It's the truth," she said.

He nodded, but only barely, and she couldn't see his eyes. She felt the slight movement of his chin against the top of her head as he held her. "Okay," he whispered softly. "It is the truth. So I'm going to say goodbye now. But I'm never going to stop loving you. I can say I'm not coming back, but I want you to understand that there won't be a day when I don't want to." He kissed her hair and held her a moment longer; then she felt him pull away slowly. She held her breath as he went out the door and closed it behind him.

Then she went to her room and lay on the bed and wept, still clinging to the scrap of paper with Jack's number, not because she was thinking about the baby, or even the future, but because it was the thing that Wyatt had left her with.

Finally she smoothed the wadded scrap, damp with her tears, out on the bed. The handwriting was Wyatt's, as precise and meticulous as his paintings. For a long time, she looked at the number and thought about everything Wyatt had said.

She awoke sick to her stomach the next morning. Vomiting into the toilet, she had the terrible realization she no longer knew what was right for the baby. The question began to make her feel desperate during the day, and a frightened part of her started to wish that someone could take the decision out of her hands.

When evening came, she found her father standing in the middle of the backyard, looking idle and saddened in the lingering twilight. Her approach was so quiet it startled him. "Hey," she whispered.

He turned to her, a swath of light from the window falling across his face. "Hi, sweetie."

"Can I talk to you? I feel . . . confused. Yesterday I was sure about what I should do, but now I don't know what's right. Do you think I'm being selfish to keep the baby? If I stay here, and have the baby, and try to work . . . Mom won't want me to be here. I know she won't ask me to leave, but she'll be humiliated and ashamed."

He stared at a heat-stricken rose bush in the half darkness, and didn't deny what Shelly had said about her mother. Finally he said, "Are Jack and his wife good people?"

"I don't know them. I think so. Wyatt believes so." She could hear the woman who lived next door feeding her dogs on the other side of the fence, pouring chow into their bowls, and she thought of the windy day at the farm when she and Wyatt had fed the dog, and collected the eggs, and made love. "Jack is almost like Wyatt's brother," she said. "The only time I've talked to him was in the hospital, and I've never met his wife. Her name's Delia."

"Your mother and I met her in the hospital."

"I know."

"She's a nice young lady."

"They're Catholic, Dad. They would raise the baby as a Catholic."

"I know plenty of good Catholics, honey."

"So you think I should do it? That I should give the baby up?"

"Yes, honey. I do. I think it would be best for everyone. Including the baby."

She looked at the rusty swing set she had played on as a child, and imagined her father hauling it off and bringing a new one, and imagined her mother out here with a little grandson or granddaughter she was embarrassed about having. She pictured herself in the back room of the feed store, surrounded by boxes and sacks of oats.

It didn't seem like a happy life for a baby. It didn't seem like a happy family.

What would she do with her life if she gave up the child? Finish her education? Join the Peace Corps?

At least with Jack and Delia, the baby would still have Wyatt around sometimes. It wouldn't be fatherless—it would have two fathers, even if that was a secret. It wouldn't be motherless either. And Delia had lots of brothers and sisters. The baby would have cousins.

She stared at the yard, the swing set. It seemed so pointless. She wished she were dead, and said aloud to her father, "I wish he had aimed better."

"Shelly."

"I do." She looked him in the eye. "I don't have the heart to call them, Dad. Would you do it for me? The number's by my bed."

"When do you want me to call them?"

"Now. Just go inside and do it. I'll wait out here."

"You're sure about this?"

"I'll never be sure about this."

# 15

# IN THOSE LONG MONTHS

Astronauts walked on the moon. Charles Manson and his cult followers murdered seven people. A music and art fair in Woodstock, New York, attracted hundreds of thousands. A hurricane battered Mississippi. And Shelly moved twenty miles down the road from Lockhart to San Marcos to be out of her hometown and away from her mother, who was incapable of responding to Shelly's emotions in any way that was helpful. She moved into an apartment with a friend who was attending Southwest State, and got a job at the concession stand of the Holiday movie theater on the square. She didn't tell anyone she was pregnant, and once a month she bought tampons and wrapped them up in toilet paper and threw them in the trash so her friend would see them and think she was having her monthly period. She wore a spandex girdle and tent dresses and had no one to confide in, no one to talk with about her broken heart. There was no one who knew her except Wyatt, and he was gone from her life.

*Rosemary's Baby* came to the theater, but Shelly wouldn't watch it. Her own future was dark enough. She feared and dreaded the moment when she would have to surrender the baby. It felt like a death sentence. There would be nothing after that. She missed her mother and needed her but didn't want to talk to her, because she felt her mother had shunned her. She felt exiled. Didn't her mother understand how painful it would be to give the baby away?

Six months into the pregnancy her parents drove to San Marcos and loaded Shelly's things into the station wagon and drove her to Beeville, a hundred miles south, where her mother's aunt Aileen lived. Aileen's husband was dead and her son Raymond was missing in

Vietnam, and she had agreed that Shelly could stay with her until the baby was born.

Aileen was kind to Shelly, but depressed about her son, and prayed all the time, and cried a lot. She was extremely thin, with arms and legs as flat as a paper doll's. She ate almost nothing but saltines with jelly, and drank Tabs all day.

On the first night Shelly was with her, they sat in Aileen's kitchen with Red, Raymond's shaggy old dog, in a heap at their feet, and made up a name for Shelly. "The neighbors are nosy," Aileen told her. "I promised your mama I'd keep things private. What about Polly?"

"Polly's okay." She didn't care what anyone called her.

"How about Polly Miller?" Aileen said.

That was all right with Shelly. It reminded her of Roger Miller, and she liked his lighthearted songs, if not "Little Green Apples," which made her cry.

"We can tell them you're from Ohio, and your husband died in a car crash," Aileen said.

"That sounds good," Shelly said. She had never been to Ohio, and doubted she'd ever go there. She doubted she'd go much of anywhere now. She might have been better off if she did live in Ohio and had a husband who died in a car crash. At least then she could grieve openly. And for someone other than Wyatt. And she could keep the baby.

"I'll tell them you don't want to talk about it. Not to ask you about it. And I'll give you a ring to wear."

"Thanks, but I have a ring." Her mother had asked her to wear it whenever she left Aileen's house.

"You can stay in Raymond's room, or sleep with me."

"I'll do whichever is better for you."

Aileen was such a sad woman that Shelly felt sorry for her. Her skinny hand cradled her weathered cheek and her eyes watered. "The last time you saw Raymond was at that family reunion in Belton," she reminded Shelly. "What comes to your mind about him?"

She didn't remember him well. That had been years ago when she was in intermediate school, and Raymond had seemed like a grown-up, though he was only about eighteen. "I remember that he was handsome," she told Aileen, though he wasn't really.

"When you were little, you came with your mama, and he threw the baseball for you. He always is good with the little ones. He's generous—that's what he is. By nature. That's what got him in trouble."

She repeated what Shelly already knew—that Raymond had gone out into the dark to help a fellow soldier who was hurt and yelling for him. And nobody saw him after that. "They think the VC got him," Aileen said. "He might have passed on to the Lord. But I have my valid doubts about it. I believe that he's still with us."

They talked a while about Raymond's job at the Reynolds plant in Ingleside and about his girlfriend, who had given up on him when she learned he was missing. She had told Aileen on the phone that she knew he wasn't coming home and that she wasn't going to spend a bunch of years waiting.

"It's a blessing he's shed of that tripe," Aileen told Shelly. "You can't ask a girl to wait ten years, but how about ten minutes? It wasn't like Raymond was out catting around. He was out killing the Communists."

"Let's look at the room," Shelly told her.

"It won't be clean," Aileen said. "I haven't been in since he went missing. I keep that door shut."

"We don't have to go in there," Shelly told her.

"We'll go in together," Aileen said.

Red got to his feet with effort—he was a massive old dog—and followed them down the hall. "Since Raymond was ten years old that dog's been sleeping with him. If I didn't keep him shut out of that room he'd lie on that bed all day waiting for Raymond to come home. That's not a good life for a dog." His shaggy hair littered the floorboards. "Come on," Aileen urged him. "You've been begging for months to get in there, and now you're draggin' your bones."

The room was dark and dusty. Cold dampness had taken up residence. There was a bed and a chair and a dresser. Shelly set her bag on the floor and watched the dog sniff around on the rug.

"Raymond's things are still in the closet," Aileen told her. "But you can put your things in there too. You remember exactly what Raymond looked like?"

"Not exactly. Just handsome."

"I got pictures we'll look at later."

"I remember he had big feet."

"Sure enough he did. His shoes are there in the closet."

Aileen left, telling Red to come with her, and Shelly sat in the chair for a minute and rested her hands on her stomach to wait for the baby to kick. "It's sad here," she said to the baby. "Aileen misses her son."

She got up and looked in the closet. A coat and a few shirts and two pairs of slacks dangled from hangers, and belts hung from a nail. Three pairs of shoes were neatly lined up. A box contained a baseball mitt and a trophy of some sort.

When Aileen had gone to bed, Shelly lay in Raymond's bed and felt so gloomy she couldn't move. Her heart was a lump in her chest. The only thing that felt alive inside her was the baby. It kicked every now and then. It got the hiccups. Shelly lay with her hands on her belly and imagined that she was dead and the baby had gone on living. She thought about killing herself after the baby was born: shooting herself with her father's pistol, or jumping from the tower onto the plaza, where Wyatt Calvert and Jack Stone wouldn't rescue her this time.

After a while Red began to sniff at the door, and she let him in. She helped him into the bed, hoisting him from behind, and slept with her arms around him. He smelled bad, but she didn't care.

In the weeks that followed, she hoped for a letter from Wyatt, even though she didn't expect one and knew that none would come. Every day, she looked in the mailbox, but the only letters that came were from her mother.

Stone-faced, she sat with Aileen through episodes of *Gomer Pyle*, and *Rowan & Martin's Laugh-In*, and *The Glen Campbell Goodtime Hour*. When she heard songs on the radio about rain, by the Cascades or Dee Clark or the Serendipity Singers, she remembered the rainy day she had sat in the station wagon with Wyatt and told him she was pregnant. When the Temptations sang about how they had "sunshine on a cloudy day," she thought of the cloudy day at the beach with Wyatt, how he had bundled her in his arms as they sat against the dunes watching the whitecaps roll in.

Before bed every night, she and Aileen held hands at the kitchen table and prayed for Raymond. "Let him walk through that door," Aileen said. "Let the phone ring and somebody tell me they've found him." Later she said, "We can pray for the baby's daddy, too."

It was months since Shelly had spoken his name aloud. "Maybe just once," she told Aileen. "His name's Wyatt." It sounded unfamiliar even to her.

"Would it help you to talk about him?"

So they did. Shelly told Aileen everything from beginning to end. She told her what Wyatt looked like, and how kind he was, and how she admired and loved him. How he had come out to help her on the plaza, just like Raymond had gone out to help someone. She talked about the portrait and said she wondered what would become of it. "I wish you could see his paintings. I wish you could meet him. You could look in his eyes and know what a good person he is."

"Keep your hand on the shoulder of that young man," Aileen prayed.

Shelly tried not to think about Wyatt too much, and imagined putting all her memories of him into a room and leaving them there. She told herself not to look into the room; she knew everything that was in there. Now and then she imagined herself going inside. She would look over the memories. Stand in the middle of her ruined life.

Her mother called her sometimes and talked about local things going on in Lockhart. Sometimes she told Shelly that people had asked about her.

"Do you think they know?" Shelly asked her.

"They wonder. I'm doing my best to stop the rumors."

Shelly's father was running for reelection as sheriff, and on the day of the election, Shelly called home to find out if he had won. Her mother was tearful on the phone, her father not yet home.

"Did he win?"

"Oh honey, he lost."

"But . . . how? Everyone was for him. Everybody loves him. Why would he lose? Mom? Was it . . . because of the rumors?"

Her mother paused before answering. "That might have been part of it. I don't know." She seemed to think better of having said that. "But it's not any use at this point to go blaming yourself."

"If he lost because of me, how could I not blame myself? Do you think it was?"

Later, her parents came to Beeville and took her out for a hamburger. Over milk shakes, her father told her he had taken a desk job with the highway department. "I actually kind of like it. I get to put my feet up."

"He's looking on the bright side," her mother told her.

"It's my fault you lost, isn't it," Shelly finally said.

"You mean, because of gossip? Not a chance." He waved his hand at a fly that was buzzing around their milk shakes. "If I had to guess, I'd say it was because I caught Burt Kemper's straight-A son urinating on Coach Allen's tires. His dad didn't appreciate that I gave him a ride home in the patrol car."

Shelly laughed.

"I knew the minute that man answered the door and saw me with his son that I had just lost that car. And I can't say I have any big regrets about it."

She wasn't reassured, but she didn't want to press the point in front of her mother, who would only undermine the peace of mind her father was trying to give her.

"I guess you've talked with Jack, or Delia, again?" She was reluctant to bring up this painful subject but wanted to know it was settled.

"I've had several conversations with Jack, and everything is taken care of, honey. There's nothing you need to do. You'll just have to sign the papers after the baby is born. Jack wants to know if you'd like to talk with Delia beforehand."

"No." She didn't see any reason to. She was going to sign the papers, and Jack and Delia would be good parents, and the baby would be better off. "It's not like I can tell them how to raise the baby. We could give each other well-wishes, I guess. But that wouldn't change anything. So . . . are they just going to come and get the baby after I have it?"

"They'll come with their attorney to the hospital."

"You mean—right away? I'll have the baby, and they'll show up?"

"You'll have a few days in the hospital to see the baby there, if you want that."

"I do want that."

"Honey? You're doing the right thing. You're giving the child a home with nice people, and a good chance in life." He patted her hand. "I'm proud of you. And you'll get past this, and lead a good life."

Sometimes, at Aileen's house, Shelly dreamed of Elaine. In the beginning she always dreamed about Wyatt, but then one day she started dreaming about Elaine instead. In the dreams, Elaine forgave her. She put her slender arms around her.

Often Shelly stood on the bed in front of the mirror that hung over the dresser, so she could see her stomach and watch the baby kick. One day Aileen found her there with her shirt pulled up. She had her hands on her belly. It was as smooth as a bowling ball.

"If you do that, you'll get attached to that baby."

"I love this baby. I love it so much, Aileen."

Aileen took her to see the doctor who would deliver the baby. He had gray hair and a small wrinkled face, and he made it clear he disapproved of Shelly for being pregnant. He examined her, then pulled the sheet down over her and told her she could sit up.

"All normal," he said without looking her in the eye. "No obvious problems."

"How will it happen?" she asked him.

"You're talking about the delivery?"

"When they take the baby. How will that happen?"

"You'll be able to see the baby, if that's what you're asking."

"For how long?"

"You'll be in the hospital four or five days, and so will the child."

"So I can hold the baby during that time?"

"If that's what you choose to do."

"How many babies have you delivered that were adopted?"

"Probably a half a dozen."

"And the adoptions turned out all right?"

"As far as I know."

"Did the mothers who had the babies ever get over it?"

He hesitated, and then consulted her file. "Is Polly Miller your real name?"

"My real name's Shelly Maddox."

"Some of them did, and some didn't."

On the way home, Shelly asked Aileen to drop her off on the courthouse square, in front of the library. She combed the shelves for a book on adoption but couldn't find one. She looked for "Adoption" in the encyclopedia but there wasn't an entry. The librarian asked her what she was searching for, and she said she was only browsing. She walked to Aileen's house while the sun sank in the wintry sky, and they sat at Aileen's kitchen table and tried to think of famous people adopted as infants. "Moses," Aileen said.

Shelly frowned at her. "It's not like his mom had a choice in the matter." She thought for a minute. "Edward Albee."

"Who's that?" Aileen asked.

"We studied his life in English. He wrote *Who's Afraid of Virginia Woolf?*"

"I never read that."

"It's a play."

"I never saw it." Aileen sipped her Tab. "Edgar Allan Poe was adopted."

"Thanks a lot, Aileen. He didn't exactly turn out right."

"Well yes he did."

"How do you know about him, anyway?"

"You think I never went to school?"

"I didn't think they'd teach you that in Cotulla."

"Ninth grade," Aileen said. "Mrs. Shirley Bergham. She was a expert on Poe." She chewed at her bottom lip. Her short hair was held at her temples with bobby pins. "And you have to look at the bright side. People adopting kids are decent people. George Burns and Gracie Allen, for instance. And Bob Hope."

"All comedians," Shelly said thoughtfully.

"Those kids must have a good time," Aileen said. "Lots to laugh at."

Shelly rolled her eyes.

"And Helen Hayes," Aileen added.

"I'm talking about the kids, and how they did," Shelly said.

"Yes you are," Aileen said. "But I think you're thinking about the mommas who gave 'em up."

# 16

# GOING OVER

Shelly's water broke in Aileen's kitchen while she was pressing oranges onto a squeezer. She was eight and a half months pregnant and didn't know what had happened. "That's your water," Aileen said while Shelly stood in the puddle. "You're going to have the baby." She drove her to the hospital and checked her in under the name Polly Miller. Two nurses came and gave her a gown and helped her get into bed. They told her to roll over, and gave her an enema, and she didn't know what they were doing. They shaved her pubic hair. The doctor came in to examine her. She labored, crying with pain. "She's going over," the nurses said.

"Please," Shelly kept begging, though she didn't know what she was begging for. She screamed for Aileen until Aileen was admitted into the room. Finally the nurses gave her an ether mask and she woke up vomiting over a bowl. "Where's my baby?"

A nurse came in with the baby wrapped in a blanket. "You take your time," Aileen told Shelly. "This is your time. You take it." They left her alone with the bundle.

Shelly unwrapped the baby and saw that it was a girl. She looked at every inch of her and stroked her hair. She talked to her, and smelled her, and sang "Swanee River" to her, the song that her grandmother had sung to her. The baby had red hair, like Shelly's mother, and a round pink face. She had blue eyes. She was quiet, and stared at Shelly's face.

Shelly's heart was filled with so much love and so much pain that she couldn't tell one from the other. Maybe it wasn't too late to change her mind and keep the baby. She could get out of bed and take the baby with her and find a ride to somewhere. Maybe someone would take them in. "Oh, sweet girl," she said. "What is your name?" She promised the child that she would protect her and take care of her. But even while she made the promise, she knew it wasn't true.

The baby cried, and Shelly soothed her until she fell asleep, and then held her a long time, watching the little fluttering veins in her throat and stroking her delicate ears and her warm cheeks. "I wish your daddy was here," she whispered.

She loved the moments, but hated the hours for passing so quickly. She cried often and couldn't control her emotions. The breast that was whole began to swell and ache, and the other one strained at its scars. Shelly was given ice packs to place between her legs and on her breasts. She slept, and then woke, and asked for the baby. The baby was always brought, but then she was always taken away. Shelly often followed the nurse so she could look at the baby through the window. She saw how tiny she was, and how her little arms flailed in the air, and how her fists clenched. How silent her cries were through the glass.

She wanted the child in her arms all the time, but the nurses wouldn't allow this. One of them let her hold the baby at feeding times and give her the bottle. Aileen said to Shelly, "That is a bad idea."

"I love her so much already," Shelly told her.

Once, she put the baby against her breast and let her nuzzle around. But the nurse came in and took her away and sent Shelly off down the hall for her sitz bath.

"You'll get through this," Aileen told her. "You're strong, strong, strong. Look what you've already went through. I shake my head sometimes."

"What will I do?' Shelly cried.

"Be in the Peace Corps, like you planned. Go around the world."

Shelly couldn't think about being so far from the child. She believed the Peace Corps was the only hope for her future, the only way to make something good of her life, but her mind would no longer summon the pictures.

Finally a lawyer came. He asked her if she wanted to see Jack and Delia before she signed the papers, but she didn't. She hoped that Delia would be a loving mother, but she didn't want to picture her with the baby. He said they were in the lobby, and Shelly said, "I don't care." She signed the papers and gave them back to the lawyer. When he started to speak, she said, "If you say anything I'll change my mind." So he took the papers and left.

The nurse who had been the nicest brought the baby so Shelly could tell her goodbye. Shelly had planned to sing to the baby and tell her stories, and wish her a good life, but instead she cried so hard that she couldn't talk and she couldn't sing. She felt as if she would choke, as if she couldn't get air. The baby began to cry too, so the nurse lifted her out of Shelly's arms with a quick, sad look into Shelly's eyes and carried her away. Shelly thought she was coming back, and was surprised to see her mother walk into the room.

"Did you see the baby?" Shelly cried, getting out of bed.

"No, I didn't—"

"Are they bringing her back? Mom? Where is she?"

"I think she's leaving, sweetie. I think they're taking her home."

Shelly ran from the room and down the hall to the lobby, yelling, "Where's my baby?" People turned to look at her; patients came to their doors. Nurses stopped in the hall. Shelly could feel that her breast was leaking, her gown had come untied. Aileen was walking in her direction, but Shelly ran past her. Her father stood in the lobby, wearing a blue jacket. "Shelly, honey," he said, his arm outstretched for her, but she avoided him and ran outside in search of Jack and Delia. The cold wind stung her painful breasts. Milk spotted her gown. The landscape all around was flat and colorless, the parking lot nearly empty. Her father had followed her. He pleaded with her to listen to him, but she ran back into the lobby and saw Jack and the lawyer coming out of an office. Behind them, a woman she knew must be Delia was holding the baby.

The lobby seemed to empty itself of everyone but Delia with the baby. The voice of Shelly's mother had trailed off somewhere, leaving only a strange silence, and Delia, who wore a green dress and held the child. Delia's eyes were sincere as she looked at Shelly. Her face was solemn, her skin brown and smooth.

And what was Shelly to do now? She knew she had no claim. She had leaking breasts and a pounding heart and sorrow so heavy she feared she would fall to her knees. She sobbed, her hands at her face. Her gown had fallen down over her shoulder. And Delia was holding her baby. There was an outward calm in the lobby, an eerie stillness, and unbearable inward pain.

Then Delia did something beautiful and serene and unexpected. She walked over to Shelly and put her arms around her, so that both of them together were holding the child. And Shelly leaned against

Delia and cried into her hair, pressed her face into her shoulder and cried against the green dress.

Her father draped his jacket over her shoulders. Her mother was at her side and smelled of the Prell shampoo she always used. Aileen's thin hands had taken hold of her elbow. Jack stood behind Delia. Shelly saw his acne scars, his mangled ear. His short hair in a crew cut. The baby was making fretful noises, her legs drawn up under the blanket. "Come, my dear," Aileen said to Shelly. "And don't you look back."

In the room, Aileen helped Shelly to dress. Her mother had brought her a new coat, and something about it tore at Shelly. She hated the red color and the way the coat closed tightly around her body as if it owned her. Her mother told her to button it because of the wind. They walked her out to the station wagon, where her belongings from Aileen's house were already in the back. Shelly got in, and Aileen kissed her goodbye. Shelly thought of the little bundle—the little pink bundle with its warm breath and blue eyes and tiny, tiny fingers.

Her father turned the station wagon out of the parking lot and started for the highway, and Shelly thought of slinging the door open. She wanted to say she had changed her mind. She put her hand on the latch and cupped her fingers around it. But she didn't open her mouth, and didn't open the door. She sat there in her red coat, and felt what she had felt that day on the South Mall, as if the blood was pouring out of her and she was back in the same place and had to lie still and play dead. But this time there was no one to rescue her, no one to hold her. Wyatt was far away and didn't know where she was or what she had just done.

"What Delia did was very nice," her mother said when they had reached the highway.

"They'll be good parents," her father said. "I'm certain of it. I know it's hard, but you've done what's right." He spoke over his shoulder. She could see his eyes in the rearview mirror, but he didn't look back at her.

She tried to think of Bolivia. Sarawak. Ecuador. All those pictures. The obstacle course—rapelling, rock climbing. The softhearted city girls killing the chickens for dinner, and Albert Schweitzer wearing his safari hat. The handsome guys on the hillside, herding sheep.

It was a different life that she could have lived. No longer part of her world. All she could see was the baby. Whole countries had fallen away.

# 17

# AQUARENA

The thought of Austin broke her heart, so Shelly didn't return to UT that year. She didn't trust herself to live so close to the baby and feel like a normal person. Too sad to make plans for the future, she returned to the little town of San Marcos where she had spent the first months of the pregnancy. She rented a cheap apartment and got a job in the gift shop at a local tourist attraction called Aquarena Springs.

Aquarena wasn't Ecuador, but a kind of a magical world of its own, with a Swiss sky ride of gondolas that floated like bubbles high over the tree-lined headwaters of the San Marcos River, and a submarine theater for underwater shows where beautiful girls called Aquamaids wore Polynesian sarongs and fed milk bottles to swimming pigs and had underwater picnics with Glurpo the witch doctor, their hair billowing luxuriously about them. Glass-bottomed boats glided among swans and ducks on the peaceful waters, looking down upon crystal springs bubbling below. Fountains sprayed water out of the river, creating rainbows in the sunlight. A frontier town next to the Visitor's Center where Shelly worked had a jail, a blacksmith shop, and a general store. The barbershop where Gene Autry had shined shoes as a boy had been hauled in from Tioga, Texas. The saloon had a player piano. For a dime, visitors could fire electric rays out of a three-shooter pistol at a life-size talking wax gunfighter. They could walk through a fun house with trick mirrors and watch trained chickens play checkers and tic-tac-toe. They could clap their hands at the "scare goats" and see them fall down and go rigid.

Shelly had been working in the gift shop for less than a week when the skies dumped nineteen inches of rain on San Marcos, inundating a fourth of the town. It was the spring of 1970, the worst flood on record in San Marcos—a town that was prone to flooding.

She had driven to work early that morning, inching her way through the heavy rain in a used Chevy Impala her parents had lent her the money to buy, the windshield wipers useless against the blanket of water. She wore jeans and a sweatshirt and tennis shoes, and carried her work dress in a bag to keep it from getting soaked.

Under a flimsy umbrella that tugged in the rising wind, lightning flashing and thunder exploding around her, she ran from the parking lot to the open breezeway between the restaurant and the gift shop. It was slippery in the breezeway, and Shelly stepped carefully here, avoiding the misty splatters. The air smelled cold and electric.

She found the gift shop brightly lit compared to the rainy darkness outside. Her coworkers, a petite coed named Miriam with a sleek bob cut, and a husky local girl named Sandi, who wore too much mascara, stood at the plate-glass windows, staring out at a deluge so heavy it curtained the river from sight.

"Nobody's going to come today," Miriam said as Shelly joined them at the window. "I wished they'd let us go home."

"I feel like we're in the submarine theater," Shelly said.

"I guess they won't be running the sky ride in this," Miriam added.

"One time when I was little I saw the trees on Lime Kiln Road completely underwater," Sandi said. "And that's just half a mile from here."

"They could not have been underwater," Miriam scoffed, turning from the window and starting to count bills into the register. She had a persnickety personality, and neither Shelly nor Sandi liked her.

"You don't know; you didn't grow up here," Sandi answered.

A man—a blur in the rain—ran alongside the windows in the direction of the restaurant. "So there are still people around," Miriam said. "I guess we won't be going home." A trickle of water slid under the door from the breezeway. "What we need is a mop." She went into the storage room to look for one, and came out with an electric fan, which she plugged in, facing it toward the door so it blew the encroaching puddle back in ripples.

They started moving the merchandise up to the higher shelves. Some of the items were heavy, and Shelly had trouble lifting them with her crooked arm. She was lifting a box of ceramic piggy banks from under the desk when the door opened with a jangle of bells. Expecting to see the supervisor, she turned. But it wasn't the supervisor that came in. It was a wave of water.

Miriam gave a confused laugh but cut it short because the water kept coming. The glass door was heavy, but the force of the flow held it open. Miriam tried shoving it shut, but the water swept her feet from under her and knocked her to the ground.

The water swirled around Shelly's ankles in muddy whirlpools. She was surprised it came in so quickly and was so cold—much colder than the river. It felt like ice water. She sloshed toward Miriam to help her up, but heard a whirring sound from the blades of the fan splashing droplets into the air, and realized that the electrical cord was underwater. She ran to pull the plug out of the socket, but the water hobbled her and she lost her balance. On her knees, she crawled toward the wall and yanked out the cord. A buzz of electricity shot through her hand, and a spidery branch of fire traveled over the surface of the churning water.

Then the lights went out. Shelly was seized with fear to be in the dark. The rising water lifted her from the floor and shoved her across the room. In a flash of lightning she saw Sandi standing on the desktop, looking toward the windows with an expression of panic. She saw her plunge into the water and drag herself against the current toward the door to the breezeway. And in that instant she understood it was the river pouring in—not the rain. In minutes, it would fill the room.

Postcards swirled around her; snow globes bobbed in eddies. Slimy things brushed at her legs. Lightning cast an eerie sheen on the water and over the trinkets on the shelves—wooden pecking chickens and souvenir teacups and jars of polished stones.

The water tugged at Shelly's sneakers and she kicked them off. "Kick your shoes off!" she yelled. The three of them tried to get to the door, but the water was up to their waists and then to their chests, and the floor slid out from under them. The postcard rack floated sideways, blocking their way. When they got hold of each other, Sandi was in the middle between the others. Shelly struggled against the current, but her left arm was weak and stiff. Trash clogged the water, and Shelly felt as if she were fighting through a garbage heap. Fish wriggled against her as she tugged at the doorframe.

For half a second after they had pulled themselves through the door, Shelly thought they had escaped to safety. But then the current grabbed them and sent them through the breezeway and toward the parking lot at a terrifying speed. Strung out and clutching each other's hands like paper dolls, they tried to hold on to each other. But the water pulled them apart, and Shelly saw the others carried away from her, their heads bobbing as helplessly as volleyballs on the current. In the flickering lightning she saw Sandi sink, and then rise to the surface, and sink and rise again, her fat cheeks stained with mascara and her mouth open.

The current tangled Shelly's hair into her mouth and eyes. Swimming sideways against the powerful flow, she angled for a nearby tree, but something rammed the back of her head and shoved her under the surface, where the deafening noise of thunder and rain gave way to a sudden quiet and a strange illusion of peace. Shelly squeezed her eyes shut and let the quiet hold her until branches and debris snagged in her hair and dragged her forward again. She tried to claw her way to the surface, but the branches trapped her and she could not get up for air. Through murky water she saw the leafy limbs in front of her face and tried to dig out of the snarl by kicking and thrashing. But the branches only seemed to close more tightly around her, scratching at her as she fought them. Her lungs ached, and she began, in a moment of panic, to think she would die. Her life had been wasted except for the baby. She was about to breathe water into her lungs when the snare of branches broke apart and allowed her to reach the surface.

The rain hit her face so hard that she wasn't sure her head was above water until, in a flicker of lightning, she saw the tree she had been trying to reach rising in front of her. As if delivering her into its branches, the water swept her there. She kicked and pulled hard with her arms, hauling herself from the current, and climbed as high as she could.

In the tree, she clung to the branches, which swayed and rocked in the wind. She peered through a shroud of rain at lightning shimmering over the parking lot, where floating cars looked like whales. She watched the dark floodwaters sweep debris beneath her. Her teeth chattered and her heart pounded; she couldn't forget how frightened she had felt when she was pinned under the surface, how strangely silent it was down there.

When the torrent finally slackened and the current slowed, she ventured down from the tree and found her friends. The river had become an enormous lake. Slowly, it began to recede. People waded in water up to their knees. They found animals dead in their cages. The talking wax gunman bobbed in two feet of water. Cars had drifted away. Fish flopped about in the buildings. But no one at Aquarena had drowned in the flood. Shelly stood in the ruined gift shop in a daze, asking herself if there was a reason why, for the second time in her life, she had come so close to death, and yet been saved.

# 18

# HER NAME IS CARLOTTA

The flood had floated twenty-four alligators out of their fenced enclosure, and they had to be rounded up. For days, while trash still hung in the willow trees along the river and Shelly swept dirty water and handled bloated souvenirs, workers carried alligators past the gift shop with their snouts taped shut and their legs secured behind their backs.

Shelly kept thinking about how it felt to be caged under the water. She didn't know why the snag of limbs had let her go. Maybe a stick, haphazardly lodged in the tangle, had shifted at just the last second. Maybe some piece of floating garbage had jostled the mass of limbs at just the right angle, just the right time. She could still feel the panic, the ache in her lungs, with the same clarity that she could recall how the flies had waded about in her blood on the South Mall. Four years ago a single inch of all the inches between the tower deck and the plaza, twenty-eight floors below, had meant the difference. And now the sudden movement of a jumble of wreckage had saved her life.

She began to wonder if maybe her life was worthwhile after all—if maybe she was meant to resurrect her old plan to join the Peace Corps. She could work at Aquarena for another year and save up her money, then move back to Austin and finish school. She could improve her Spanish. In the Peace Corps, she could do some good in the world.

The debris was cleared, the spring showers washed the mud from the trees. Often at the end of the day Shelly took the sky ride, or the ferry, across the river and walked the Aquarena trails under tall trees shrouded with Spanish moss through a wonderland of gardens to historic sites—a replica of the tower of an old Spanish mission that had once stood on the banks, a gristmill powered by water, the log cabin of an early pioneer who had fought in the battle of San Jacinto and served the Republic of Texas and later bought this property on the San Marcos River. These days, a white-haired glassblower in a coat and tie and captain's hat fashioned works of art for the visitors in that cabin. Sometimes he tied a blindfold around his eyes to show that he could create by touch alone. He talked to Shelly about blowpipes and paddles and thermal stress.

She became friends with the Aquamaids, who could hold their breath for two minutes underwater and casually sip air from a bubbling hose, and with the college guys who played the clownish witch doctor, and with the waitresses in the restaurant and the guys in uniform, who swung open the doors to the gondolas and swung them shut and shoved the bubble off to glide out over the water.

On her baby's first birthday, in February of 1971, she rode the sky ride across the river and back so many times without stopping that she lost count of the number. Gazing down at the glassy river, at the swans drifting in formation, at the canopied tour boats, Ralph the pig performing his swan dive from the belching fiberglass volcano, she wondered if there was a birthday party for her baby, and what Delia and Jack had named her. She tried to picture the baby eating birthday cake. She wondered if she could walk yet, and if she could say any words.

In the spring, Shelly was alone at the register in the gift shop on a slow weekday morning when the tinkling bells announced that someone was at the door. She looked up to welcome the visitors and for a dizzying second didn't quite place the family of three—a father and mother and a child on the mother's hip. Because this was not where they ought to be, and the child was not an infant now, wrapped in a pink blanket.

Jack was holding the door open as Delia stepped inside. Shelly's eyes remained on the child. She steadied herself at the counter. It flashed through her mind that she shouldn't be seeing the baby—that there was something illicit in this. It was as if she were looking at one of the trick mirrors in the fun house, and the image was out of place or folded backward in time somehow. Something was not as it should be.

Except that everything was. The baby had orange curls and perfect skin and a perfect button nose, and her sturdy little legs were wrapped around Delia. She took in the sunny shop, the light from plate-glass windows pouring across the shelves of trinkets, and kicked her legs to get down. "Down," she said, "get *down*." Delia set her down, and she toddled toward an array of Indian drums and plastic tomahawks.

And Delia turned and saw Shelly. Jack's hand was still on the door. He, too, was looking at Shelly.

The child plopped down on the floor and took up a plastic tomahawk decorated with feathers. Her mouth made a perfect O as she riffled her fingers across the feathers.

Delia said, "Shelly? Hi."

Shelly replied so quietly she hardly heard her own voice. "Hey Delia."

They stared at each other. "It's hard to believe this," Delia said.

"Yes, it's kind of strange."

"You're working here?"

"Yes. She's beautiful."

Delia turned and looked at the child. "She is, isn't she?"

The sunlight made a halo out of the girl's wispy curls while she examined the bright feathers on the shaft of the tomahawk.

"Is this awful for you?" Delia asked Shelly. "To have her here?"

"It's like a miracle," Shelly said. "It's wonderful. I love having her here. And she looks like . . ."

"Like who?"

"Like my mother, a little. Maybe it's just her hair that does. But her skin is the same, too. It's fair like my mother's. Oh, I never thought I'd see her again."

Jack allowed the door to swing closed, jangling the bells. He smiled at Shelly.

"What did you name her?" Shelly asked.

"We named her Carlotta," Delia said.

"Carlotta Stone," Shelly repeated. "That's beautiful." She had tried to guess at the name, but had never thought of Carlotta. "It's perfect. Is it a family name?"

"My mother's," Delia said.

The child picked up a souvenir ashtray and studied the picture on it. "Moke!" she said, waving the ashtray at Jack.

"Because I smoke," Jack explained.

He tried to coax her to give him the ashtray, telling her it would break if she dropped it, but she clutched it and shook her head, saying, "Have it, have it," until he distracted her with a Barbie-size doll dressed as a mermaid that he took from the top shelf, and she surrendered the ashtray. The doll had eyes that opened and closed, and Carlotta played with them, prying them open and gazing into the glassy orbs.

"She likes anything shiny," Delia said.

Jack stacked the ashtrays out of her reach while Carlotta nestled the mermaid into her lap and plucked aggressively at the feathers on the tomahawk. Delia said, "Sweetie, don't pull those feathers out." When Carlotta saw her coming to take the tomahawk she shrieked excitedly, yanking a handful of feathers. Delia tried to pick her up, but Carlotta sprawled on her back, turning herself into limp weight. Jack lifted her up while Delia brought the tomahawk to the counter. "We'll need to buy this," she said with a rueful smile.

"Can I buy it for her?" Shelly asked. "I can glue the feathers back on." Searching under the counter for glue, she felt as if none of this really was happening—it seemed impossible to be seeing the child up close and in real life instead of in memories and dreams. She only remembered her wrapped in the blanket, making the little mewling sounds.

And now Carlotta had started to fuss and squirm in Jack's arms. Shelly picked up a snow globe from a cluster for sale on the counter, shook it, and offered it. Carlotta dropped her handful of feathers to take it, and brought it close to her face to study the falling snowflakes. It was a water scene with a background of painted ferns and mermaids and a small plastic floating figure of Ralph the swimming pig. The snowflakes made no sense in this underwater scene, but the child was transfixed, and shook the globe to watch the flakes and the tiny pig floating in the water. She looked directly at Shelly, almost as if she remembered her, and Shelly saw that her eyes had remained blue.

"So, do you want tickets to the rides?" Shelly managed to ask. "Have you been here before?"

"I was here as a kid, in the forties," Jack said, and she wondered if maybe he had come on a family outing, perhaps with Wyatt along, and the idea gave her a heartbreaking feeling. The place had been her escape from thinking of Wyatt, and she didn't want to envision him here as a boy, peering into the green waters or running along the trails in the Hanging Gardens across the river.

Jack was mercifully unforthcoming. "Mostly I just remember the pig."

"You'll want tickets to the underwater show, then," Shelly said.

"I think we'll want tickets to everything."

"Carlotta will love the glassblower," Shelly suggested. "He's in the cabin across the river. Tell him Shelly asked if he'd make a goose with a golden egg. It's amazing to watch him do that. And you might take the ferry over instead of the sky ride. A lot of kids get scared on the sky ride."

"I'm more likely to get scared than she is," Jack said, pushing Carlotta's curls out of her eyes.

"She's adventurous," Delia added.

Carlotta was still peering into the snow globe and shaking it every few seconds.

Jack paid for the tickets, but Shelly didn't allow him to pay for the tomahawk. "And I want to give her the snow globe, too," she insisted, dreading the tinkling of doorbells that would mean the magic was over, and would leave her to think of Carlotta every time the bells jangled again.

When the moment of parting came, Shelly was unable to speak. What words could do justice to her feelings? Delia thanked her again for the gifts, and was already at the door, Jack behind her, carrying Carlotta, who was shaking the snow globe, when Shelly called impulsively after them. "Will you stop back in after you've seen everything?"

Delia turned and looked at her but didn't say anything for a second. Shelly wished she could reel the words back in so that these beautiful moments would not have an awkward ending. But then Delia said, "Why don't you join us for the submarine show?"

She gasped at the thought. "I'd love to! Oh Delia, that is so nice of you! I'll get someone to fill in for me. The show starts at noon. I'll wait for you at the submarine."

When they left, she ran to the restaurant and traded hours with a waitress named June. "I'll take your whole day on Sunday if you'll fill in for me at the gift shop for an hour today," she promised. She primped in the bathroom and put on lipstick, then waited on customers, dusting every shelf and singing songs to herself—even "Swanee River," which she had been too sad to sing that last day in the hospital. Nothing seemed sad now. She felt as if she had been living the last year in a play, and now the lights had come on and she could see a world out there. Everything she was living was only a small part of the real picture. There were possibilities that she had not thought of. She could even just walk off the stage and into the world. What Charles

Whitman had done to her, and the love affair with Wyatt, and having to give up the baby wasn't her whole life—there would be chance meetings and other surprises. Because here she was, on a sunny spring day, and her baby, now beautifully named Carlotta, with orange curls, had been carried back into her life by the same people who had carried her out of it, and Shelly was going to sit with her and watch a swimming pig in an underwater show.

At noon, she was waiting outside the submarine theater when Jack and Delia came walking up the path, Carlotta perched on Jack's shoulders. "How has it been?" Shelly asked them.

"We've had a very fun time," Delia said.

"Goat," Carlotta said. "Chicken. Ball."

"Yes, the chicken plays basketball," Shelly told her.

Carlotta pointed at one of glass-bottomed tour boats anchored at the dock and lowered her voice to a whisper. "Fish swimming." She opened her mouth in imitation of a fish, revealing four small teeth. Then she seemed to remember something, and shook her head vigorously, pounding her fist on the top of Jack's head. "No, no, Lotta," she said loudly.

"She's telling you she was evicted from the saloon for beating on the player piano," Jack said. "We're hoping it's the last time she's thrown out of a bar."

The entrance to the theater was a thatched roof flanked with crossed spears. A girl named Jenny, wearing a flowered sarong and greeting the dozen or so ticket holders, came over to talk with Shelly. She chatted with Jack and Delia about the show and gave Carlotta a handful of corn to feed the ducks while waiting. It was a breezy day and not too warm. Willows along the bank swished their long limbs over the ground. When the submarine surfaced, the audience on board exited by a ramp, and a guide invited the waiting crowd aboard.

"Hey, Shelly!" the guide said when he saw her. "Aren't you supposed to be working?'

"June's filling in for me. I want you to meet my friends Jack and Delia Stone, and their little girl, Carlotta."

"Welcome!" he told them. "Right this way. Watch your step."

The submarine was a long rectangular theater built to descend as water was let into the ballast tanks. Several rows of bleachers faced a wall of windows that revealed a view of the fiberglass volcano.

Shelly sat in the front row with Jack and Delia as Carlotta ran up and down in front of the glass with three other small children. Beyond the window, a Polynesian maiden emerged from the cave of the volcano, coaxing Ralph the pig behind her with a milk bottle. The volcano suddenly emitted a puff of smoke, and Carlotta stopped running and stared at it. A rumbling sound crackled over the loudspeaker, followed by a deep voice saying, "The volcano is angry. It will erupt and create great danger if Glurpo the village witch doctor cannot appease its anger."

The witch doctor, a college student whom Shelly knew as Brad, appeared on top of the volcano, wearing a necklace of shells and a loincloth and waving a spear over his head. He fumbled the spear and dropped it, then picked it up and dropped it again, and he did this several more times while the audience in the submarine laughed. "Our fate is in the hands of Glurpo," the recording said.

The submarine began to descend. At the first sensation of movement, Carlotta climbed into Delia's lap and watched as the waterline crawled up the window and the Polynesian girl dived into the water. Ralph performed his famous swan dive after the girl, creating an explosion of underwater bubbles, his legs paddling furiously and his snout straining after the bottle. The magnifying aspect of the water, in the split-level view as the submarine descended, made Ralph's pink underside look disengaged from the rest of him, his cloven hooves pulling furiously at the water and his rump muscles straining. Corn was tossed to the ducks from above, and they dived deep, stretching their necks for the kernels that fluttered toward the bottom. Carlotta was so thrilled with the anomaly of the upside-down ducks that she shook her snow globe furiously and climbed out of Delia's lap to get closer to the window. Turning to look at Shelly, she said, "Ducks coming!" as seriously as if she were announcing the queen of England.

Shelly whispered, "Yes, look at them," and watched the child's warm breath clouding the glass.

When the theater was entirely underwater, a second Aquamaid emerged from a gigantic clam that was anchored to the bottom of the river. She carried a drawstring bag and sipped air out of a hose in a swarm of bubbles that floated upward. High above her, on the surface, Ralph's hooves paddled back toward the volcano, and the girl who had been swimming with him descended and performed a languid ballet with the girl from the clam shell, their long hair floating about them and their air tubes drifting alongside.

Watching Carlotta at the window, Shelly wanted to pull the child into her arms. She had never felt so much longing for anyone, except for Wyatt, and that had been illicit. This was pure.

The Aquamaids spread a cloth over a tabletop and opened the drawstring bag, removing bananas and clusters of grapes and sticks of celery, on which they slowly dined, wiping their mouths with napkins. They drank from bottles of soda pop and took delicate sips of air out of their hoses, letting the bubbles shimmer up to the surface. Glurpo splashed into the midst of their picnic, his large flippers thrashing about in the water, the fringes of his loincloth attracting schools of fish. Shelly could see him glancing at her through his diving mask, and she gestured toward Carlotta so that he would take note of her. He swam to the window, pressed his mask to the glass directly in front of Carlotta, and blew bubbles into her face until she let out a squeal of happiness.

Shelly wished she could stay here forever, under the surface, as in a dream, in a make-believe place with a swimming pig and a fake clam and college girls in sarongs, and Carlotta.

But the Aquamaids had finished their picnic. They shook their napkins in a dreamy way and ascended slowly, trailing their hoses. The submarine began to rise.

Feeling the upward movement, Carlotta shook her head and said, "Down! Down!" When the surface began to take over the view, she put both hands against the glass as if to hold the waterline in place and stop its descent on the window. She squatted to see the last underwater remnants, pleading "Down, down," until the theater jolted to a stop at the surface and she flung herself into a heap and cried miserably while Delia knelt beside her and tried to comfort her. People had to walk around her to exit, and Jack finally lifted her against his shoulder and carried her out as she wept.

Shelly felt wretched, watching this. She wanted to go back down, down, herself. Seeing the underwater show through Carlotta's eyes had made her fall in love with the lovely vision—the backward curve of the Aquamaids as they performed their synchronized ballet, and the unhurried swarms of perch, and even Glurpo and his ridiculous act.

"Maybe you can bring her back again," she suggested to Delia over Carlotta's cries as they exited the ramp.

"I think we'll have to," Delia said.

When they were on solid ground, Shelly purchased a nickel's worth of duck feed from a dispenser near the boats and gave it to Carlotta to distract her from pouting, and then lingered, feeling self-conscious and extraneous to the family but wanting to watch Carlotta toss the pellets to the ducks. "Are you going on the sky ride?" she asked.

"She's getting pretty cranky," Delia said. "We should probably do that another day. It's her naptime. She's been teething."

Carlotta toddled off after the ducks, and Delia ran after her. Jack and Shelly sat on a bench near the sidewalk. Two boats were tied at the dock in front of them, and a third moved slowly toward them on the water, the passengers peering down into the viewing window. The guide's voice boomed through a microphone: "As we pull into the shaded area under the trees, you're about to see a school of the famous monkey fish. These are a rare kind of fish, because if you wave at them, they'll wave back." The passengers waved and broke into laughter.

"It's their reflection," Shelly explained. "Since they're in the shade of the trees."

Jack chuckled. "I gathered."

They watched the passengers disembark. Down the dock, beyond the boats, Delia and Carlotta had paused to watch the swans on the water.

"It's like heaven being with her," Shelly said. "And not as hard as I would have thought. She's so happy. Thank you for including me. Seeing you and Delia with her reassures me."

"I have a lot of respect for how you and Wyatt handled things," Jack said.

"Wyatt couldn't have lived with himself if he had left Nate," she said.

"Maybe not. But a lot of women would have asked him to."

She folded her hands. "I try not to think about him so often. It's too messy, and hopeless." She waited a moment. "But is he okay?"

"He's okay."

"He's in Provincetown?"

"Yes."

"Has he met Carlotta yet?"

Jack looked at her solemnly. "How will it make you feel to know?'

"It doesn't matter how I feel. I just want to know."

"He's been to visit us twice."

"Oh." She tried to picture him with Carlotta. "Were Elaine and Nate with him?"

"No. He came on his own."

They watched Carlotta trying to pet a spotted duck that squawked and waddled in circles around her. "She doesn't look like Wyatt," Shelly said. "I keep trying to see if she looks like me. I don't think so. And not like my mom, either, except for her hair color. That's exactly like hers." After a moment she said, "I know Delia's good friends with Elaine, and I hope that doesn't make her resent me."

"Shelly. You gave us Carlotta. How could we resent you?"

"I hope Elaine never knows about me. I worry she might find out. You don't think there's any chance she would, do you?"

"Not unless he tells her. Or unless she were somehow to see the portrait."

"You know about the portrait?"

He nodded.

"What do you know about it?"

"It's in Provincetown, as of a few months ago. Wyatt asked me to ship some paintings he'd left at UT, and it was one of them. I took some of the paper off to be sure it was his, and I saw what it was. I didn't think he should have it there, but he said he was going to keep it in a closet in a studio he's renting, and Elaine wouldn't see it."

"Oh." She leaned back, looking up into the spring foliage overhead and thinking how the painting would probably always be going from one hiding place to another—at least until Wyatt got rid of it. And of course he should get rid of it. But she felt a renewed pang of longing for him, knowing he hadn't brought himself to do that yet.

"What about his career—how's it going?"

"Not so well. He's not painting popular stuff. Unfortunately, I think he's seen as a draftsman by the artists there. An illustrator. Tempera's not exactly in style."

"So he's not making much money?"

"No. A restaurant owner commissioned a seascape for a fair amount of money, and Wyatt painted what he tells me was a masterpiece—a sunrise over the water. But the guy said it looked too much like a photograph and he wanted an old ship of some kind painted on it to make it more like an old-fashioned seascape. Which Wyatt refused to do. He told him he wasn't putting a goddamn ship in the painting, and that blew the deal." Jack shook his head. "The more dismissive people are, the more stubborn he gets."

"Could he paint in a different style if he wanted to?"

"Of course. He used to paint with watercolors when he first started. Anyway, he's frustrated. He's got to figure out some way to make a living."

They sat watching Carlotta and Delia with the ducks, and thinking about Wyatt.

"Are you going to tell him you saw me?"

"I've been wondering that myself."

"What do you think?"

"I probably will. Unless there's a reason I shouldn't. What do you think?"

"I guess I'd like him to know."

The boats on the still water reminded her of how everything around her, now dry and placid, had been under the raging flood-waters. Maybe she had been spared from drowning just so she could have this day with Carlotta. Or maybe there was something more.

"Jack?"

"Yes?"

"Do you think today was more than a chance encounter?"

"I'm not sure I believe in providence, if that's what you mean. But I am glad we saw you."

"I have a question."

"Okay."

"I don't know how you'll feel about my asking." She realized her heart had started to race.

"Go ahead."

"Seeing Carlotta today . . . it makes me wonder if it's not possible . . . to do this. To see her again." She waited, but he didn't say anything. He watched Carlotta tossing pellets, one by one, to the squabbling ducks.

"I'm going back to school next fall. Maybe I could play with her at a park in Austin. Maybe just . . . now and then. Or . . . sometimes in the future. I know it would be complicated.'" He didn't respond. "You're thinking about the possible problems?"

"The possible problems are so many I can't even begin to think about them."

Delia was putting another nickel into the feed dispenser on the riverbank, helping Carlotta turn the knob, the pellets spilling into their hands.

"It would lead to something we couldn't easily handle," Jack said. "Any of us. It would have to. Because I don't think you'd want to see her just once or twice and then stop."

"I could do that."

"But what would be the point of seeing her in a park a couple of times?"

"I haven't thought it all through, but today was so much more manageable than I would have imagined. I know that's because you and Delia were gracious about it and made it easy. But also . . . It felt right. And now it feels possible that maybe I could see her sometimes. At least it doesn't feel impossible."

"I wish it could work, Shelly. Honestly. But who would we tell her you were?"

"You could say you knew me from college—that you came to my rescue that day and we've known each other ever since. And then leave it at that. I'm not talking about trying to play a huge role in her life."

"No, and you didn't intend to play a huge role in Wyatt's life, either. But when you love someone—"

"When you love someone, you do what's right by them, and I did what's right by Wyatt."

"Eventually, you did."

"And I would do what's right by Carlotta. Didn't I give her up to you because I thought that was right? I know I don't have any right to be asking you about this. You've been great to me today. But something in me just believes some good is supposed to come from today. Why would this chance be put in front of us, if we weren't supposed to take it?" She watched Delia, near the water, lift Carlotta and nestle her into her shoulder, the child's fluff of hair falling against Delia's neck like a blown dandelion, her eyes closing as she relaxed in her mother's arms. Cradling her, Delia walked across the stretch of grass toward Shelly and Jack.

"This looks like a deep conversation," Delia said with a smile when she reached them. "Can I join in?" She stood in front of them, holding Carlotta against her and shifting her slender hips from side to side as she rocked the baby to sleep. "It looks like a serious talk."

"Yes, but it's over," Jack said.

Delia looked at Shelly. "It doesn't seem like it's over."

"It is," Jack said. "Shelly was asking if she could see Carlotta again, and I told her I didn't think it was a good idea. Things are already complicated enough."

"Are we talking about just once?" Delia asked.

"We're not talking about once, or twice, or anytime," Jack said. "It's just not going to work."

Delia smoothed her fingers over Carlotta's forehead and over her closed lids. "But look what Shelly's done for us. Look who I have in my arms, because of Shelly. If she thinks she could do this without it causing a problem, then I believe her. She's already proven she'll do what's right for Carlotta."

Jack looked at Delia and then Shelly, and back again at Delia, and then lifted his hand in a gesture of impatience. "Am I the only one who sees all the ways this could go wrong? It won't work. It just won't."

Delia stroked the curls away from Carlotta's face. She was silent for a moment. Finally, in a voice so hushed she seemed to be talking to the sleeping child, she said, "Maybe not. Maybe you're right."

Shelly thought this was the end of it—the magic was over. Her coach was a pumpkin again. She put her hands on her knees, and stood up.

And then Delia said, lifting her gaze from Carlotta to look directly at Jack, "But it would be a shame, and a waste of love, not to try."

# 19

# DAN

At the end of the summer, Shelly left San Marcos and moved to Austin, where she rented a duplex near campus, registered for the fall semester, and found a part-time job as a cashier at Nau's Pharmacy on West Lynn Street. When she was settled in, Delia called and invited her over. The two of them spent the afternoon watching Carlotta toddle around on the shag carpet of Jack and Delia's apartment.

Shelly began seeing Carlotta almost every week and baby-sitting for her on weekends so Jack and Delia could go to the movies. She took her to eat corn dogs and soft serve and to swim at Deep Eddy, where Shelly wore a swimsuit that allowed her bent arm to show, as she had not done before. Carlotta kicked around in an inner tube and afterward would sit with Shelly on the grassy slope and play doctor on Shelly's arm, and comb her hair, which had grown long. They walked the trails at Mayfield Park, where Carlotta was mesmerized by the shimmering plumage and strange cawing sounds of the peacocks.

Delia started inviting Shelly along on family outings. Jack didn't like the idea at first, but he liked Shelly, and after a while he stopped objecting. They went out for Mexican food, and hamburgers, and visited a pioneer farm where Shelly and Delia and Carlotta made cornhusk dolls and watched a litter of suckling piglets tug at the teats of a huge sow.

Many places in Austin reminded Shelly of Wyatt, but now the memories fell into order like stepping-stones that led to Carlotta, and Shelly was not so troubled by them. She wore her hair braided, and wore hippie dresses and no makeup, and often felt happy. She told herself that the things she had lost in her life were supposed to be left behind: If she tugged her losses around, she would haul a heavy burden and still have an empty life. It had been more than two years since Wyatt went to her home in Lockhart and told her about Province-town. It was time to stop thinking about him.

But it wasn't so easy to do so. She went on dates, but her thoughts were still tethered to Wyatt. She sat through parties in smoky apart-ments, looking at psychedelic posters glowing in black lights while the music of Jimi Hendrix and Buffalo Springfield pounded the walls. Everything about the parties seemed witless and superficial compared to the quiet intimacy she had known with Wyatt. The song "Rainy Days and Mondays" was always playing on the radio, and even the title reminded her of Wyatt.

When spring came, a middle-aged skinny brunette named Nancy, who always arrived at work at the pharmacy wearing foam curlers, offered to set Shelly up on a blind date with a geologist named Dan Hadley. "He works with my brother at Radian doing environmental assessments—I'm not sure of what," she said, standing over the bath-room sink and pulling the curlers out of her hair. "He's got sandy blond hair and he's built nice."

"Maybe another time."

"Somebody's going to nab him. He's not your run-of-the-mill. Girls fall for him all the time."

"I'll think about it."

"Don't think for long. He's from a big ranch in Montana. His dad was the foreman. He can do anything, fix anything. He fixed our sep-tic tank. He went to UT."

Shelly met Dan on an April afternoon at a boat dock on Town Lake, and they walked on the hike and bike trail, swatting mosqui-toes. The trail was new and incomplete, so they turned around before they got far, and sat on a low dock, watching the sun go down, the water lapping beneath them.

Dan had reddish blond hair and a mustache, and gold flecks in his irises. His eyelashes were tawny. Shelly's first impression was that he was stodgy—there was nothing stylish about his clothing. He wore jeans without any bell to them and a plain shirt, and his hair was barely over his ears.

They talked about UT and about Nancy, who had set them up. Dan asked what Shelly planned to do after she graduated.

"I'll probably end up staying in Austin awhile," she told him. Now that she could be with Carlotta, the Peace Corps seemed more like a dream from her past than something that might come up in her future. "What about you? How did you get interested in geology?" The warmth of the evening and the sun sinking into the trees on the far side of the lake made her feel drowsy and peaceful.

"I guess from growing up in Montana. Have you ever been there?"

"I've never been out of Texas."

"Have you seen mountains?"

She shook her head. "Hills."

"Then let's think closer to home, and I'll show you why geology is so interesting. Under this dock—what's there?"

"Water."

"And under that?"

"I guess, mud."

"And under the mud?"

"Sorry, I'm stuck in the mud."

He laughed. "Under the mud is the tip of a huge underground reservoir called Edwards Aquifer. It's made of honeycombed rock eaten away by chemical reactions of water and limestone. The water under this dock has traveled through hundreds of miles of channels in the aquifer and bubbled up through Barton Springs, and flowed into the lake. One of the great things about geology is being able to visualize that whole dark journey."

Shelly gazed pensively at the lake, tinged pink and yellow by the setting sun, and tried to imagine the waters flowing through the murky subterranean world Dan had described. "How many years is an average drop of water trapped under there, in the aquifer?" she asked him.

"Two hundred, give or take. A long time."

They lay on their bellies and peered beneath the dock at the fish nibbling on weeds. Shelly talked about the glass-bottomed boats at Aquarena Springs and told Dan she would take him there and show him around. She trailed her fingers in the water, and seeing him notice the crookedness of her arm through the sleeve, decided to get the question out of the way. "My arm's a little crooked. I was one of the people Charles Whitman shot."

He looked at her sincerely. "Nancy told me. I'm sorry that happened to you."

"It seems such a long time ago. What else did Nancy tell you?"

"Ohhhhhh—" He pretended to stall. "Just that you were stubborn and not likely to agree to a date."

"I have a very full life," she said, teasing him. "Lots of homework. Half a duplex. Pharmacy customers. I have to help them find tweezers and nail polish. It's all very demanding."

"How about tomorrow night? Any demands on you then?"

He took her to see *What's Up, Doc?*, starring Barbra Streisand and Ryan O'Neal. She liked him better than she had liked anyone else she had gone out with, but couldn't forget that he wasn't Wyatt. He was not as tall as Wyatt, and didn't wear glasses, and his hair was a lighter color. His jaw was broader. When she looked him in the eyes, she felt as if she had wandered into a place she didn't belong, because his eyes were not Wyatt's.

"Tell me about him," Delia asked her at the park one day while they watched Carlotta on the slide.

"He's nice. I like him. Nothing will come of it," Shelly said.

"Because you don't like him enough? Or because you don't want to?"

But Shelly couldn't answer that.

Dan took her to dinner, and afterward lingered with her on the doorstep under a hazy lightbulb and talked about his family. Shelly talked about Lockhart and noticed that his laugh had a quiet, intimate tone, and that he smiled while he listened to her. One of his front teeth was crooked in a way she found appealing.

After Dan left, she lay on her sofa and missed Wyatt. She didn't have any pictures of him, and his face was less and less clear. She missed the way he had made her feel. Dan had stirred up an old sense of longing that she had forgotten.

By the end of the week, she kissed him. His kiss was different from Wyatt's because of the mustache, but it was nice, and gentle, and afterward he held her quietly and neither of them said anything for a while.

He began to show up at the pharmacy to have lunch with her at the counter. They had burgers and strawberry milk shakes. Sometimes he came from work outdoors, and his boots were scuffed and muddy, and he had an earthy smell that she liked. Wyatt had not been so much of an outdoorsman, and while she liked this characteristic in Dan, she was sorry the comparison put Wyatt in a less favorable light. She reminded herself that Dan had no artistic talents.

One night she cooked dinner for him, and afterward they were drinking beer and kissing in her tiny kitchen when he began to unbutton her summer dress.

"I'm nervous about it," she whispered. "It wasn't only my arm that was hurt. My breast has a lot of scars."

"You're beautiful," he told her. "I like everything about you."

But she was thinking of Wyatt, and feeling as if the scars and the rest of her still belonged to him. He had held her in the beginning when she was bleeding, and later had painted the portrait showing the wounds and imperfections, as if he had formed them with his hands and in that way had claimed them. Only because she was injured had she come to know Wyatt, and to give birth to Carlotta. She would easily choose to suffer all the pain again just to arrive at the place in her life where she now was, with a happy little girl she loved and could often spend time with. From moment to moment she had regretted so much, but looking back now she regretted nothing and was reluctant to let Dan see those parts of her that belonged to Wyatt.

Still, she wanted him to keep touching her. Wyatt had looked at her for months before he could put his hands on her, and everything between them had been difficult and burdened by the inescapable guilt. With Dan, it was all so easy by comparison. She slipped his hand into her dress and allowed him to feel the raised scars and the indentation in the flesh, and she flipped the light switch off as he unbuttoned the dress all the way down and moved his hands over her. But then she fastened the buttons and turned the light back on. "I can't explain it," she whispered. "There's just . . . a lot I haven't told you." She wanted to tell him about her affair with Wyatt, and about Carlotta, because keeping that secret from him had started to feel oppressive. And yet the secret didn't belong only to her. It belonged to Wyatt too, and to Jack and Delia. She couldn't jeopardize Wyatt's marriage, and betray Jack and Delia's trust.

"It's all right," he assured her. "It's all right."

She circled her arms around him.

"Is it so bad?" he whispered.

"I want to tell you some things, but I can't."

He urged her to try. But if she told him about Carlotta, there would be too many inevitable questions and no satisfying end to them until she had told everything. She couldn't open up half the story and say only that she had a child, and not say where the child was, or who the father was. It might have been possible to give only a limited part of the story if she weren't still involved with Carlotta, but she was deeply involved with her, and nothing could make her give that up, or risk it.

Dan told her she was like the aquifer with all those dark channels that he knew were there but wasn't able to see.

When he was gone, she felt more alone than usual and more uncertain about the future. She hoped she was doing the right thing to be so involved with Carlotta. It wasn't as if Carlotta could live her life two ways—one with Shelly and one without her, and then choose the one that worked out best. That choice was up to Shelly. And no matter how she thought about Carlotta's life, or her own, or Jack's, or Delia's, or even Wyatt's, and rearranged the pieces into different puzzles showing far, far different futures, she didn't believe the child would be better off without her. And Dan would complicate the picture. What if she fell in love with him? Wyatt's marriage might come undone someday, and he would come back to her if that should happen.

For a while, sorting clothes she had brought from the Laundromat, she considered going to Jack and asking him if he thought it was possible Wyatt would ever come back to her. But she knew she wasn't the kind of person who would ask that question or live her life waiting for someone's marriage to fall apart. And Jack would never talk to her about this anyway.

Besides—and she came to this gradually, and tearfully, lying in bed in the dark—she was more ready than she had supposed to leave behind that part of her life and take her chances with Dan.

A few nights later, he took her to Mount Bonnell, a high lookout with a view of the winding river and the lights of Austin and low distant hills rolling to the horizon. The air was scented with cedar and mountain laurel, the moon so thin it barely existed. A scattering of filmy clouds moved rapidly overhead. Shelly and Dan stood with their arms around each other and watched the night over the river. Dan talked of how the place had once been called Antoinette's Leap, for a girl who 140 years ago had flung herself from the precipice to escape Indians, and of how George Custer had brought his wife here for picnics. "The view is even better in daylight because you can see the turkey buzzards soaring down there."

There was no one around now. The only sounds were the pulse and drone of insects and the breeze sliding in from the dark, and their own unhurried voices. They found a comfortable place to sit with their backs against a rock, a short distance from the main lookout. Dan hummed the tune of "Dancing in the Moonlight," but then he fell silent and kissed her. For a long time they kissed. He moved his hands over her belly, and she longed to tell him she had carried a baby in there. He kissed her breasts, and she remembered how she had secretly nursed Carlotta the one time, and she wanted to tell him this too. But she felt she had a sacred duty to such a fragile secret and to the people who trusted her. She pictured the wild leap of Antoinette, and lay down on the ground with Dan, and made love with him, and afterward lay in his arms, staring up at the stars, feeling off-kilter and deeply in love but also engulfed by sadness and disoriented by the wide, dark view of the sky. The affair with Wyatt was finished now. Before, it had only been over.

# 20

# PAINTING OVER

In Provincetown, Elaine had become impatient with the hassle and embarrassment of living in a house owned by her parents. Twice, her parents had come for vacations, and Wyatt had insisted on hauling Elaine and Nate with him to a motel across town to be out of their way.

Money was more of an issue than ever, and Elaine began pressuring Wyatt to paint in a more profitable style or a less time-consuming medium. Sculptures? she suggested. Anything but tempera. Anything that would sell.

"That's like telling a journalist he has to write something besides journalism—that he has to write poetry," Wyatt argued. "Or telling a guitarist to play the drums."

He took a teaching job at a community college in West Barnstable, an hour away from Provincetown, and relegated his painting to the predawn hours. At four every morning, he left the house and walked to a rented studio on a side street, where he painted small, perfect likenesses of landscapes and objects. By 6:00 a.m. he was on the way to teach class. His students idolized him as an artist and a teacher, but galleries appeared to be interested only in Warhol and his legions of imitators, and in angry Abstract Expressionists trying to paint like Jackson Pollock.

For Wyatt there was no such thing anymore as waiting for the perfect light to paint by—he saw the sun come up and go down from the car windows on his way to and from the college. His dreams began to die quietly on those car rides, and his self-belief to wither. On weekends he took photographs he intended to paint from, but he rarely had time to look at them afterward. Rolls of film he couldn't afford to develop piled up on his dresser.

Elaine talked of having another baby, and although Wyatt was determined to be the husband and father he would have been had he never known Shelly, secretly he found it difficult to think about having a second child when he already had Carlotta. He was enamored of Carlotta. The two times he had seen her, he was awestruck by her red flyaway curls and her droll expressions. She was another love that he couldn't keep close.

Sometimes he allowed himself to believe he might at least see Shelly the next time he went back to Austin for a visit. The distance and the silence between them made everything that had happened seem unreal, and this sense of unreality was deepened by the fact that he had no one to talk with about her. Jack had made it plain that he wouldn't talk about the affair or about Shelly at all. The only news he would give Wyatt about Shelly was that she was spending a lot of time with Carlotta now, and had become friends with Delia, and was back at school and working part-time and getting on with her life.

Wyatt considered calling her. And yet this would only be selfish. What right did he have to ask for assurances that she was okay? If she wasn't okay, what could he do?

The longer he resisted calling, the less he could see how either of them would benefit from it. What was there to say? That he was sorry? He still loved her? None of it mattered. He was still married, and she had given their child away.

And soon he would have to give up the portrait as well as Shelly. He shared a studio with two other artists, and the rent was going up, and Wyatt couldn't commit to another year. He had stored the portrait of Shelly there, along with his other paintings from Texas, all still in the wrappings Jack had shipped them in.

Stymied over what to do with the portrait, he took Elaine to an art show on Commercial Street and walked around with a glass of wine, looking at paintings he didn't like and mulling over the problem. The gallery was crowded with luminaries from the Cape School of Art: Henry Hensche was rumored to be coming, and several people reported that Robert Motherwell might show up and that Cookie Mueller, the vagabond actress, had already come and gone. A man claiming to be a member of the Native American Church, wearing moccasins, sporting a ponytail, and carrying a plastic bag of cactus buds, set up a canvas tepee on the beach behind the gallery. Partygoers took their shoes off and, carrying their martinis, went out to eat peyote.

Wyatt wasn't interested in the peyote. He figured the man was a fraud and the whole scene a caricature of the town's affectations. Watching people loiter on the beach and vomit into the ocean from the bitter taste of the cactus, he tried to convince Elaine to go home with him.

"You go on," she told him. "Pay the baby-sitter." She walked off down the beach with a young artist she had been flirting with, and Wyatt watched her run in and out of the frothy waves, her legs lovely and thin. She held her skirt up, her hair pulled by the wind. He thought she might eventually turn and call to him or come back, but she didn't. He remembered the November day on the beach at Port Aransas with Shelly, and stood listening to the dark waves, watching Elaine wander away.

Finally he left the party and walked to his studio. On his worktable lay a half-finished painting of the UT tower from the viewpoint of the South Mall plaza. He had started it months ago and had eventually scrapped it as a failure, frustrated that he couldn't make the tempera look anything but flat and antiseptically pale. It had occurred to him the painting should be done in oil or in a combination of paints that weren't so starkly precise as tempera, and he thought maybe he would try that someday. Or maybe what was needed, more than a different style or a different paint, was an entirely different view from the plaza. While he was painting, he had felt as if the image with the strongest hold on his mind was behind him instead of in front of him, and he had finally realized he was thinking of the face looking down from the third-floor window of the English building. He had seen that face in only a glance that day, just before his glasses had fallen to the ground, and possibly the memory had lasted merely because it was the final thing he had seen with absolute clarity. But he felt there was something more to it. The face had snared his attention the moment he saw it, even before his glasses fell; it had seemed to mean something. In retrospect it seemed to express more plainly than any view of the tower the fear that he himself had felt during that hour and a half of the shootings.

Someday he might try to create that face in a painting. But he wasn't up to the task now, as a struggling artist whose work didn't sell. He owed the memory more than that, and in some way he couldn't define he owed the face in the window more than that.

Leaving the rejected painting, he turned his attention to the reason he had come to his studio, taking from the closet the box in which Jack had shipped the portrait of Shelly. He pried it open and removed the portrait wrapped in butcher paper, and then peeled off the paper and set the painting upright on an easel.

For a long time he looked at it, battling with his memories and studying the paint to see if he could possibly apply clothing the way Shelly had wanted when she first saw the painting.

After a while, he started mixing pigments. The original paint had set and hardened over the years, so he placed the painting on the table and rubbed it gently with a damp cheesecloth to soften the surface. Then over her naked breasts he began to paint from memory the smocked blouse Shelly had worn that day at the beach.

The portrait resisted being painted over. The paint was almost too thick as it was—he had failed to make the layers as delicate as he should have. The new paint slipped and beaded. It had a different sheen. He had to layer it thickly, coat over coat of ultramarine.

He worked like this, at intervals, for several days, covering over the body he loved, clothing Shelly in blue.

When he was finished, he called Jack from his college office to ask for Shelly's address. "I have something I want to send her."

"Why would you be sending her something?"

"It's the portrait. I can't keep it any longer."

"You can't send her the portrait!"

"Well unless you want to store it—"

"I don't want to store it. She's happy, Wyatt. Leave her alone."

"You're so goddamn self-righteous, Jack. Can I please just have the address?"

Finally Jack gave it to him. "I hope you're not trying to start any-thing."

"Give me some credit, will you?"

"I told you I'm not going to be the bearer of information."

"You're not going to be the bearer of anything. But just tell me—how is she?"

"She's fine."

"Fine? Goddamn it, how is she?"

"She's dating someone."

He should have known this news would be coming sooner or later. But it settled hard.

"Just dating? Or . . ."

"She's involved with him."

"Who is he?"

"A geologist. He went to UT, but I doubt you know him. I haven't met him. She's told us about him. Apparently he's a nice guy."

Wyatt left the office and walked. It was a warm day; he walked the roads of Sandy Neck Barrier Beach along the Great Marsh where the seabirds soared over the water, and he walked past the old Congregational meetinghouse in the village, past the train station in Shark City, and through Finn Town. For hours, he walked.

# 21

# AN UNLIKELY GIFT

The box was waiting on Shelly's doorstep when she got home from work. She took it inside, and when she unwrapped the painting and saw that Wyatt had painted over her naked breasts, she felt flustered and overwhelmed, recalling those moments in the studio and how desperately she had wanted him while he was painting her.

He had tucked a letter into the frame.

Shelly,

I'm sure this is the last thing you were expecting to see again, and I hope you don't mind my sending it. If there were any way for me to keep it, I would. The changes don't improve it, but I thought they might make it more likely that you could find a home for it somewhere. If you can't, please don't let it become a burden. Do what you need to.

I'm sure you know from Jack and Delia that it's been a while since I've seen Carlotta. She is beautiful and it makes me happy to think of you two together. She'll grow into an even better person because of having time with you, and having your influence in her life. I wish I could be in Austin and with her more myself, but it's better this way for everyone.

I heard from Jack that you're dating someone and that he's a nice guy. Honestly, Shelly, you deserve that more than anyone. I won't say anything else about this or I might say too much, but I hope you know my feelings haven't changed, and that I want you to be happy, and that I understand your happiness has to involve someone besides me.

As for things here, Elaine and Nate and I are all right. It was probably a good move for us to come here.

You take good care of yourself.

Love, Wyatt

Holding the letter against her, she cried at how final it sounded—less like a letter saying goodbye and more like a note from someone who had left a long time ago. She knew he only meant to let her know that it was all right for her to get on with her life, but she wasn't sure she wanted Wyatt's blessings about that.

The painting, through her tears, was not as pretty as she'd remembered. Covering up the scars had diminished it somehow. And she didn't like the girl there in a studio looking into the eyes of someone else's husband. She regretted many things about the portrait perched on the chair in front of her in her little duplex apartment—how it came to be, who she was at the time—regretted everything except having Carlotta. She wished Wyatt hadn't sent it. But here it was, and what could she do?

She wrapped it back up and carried it out to her car, then drove to Beeville, pulling into Aileen's driveway after midnight.

"Oh dear, what's wrong!" Aileen exclaimed when she answered her knock. "Come in. What have you got there?"

Shelly carried the painting inside and propped it on the kitchen table. Aileen marveled at it. "If I didn't know any better, I would think that was the real you up on that table."

"It used to be a lot prettier," Shelly said regretfully, pointing out the brushstrokes where the new paint intruded over the old. "Anyway, I brought it because I was wondering if maybe you could keep it for me."

They put the painting away in the closet of Raymond's bedroom, pushing it back behind the clothes he had left when he went to Vietnam.

Aileen gave Shelly a Tab, and they sat in the kitchen and talked about Carlotta and how Shelly adored her, and about Raymond. "I think he's still alive," Aileen said. "I have a hope that he might be. I get that sense, every day." But she sounded as if she was saying this more from habit than hope.

Shelly told Aileen she wished she could talk to her mother like she could talk to her. She couldn't forget how her mother had sent her away when she was expecting. "She was so concerned about Daddy's job and what everybody would think. I haven't told her I'm seeing Carlotta, because she would disapprove. But I miss talking to her like I used to. I feel like having Carlotta made her love me less. And maybe the way she acted made me love her less, too."

"Your mom's all right," Aileen said. "Just not the strongest. Ever since she was little, everybody could push her around. She was cute, though, I'll give you that. Little redheaded thing."

They talked about Dan, too. "I want to tell him about Carlotta, but I don't know if I should. Not unless I'm sure we're going to get married. And I keep thinking how it could change things if I marry him. What if he got a different job, somewhere besides Austin, and we ended up moving? I wouldn't be able to see Carlotta."

Aileen shook her head. "That's too much thinking. You tell him about that little girl, and you marry him if you love him. What else are you going to do? Live your whole life with nobody? Carlotta is going to grow up and have her own life and her own babies. You can't follow her everywhere she goes her whole life. Let's pray about it."

She took Shelly's hand on the table. "Lord, give Shelly some wisdom. Let her do what's right." They prayed for Aileen's son. "Let him come back," Aileen said. "Let him walk through that door."

Shelly slept for a few hours in her old bedroom. Red had since died, and the room was lonely. Even Raymond and Wyatt, who used to haunt Shelly in this room, didn't seem to be here anymore.

She left before daylight to get back to Austin in time for her morning class, driving through the moonless predawn on the flat south Texas roads, through miles of cornfields and small towns.

# 22

# DUE WEST

Delia came to the pharmacy a few days later to talk to Shelly. "There's something I've been dreading to tell you," she said as they sat at a corner table. "Jack has been offered a job, so we might be moving."

"Where?" Shelly asked when she found her voice.

"Alpine, out near Big Bend. There's a college there—Sul Ross— that's been looking for someone to teach American history. We drove out last Friday for the interview, and it went pretty well. They liked Jack. We looked around and saw an old farmhouse we could buy with the money Jack's grandmother left him. It could be a great place for Carlotta to grow up. But if we moved, we would want you to come visit—the same as you do here, only you could stay longer. Oh, Shelly, I can see how you're taking this."

"How sure is it, that you're going?"

"Pretty sure, honestly."

"When would it be?"

"Soon. This summer. Before the fall semester."

"How far is it? How many hours?"

"We drove it in seven."

"Seven? That's so far!"

"You could come for whole weekends. If we bought the farmhouse, it's a big house and you would have your own room."

She could follow Carlotta to Alpine if she wanted to, and graduate from Sul Ross instead of UT, and get a job in the area. But even as the idea occurred to her, she knew it was pathetic and absurd. The only option that made any sense was to stay in Austin and go to Alpine to visit sometimes. But how often could she really do that?

"And Jack wouldn't mind if I come visit?"

Delia hesitated. "Honestly, he thinks it would be complicated because Wyatt and Elaine would be coming sometimes, too. Not at the same time, of course. But he thinks we could work it out. He knows how much Carlotta loves you."

They tried to talk over the options and logistical problems, but Shelly was too stunned and sick at heart to think clearly.

She finished her shift after Delia left, and skipped her afternoon class, unhinged by the vision of what it would be like to stay behind in Austin if Carlotta was no longer here.

She had promised to meet Dan at El Matamoros for tacos that night and to stay at his apartment as she often did, but now she regretted the plan. She didn't want to carry the deceit any further, and yet this wasn't the time to tell him about Carlotta. It would be a hard truth for him to hear at any time—that she had a child she had kept secret from him, and that the father was a married man whom she had loved so much that she would have married him if she could. She wanted to tell him thoughtfully, keeping only his feelings in mind, not as an outpouring of her own grief and confusion over Carlotta's leaving Austin. She called to cancel their date, but couldn't reach him.

When she met him at the restaurant, she tried to act as if nothing unusual was on her mind. From dinner, they went to a beer joint called Threadgill's to listen to Dan's friend play guitar. The music was soulful, and when Dan remarked on how quiet Shelly was, she said, "The songs are awfully sad."

They stayed at his apartment for the night, and after they had made love on the sofa, Dan became quiet, his arm looped over her naked body, and asked again if there was something on her mind. She almost told him, but the couple next door had started to argue, their voices penetrating the wall, and she let the chance go by.

"There's something," he said the next morning, holding her gaze. "There is. There's something." From the TV in the living room the Monkees were singing their theme song. He turned his back on Shelly and pulled his jogging pants and a T-shirt out of a drawer and put them on. He shoved his feet into running shoes, yanking the laces. "Is it someone else?" he asked bluntly, angrily, glancing up at her as he tied the laces.

"No." She shook her head. "It's nothing like that."

"When you're ready to talk about it, let me know."

He walked out of the room, and she heard him go outside. She knocked her head back slowly against the bedroom wall. It was ridiculous behavior, but she continued to do it, her eyes shut tightly.

Then she left the apartment and started walking through the neighborhood in search of Dan. It was nearly summertime, and hot. She was twenty-five years old and afraid of losing him and afraid of losing Carlotta. Her life was about to change, and she was afraid to think about it. She listened to the mourning doves making their throaty sounds in the trees, and then saw Dan running toward her around a shady corner. He slowed when he saw her. A thought of Carlotta, as transitory as the sun's glare on the parked cars or the small, perceptible shift of leaves in the heavy stagnant air, came to her, and she feared she would later wish she had set this moment into reverse.

He was breathing hard when he reached her.

She would remember the questioning look, the squint, the way he jogged in place before he stopped. "I love you," she said, and almost left it at that. "And I have a daughter. I had an affair with a married man named Wyatt Calvert, and got pregnant, and his cousin adopted the baby. His cousin's name is Jack Stone; he and his wife Delia are raising the baby. Her name is Carlotta. She's two and a half years old. I see her once or twice a week. Wyatt doesn't live in Austin anymore. He moved away."

Sweat dripped from Dan's face. He stared at her.

"I wasn't planning to tell anyone—ever. That was before I met you."

When Dan spoke, his voice was softer than the bloated sounds of the doves, and his expression kept the same perplexed scrutiny.

"Are you still in love with him?"

"No."

"He's still married?"

"Yes."

"Have you seen him since the baby was born?"

"No."

"Was he a student at UT? How do you know him?"

"He and his cousin Jack carried me off the plaza when I was shot."

Dan looked away from her, and wiped the sweat from his face with his palm. "Does he come here? To see the baby?"

"He's been here, yes. When I was living in San Marcos. I didn't see him. He lives in Massachusetts with his wife and son."

He shook his head, as if trying to shake off what she was saying.

"He's not in my life anymore."

"Okay. Well." But he didn't move. "You couldn't have told me sooner?"

"It didn't seem right."

He looked at her. "Are you all right?"

"You mean from telling you this?"

"I mean from when it happened. Are you all right?"

"If you are."

When they got to the apartment they closed themselves in the bedroom. Dan didn't ask about the affair, which he didn't want to talk about. He asked how Jack and Delia had adopted the baby and why Shelly had kept so many secrets from him. Shelly herself couldn't believe how many secrets there were until one by one she handed them over: the pregnancy, the adoption, her reunion with Carlotta, and now her fear of losing her once again. Her eyes burned with tears. Dan was dazed and asked if Wyatt was the reason she had kept these secrets. "Were you hoping he would come back?" In a moment of bitterness he asked if he was the consolation prize for losing Wyatt. His jealousy was raw and obvious.

It was the oddest thing, but facing Dan's pain and standing exhausted in front of him, the story spread out between them, her face streaked with tears, she felt a sense of peace and salvation that was deeper than any she'd felt in all those six years since Wyatt Calvert had first lifted her into his arms.

# 23

# LIZARD MOUNTAIN

The same feeling of pending loss hung over those summer months as Shelly had battled when she was pregnant and knew she would be giving the baby up to Jack and Delia. The difference now was having Dan to turn to.

He wanted to wait and meet Jack and Delia at a later time, when they were settled in Alpine, but he and Shelly both felt he should meet Carlotta before the move.

They met, for the first time, at Pease Park. Shelly was pushing her on the swings. Carlotta was two and a half years old, pumping her legs to make the swing go higher and squealing at the air in her face. Pulling her to a stop, Shelly said, "Carlotta, this is my friend Dan Hadley."

Carlotta glanced at him, her legs still out in front of her as if for momentum, and told him joyfully, "Push me higher!" And he did. The three of them walked along Shoal Creek, looking for tiny marine fossils.

Throughout the summer, Dan listened to Shelly debate with herself about how often she should visit Alpine after Jack and Delia moved. "It presents such a huge problem about what's right for everyone. What's best for Wyatt's family is if I don't go at all. And I think Jack probably wonders if that wouldn't be best for Carlotta, too. She's young enough that she would forget me. But it doesn't seem right to drop out of her life like that. If I didn't think I should be in her life, I never would have started seeing her in the first place."

Finally she proposed a plan to Delia. "What if I come once a year, and stay for a week or so? Maybe in the summers. It might be simpler for everyone than if I'm constantly popping in and out."

"But wouldn't it be hard for you—not to see her more than that?"

"I don't think I can justify seeing her if I'm being selfish about it."

She said goodbye to Carlotta the afternoon of the move. Jack had borrowed a pickup and had already hauled two loads to Alpine, and now the truck was packed with most of what was left and parked at the base of the shabby steps that led to the emptied garage apartment. Shelly sat with Carlotta in the truck's cab, watching her pretend to drive. Carlotta had on a pair of Delia's sunglasses with large frames, like the ones Jackie Onassis wore.

"I won't be going with you, you know," Shelly told her, keeping her tone light. "But I'll come see you, and you can show me your new house and the beautiful mountains."

Carlotta turned the radio dial and bounced on the seat to music she pretended to hear. She shook her curls and didn't pay much attention to what Shelly was saying.

The forced casualness of the parting was difficult for Shelly. She said goodbye to Jack and Delia while they all stood in the bare living room, Delia holding a rag, Jack sweaty and dirty from carrying boxes.

She didn't break down until she got home to her duplex and found that Dan was waiting there, having left work early to be with her and try to cheer her up.

The days passed slowly after that, but then the weeks and months sped up. Shelly talked on the phone long-distance with Delia and Carlotta sometimes, and Delia sent her a Polaroid of Carlotta sitting in a porch swing at the farmhouse.

Shelly could pick up her old plans to apply for the Peace Corps if she wanted to now. The dream had been delayed by the shooting and stalled by the love affair with Wyatt, and then halted by the pregnancy. She had managed to resurrect it briefly at Aquarena, and then had abandoned it when Carlotta had come back into her life. Now she was close to finishing school—she could go anywhere she wanted. She could apply to the Peace Corps. Dan said he would wait for her. But she was already too far away from Carlotta, and she didn't want to leave Dan.

Just before Christmas she married Dan in a ceremony in an old Victorian house that had been converted into a restaurant called Green Pastures. It was the end of 1972. Their friends and coworkers came to the wedding, and Dan's parents and several members of his family drove from Montana. Shelly had not met them before. They were pleasant and unassuming and seemed happy about the marriage. Dan and his brother shared the same quiet, understated sense of humor.

Shelly's parents came too, driving in from Lockhart with some of their friends. Aileen came from Beeville, more dressed up than Shelly had ever seen her. Nancy, from Nau's Pharmacy, sat up front with the family, and afterward told everyone how she had first talked Shelly into going out with Dan. "She wasn't going to do it. She didn't want to go on a date with anybody. I had to push her. I had to brag on him."

With Dan's savings they made a down payment on a small frame house in Austin's Hyde Park neighborhood, not far from the university, and in the spring Shelly graduated with a degree in English and a minor in Spanish. She found a job in the front office of the Helping Hand Home for Children—a small facility occupying a block in her own neighborhood. She didn't work with the children, who were mostly from abusive or neglectful situations and in the care of therapists, but many of them hung around her desk during the day and talked with her when they were waiting for the bus to take them to school or on outings. She grew to love them.

In blistering summer, she took a week off, and she and Dan drove west through the scruffy hill country of central Texas, the sun in their eyes and the windows down. They stopped at a filling station in Johnson City, ate burgers at a diner in Junction. Farther west, Shelly saw mountains for the first time in her life, and her heart began to pound because she was getting closer to Carlotta. She could tell that Dan was nervous about meeting Jack and Delia, so she tried to put him at ease by asking about the land formations they were passing. He said something about Precambrian times and the Permian Sea, but his manner was rote and uneasy. Even his knowledge of the land couldn't make him feel at home where he was going.

"I think I'm being selfish to want you to come with me," Shelly said at last.

"It's not that. There's something I have to tell you."

She looked at him from the side, waiting for him to say what was on his mind. He seemed unnaturally still, one hand tight on the wheel.

"I've been needing to tell you this since the day I met you," he finally said, with only a glance in her direction. "I was there that day. In the English building. I saw you."

It took a moment for her to realize what day he was talking about.

"And I didn't go out to help you. I didn't know you, but that isn't the point. The point is, I was a bystander. I watched. I can't explain it. There's no excuse. I was afraid of being shot."

She was too stunned to speak at first. The memory of a face she had seen in the third-floor window of the English building that day came to her. The face had seemed to be looking at her, and she had felt strangely as if she could see herself through those distant eyes. Could it have been Dan's face? Perhaps not. It could have been anyone's. "Anybody would be afraid of being shot," she said.

"No, not anybody. Not Jack. Not Wyatt." She could see how he struggled.

"Pull over," she said. "Let's talk."

But he didn't pull over. Nor did he turn to look at her.

"You've never told anyone you were there?" she asked him.

"Is there a reason I would want to?"

"Well it doesn't make any difference in how I see you."

"So you say."

"Give me some credit," she said. "Look, there are people who would run into a burning building to save someone, but wouldn't risk being shot at, and people who would get shot at but wouldn't go into a burning building. It depends on a thousand things how people react— maybe just whether or not they've had coffee that morning, or a good night's sleep."

"I guess it's lucky Jack and Wyatt had their coffee."

"Stop it. I love you. It's ridiculous for you to beat yourself up about something that happened ages ago."

He had both hands on the steering wheel now, and still hadn't turned to look at her. "It was the most shameful thing I ever did. To stand there in that window and watch other people risk their lives to help."

"But you've proven yourself in a thousand ways. You don't have to feel ashamed of one moment for the rest of your life."

He glanced in her direction. "I can't feel entirely otherwise."

It occurred to her that Carlotta would not have been born if it had been Dan, instead of Wyatt, who had come to help her. "I don't think less of you, and I don't have any regrets about how it happened."

"Because it allowed you to meet Wyatt."

"What—you think I love him more? Because he came out on the plaza? You think I'm only capable of loving one person my whole life? I don't care that you didn't go out on the plaza. It makes no difference to me one way or the other. I do care that you have this undeserved feeling of shame about it. How many people do you think were on campus, and how many of those do you think ran out there while he was shooting? Not many. Who knows why Wyatt and Jack did? Not because they're braver. I know both of them very well, and I know you, and they're not braver. Maybe they just acted together because they knew each other, or maybe Jack went out there because he'd been in Vietnam and he was used to gunfire, and Wyatt followed him—I don't know. I *do* know that neither of those guys are any better than you." She turned the vent onto her face for cold air. "You're not a coward, and I'm not going to feel sorry for you as if you were."

They drove in silence for a while, and eventually Dan seemed to relax a little. When he spoke, he sounded amused. "That wasn't exactly the response I expected."

"Well, it's hot in this car," she said.

"I do feel like I won the princess without slaying the dragon."

"Hardly a princess."

When they arrived in Alpine, Shelly squinted in the dimming light at directions she had taken down from Delia over the phone. Across from a Coca-Cola bottling plant and an old roadside map and curiosity store called Apache Trading Post, they turned onto a narrow road bordered by goat and horse paddocks, tin sheds and fenced yards. Pickups and trailers sat parked in the yards. As they turned onto a dirt road, their headlights scanned a shaggy overgrowth of lantana bushes and a spindly tree with dangling seedpods.

Ahead was an old two-story farmhouse with dormer windows and a wraparound porch. The lights inside were shining. A small mountain rose from the darkness behind the house. Dan pulled into the gravel drive and shut the motor off, and Shelly studied the large house in the fading light and noticed movement and the jostle of chains supporting a wooden swing on the lighted porch. A child peered out from the railing spindles, the light glinting on her red hair.

"There she is," Shelly whispered. It was almost a year since she had seen her.

Dan reached over and squeezed her hand, and then Shelly got out of the car and waved at Carlotta. "Hi, sweetie," she called softly.

Carlotta didn't move from the porch at first, but when Jack and Delia came out she ran down the steps toward Shelly, looking back to see that they were coming too. She was three and a half years old now, barefoot, in a faded dress, her tangled curls flopping around her shoulders as she ran. Shelly leaned and scooped her into her arms, folding the warm little body against her.

"Leave the bags for later," Jack said as Dan opened the trunk. "We'll take care of all that later. Delia's made plenty of food, if you haven't eaten. Come on in."

They all traipsed up the porch steps and into the house, talking about the drive and the need for rain, Carlotta silent and casting furtive looks at Shelly. Shelly's first impression of the house inside was the chandelier in the front hallway speckling the walls with light and shining down on the massive newel post at the base of the stairs.

Delia led the way upstairs and into a corner bedroom lit by a table lamp with a tufted shade. The window shutters were open, the glass reflecting the lamplight, and Shelly stood close to the window and cupped her hands to see out past the reflections.

"Now that I see you, I think we've met before," Jack told Dan. "We were on a committee to recount votes for a student government election."

"Oh, that's right," Dan said. "When was that—in sixty-four?"

Gazing out over the carport at the sheen of a tin barn in the dwindling light, Shelly was awestruck. "This is beautiful, Delia." She crossed the room to a window on the adjacent wall. Two fat limbs of a cottonwood with craggy bark and large triangular leaves nestled close to the glass, framing a view of the small mountain rising out of the flat terrain. Carlotta came to the window and stood next to Shelly, cupping her hands in the same way to fend off the interior light.

"Lizard Mountain," Carlotta said in a droll tone, keeping her nose to the glass, "looks like a lizard."

"Yes, it does," Shelly agreed.

"He has eyes," Carlotta said. "He has a tail."

At dinner, Carlotta sat beside Shelly and talked about her horse named Freckles while Jack and Delia talked with Dan. Afterward they sat out on the porch until late, Jack smoking his Camels, their conversation punctuated by the creak of chains supporting the swing and the high-pitched chirrups of crickets out in the darkness beyond the glow of the porch light. When the others had gone inside, Shelly stayed out, talking with Jack.

"I like Dan," he told her. "He's seems solid."

"Very solid."

"And you look happy."

"I am. I hope you know how much I appreciate your letting us come here. I know it would have been easier for you not to."

"True." He drew hard on his cigarette and exhaled slowly. "But we would have missed you."

The house was quiet when Shelly went inside. Dan was already sleeping, and Shelly returned to the window of their bedroom, sliding it open to feel the breeze and hear the rustling leaves and the pulsing sound of insects. The mountain sat hunched against the horizon, a dull black under the shimmering stars, the moon three-quarters full and lighting the mountain dimly.

The longer Shelly looked at the mountain, the more she wished it wasn't there. It appeared hostile in this light—a dinosaur-lizard observing her with a small, immobile eye. The eye was formed by an odd stacking of rocks or a growth of trees or maybe a cluster of shadows from the tepid moonlight. Its stillness seemed aggressive. After a while she realized that the mute and staring aspect reminded her of the tower.

She closed the window and latched the shutters. Crawling into bed with Dan, she took his hand and slid it up under her nightgown and settled it onto her stomach, then lay there eyeing the room in the pallid light through the shutters. The dresser had a marble top and wooden drawer pulls carved to look like walnuts. A small rug covered a patch of floor. Mulling over her earlier conversation with Dan in the car, she thought how hard it must have been for him to keep to himself the shame he had felt all those years.

She wanted him to wake. She wondered if Wyatt had been here to this house, and if he and Elaine had perhaps stayed in this same room. The idea troubled her, and to dispel it she rose on her elbow and kissed Dan's forehead, and then his mouth, and laid her head on his shoulder. Finally she moved his finger in a circle around her naval, and he woke up drowsily and made love with her.

When she woke in the morning, Dan had gone downstairs, and she opened the shutters and studied the mountain, plainly visible now in the morning sun: a jumble of sharp rocks darker and rougher than the flat land around it. Off in the distance were larger, imposing mountains, but they were pale against the sky.

Dan returned to the room while Shelly was getting dressed. "You want to go with me on an interesting outing?" he asked her. "Jack called the people who own Lizard Mountain, and they said we're welcome to hike over there. It's a volcanic dike that was probably active thirty million years ago. It used to have water, and still has depressions with plants and wildlife. Like its own relic ecosystem. Can I talk you into coming?"

They talked it over, but she decided to stay with Carlotta. She watched him from the window as he hiked out through the yellow grasses with his backpack. He turned and waved at her, calling, "Are you sure?" And she waved at him to go on.

She went to the grocery store with Delia and Carlotta and hung around the barn as Carlotta fed the horse oats out of a bucket and braided his mane. In the afternoon she ambled through the house, looking at knickknacks and photographs and all the different views from the windows. The parlor had a library alcove paneled in dark wood, and there on a shelf she discovered a framed photograph of Wyatt with Elaine and Nate. The three of them, wearing coats, were standing before a storefront window that reflected a narrow cobbled street. It was obvious in a glance that Elaine was pregnant.

Shelly stood staring at the picture. She tried to tell herself she didn't mind about the pregnancy and shouldn't feel hurt that she had not been told. Wyatt's marriage had nothing to do with her. And yet of course it did. The baby Elaine carried in the picture would be Carlotta's half brother or sister.

She picked the photograph up and studied it closely. Wyatt looked no different from when she had last seen him four years ago. He wore the same navy pea jacket he had always worn, and his hair fell at the same length over his ears. His sideburns were a little shorter than before. Nate stood exactly in front of him, his head cocked to the side and a sweet smile on his face, Wyatt's hands resting on his shoulders. Shelly examined Nate's features to see if they resembled Carlotta's, but she couldn't tell if they did. Elaine, standing very close to Wyatt, wore a long black coat and boots and a gray cloche hat that came down low on her forehead, covering her eyebrows. Her hair flowed out from under the hat, the ends fluttering around the bulge of her belly. She was as lovely as Shelly remembered.

A small noise made Shelly turn, and she found Delia looking at her.

"When was it taken?" Shelly asked.

"Last winter. The baby's a month old now."

"A boy or a girl?"

"A girl. Her name is Margaret and they call her Maggie. I'm sorry, Shelly—I wanted the chance to tell you before you saw the picture. I should have told you last night."

"Maggie Calvert," Shelly said. It was a good name. She put the picture back on the shelf. "It's all right. I'm married, you know? I'm happy. I'm not still in love with Wyatt. Can I ask you something, though? Have they been here to visit?"

"Yes, when we first moved in."

She wished the answer had been no. "I guess Carlotta enjoyed having Nate here."

"Yes, she did. Of course he's two and half years older than she is, but they had a good time together."

Late in the afternoon, Dan returned and stood in the kitchen with Delia and Shelly, guzzling lemonade and talking about the hike. "It was like a safari," he said. "At one point I was looking at a fox, a hawk, and a coyote all in the same view. I almost stepped on a rattlesnake. It's its own biological island over there. I'd love to know if anyone's taken cores from the pond deposits or if they've dug test holes."

Toward evening the heat began to lift. Jack returned from the campus, and Dan and Shelly followed Carlotta around the property on a rock hunt. "I understand that you like to collect things," Dan told Carlotta. They filled their pockets with pebbles and stones and lined them up on shelves in a cabin down the road that Carlotta used for a playhouse. Dan told Carlotta the scientific names for the rocks, and she repeated and memorized them and made up common names of her choosing: Esmeralda and Sammy and Juan.

Later, Dan came into the bedroom and stood quietly looking at Shelly as she knelt before her suitcase, searching for a nightgown. "That picture on the bookshelves downstairs," he said solemnly. "Is that Wyatt?"

She sat back on her heels. "Yes. With Elaine and Nate."

"And you're not in love with him anymore?"

"Not in the least. I'm in love with you."

"You're sure?"

"I'm sure." Looking at him, she was sure.

He sighed, and half-smiled. "Just checking."

## 24

# MADELINE

Two years later, at Brackenridge Hospital in Austin, Shelly had a little girl whom she and Dan named Madeline.

The baby was tiny, and tenacious. She clung tightly to Shelly's fingers. She didn't look like Carlotta, who'd had pink skin and wispy cowlicks of red hair at birth. Instead she was pale, with straight black hair. Her lashes were long and her eyes dark and enormous.

Shelly's mother came, and seeing her by the hospital bed reminded Shelly of the days after the shooting and the night when she woke from her terrible visions and fled to Jack's room, and found Wyatt there.

Shelly was peaceful now, nursing the baby, though the ruined breast strained at the scars, tingling as if to produce milk though it could not. Madeline drew her head back, kicking with fury, and pushed her tiny nose up to the other breast, latching greedily onto it and settling happily into rhythmic suckling.

"I'm sorry, honey," Shelly's mother whispered.

Shelly stroked the baby's soft face. "There's plenty of milk. She's doing fine."

"Not about that. I'm sorry for what I did. The last time." Tears began to flow down her mother's freckled face and into the lines around her mouth, and Shelly remembered how her mother had not wanted her in their home at the loneliest time of her life, and how she had brought the red coat to the hospital as if a new coat could replace a baby, and how she had sat in the front seat of the station wagon without turning to look at her daughter whose heart was broken.

"Can you ever forgive me?"

"I'm not mad at you anymore, if that's what you mean."

"It isn't, exactly."

Shelly stroked the baby and kept her voice down so as not to disturb her. "I understand why you didn't want me in Lockhart—I understand about Daddy's reelection and everything."

"I didn't blame you for the fact that your father lost."

"No, but you let me blame myself. Mom? Why couldn't you have been with me?" She looked at her mother. "I needed you. I really, really needed you."

Her mother was crying harder now.

"You weren't even there when the baby was born. You came the day I gave her up. You showed up after it was over."

"I want to think I would do it differently now if I had the chance," her mother said. "I wish I could go back. I hope the baby is okay. Do you ever hear?"

"Mom?"

"Yes."

"I see her sometimes."

"You mean you dream about her?"

"I see her. I go and see her. They're living out near Big Bend, and Dan and I go and visit them."

"You visit Jack Stone and his wife?"

Her mother had stopped crying, a look of disbelief on her face.

"We're friends," Shelly said. "We're all friends."

"But when . . . How did that happen?"

Shelly told her how Jack and Delia had walked into the gift shop at Aquarena with the little girl.

"But how can it end well?" her mother asked. "I just worry about how you would feel if . . ."

"Why can't you just be glad for me?"

"What is she like? What does she look like?"

"Honestly, Mom, she has your red hair. And she's getting freckles."

Her mother stared at her, and then got up. She seemed not to know what to do or what to say, and finally, as if to do just anything, she lifted Shelly's breakfast tray of cold eggs and toast and carried it to a table beside the door. She moved a vase of flowers that was too close to the edge of the sill. Without turning, her hands still on the vase, she said, "Do you think I could ever see her?"

Shelly looked down at Madeline, who was falling asleep as she nursed. "Maybe someday. But I have a picture of her in my billfold. You can take it and show it to Dad if you'll bring it back tomorrow."

Tucked behind the driver's license was a photograph of Carlotta that Shelly pulled out and showed to her mother. Carlotta was perched on the barn fence, wearing a straw hat, leaning toward the camera. She was five years old.

———

In the years that followed, as Madeline grew up, Shelly and Dan took her to Alpine every summer, where she tagged along with Carlotta, who taught her to mount the horse bareback by climbing on from the fence, and to dance the hokey pokey and make mud pies with water scooped from the trough.

Shelly continued to work at Helping Hand three days a week while Madeline went to day care. She liked the people she worked with and was attached to the children, and she missed those who found their way into foster care or back to their families.

Sometimes she took Madeline to see Aileen. One winter Saturday while Shelly was on her hands and knees replacing Aileen's bathroom floor with new squares of linoleum, Madeline wandered down the hall into a room she had never seen anyone else go into, and found herself alone. It was quiet in there, and though she was only four years old, she knew immediately that this was a serious place. The shades were drawn. There was a bed and a chair. A round mirror hung from a chain over a chest of drawers, too high for her to see into. She sat on the bed and swung her legs and stared at the closet doorknob. It was glass and looked like a bubble of light in the dim room. She heard her mother calling, and scrambled off the bed to hide in the closet, closing herself in.

The place was dark except for lines of light around the door. Madeline stood on her toes and felt the wall for a switch, but all she found were belts dangling from a nail. Clothes hung down around her. Everything in the closet felt cold and smelled cold. She felt something tickle her neck, and she let out a peep, but it was only a shirtsleeve. She sat down among the shoes. They were men's shoes—big and dusty-smelling. Scooting back, she felt as if the wall were falling down on top of her, and she yelped and threw her hand back to stop it. She turned to look, and saw a face behind her and was startled until she realized this was only a painting. She couldn't see well in the dark, but it was a lady's face. She moved over and sat beside it and leaned back against the wall, pulling her knees up to make herself small.

After a while, she heard her mother enter the room, and whispering to the painting "Shhhhh, that's my mommy. She's coming," pressed her finger against the painted lips. Side by side with the painting, she stared anxiously at the door. She could hear her mother out there.

"Madeline, honey?" her mother called.

"Make her go away," Madeline whispered to the painting. "Make her not find us." Miraculously, immediately, her mother left the room. "You did it," Madeline told the painting. "You did it!" She could hear her mother calling her from far away, and scrambled out of the closet to reappear in the kitchen.

"Sweetie, you scared me! Where were you?" But Madeline didn't tell her mother where she had been.

After that, Madeline went to the closet every time she visited Aileen's house. No one ever knew she was there. She talked to the lady in the painting about her wishes, and sometimes they came true. "You're a fairy godmother," she told her.

When she became tall enough to turn the light on from a string inside the closet and part the clothes and study the painting and realize, with a sinking heart, that this was not her fairy godmother but in fact only her real mother, much younger and different somehow, wearing a blue top and smiling at someone else, she stopped going to see the painting. She looked in on it sometimes, ruefully, suspiciously, feeling betrayed.

# 25

# THE MARFA LIGHTS

In Alpine in the summers, Madeline and Carlotta gathered rocks to add to Carlotta's collection. They slept in the same bed. Carlotta drove Madeline around the property in a golf cart, and they had pajama parties with Carlotta's friends. Carlotta talked a lot and told ghost stories and showed Madeline how to string beads for bracelets and necklaces.

At times, when Shelly was home in Austin, the feeling that something was missing came over her, and she found herself looking around for Carlotta and wondering what her life would have been with Wyatt, as if a ghost family tagged along with her own. She wondered if Carlotta would ever learn that she was her mother, and what would come of it if she did. If it were in the distant future, would it even make a difference in how anyone felt? They were all so settled in the way things were, and it was plain the affair was over.

But of course the old transgression remained—Carlotta was living proof of that. And just knowing about it could be destructive for so many people. Elaine and Wyatt went to Alpine as often as Shelly did. Their children played with Carlotta. How would Elaine feel toward Carlotta if she learned the truth? How would her children feel? Suppose that after everything, the affair still doomed the marriage. How would Carlotta feel to have come from a destructive love affair?

It was already unclear how she felt about being adopted. On one of the trips to Alpine, when Carlotta was eleven years old and Madeline was six, Jack and Shelly drove them over to Marfa to try to glimpse the mystery lights at the edge of town. They parked beside the road and everyone climbed out of the car and stared into the night, waiting for the legendary orbs of bouncing light to make a rare appearance.

Carlotta trekked off by herself, squatting down in the grass apart from the others: a beautiful child staring fixedly into the dark Chihuahuan Desert. While Madeline pointed out car lights and twinklings and distant glimmers that were only possibly there, Carlotta sat in the prickly grass and stared across Mitchell Flat toward the Chinati Mountains.

On the drive back home Jack teased her about how seriously she always took these outings to Marfa. She sat in the backseat, against the car door, her curls swirling about her face in the warm breeze from the open window, her eyes blinking in the dark, and she replied in a somber voice, "The reason I want to see them is to know they're out there. I can't know for sure, if I don't see them."

One night when the others had gone to bed, Shelly browsed the bookcase at the top of the stairs and noticed, in a stack of oversized art books on the bottom shelf, the title *Tempera in Modern America*. She knew from Jack and Delia, and from an article she had read about Wyatt in a UT magazine, that his paintings had begun to sell, so she pulled the book from the stack and scanned the index for his name. Several pages were listed. Sitting on the floor under the murky hallway light, she turned to those pages.

The first of the paintings took her breath. It dominated a full page and was different from anything she had ever known him to paint. It appeared to be painted partly in oil. The title was *1966*, the subject was the tower as seen from below on the South Mall plaza. It was not Wyatt's usual realistic rendering, but contorted and complicated, the tower tilted, the rows of windows lopsided, the sky an innocent crayon blue that a child might choose. Only the red tiles of the roof of the main building, interlocking like a woven basket, and the clock face and the speckling of the white stones looked realistic. They clashed with the strange asymmetry.

Shelly had the sensation of time flipping backward, as if the floorboards beneath her had turned to the pebbled cement of the plaza. For years she had tried to leave that place behind, but this painting made her feel that she had not gained any distance at all and was back in that terrible blazing-hot world with its sickening smell of blood.

Quickly, she turned the page. Some of Wyatt's other paintings were similar: perplexing images, tempera he had combined with pale washes of watercolor and textured features in oil. The more recent resembled those he had painted during the years she knew him—tempera only, authoritative and unerring. It seemed as if he had made a name for himself by depicting the world as a hodgepodge of distortions, and then had returned to factual landscapes. Tree trunks. The study of sunlight on veined leaves. She preferred these.

In the morning she wandered behind the house with Madeline and Carlotta to visit a small fishpond Jack had dug. The pond was an imperfect oval, half-shaded, littered somewhat by droppings from the branches overhead, the bottom covered with colorful rocks and pebbles and the surface lush with floating hyacinth and lilies. Jack had laid large stones around the edges, and Madeline lay belly-down on one of these, peering into the pond, her small chin on her palms, the tips of her dark hair dripping into the water.

Carlotta prowled the perimeter, kneeling periodically to skim debris from the surface with a fishnet and peer into the depths and speculate about whether or not raccoons had raided during the night. "They don't come every night," she said. "Sometimes bobcats come. I had one fish named Becky with black spots, and all we found was her head."

The fish were small and mottled. Carlotta identified the red-and-blue shubunkins, the orange comets and gold bitterlings. Her favorite was a small Sarasa missing part of its tail. "We had mosquito fish but they died." She talked with surprising authority for an eleven-year-old, naming the genus and species of fish and their characteristics with the same eager command of knowledge that she brought to her rock collection, as if she imagined the world in categories, the objects organized and specified and as perfectly delineated as the objects in Wyatt's paintings. In many ways she was like Wyatt, enchanted by the visual world. But something restless and driven in her reminded Shelly of herself before the shooting and before she fell in love with Wyatt. Shelly had discarded so many dreams of travel and adventure, and had never gone back for them, and now it was as if Carlotta trailed along behind her, picking them up. Each time Shelly saw Carlotta, the child was more like her.

"I would like to be a fish, but not in a pond," Carlotta said. "In the ocean, where there's coral." She went on for a while about coral, and about how whales were not fish. Madeline protested about the whales, but Carlotta explained how the blowholes were like nostrils and some whales had two and some had one.

The day was warm; sunlight glinted in the ripples stirred up by Carlotta dragging the net through the water. A train not far away blew its horn. The fish propelling themselves in figure eights in and out of the lilies and underwater shadows reminded Shelly of Aquarena and the submarine theater and how Carlotta had stood at the expanse of glass, transfixed by the graceful ballet of the Aquamaids, pleading to go back down, down, as the theater rose to the surface.

In the warmth and peace of the morning, Shelly had grown sleepy standing over the pond and responding to the sweet chatter of the two girls. She was jostled alert when Carlotta said, "It's possible my other parents might live by the ocean."

Madeline's face, with its large eyes, came up from its little perch on her palms. "You have other parents?"

"I have four parents because I'm adopted," Carlotta told her, leaning out over the water to skim leaves from her reflection. "I have my real parents and my imaginary parents. I imagine all kinds of things about those. The mother who had me wasn't married so she gave me to my parents so they could raise me."

"Where is she now?" Madeline was incredulous.

"I think she might be in Beeville. That's where I was born."

Madeline pulled her legs up and sat cross-legged. "My mommy's great-aunt Aileen lives in Beeville," she said. "We go see her sometimes."

"You've been to Beeville?"

"Mommy takes me."

Carlotta turned to Shelly. "Would you take me too?"

Trying hurriedly to cobble the options together—all the things she might say—Shelly answered, "Your mother and dad should be the ones to take you, if you go there sometime."

"Maybe I would see my imaginary mother," Carlotta said. "She might be walking along the street and would look just like me, and I would know who she was. Or maybe I would see her, but wouldn't know who she was." She stared into the water. "Do you see that fish under the lily pad?" she asked Madeline. "His name's Robert. Watch how he moves his fins. It's very graceful. I'm going to learn to scuba dive when I grow up. There's no place around here to swim. Cow ponds, that's all, and you wouldn't get in those, you'd get tetanus or something. One time there was ice on the top of the fish pond, and we could see the fish through it. My dad's cousin Wyatt took pictures so he could paint what it looked like. He's a famous painter. His wife is very good at horseshoes. They have a son named Nate who's older than me, and his little sister is afraid of bugs. They live on a beach and can swim every day if they want to. You should meet Wyatt someday because he helped save your mother when she got shot in the arm." Carlotta lifted the net and held it, dripping, above the water. Her eyes, for an instant, looked like Wyatt's. "Isn't that right, Shelly?"

The fish meandered torpidly in the mossy pond. The train was blowing its whistle from farther away now. Shelly nodded. "That's right."

"He's tall," Carlotta told Madeline. "Sometimes I wish I lived near a beach. Alpine used to be underwater. Your dad told me that. That's one of the special things about fossils—sometimes they used to be seashells."

# 26

# THE SECRET SIDE OF THE MOON

On a field trip to Big Bend in the seventh grade, Carlotta discovered a perfect fossilized oyster, still in its shell, embedded in the high wall of a narrow canyon. She had ridden two hours on the school bus with two dozen other thirteen-year-olds and a teacher, and was hiking through the canyon with the disorderly crowd when she found it. It was a cold day, and the noon sun shone directly down onto the canyon floor, lighting the dry streambed in which the students were walking, and creating shadows in the cracks and crevices of the walls.

The hike had become something of a slog for most of the students, with many stops and starts for the teacher to lecture. Several lagged behind, and some ran ahead, causing the teacher—a young man who was new to the school—to constantly count heads and call to those who were missing, admonishing them, "Stay with your buddy!"

During one of these pauses, while the teacher counted the students, Carlotta turned and studied the layered rock of the wall behind her and saw the edge of the oyster shell, ghostly amid remnants of other sea life—clams, sea urchins, snails, and corals all turned to stone and having the bleached look of dead things. What caught Carlotta's eye was that the oyster shell appeared to be entirely whole, the halves clasped together. She pictured the canyon at the bottom of a deep sea, filled with plants and schools of fish and thousands of little creatures like this one burrowed into the shelf of rock. Turning to see that no one was looking, she pried it from the crumbling limestone and tucked it into her coat pocket. When the group began walking again she drifted to the back and pulled the fossil out of her pocket to get a better look, and the two halves fell miraculously open, parting to reveal the smooth stone mollusk that for thousands of years had been safely encased in its home.

She stopped walking, amazed, feeling the oyster with her thumb. It was shaped like a tongue and adhered to the bottom half of the shell. The top half she lifted and replaced—a perfect fit. How astonishing it was! And how fortunate that she had found it. What could it mean?

On the bus ride back to school she played games with her friends, and sang songs and laughed happily, but all the while she fantasized how one day she would give this beautiful little frozen oyster as a gift to the mother who had given birth to her. For thousands of years this perfect thing had been waiting, a symbol of how things fit together and belonged one half to the other, so that even when they were pulled apart they still could be placed together again, and the curves and edges would simply settle against each other. She imagined she would walk along a beach somewhere with her mother, and pull the oyster from a little silk bag and present it to her. Or they would be sitting under an open sky, or maybe by a campfire, and she would pull it out of her pocket and show her mother how remarkable it was, and how the halves fit and the creature inside was still whole.

Over the years, Carlotta's fantasies about this scene would change, even while the fossil remained exactly the same, every ridge and curve familiar to her and always a source of hope and endurance, which for her were the same thing, because she anticipated with a kind of buried excitement the day when she might meet her biological parents.

Sometimes she would pretend those parents were watching her. They could be anywhere, such as the grocery store, or in another country. Or they could still be in Beeville. She liked to wonder, and she believed someday she would find out, but she didn't feel in a hurry, because learning the truth would cost her the possibilities. Thinking about her biological mother was like thinking about the far side of the moon. She could imagine the far side had running water and exotic landscapes, but in reality she knew that if it swung around, and the sun shone on it, then likely it would only resemble the near side. And the moon would offer nothing to dream about anymore.

When she turned sixteen and had a boyfriend, and was at odds with her parents and no longer believed in the teachings of the Catholic Church, the mystery of her biological mother taunted her, and there were times she almost told her parents she wanted to go and find her.

She distanced herself from Delia, who was different from her in countless ways, and then felt lonely and unhinged for having done so. Sometimes it felt as if being adopted was like being spun around and blindfolded and turned loose in the world. Just twenty-five miles away in the Davis Mountains the telescopes of the McDonald Observatory peered upward through the blackest skies on the North American continent, and Carlotta sometimes went there with her father and looked at the crystal stars and imagined herself as one of them, a tiny pinpoint in the vastness. She loved the constellations because they gave the pinpoints a reliable place in the chaos.

But by the time she turned eighteen, she had come to enjoy the dizzy freedom of being rootless and no longer felt tied to Jack and Delia solely because they had raised her, but because she loved them. She wore skimpy hippie dresses that fell softly around her tall and statuesque figure, and read books about Buddhism. She studied rocks and crystals and their mysterious powers, and arrived at a philosophy that was grounded in the theories of Plato, Aristotle, and Kant. Having no interest in obscure logic and no confidence in ancient figurings, she did not read deeply into the works of these philosophers, but plucked from their writings the concept of a final cause, and believed that her own final cause would become the search for her parents. The only problem with a cause that was final was that it would come to an end, and she wanted to carry this one for a while longer. She liked wondering who her parents were. She wanted to travel, and have adventures, to learn to scuba dive in deep waters. She wasn't ready to find answers, and wasn't ready, just yet, to look for them.

She graduated from high school and spent a year learning how to use lapidary equipment from a jeweler in Marathon, driving the half hour there and back in an ancient Chevy pickup she bought from a rancher in Marfa. She cut rocks in a shed in back of the jeweler's house, and made necklaces and belt buckles and bookends.

In the fall of 1989 she moved to Austin and attended UT, living with three friends in a ramshackle house on the south end of town. When she needed a quiet place to study she often stayed with Shelly and Dan, whom she knew as intimately as she knew her aunts and uncles. She made delicate necklaces of threads knotted with seed pearls and glass beads and gemstones, and on Saturday mornings she would set up a table alongside other venders on the Drag and sell the jewelry. Madeline sometimes helped her. Madeline was in middle school, intense and studious, with a watchful disposition. She played the flute in the school band and managed props for the Drama Department, so Carlotta sat through high school plays and sight-reading contests. Carlotta loved playing the older sister to Madeline and being with Shelly. She could talk to Shelly in ways she couldn't talk to her own mother.

Dan often took Madeline on weekend campouts, and for her fifteenth birthday she decided on a family campout at Enchanted Rock, in the hill country, and invited Carlotta along. Shelly forgot the candles, so they stuck twigs in the cake and set them on fire. They laughed, trying to put out the flames, then licked the icing from the charred twigs.

Carlotta dated in college, a little recklessly, and broke hearts. She took scuba-diving lessons and pored over travel magazines. She dreamed of diving in Malaysia and the Great Barrier Reef and the Red Sea, and in the summers drove with friends to Florida to camp or stay in cheap hotels and dive in Ginnie Springs or at Pennekamp Park. The summer before her senior year she had the chance to go to Belize with friends and dive at Blue Hole, but her parents urged her to find a job and to start planning how to support herself after graduation.

"It doesn't seem right to have the chance to go and not take it," Carlotta complained to Shelly as they stood in a campus parking lot, Carlotta holding a pair of jumper cables that Shelly had brought her. She had come out of class, to find the battery in her old truck dead.

"But your parents have a point," Shelly told her.

"And I can tell you don't agree with it," Carlotta said from under the truck's hood as she attached a clamp to the battery. "You think I should go."

"I think it should be between you and your parents."

"You never wanted to travel?"

"Oh, I guess I did. I thought about joining the Peace Corps."

Carlotta straightened and looked at her. "You did? I didn't know that. Why didn't you do it?"

"Well, the shooting, for one thing."

"So then you never went?"

"It wasn't a real loss. Looking back, it wasn't."

"It sounds like one. I have an idea. Why don't you and Dan go somewhere, and I'll stay with Madeline?"

"We might just do that someday. But in the meantime, I'm not taking sides about Belize."

Eventually Carlotta talked her parents into paying for her plane ticket, and promised to get a job as soon as she graduated.

In Belize she fell in love with an Australian archaeology student named Sean, who was involved in excavating a pre-Mayan farming community. She stayed in Belize after her friends went home to Texas, and hiked with Sean through rain forests and the ruins of Mayan temples. When he returned to Sydney, she didn't want to go home, so she took the ferry to Ambergris Caye and hired on with a dive shop in San Pedro. She hung about the markets, uncertain whether she was in search of something or in flight from something. Oddly, she often found herself thinking about Alpine—the dry air there, the sound of the train, and the unpretentious way of the people. She missed her mom and dad and wondered why she would come so far just to want to go home. An old woman she met in the market taught her to weave baskets, and on days she wasn't working, she made jewelry from shells and coral and sold it on the beaches outside the hotels, sitting under the coconut trees, her freckles darkened by the sun, her hair a flaming orange. She wandered through shell shops, drawn to the clutter and texture and colors, and was browsing in a shop filled with jade and emerald jewelry, in an alley that led to the beach, when she realized what she wanted to do with her life.

The minute she thought of it, her heart started to race. She looked around the shop and made a mental note of how the shelves were arranged, and pictured an old adobe storefront next to a picture-framing shop on a backstreet in downtown Alpine that had long been up for sale, and thought about the jeweler in Marathon who had taught her to use lapidary equipment. Alpine just happened to be near places rich in petrified wood and fossils, and nearly in the shadow of the Glass Mountains, the very name of which filled Carlotta with awe and a sense of reverence. She could make necklaces and belt buckles and bolo ties with her own hands. She loved exquisite objects and discovering things and assembling collections and polishing stones. Was it any wonder? Her name, after all, was Carlotta Stone. She could call the shop Carlotta's Stones.

She returned to Austin at the end of the summer and registered for fall classes, and talked to Shelly about her plans. "I'll take a business class," she told her as they sat in Shelly's kitchen. "I keep designing the shop in my head—exactly where I would put everything. It's like I've been moving in this direction forever. I just didn't realize it happened to be in a circle. I know that area. I know the rocks, the fossils, the people. The building needs some work, so it's cheap. It's been for sale forever. And I could live upstairs. And we're getting tourists out there now, you know."

Shelly cradled a coffee cup and leaned back against the kitchen counter and looked at Carlotta thoughtfully, moving her thumb up and down over the smooth porcelain of the cup.

"It's strange, I always had this idea of leaving Alpine and living near the water," Carlotta said. "But now I'm excited about the idea of going back. I guess that's okay as long as it's not a retreat."

"What would it be a retreat from?"

"Oh, I'm not sure. Something." After a moment, she said, "I've considered trying to find my biological parents. I dream about it. But then I never seem to do it."

"Oh?" Shelly steadied her thoughts. "Is that because you're worried how your parents would feel about it?"

"No, not only that. I feel like I'd lose something if I found them. Some part of myself—something like that. And it doesn't seem right to go looking for someone who's not looking for me. It's not like they don't know about me. My mother certainly has to."

Shelly was still moving her thumb over the porcelain. "How do you feel about all of that?"

"Like Pandora probably felt about the box," Carlotta said. "And who knows what would fly out of it?"

The day before classes started, Carlotta got in her pickup and drove three hours south to Beeville, where she asked at a gas station for directions to the hospital. She stood in the hospital lobby and looked around and said to an elderly woman at the reception desk, "I was born here."

It was a small-town hospital. Nothing special. She wasn't sure what she had thought she would see.

# INTO THE WOODS

# 27

Madeline began to feel as if Carlotta was always in their house—as if every day when she came home from school her mother and Carlotta were in the kitchen, discussing plans for Carlotta's store. Madeline would walk in and put her books down and find the two of them talking about financing or suppliers or the pillows that Delia was needlepointing to add to the merchandise.

"She's over here so much," Madeline said to her mother one night after Carlotta had left.

Shelly was unloading a stack of clean clothes from a laundry basket into Madeline's chest of drawers. "Yes, lately she has been," she agreed, placing the clothes in the drawers. "Her friends aren't business types, so she doesn't have many people to talk to about the store."

"I didn't know you were so much of a business type."

Shelly sorted the socks. "Does it bother you that she's over here a lot?"

"It does when it seems like she lives here."

"I thought you liked having her over."

"I just wonder why she isn't planning the store with Delia. You're not her mother."

Shelly turned and looked at her. "Delia's in Alpine, and I'm here. Honey? Do you think you and I aren't spending enough time together?"

Madeline shrugged. She was sixteen, and didn't want to spend more time with her mother. Still, she wished her mother had seemed upset about that. Instead she seemed happy to work at the Helping Hand Home and then come home and talk to Carlotta.

How had Carlotta become like part of their family? She existed in their lives in some important but veiled way that Madeline couldn't make out. There seemed to be gaps, and places where the pieces didn't quite fit. Apparently, Jack and his cousin Wyatt Calvert had rescued her mother when she was shot by the sniper, and afterward her mother was bonded to Jack for life. But why? And why wasn't she bonded to Wyatt? And why had Madeline never met Wyatt? She had seen pictures of him at Jack and Delia's house and knew he was Jack's cousin and a famous painter, and that he came to Alpine sometimes with his wife and two children. But when she asked her mother about him or said she would like to meet him, or suggested they buy one of his paintings, her mother offered brief answers about how Wyatt lived so far away and how they couldn't afford his paintings.

He had saved her mother's life, and so, in a way, he was important to Madeline's, and it was odd that she'd never met him, and odd that her mother didn't talk more about what had happened. When Madeline was seven years old and curious about her mother's scars, her parents had taken her to the South Mall plaza under the UT tower and explained that the shooter was dead, that there was no more danger, and it had all happened a long time ago. Her mother had said the injured arm worked perfectly well enough to hold and hug her sweet Madeline, and then they had taken her off to throw pennies into the fountain.

The explanation had been plenty at that age, but now, in retrospect, it seemed dismissive and thin. It wasn't as if Madeline was preoccupied with this distant event in her mother's life, but she felt shut out of something about it, and sensed that Carlotta was somehow linked to whatever was being kept from her.

When Carlotta finished college that spring, Jack and Delia came to Austin to see her graduate, then helped her move her things back to Alpine and into the small apartment space on the second floor of the stone building that would become the store. Carlotta collected the merchandise and made jewelry from stones. She stocked the shelves, installed rows of bright track lighting that made the place sparkle, and sent out invitations for the opening.

Madeline dreaded the opening. It would mean at least a six-hour drive each way with her parents, and a party with a lot of people from Alpine whom she didn't know.

So when her high school drama teacher called to say her class had been invited to perform a summer production of *Into the Woods*—a play they had performed three times already in the high school auditorium—for a larger audience at the Paramount Theater downtown, Madeline was, for a moment, thrilled to hear that the date was the same as Carlotta's opening. She was essential to the production, in charge of costumes and a complicated array of props; she would have to stay and be part of it.

But then it occurred to her that her parents would have to choose one event over the other, and that her mother might prefer to go to Alpine, having seen the play three times already at the high school. Madeline didn't need her at the play, but wished she would want to be there, and suspected she would only pretend to want to.

She found her mother outside, dragging the garden hose attached to a sprinkler dribbling water. "Mr. Barrientos called. The Paramount wants us to do *Into the Woods* this weekend."

She saw the pride in her mother's smile, and then the consternation. Saw her put the sprinkler down. It spurted a little stream at her mother's ankles. "That's great! But . . . this weekend?"

"Yeah, this weekend."

"Which day?"

"Saturday."

"What time?"

"At one."

She could see her mother calculating the hours for the drive. The water sputtered around in a small circle.

"I know it's the day we're supposed to go to Alpine," Madeline said. "If you need to go without me, it's okay."

"Oh, I want to go to the play, Madeline. This is awful."

She probably did want to, but she probably wanted to go to Alpine more, Madeline thought. "You should go. I can tell you want to." She watched her mother standing in the bright sunshine in blue jeans and an old T-shirt, her hair tied back, her shoes sopping wet now. "I don't want you to pretend you'd rather be here, when I know you want to be there. You've been helping Carlotta from the beginning. You should go." It was more a brush-off than permission.

"Honey, let's talk about this. I think you're feeling—"

"She's not your daughter, Mom. I'm your daughter. And I don't think you should stay for the play when you've already seen it, but I just wish you wanted to. And obviously you don't. So I'd really rather you go."

Her mother spoke clearly and slowly. "I am not going to Alpine. I would rather be here. It's a big day for you, and I'm proud of you."

"You're more proud of Carlotta."

"Madeline, how could that be true? Listen to me—"

"I don't want to listen. There's something about you I don't get, Mom. It's like you're not telling me something." She paused after saying this, giving her mother time to agree that yes, there was something, or to assure her there was not. But her mother only stared at her with a look of astonishment. "Sometimes I feel like I don't know you," Madeline said. She could see her mother trying to collect herself.

"Honey, everyone at sixteen feels like they don't know their mother. It's normal . . . It's . . . expected . . ." Madeline watched her fumble for words. "But I didn't know you felt that way."

"And that's my point. You have no idea what I feel."

"I guess maybe I don't. I haven't. Oh, honey. This is out of the blue."

"For you it is. Not for me."

It frightened her how lost her mother seemed for words. She went to her room and closed the door. Her mother knocked and pleaded with her to open it, but she didn't.

Later, Madeline heard her father pull into the driveway, and went out and climbed into the passenger side of his Bronco. On the radio Tina Turner was singing "What's Love Got to Do with It?" Her father turned the motor off. "What's up?"

"I said a bunch of stuff to Mom."

"What kind of stuff?"

"About Carlotta."

"What about her?"

"I'm jealous. There, I've said it. It's like sibling rivalry, only she's not my sister. I feel stupid, telling you."

He took the key from the ignition and settled back against the door. "You can't possibly think your mother loves Carlotta more than you."

"She spends more time with her. And they have more in common. I can't say what, exactly, but they do. And there's some mystique about Mom that I don't get—that goes back to what happened to her. I can't figure it out."

"Madeline, your mother loves you more than she loves anybody else on earth, and that includes me, and it certainly includes Carlotta."

"Well, we'll see. She has to decide whether she's going to Carlotta's opening, or going to my play again. We're doing it at the Paramount at one o'clock on Saturday. She says she's going to stay and see it, but I don't want her to unless she wants to."

"And she says she wants to? After we've seen it three times already? There's proof of how much she loves you." He shook his head. "Does that mean I have to see it again, too?"

"I'm not joking, Daddy."

"Okay. If you want my advice, I think you should give her permission to go. Take it out of her hands. Don't make it a test. She's already said she'll stay. I'll stay and see the play again, and I can even record it so your mom can watch it later. If it starts at one o'clock it should be over by three, and then you and I will leave for Alpine and maybe make it for the tail end of the party."

"I already told Mom to go."

"But you didn't mean it. And she can read you."

"How about if she goes, and we don't try to make the tail end of the party?"

"That's okay too. I don't care either way. But Carlotta would probably like to have you there. And she came to your birthday campout at Enchanted Rock."

"She didn't have to drive twelve hours for that. And I wished I hadn't invited her. Mom had more fun with her than she did with me."

"You looked like you were having a good time. Remember, your mother forgot the candles, so we burned twigs?"

"That was Carlotta's idea."

"Okay, Madeline. What do you want to do? I'm game for whatever. Go, or stay. I'm with you."

"I don't know." She stared past him. The Bronco's windows were splattered with dried mud from somewhere her father had worked earlier in the week, and it obscured her view of the neighborhood houses. "All right. I guess we should go." She sighed aloud. "So what do I tell Mom?"

"Tell her you've decided you don't want her to sit through the play another time when she has an obligation to be in Alpine. And that you and I will hit the road as soon as the play's over. Go tell her now, while I hose down the car."

"Are you sure you don't mind seeing it again?"

"I love seeing bad plays four times in a row."

She had to smile. "It is pretty bad, isn't it?"

"The costumes and the props are worth it."

Madeline sat in the Bronco for a minute while Dan uncoiled the water hose and started spraying the windows. Finally she went into the house to look for her mother. She found her staring at a row of soggy impatiens in the backyard, and spoke to her from the doorstep. "I talked to Dad, and I want you to go to Alpine."

Her mother looked up. "No, honey. I'd rather see the play."

"No, really." She couldn't bring herself to sound convincing.

Her father came up behind her and spoke over her shoulder. "Madeline and I agree you should go. You've been part of the planning. We'll come late, after the play."

Shelly shook her head. "I've made up my mind—"

"So has Madeline. And she's as hardheaded as you are. Now, have either of you made any dinner, or am I on my own?"

Standing in her wet shoes, the sun hot on her face, Shelly met Dan's eyes over Madeline's shoulder. "There's a pot of chili on the stove, but I haven't made the corn bread yet," she said.

"I'm not hungry," Madeline said, and turned and went inside.

Dan and Shelly went into the bedroom and closed the door, then went into the bathroom to be certain Madeline couldn't hear their voices.

"This is horrible," Shelly whispered. "It's my fault. I haven't handled things right, or she wouldn't feel this way."

"I'm not sure there was a right way to handle them."

"Have I poisoned things with Madeline?" It was such a painful thought. Could it be true that she favored Carlotta? She loved both girls so intensely her feelings for them could not be categorized or quantified or adequately compared. She had raised Madeline—she was closest to her, and knew her the best. If pressed to decide, she would probably say she loved her the best. And yet her longing for Carlotta had been deeply implanted during the early years of dreaming about her, and missing her, and rationing the visits with her—all long before Madeline was born. And now Carlotta, as an adult, loved Shelly's company, while Madeline, as a teenager, was absorbed in her friends and herself. "Have I done it all wrong? I don't know how to get back from this."

"You haven't done anything wrong," Dan said. "Don't do that to yourself, honey. We just have to decide where to go from here."

"Well, not Alpine, for one thing."

She expected him to agree with that, but instead he looked at her thoughtfully. "I'm not so sure. At this point, since she knows you wanted to go, it might just legitimize her concern if you don't. Like you're making a point that doesn't have to be made."

"But what can we do to reassure her?"

"I know what we can't do. We can't lie to her when she's basically straight out asking about this. I almost lied to her in the car. That can't happen."

"Are you suggesting we should tell her about Carlotta?"

"I'm suggesting she's bound to find out at some point, if she's asking questions like this now."

"What did she say to you in the car?"

"That she's jealous of Carlotta. And she thinks you're hiding something."

"She's not ready for the truth," Shelly said. "If she's jealous now, think how she would feel if she knew Carlotta really is my daughter."

"Better than if she learned years from now that we'd lied to her when she was asking for the truth in every way she knew how. If she weren't asking, that would be different."

"But can you imagine how hard it would be for her to be around Carlotta and know the truth, when Carlotta doesn't know it?"

"Maybe Carlotta should know it."

She stared at him, uncertain if he was serious.

"Maybe it's time to tell her."

"She doesn't want to know it. She has a lot of conflicted feelings. We'd be throwing information at her that she doesn't want."

"It's not like she'd be finding out her parents were criminals, Shelly. And I assume Jack and Delia haven't planned to lie to her if she were to start asking. I know it could be a problem for Wyatt if she finds out, but I'm not worried about Wyatt. He did what he did, and he might have to end up answering for it. Most of us do."

Shelly sat down on the edge of the tub and tried to think. When she finally lifted her face to Dan, she whispered, "Maybe we should talk to Jack and Delia on Sunday and see what they think."

"We should plan to do that."

"And I guess Jack could talk to Wyatt. And maybe at some point this summer we could sit the girls down—either together, or apart—and . . . maybe . . ." She couldn't imagine saying the words to either of them.

"And talk to them," Dan said.

"Yes. But do you see all the ways this could unravel?"

"Quite clearly, honey."

# 28

# THE DEVIL'S SINKHOLE

On Saturday morning, before she left for Alpine, Shelly went to Madeline's room and asked if she needed clothes washed, or last-minute errands run, and if she wanted eggs and toast for breakfast.

Madeline shrugged at the offers. She stayed in her room afterward and didn't do anything to make her mother feel better about leaving. She was at the mirror in her bathroom, brushing mascara onto her lashes, when her mother came and told her goodbye. "I love you, honey. I'll see you tonight."

"Okay."

"Your dad said he'd record the show so I can watch it later."

"That's nice." She barely glanced at Shelly's reflection.

"Honey, obviously you're upset. I don't want to go if it's going to make you unhappy."

Madeline knew she had taken the grudge too far. "I want you to go." But she wasn't reassuring, and didn't intend to be.

When Shelly had finally kissed them both and started for Alpine, Dan and Madeline drove to the high school and loaded a Styrofoam cow, a harp, a painted wooden chicken, and six small wooden birds on marionette strings, along with dozens of other props, into the Bronco and the teacher's van. They met the teacher at the back entrance of the Paramount and hauled the props inside. Madeline thought she should be happy to work in an actual theater instead of the school auditorium, but her mother's absence ruined her mood and spoiled the day.

They had planned to leave as soon as the play was over, but the students assigned to help the teacher transport props and costumes back to the school skipped out on the job, so Dan stepped in. "No problem," he told the teacher. "It won't take long."

After they had gone to the school and unloaded everything, the girl who had played the baker's wife discovered she needed a ride home, and since no one else offered to take her, Dan said he could do it.

It was nearly five by the time they left town, stopping at McDonald's on the way out and then heading west into the hill country. The land was rocky here, covered with cedar and live oak, the hills folding into one another like kneaded dough. The bluebonnets had disappeared in the heat, but the roadside was still colorful with red and yellow summer flowers. The relentless sun was in front of them, so Madeline climbed into the backseat to escape the glare. After a while she dozed off, and when she woke, she asked groggily, "Where are we?"

Dan said they were past Fredericksburg and almost to Interstate 10. "And we have a decision to make. We're not going to be there in time for the party, so we can get there when we get there, or"—he glanced at her over the seat—"we can do something special and go see bats."

"Bats? That doesn't thrill me."

"Flying out of a cave," he said. "A sinkhole, to be exact. It's state property, but I have permission. I've worked there."

"Is this your attempt to cheer me up about Alpine?"

"It's my best offer."

"Bats."

"Thousands of them. Flying up out of a huge hole in the ground."

"How far out of the way?" she asked.

"An hour."

"You always mean two hours when you say one."

"What's the hurry?"

She thought about that. She didn't care if they got there at all. "True. Okay. Should we stop and call Mom?" She climbed into the front seat.

"We'll call her afterward. The bats come out at dusk, so we're going to have to hurry."

They drove in silence for a few miles before Madeline summoned the courage to ask what she wanted to. "Daddy? About our conversation the other day. When I told you I felt like there were things about Mom that she wasn't telling me. Are there?"

"I think you know your mom pretty well."

"There's not something?"

"I'm sure there are things about all of us that would surprise the rest of us. I'm also pretty sure your mom could tell you anything about herself, and you would find her to be the same mom who loves you more than her own life and would do anything for you."

"Except go to the play."

"Except go to the play for the fourth time when there's somewhere else she's needed. And she did offer. Come on, sweetie."

"It's just that there's something about her that feels out of bounds. Like a line I can't cross, or something. Some secret."

"Plenty of secrets. Plenty of things that could surprise you. Not about her character—that's always going to be solid. But certainly about her life. I bet there would be some things about your life that would surprise her, too. For instance, on just a small scale, how did those beer caps happen to get in our backyard last weekend when we were out and you had your friends over?"

"You found those?"

"Seven, to be exact."

"Those guys who came with Carol were drinking."

"Next time tell them to drink in somebody else's backyard."

"You didn't tell Mom?"

"No."

By the time they reached Highway 41 toward Rocksprings, the sun had gone below the horizon, but the sky was still light. The land was flatter here, and there was almost no traffic for a long stretch. Madeline got behind the wheel to practice driving. Finally her father directed her onto a white caliche road. "Easy on the clutch," he said. She drove through an open gate and rolled her window down, flooding the car with the pungent smell of cedars. The sky had turned purple, and a scooped moon was rising over rocky pastureland dotted with scrub oak and prickly pear.

Rounding a curve, the car lights suddenly swung onto a figure running toward them down the road. He was young—a teenager—and a harness of some kind dangled off him. He waved his arms wildly. "My girlfriend's down the hole! I can't get her out!"

Madeline pulled to a stop and the boy came to the window. He was thin and wore a ball cap with a logo for Detroit Diesel, and his hands were bleeding. The fingernails looked like they'd been scraped off. One was attached but bent all the way back. He was panting hard and sweating. "She's hanging from a rope down the hole and she's hurt—I think her ribs are broken!" he cried. "I can't get her out! It's the wrong kind of rope—she's twirling in circles. She can't breathe right!"

"Get in the car," Dan said, and changed places with Madeline. He drove so fast she shut her eyes. When the car stopped and Madeline opened her eyes, she saw her father running with the boy, the headlights tossing their shadows into patches of prickly pear. The light shone on cactus needles and skimmed through yellow grass, then dropped away abruptly, plunging into an abyss.

Madeline got out and steadied herself. The monstrous hole might have looked like nothing more than a still pond of black water on the level landscape if the moon had been reflected, but the light of the moon fell into the hole just as the headlights did—suddenly and totally. An old white pickup, missing its tailgate, was backed up to the cavernous pit. It gleamed in the light of the rising moon, its back end drooping lopsidedly where one of the wheels was over the edge. A rope tied underneath stretched down into the pit. Madeline heard a sound—a high, thin wailing coming out of the hole—an echoing supplication circling up from the depths along with the rank smell of bat guano and drifting into the open spaces over the rocky pasture.

"Amanda!" the boy screamed down. "We're here! I got help!" He paced at the edge, fretfully yanking the ball cap off and on, his eyes darting with fear.

"Does her harness have leg straps, or is it like yours?" Dan demanded.

"It's the same as mine. Oh God, can we get her up?"

"No leg straps?"

"No sir, it's a telephone harness like this one. My dad works at the phone company so I just—"

"Is that the only rope you have?"

"Yes sir. But I've got a Jumar too."

"How long has she been down there?"

"We went down a few hours ago and—"

"I mean how long has she been hanging there?"

"I've been trying to get her up—"

"How long?"

"A long time. Is she going to die? Oh God, is she—"

"Tie your shoes."

"Sir?"

"Tie your laces."

The boy squatted to tie them.

Madeline watched her father crawl half under the truck and examine the rope where it stretched over the rim and down into the hole. She approached but held back from the edge, afraid of what she would see. The girl was calling from below, her voice an echoing moan.

"We're here!" the boy screamed down to her. "We're here!" His teeth were chattering. Swallows circled overhead, laying their wings flat against their bodies and diving jetlike into the opening.

"How did she get there—did she fall?" Dan demanded as he got to his feet.

"We were down there and she was scared to come back up so I came up to show her, but then it was hard for her to climb, and she was tired out when she got up here—oh God!"

"She fell from the top?"

"Yes sir, she was standing right here, and then . . . She was trying to get the rope off and it got tangled around her feet or something, and then she just—"

"Okay—"

"She just was gone! She didn't fall all the way to the bottom 'cause the rope got tangled up in the Jumar! I got one Jumar here, but the other one's down there and the rope's wadded up in a rat's nest under her butt. She's spinning! Ah God! Do you see her? I'm so scared!"

"Settle down and get hold of yourself."

"And I couldn't go nowhere for help 'cause she's tied to the truck. I tried driving it forward to pull her out but it seemed like the rope was going to get sawed off by the rim, and I tried backing up to lower her down, but she's about a hundred feet up from the bottom—and my wheel went over. I'll do whatever you say. I'll do—"

"Listen to me."

The boy bent over, breathing hard, his hands on his knees.

"Look at me."

"Yes sir."

"Straighten up. Look at me. Calm down. We're going to help her."

Madeline wanted to run from here, to get back in the car and hide her face and shut her eyes. She wanted to be anywhere but here in this descending darkness. "Do you want me to drive for help?" she called to her father. She had never driven alone before, but thought that she could do it.

"No, there's no time."

The girl was pleading from the hole, her voice a freakish wuthering sound rising out of the depths.

The boy said, "I can try to pull the truck forward—"

Dan had started running toward the Bronco. "Don't touch the truck," he said over his shoulder. "We can't risk cutting the rope. We'll do it another way."

The Bronco's headlights shone like stage lights. The boy's hands bled. His fingernail extended straight up from his finger, and Madeline couldn't look at it. She got on her hands and knees and crawled to the edge of the pit to see down into it. The depth shocked her. This was more than a hole. It was an entrance to another world. Dizzy, she settled flat on her belly.

The overhang on which she lay was three feet thick and dropped away into nothing. Below, the girl hung so far down in the dusky light that she looked like a tiny acrobat, revolving in a slow circle, faceup, her head bent back, her hair flowing, her legs swinging loose.

Madeline stared at the overhang that encircled the empty space. The truck was a few yards away, the rear of the open bed sagging over the precipice, the rope tied to the axle stretched tight across the lip and then descending straight down, as if the weight that hung from it could drag the truck backward into the hole at any moment. The walls deep down were darkly shadowed, trickling water, overgrown with spongy moss. Mud nests of swallows hung in clusters on shallow ledges. Twilight ventured only as far down as the girl, who dangled over a cushion of darkness.

Dan got in the Bronco and drove it up close to the edge, aiming the headlights at the pickup. He grabbed a tow strap from the back of the Bronco and handed Madeline a flashlight. "Stay on your stomach as long as you're at the edge."

"Amanda!" the boy screamed. "We're going to get you out!"

Lying on the speckled limestone beside tufts of speargrass, Madeline shone the flashlight into the cavern. Warmth leached out of the stone against her stomach as twilight turned to night. The girl became invisible, the rope vanishing into the dark like a fishing line in murky water. She was only a voice now, calling the boy's name faintly. She whimpered, feebly calling that she couldn't breathe, she couldn't feel her legs.

Madeline swung the light onto the tow strap as it slithered into the dark. She could see no way her father could climb down into the hole and bring the girl back up. Even if the strap proved long enough, and he managed to tie it onto something and get down over the treacherous rim, how could he rescue the girl? He knew about rocks and climbing from his work, but he wouldn't be wrestling with rocks down there. He would be wrestling with air. There was nothing even to shove his feet against once he dropped over the edge.

A small dark object fluttered up through Madeline's beam of light, like a leaf carried up by a gust of wind. A curious stirring sound rose from the hole. The smell was dank and putrid, as if the hole had started to breathe, and the girl below called out, her words lost in the eerie beat of wings and a strange collective chattering. Dan shouted down, "I've lowered a tow strap down there. Can you see it?"

Her answer had a vibration, as if distorted by the pattering wings of the bats. "No, I can't see it. I can't breathe. Please help me."

Madeline watched her father in the bright headlights as he stood holding the end of the tow strap. It would reach no farther down. His shadow stretched over the limestone and dropped over the rim as if tumbling into the hole. He pulled the useless tow strap out and tossed it onto the ground.

The bats rose in greater numbers, interfering with the moonlight. Madeline swiped at them, crawling backward from the hole, and got to her feet. The night was drained of color, reduced to the white lights and the white truck, the white moon, the dark bats. Her father appeared in front of her, setting his hands on her shoulders, but she couldn't make sense of his words. The bats frightened her, stirring a hot, foul breeze as they whirled around her.

"Do you understand?" her father asked above their muffled piping. "It's our only chance to get her out before she suffocates from the rope."

"What are you going to do?"

But then, looking at his face, she knew.

The boy stepped in and out of the light, shouting into the hole. Bats blackened the air, spiraling toward the moon. Madeline looked at the truck, its back wheel over the edge. She looked at the rope, the hole. Guano fell from the sky, drifting through the headlights' glare like flakes of snow.

"Don't, Daddy." Her voice shook.

He closed his arms around her, and whispered, "Madeline, I have to do this. I have to. I'll use the tow strap to get down over the edge; then I can get on the rope and go down and bring her up."

She pleaded with him. "The rope won't hold you both . . . You said it could break—"

But he was talking with the boy now, getting things from him, strapping the boy's harness around his own waist.

She felt alone already. She wanted the girl to stop calling for help—to fall . . . to die . . . anything that would stop her father from going down in the hole.

He held something up for her to see. "This is a Jumar; it goes on the rope. Guess who invented it?"

He spoke as he tied things and made knots, doing his story thing again—the trick he had always done. When she was younger and frightened, he would distract her with some nonsense story. "I don't care, Daddy."

"A birder. A Swiss man, so he could sit in trees."

"Daddy, I don't care—"

"He would use a pair of these to climb up and down a rope tied high up in a tree, and perch there with a bottle of wine and binoculars and watercolors. The villagers thought he was a lunatic."

Madeline looked at the thing he held in his fist—gray, metal, alien.

"This is a handle, see? And here's the jaw." He opened it and showed her the teeth. "It grabs the rope. Then I can stand in the stirrup." He held up a dirty white sling attached to the Jumar. "See how easy it is?"

But she couldn't imagine her father standing on one foot in the midair dark.

He was cutting a piece from the tow strap with his pocketknife and tying it into a loop. "The only problem is, I need two," he said as he worked. "One for my right foot, one for my left. They slide up the rope. It's like walking. I can go up or down. Simple. So here's my second stirrup."

"Please, Daddy," she whispered.

"We can do this," he said. "I'll use the tow strap to get down over the rim, then move onto the rope and go down and untangle the girl so we can lower her down to the bottom where she can breathe. If I can't untangle her, I'll bring her up." He hugged Madeline, the sling flapping against her back. The strength of the embrace surprised her. Don't let go, she thought. But he already had.

She held the light as he adjusted the harness and cut another section from the strap. He did his magic with it, looping it into a seat that he wrapped around his thighs. He told the boy to give him one of his shoelaces. The boy was leaning over the hole, his hands on his knees, and he looked at Dan skeptically for only a second before backing away from the hole, untying a shoelace, and yanking it from his shoe. Dan took it and tied the ends together. "The poor man's substitute for a Jumar," he said. "It's called a Prusik loop. Guess who invented it." He flashed a smile at Madeline.

"Stop it, Daddy."

"Looks pretty Mickey Mouse, I know, but it works."

Everything was happening too fast for Madeline to make sense of. She quit trying to understand. She just wanted it over. He crawled under the truck and tied the tow strap to the axle, alongside the rope. Madeline crouched, peering under, breathing the sickening odor of axle grease and shining the beam on his hands to light what he was doing.

There were no more jokes when he came out from under the truck. He tossed the slack end of the tow strap into the hole, looped the shoelace around it, and backed up to the abyss. Slowly he put his weight on the strap, causing the knots to creak and the truck to groan. He didn't look at Madeline, as if he didn't dare. Drawing a deep breath, he began to lower himself over the edge.

Madeline centered the flashlight's beam on her father as if it were a tether that would hold him. He looked sturdy with his feet planted against the vertical rock. But where the rim lipped under, there was nothing to put his weight against. He bent and clamped the boy's Jumar onto the rope, taut with the girl's weight, fished one foot into the stirrup, and studied the frayed section of rope stretched over the edge above him. Carefully, staring up at the fray, he stood on the stirrup, testing if the rope would hold.

When it did hold, he released the tow strap and allowed it to swing free, committing himself to the frayed rope. One step at a time, revolving slowly as the rope spun, he walked down into the underworld.

Everything was in and out of the light now. The moon moved in the sky, the bats flew, the stars blinked into existence. Down below, the shaft of Madeline's light pierced the dark void.

She heard the boy moving back and forth along the rim, but did not look at him. He had led them to this danger; he should be the one going down. Her father became smaller and darker, and finally the beam no longer reached him. "He'll be okay," Madeline whispered to herself. But that would depend on the rope.

A rock under her hand moved and skated off the edge. "Daddy," she shouted, "I'm sorry! I'm sorry!" The rock made a small clap at the bottom. Her father's voice, muffled by distance, echoed upward—"Everything's all right"—and Madeline realized he wasn't talking to her now. He was talking to the girl.

She heard their voices as he struggled. The rope creaked and twirled. Beside the truck, the boy talked to himself. Madeline dug her elbows into the rock, searching the dark with the light. The beam sputtered. She knocked the flashlight into her palm to bring it back to life. She could hear in their faint voices that her father had failed to lower the girl to the bottom and was trying to bring her back up. Slowly, out of the blackness, he appeared like an apparition, shouldering his way into the light, the girl attached to his harness, dangling just beneath him in her nest of dirty rope.

Inch by inch, he muscled higher, escaping the darkness, his rope swinging in and out of Madeline's light. Watching his face take shape, Madeline felt hope.

Again, the flashlight flickered and dimmed. Again, she smacked it into her palm and angled it down to spotlight her father as he struggled upward. The light was all she could offer him.

As he neared the top, the girl's weight pulling at him, his body buckled and quivered with the strain. He wiped the sweat from his eyes and gasped for air.

The girl he was hauling up from the depths was motionless, her mouth gaping. She was homely. Limp. She moaned, her head canted to the side.

"Amanda!" the boy shouted. Leaning over the edge, he scuffled dirt over the rim, a cloud of tan dust falling through Madeline's light and into her father's face.

"Get back!" Madeline shouted at him.

"Light . . ." her father gasped, "the tow strap."

The dull light was his guide. She shook the flashlight hard, superstitiously now, and shined it at the tow strap.

But the strap dangled out of his reach. The rope supporting him groaned as it loosened and scraped at the rock. The smell of guano poisoned the air and made the night seem deeper. Hurry, Madeline thought.

Her father had come to the underside of the rim, and his Jumar and knots would go no farther up on the rope. He tried to worm them higher, but the rope clung to the rock as if it were welded to it. He bucked at it and managed to wedge his fingers next to the stone, but the rope ground at them and made them bleed, and he had to pull them free.

The boy talked to the girl. "You're close now. You're going to make it."

Madeline wanted the courage to crawl closer and stretch out her hand to her father. She felt she could almost reach him. But even she and the boy together would not be able to pull him up over the three-foot rim. Only her father could solve this final hurdle. The only thing she could give him was the vanishing beam.

The boy cried out, "Amanda!" his voice shrill with panic. "Oh God, is she breathing? She's not breathing!"

The girl suddenly pitched sideways, jerking Dan and jackknifing him backward. He tried to right himself, pedaling in the empty air while the girl swayed and rocked, her limbs flailing out from the ropes.

Swinging her light at the girl, Madeline saw her eyes were shut and her mouth was no longer gaping. Her jaw was clenched hard, as if she were thrashing and flailing in some terrible nightmare.

"She's dying!" the boy cried. "She's having a fit or something! Get her up! Oh God, get her up!"

Madeline watched her father struggle against the wild, haphazard movements. "Give me the tow strap," he shouted.

The girl had become still.

The boy tried to pull at the rope, but it clung fast to the rock. The uprooted fingernail tore free of his hand and stayed upright on the edge of the limestone, balanced there like a moth's wing.

"The tow strap . . ." Madeline heard her father gasp. "Shove it over!"

The boy slung it to him, but he missed it, and snatched again, and on the third try hooked it with his raw palm, pulled it closer, tied it to the ropes that held the girl. His arms twitched. His legs bore down on the loops. When he had tied the girl onto the strap, he jerked at the knot to test it, then wrestled his pocketknife out of his jeans. He struggled to open the blade. His fingers were bent at strange angles and his hands bled, so he pulled the blade up with his teeth. Blindly, he sawed beneath him at the rope connecting him to the girl. She was motionless, her knees doubled against her chest. The rope squeaked on the rim.

Finally the knife cut through and Madeline saw it fall from her father's hand and disappear into the dark below. The girl fell away too, swinging wildly into free space, the tow strap catching her weight. She rocked there in her knotted nest, as still as a rag doll wrapped in knitted yarn.

"You're going to make it!" the boy shouted. "You're safe now!"

But how would they get her up over the rim?

"Daddy," Madeline whispered. She wanted to see his eyes.

He swam his way back and forth and latched one hand onto the mass of ropes around the girl. "Pull," he said to the boy, putting his shoulder up to the jumbled mess and trying to shove the girl upward.

The boy clawed at the tow strap, but it held taut against the rock, and Madeline's father released the girl and let the tow strap have her. Her face was turned to the light. It was dirty. Narrow. Her eyes half-closed. He was alone now, on the rope.

"Here's . . . what happens." His voice was strained, foreign to Madeline—he didn't sound like her father. His words were disjointed. "Madeline. Get in the truck. Set . . . the emergency brake. Pull the truck forward . . . Son, you get hold . . . of the strap and . . . guide your girl up over the rim."

Madeline didn't budge. "You said it would cut the rope if we drove." The rope was his rope now. The tow strap was different. It was strong. It could hold. It would hold the girl.

Her father labored for breath as he spoke. "Be sure . . . the brake is set . . . Do you know . . . how to check it?"

"I think so. But you said—"

"It's set," the boy said. "Can you drive a standard?"

"Yes," Madeline said.

"Be sure . . . about the emergency brake," her father gasped. "It's the smallest pedal . . . by the door . . ."

"I know where it is—"

"Push it . . . hard."

"Okay."

"Don't use . . . first gear. Use second. Left . . . and down."

"But the truck will jerk."

"Doesn't matter. First gear is"—he struggled to breathe—"too near reverse. Don't stall . . . or drift backward. Give plenty . . . of gas. Let the clutch out slow."

"Daddy?" Her voice was a choked whisper.

"Nice and . . . slow, Madeline."

She tried to make her voice louder. "Daddy?"

"It's our only . . . chance," he said with a note of impatience now. He raised his eyes, looking directly into the yellow beam. "Madeline, honey? . . . Do this."

She set the flashlight down at the edge of the hole and walked to the truck. The seat was too far back, but moving it could jolt the truck, so she left it where it was. Sitting forward on the seat, she pushed the emergency brake down hard with her foot, all the way to the floor. She pushed the clutch down, and turned the key. At first the truck refused her. It kicked and almost stalled before it idled. Her hands shook on the gearshift as she moved it left, then down. She pressed the accelerator and slowly, slowly, her legs trembling, took her weight off the clutch. Closing her eyes, she felt the grating spin of the wheels beneath her and heard the grind of rocks spewing backward into the hole. "Please. Please. Please." She prayed for the rope to hold.

She felt the truck lurch forward, and heard the boy shout. She opened her eyes and realized she was several feet farther from where she had been. Flinging the door wide open, she ran back toward the hole. The boy was kneeling beside the girl, who lay on the ground in her mess of ropes like a creature caught in a net. Her arm rose up in the light, as if she were coming to life.

The grass moved in the breeze, making a whispering sound.

The flashlight lay at the edge of the hole, the pale beam marking the edge of the world.

The ragged, severed end of the rope her father had been hanging from curved lazily through upright tufts of speargrass sprouting between chinks in the mottled limestone.

# 29

# NIGHT JOURNEY

In Carlotta's shop, cross-sectioned slabs of transparent rock as thin as wafers dangled like chimes from the ceiling, peacock feathers arched from vases, smoke curled from sticks of incense. Books and figurines and bins of polished stones crowded the shelves along the adobe walls, rattling with vibration when trains clattered along the tracks.

Carlotta wore cowboy boots, a gauze skirt, and a flannel shirt. Her hair swung down her back from under her cowboy hat as she put her arm around Shelly and walked her through the shop to introduce her to friends and townspeople. Her high school principal and several former teachers were there, as well as Jack's colleagues from Sul Ross and Delia's friends from church. The cats that lived in the frame shop next door wandered over and ate scraps of sausage that people fed them.

When the party began to wind down, Carlotta invited several friends to the house, where they stood around in the kitchen, drinking beer and eating chips and queso. Jack and an old-timer went out back by the fishpond, long since dry and abandoned due to raccoons, and talked about real estate. Delia had recently converted the old cabin Carlotta had once used as a playhouse to a small guest house, and Shelly walked down the road to look at it, shining a flashlight in the wheel ruts and out across the bee brush and Spanish daggers and stalks of tall agave. Clumps of johnsongrass sprouted in the humped center of the road, and insects chirped in the tall grass along the edges. Night birds called from mesquite trees. In the distance, Lizard Mountain rose in the darkness; at night it was only a jagged pile of rocks jutting into the blue-black sky.

Rounding a bedraggled row of willows and a screen of bushy junipers she saw the cabin, milky white in the moonlight. She climbed the three small steps to the porch and turned the light on as she entered, illuminating a sparsely furnished room that still smelled of fresh paint. Sitting on the edge of the bed, she felt she shouldn't have come to Alpine; she should have gone to Madeline's play. She wished that Dan and Madeline would hurry up and arrive. Being here without them felt wrong. Something in general felt wrong.

By one o'clock in the morning, Shelly was pacing in her room at the house. She went through every plausible thought: Maybe they had run out of gas or the car had broken down. She called home to Austin in case they had turned around, but the phone only rang in the empty house until the machine answered with Madeline's voice saying to leave a message. Jack called the local police and had them check with the Highway Patrol. They said there had been no accidents between Austin and Alpine. "Could Dan have taken a detour?" Jack asked Shelly.

"If he had, he would have called me by now."

The minutes dragged on and on. She paced in the hall and back and forth on the porch, unable to stop moving. Carlotta stayed close to her, quiet and worried, but Shelly hardly felt her presence. She was alone with her fear. Delia sat by the phone in the bedroom. Shelly was pacing out in the gravel drive when she heard the faint ring of the phone inside and ran up the stairs to Jack and Delia's room, with Carlotta behind her.

Delia was listening to a voice on the phone, her palm pressed to her face. She handed the phone to Shelly.

"Yes?" Her heart was pounding hard.

"Ma'am? I'm Stephen Cates, the sheriff in Rocksprings."

"Yes."

"I have your daughter, Madeline, here, and she's all right. But . . ." He cleared his throat. "Well, ma'am. Your husband . . . He . . . he went down in Devil's Sinkhole to help someone out, and his rope broke. He fell."

"Is he all right?"

"No ma'am. He . . . he's not. He's . . . deceased."

Jack took hold of her arm, but she was as stiff as a scarecrow.

"Your daughter needs to talk to you, ma'am."

"Mom?" Madeline sounded four years old.

"Honey?"

"Mom?"

"Madeline, where are you, honey?"

"Mom?" Madeline's voice trembled. "Mom? Daddy went down, to get a girl out, and . . ."

Carlotta took hold of her hand, and Shelly pulled it back and bent over, clutching her stomach. She kept her voice calm as she spoke into the phone. "Honey?" It wavered. "I'm coming to get you. Tell me where you are."

"The hospital in Kerrville."

"The hospital?"

"The basement. The morgue. Mom?"

"I'm here."

"Mom?"

Jack took the phone. Shelly heard him talk to Madeline and then to the sheriff, heard him mention Devil's Sinkhole. Delia left the room and came back with Shelly's purse.

"Jack will take you," Delia said. "Carlotta and I will take your car and meet you in Austin."

Shelly caught hold of Delia's hand. She wanted her comfort—her faith.

Everything had an unnatural clarity as she walked out to the car. The buttons on her sweater, her hand tugging the door handle, the moon with a part missing, the pinpoint stars. She sat in the passenger seat, so still at first that the only movement she felt was her own blinking. Car lights grew bright in her eyes on the highway. She stared them down. Passing through town, she saw the familiar places. The road came in segments. Jack turned here. Turned there. Shelly rocked forward and back in the seat as if this would speed her to Madeline. She kept her arms wrapped around herself and thought if she spoke she would scream. She tapped her feet on the floorboard and knotted her hands together. When the town was behind them, the road stretching ahead, the shape of mountains off in the distance under the moon, she forced the awful questions: "What did the sheriff tell you? Where is Devil's Sinkhole?"

"An hour south of Kerrville. Outside Rocksprings."

"What was he doing there?"

Jack could only repeat what the sheriff had said—that Dan and Madeline found a girl caught down in the vertical cave. She was caught on her rope and injured. Her boyfriend, up at the top, was trying to get her out when Dan and Madeline got there. Dan rigged himself with the boy's harness and went down to get her. He managed to get her out, but the rope broke and he fell.

The anxiety to reach Madeline became intolerable. Shelly plucked at her hair and pounded the dashboard. When Jack pulled into a truck stop for gas, she got out and kept walking. He picked her up on the road. "What was he doing at Devil's Sinkhole?" she asked him. "Why did he go there?" She rolled down the window, drowning herself in air and searching the moonlit landscape.

At the Kerrville hospital, Shelly got out of the car before Jack pulled to a stop. She hardly paused at the front desk long enough to ask where the morgue was, and was sent to the service elevators. She went down without waiting for Jack. The doors opened into a dim basement crowded with exposed pipes, discarded equipment, and hospital beds. A path the width of a gurney led to a door with a frosted window. Beside this door, Shelly found Madeline and the sheriff seated side by side in metal chairs, Madeline staring blankly at Shelly as she approached. Only when Shelly flung herself down in the chair beside her daughter and wrapped her in her arms did Madeline cling to her and sob against her shoulder. Shelly stroked her hair. "It's all right, baby." As if it could be.

The sheriff was tall, with gray hair and a gray mustache. A mole on his neck was the physical characteristic Shelly would later remember clearly about him. He held his hat in his hands. "We're still working on how this happened. The short of it, ma'am, is that your husband saved the girl. I know her family; they're from my county. Good people, ma'am. You can be sure your husband's sacrifice is deeply mourned and greatly appreciated. I'm sorry to ask it, but we'll need you to identify the body."

Jack came down and Shelly asked him to stay in the hall with Madeline. "I don't want to leave her alone." The Sheriff told her he would get someone else to stay with Madeline so Jack could go into the morgue with Shelly, but before he had finished making the offer, Shelly turned and walked in alone.

The Sheriff followed her. The air inside was frigid and saturated with chemical smells. An attendant stood beside a gurney on which a body lay under a sheet. "I should tell you, ma'am," the sheriff said. "I should warn you. Your husband fell a long way down. There's damage. It's extensive."

Shelly stepped forward and lifted the sheet away from Dan's face.

The bruises made the face black. His skull was flattened and lopsided. Pieces of bone protruded. A gash on his cheek splayed the flesh open. His nose was off center, his jaw unhinged. His tawny eyelashes lay against his purpled skin like golden butterfly wings.

She took a step back, and then forward, and leaned over him, and took his face in her hands. She kissed his forehead and found it as cold as the room. She kissed him repeatedly on the bruises and the broken bones until the sheriff tried to coax her away, and she flung her arm at him.

"Ma'am—"

"No." Smoothing her hands under the sheet and over his broken ribs, she felt his arms and fingers, and tried to hold his hands, but they were hard and unyielding. She kept expecting his eyes to open, his head to turn, and pulled the sheet farther back and stared at his chest, as if it might fill with breath. She placed her hand on his heart and thought she could feel a heartbeat, but knew there was none.

Finally she let the sheriff cover the body, but when the attendant started to roll the gurney away Shelly broke down and grabbed the rail, crying out, "What will happen to him?"

The sheriff stood holding his hat. "He has to be taken to San Antonio for an autopsy. The JP has requested that. It's standard."

"We don't need an autopsy. We know how he died."

"Yes, we do, ma'am. And we need to know which of the injuries killed him. I know it doesn't seem necessary, but they'll do a toxicology report. That's just standard, ma'am."

"No drugs or alcohol were involved," she told him. "I can promise you that. He wouldn't have been drinking—"

"I'm sure that's true, ma'am. But they need to have it on record. You might think I'm presumptuous to say it, but I think you'll want to have the record in case it ever eases your mind to know exactly what your husband died from—if it was head trauma, or what exactly it was. Maybe you don't want to think about that right now, but if we don't find out, it's possible there might come a day you can't think of another thing."

He talked about paperwork, but she found it impossible to concentrate on what he was saying. "I need to get back to my daughter."

Later, she walked Madeline out to the car and got in the backseat with her, and Jack drove them to Austin.

Wrapped in her mother's arms, Madeline felt as if nothing was real, as if she was playing the part of a girl whose father had just been killed. She had thought the presence of her mother would be the answer to something, or the end of the grief—that her mother would take her into her arms and somehow the death would be over.

When they arrived home they found Carlotta and Delia waiting in the driveway in Shelly's car. They went into the house, and Madeline looked at her father's things, all where he had left him, his books and papers, the mug from his morning coffee still in the sink. She walked around the house in a daze. Shelly cried against Jack's shoulder in the kitchen, and turned the stove on to make tea but forgot to put water into the kettle.

Standing before her father's reading chair, Madeline broke down and wept terribly, and her mother came and held her tightly. She broke away and cried so hard she sounded like she was screaming. She saw how stricken her mother was and wanted to make things right again, but knew she never could, and knew her mother could not make things right either. Her mother's tearful words of consolation were as empty as air, as empty as the space her father had fallen into. And Madeline knew then that the death would never be over. Nothing would ever be over. Her father would never come home.

Delia encouraged Madeline to eat, but she could not. Carlotta ran a bath for her. She lay in the tub, staring up at the ceiling and trying not to think about the terrifying depth of the sinkhole, the girl's voice echoing up from the dark, the rising of the bats, the clarity of her father's face in the beam of the flashlight when he told her to drive the truck forward. "Madeline, honey? Do this."

She put on jeans and a bathrobe and walked, in the dark, down the street to the corner and back, trying to comprehend a world without her father in it.

She was unwilling to get into bed, and awoke in the night on the sofa. Shelly held her and talked to her. All night she stroked her and whispered to her, and soaked her hair with tears. Madeline wanted to blame her for what had happened—for her choice to go to Alpine. But she needed her too much, and she feared with a sickening horror and self-loathing that the fault was her own. Her father had gone to Devil's Sinkhole only because she was being childish. He had wanted to distract her from the jealousy over Carlotta, which now, obliterated by her pain, she remembered like a distant nightmare, pitiful and obsolete.

"I drove the truck the rope was tied to," she whimpered to her mother. "It was me. Daddy told me to do it."

"Nothing is your fault, honey. Nothing is your fault. You were both helping the girl."

And while Shelly held on to Madeline as tightly as she could, she felt in some way she had lost her, because Madeline was alone in a world with her memory of what had happened, and Shelly could not be there with her. She struggled to put together a puzzle of blank pieces, and even when she had them in place, they couldn't create a picture. She had never seen Devil's Sinkhole, had not laid eyes on the girl Dan had saved. She had not been there when he fell. She was blind to his death. She was even blind to her own terrible, dark grief, because all she could see in front of her, stretching out for years and years, was Madeline's.

# 30

# THE LOST YEARS

Part of the trouble for Shelly was simply knowing the sinkhole was there, a few hours' drive away, a dark presence day and night. She could not picture it and could not bring herself to think of ever going to look at it, but the fact of its existence haunted her. She felt unbearable guilt for what had happened there. Her decisions that had set Dan on that road to Devil's Sinkhole had begun so far back in life that she was unable even to trace them. Her nights were filled with frightful dreams of Dan falling into the dark abyss.

He was lauded as a hero on the nightly news and in newspaper headlines—HEROIC GEOLOGIST DIES IN RESCUE—his death a shocking blow to his parents and coworkers and everyone who knew him. Shelly held his funeral service outdoors because she knew he would want that. His friends gave moving tributes, speaking of his kindness and professionalism and extraordinary character, and one of them played guitar solos of "Everything I Own" and "Let it Be." It was a crowded ceremony, under a stand of oak trees, on a scalding day.

In the months afterward, Shelly devoted herself to Madeline and immersed herself in the office work at Helping Hand. She knew all of the children there, saw them as they came and went from their daily activities, helped to arrange for their appointments and schooling and foster care. She talked with the young therapist, named Molly, about the children's sad wounds and enormous needs. She asked Molly for advice about how to help Madeline cope with the trauma of what she had witnessed at the sinkhole, but everything Molly suggested involved Madeline talking about that night, which Madeline wasn't doing.

And still the sinkhole was there, always a dark place on a dark horizon. Shelly wondered if going to see it in daylight would make it seem less frightening and diminish it in her consciousness. A friend she had known since Madeline's preschool days offered to take her there. "We could face it together," she said. But Shelly felt as if the place had power enough to draw her down into an invisible, expansive depth from which she would never come back.

On long weekends during the year and for whole weeks during the summer, she and Madeline escaped to Alpine. Madeline's envy of Carlotta had been swept away in the flood of grief, and she regarded Jack and Delia and Carlotta, and the fresh air of west Texas—so familiar since childhood—as a refuge.

Shelly talked with Jack and Delia about Dan's belief that it was time to tell the girls the truth about Carlotta, but in the end the three of them agreed that Madeline's world had been shattered enough as it was. Madeline needed her mother. She also needed the Stones, who along with her mother and grandparents were the closest she had to family. Learning the truth now could only strain the relationships she was dependent on.

During the visits to Alpine, Madeline sat in the porch swing, lost in romance novels, and Shelly took walks on the country roads with Delia.

The hardest part of the trips was passing the highway exit to Rocksprings, coming and going. Madeline became quiet, and fidgeted with the radio in search of a clear station, or sat stone-faced in the passenger seat as if she didn't see the highway sign. Shelly was always grateful to leave that stretch of road behind.

When Madeline turned eighteen in 1993, she decided she wanted to be an elementary school teacher, and she earned a college scholarship from Trinity University in San Antonio. Shelly helped her settle into the dormitory, then drove back home to Austin and started her life alone in the house that she had bought with Dan. For two years, she had battled Madeline's sorrow with a fierce maternal instinct that had helped her to survive her own. Now she sank deeply and suddenly into a frightening depression. Most of her friends and the people she worked with at Helping Hand were married, and Shelly was single now, a forty-six-year-old widow. She started drinking at home in the evenings, first wine and then vodka. She knew exactly what was happening: Her daughter was gone, and she felt melancholy and hollow, with too much time on her hands, having to face the fact that she was alone.

One rainy day she came home from work and found in the dripping mailbox a padded envelope from Texas Parks and Wildlife that contained a small but weighty object. She took the envelope inside and opened it, making a little cry of alarm when the pocketknife that she and Madeline had given to Dan one Christmas, engraved with his initials, dropped onto the kitchen table.

She let it lie there, reluctant even to touch it. He had always carried it with him, and she had wondered why it was not among the items returned to her by the sheriff, or by Jack when he had retrieved the Bronco from Rocksprings to sell it for her. She had wondered where the pocketknife was.

In the envelope, she found a letter from a biologist explaining, with condolences, that he had discovered the knife in the sinkhole when he was studying water bugs in the underground lakes. "It was on the rocks in the scree pile. I thought from the initials that it might have belonged to your husband."

She poured herself a drink and sat at the table, looking at the object, so familiar, and still not touching it. She could remember so many times that Dan had pulled it out of his pocket and used it to sharpen pencils, or peel oranges, or shave down kindling to roast hot dogs on campouts. Uncertain whether to ever show it to Madeline, she finally picked it up and held it next to her heart.

When Madeline was home for spring break, Shelly decided to tell her about the knife. "Something came in the mail, honey," she said, choosing her words carefully one day at noon when they were in the kitchen. Madeline had slept late and was just now drinking her coffee. "I haven't known whether to show it to you or not. It's your father's pocketknife. Someone found it in—"

The blood drained from Madeline's face even before Shelly finished the sentence, her skin becoming as pale as chalk against her dark hair. She reached for the kitchen counter to get her balance. Tears welled in her eyes, and she said in a breathless whisper, "I don't want it. I don't want to see it. Mom?" she cried, her voice childlike. "He used it to cut the girl free from the rope. So she would be safe. So he would be the one to fall. I saw it drop out of his hands after he did that."

It was the most she had ever spoken about that moment that Dan fell, and Shelly could see in her face how clear the memory was. Her father had dropped through the same vacant air as the knife, and onto the same rocks.

After that, the knife began to seem like a curse in the house. It had been such a part of Dan's daily life, and Shelly couldn't bring herself to throw it away. But how could she keep it when it could create such unbearable visions for Madeline? She could hide it away at her parents' house, or Aileen's—but what for? What future use could she possibly have for such a memento?

When Madeline was back at school, Shelly drove to the cemetery and buried the pocketknife next to Dan's grave.

On a Saturday afternoon shortly before Thanksgiving, Shelly came home and discovered an old green Plymouth parked in front of her house, a girl holding a baby leaning against the hood. The day was chilly and overcast, but the girl wore a pale summer dress that was modest and out-of-date as well as out of season. Her dishwater hair, thin and flyaway, danced around her face in the autumn breeze. She looked as if she was dressed for a country church service, except that her low-heeled white pumps were scuffed. Shelly assumed she'd had car trouble and was waiting here for someone to help her, and yet there was something about the girl that made her appear misplaced rather than merely inconvenienced. "Can I help you with anything?" Shelly asked her.

The girl approached from across the lawn, carrying the sleeping baby. "Are you Mrs. Hadley?" she asked with a timid and slow Texas lilt.

"Yes."

"I don't know how to say this, exactly, ma'am, but my name's Amanda Shultz, and I'm the girl your husband saved." Her face was thin and plain-featured, her expression somber. "I found your address in the phone book. I hope it's okay I came."

Shelly set her purse in the grass as if she was going to sit down with it, and then she picked it up again, unprepared for this moment. The girl had stepped out of a nightmare and here she was, holding a baby, wearing a summer dress and white pump shoes.

"I was afraid if I called ahead, you'd tell me not to come. I . . . just needed to talk to you for a minute. If that's okay."

"Would you . . . want to come inside?"

"Either way's all right with me. I can stay out here." She shifted the sleeping baby in her arms.

"No. There's no need for that. Come inside."

The girl followed her in, and Shelly showed her into the living room. "I'll bring you something to drink."

"Thank you, ma'am. But I don't need something."

"It will just take me a minute." She went to the kitchen and tried to wait for her heart to stop pounding so painfully. She wanted a drink. Instead she filled a glass with ice and poured some tea from a pitcher in the refrigerator, then took it out and set it on the coffee table in front of the girl.

The baby was making snuffling noises, and the girl took a pacifier out of her purse and touched it to his lips until he latched onto it and drifted back to sleep.

"What's your baby's name?" Shelly asked, seating herself across from her.

"Cody. After his daddy."

"He looks like a sweet baby."

The girl took a sip of the tea. "That's good tea. I guess you're wondering why I came here. It's not something big I have to say, just that I . . . Well, I wanted to say . . . I guess I just needed to say how sorry I am for what I did and that I wished it hadn't of happened. It was my fault. Me and my boyfriend's. He's my husband now, but then . . . we was just stupid in what we did. It seemed like a pure lark at the time—like we'd go down there and look around and come up and go and tell our friends about it. And then it was all so terrible, and your husband . . . well, what happened, you know. I can't forgive myself. That's what I came to say. I wouldn't dare ask you to forgive me when I can't forgive myself, but I wanted you to know how sorry I am. How bad I feel." She had started to cry.

Shelly wanted to offer some reassurance, but she was too staggered by the girl's presence to know how to respond. "Amanda—"

"I don't expect it to mean much to you, but I had to say it. My mama said not to come here, that you had enough to worry about without me showing up to remind you about it, but I just can't feel right until I've said it all. I wanted to say I'm religious now. I'm married to Cody, who was with me that night when it happened, and we go to church and Sunday school, and people is always telling me I owe my life to God because I came so close to dying. And I say it wasn't God that showed up that night; it was Mr. Hadley. And they say maybe God sent him. But I say why would He do that? It was me that went down there. Why should Mr. Hadley pay for what I did? I can't make it right in my mind. I'm not that good of a person that ought to get saved by some-body. And I can't quit thinking about why he did such a thing, and if

I can ever be worth it. My mama says maybe my baby'll turn out worth it, so I'm hoping that might be the case, but it makes no sense to me why Mr. Hadley would have to die. If God had of wanted a hand in it, He might of just changed my mind about going down there in the first place." She frowned, and settled her gaze on the far wall. "Is that over there a picture of Mr. Hadley?"

Shelly turned and looked at the picture.

"And is that your daughter with him?"

"Yes, it is."

"She was a help to me too." She gave a forlorn smile. "What can I do to make it okay in my mind? Do you know what I mean?" Tears ran down her face, and she rubbed them off with her palm. "I guess you can't know, really."

"Maybe I can. A long time ago, there was someone who saved my life. Actually, there were two people who saved me, and one of them was badly hurt when he did it."

"Did he die?"

"No."

"And did you make your peace with it in your mind?"

"I guess the only way I made peace with it was to quit trying to make sense of it."

Amanda laid the sleeping baby down on the sofa next to her. She tucked the knitted blanket around him and took another sip of the tea. "Can I look at the picture?" she asked.

"Sure. And he's in some of the others, too."

The girl got up, leaning forward for a second with a small catch in her side as she rose.

"Are you all right?" Shelly asked her.

"Oh yes, I am. It's only when I just stand up that I feel it. Two of my ribs were broke from the rope and it's just scar tissue inside. I can't hardly catch my breath sometimes." She straightened slowly, then crossed the room and studied the wall of family pictures, moving from one to the next. Shelly got up and stood beside her and told her about them.

"He looks different from what I thought. The picture they had in the newspaper looked different. Your daughter has got pretty eyes. Where is she at right now?"

"She's away at college."

"Really? I might go to college myself when my baby gets old

enough. There's one in Uvalde. It's more than a hour away from where I live, but if I had time I could do it."

The baby woke, kicking his blanket off, and Amanda went to the sofa and gathered him up. "I guess I better go on before he starts squalling," she said, working the pacifier into his mouth again. "He can be awfully loud when he's hungry. I got a bottle out in the car."

"I'm afraid you didn't find what you came here to find," Shelly said regretfully.

"Well. But I'm real glad I came." She stroked her baby's face. "It means a lot to me that you were so nice. And I liked seeing the pictures. Now I can know what he looked like."

When Amanda had gone, Shelly stood in front of the wall of photographs, looking at the faces, feeling that she could make no sense of her past, and that she had failed to face the present. Finally she got from a cabinet the video Dan had made of Madeline's play at the Paramount, which Jack had returned with the other items he had retrieved from the Bronco. Drinking a shot of vodka, she sat in front of the television and tried to lose herself in the scene before her, as if she could concentrate hard enough to turn the screen into a stage, and go back in time, and be there in the theater with Dan. She pictured Madeline scrambling with props behind the curtain, and tried to envision the people around her, the ornate domed ceiling, the red-cushioned seats. She closed her eyes. The sound quality of the video was indistinct, the music raspy and distant and most of the lines too faint to make out, but she heard clearly Dan's gentle laughter at the parts meant to be funny, his whispered conversation with the people seated beside him. "No, she's not in it; she's in charge of the props," he said, and "Is this thing making an irritating noise?" She wept, and curled herself on the couch and kept her eyes closed, and listened to the entire play so she could hear every word that Dan had spoken and be with him on that last day of his life in the only way she now could.

A week later she went to the library and combed through books on Texas caves and geology until she found pictures of Devil's Sinkhole, and forced herself to look at them.

The first was an aerial view taken from high above. The sinkhole was pitch-black and oblong in shape, surrounded by stubby vegetation that appeared to be cedars. The caption said the depth exceeded three hundred feet.

On the opposite page was a diagram of the interior—a huge, vacuous pit. Below ground level, the space bulged out like a fishbowl. From the bottom rose a mountainous dome of rubble, which the caption explained was created thousands of years ago when the surface had caved in. Tracing a line down from the rim, Shelly could see that Dan had fallen onto the side of this subterranean mountain. "The scree pile," it was labeled. The caption said the rubble was covered in slippery bat guano. Creatures found nowhere else on the earth—shrimplike crustaceans and carnivorous beetles—dwelled in the underground lakes that flowed at the base of this pile of broken rocks. A tiny standing figure was drawn to scale on the peak, indicating the frightening size of the cavern.

The final picture was taken from deep within the cave, the camera angled upward toward the circle of sunlight. Shelly thought of Dan as he had fallen, lying there at the bottom. She studied the slant of the sunlight, wondering from which direction the moon had been shining that night, and if it had cast its light over his body.

The next weekend she got in her car and started for Rocksprings. She drove through Johnson City, Fredericksburg, and Kerrville, holding the wheel tightly and watching the monotonous road under the gray sky. At the Rocksprings exit she pulled to the side and stood in the dry grass, holding her coat closed against the wind. She tried to summon her courage, but the longer she stood and contemplated going to the sinkhole, the more terrified she became. For an hour she paced in the winter grass, got in and out of the car, braced herself against the wind, pictured the place. She imagined herself driving up to it and getting out of the car and walking up close to the edge, looking down into the dark.

When she finally drove on, it wasn't in the direction of Rocksprings and the sinkhole, or back to Austin. She drove straight on to Alpine, where she arrived stunned by her own weakness and the severity of her fear.

Bundled in a blanket, standing out on the porch that night while Jack smoked a cigarette, she told him about the girl's visit and about the pictures she had seen of Devil's Sinkhole, and talked about how lost she felt, and how she couldn't stop blaming herself or get rid of the notion that her insistence on being involved with Carlotta had led to Dan's death. "I can spin it out in my mind any way I want to," she said. "But it all lands in the same place."

He listened without saying much, leaning back against the porch rail and blowing the smoke into the cold air.

After a long pause, she said, "And I think I'm drinking too much."

He drew on his cigarette. "I know it."

"I want to stop it."

"Okay. Then stop it."

"It's not so easy. Look at you, with your Camels."

"True enough. I'll make you a deal. If you'll keep it to one drink a day, I'll keep it to one cigarette."

"You can do that?"

"I'm already down to two."

"So if, sometime, I have more than one drink, I'm supposed to call you and tell on myself?"

"That's right."

"And you trust me to do that?"

He drew the smoke in, and blew it out slowly over his shoulder. "I've known you a long time, Shelly. I'd trust you to do anything you said you would."

# 31

# ANDY

Madeline earned her master's from Trinity at an accelerated pace and returned to Austin to share an apartment with a friend and find a job. Having already completed her student teaching and certification, she was hired as a substitute and then as a full-time fourth-grade teacher at Casis Elementary in the west Austin Tarrytown neighborhood. Her friends told her she would never have a social life if she spent all day with fourth graders, but on a trip to a luggage store in the mall she struck up a conversation with a customer named Andy Fischer—a handsome man three years older than she was, with dark hair and olive skin. Before long, they were dating.

Andy had recently divorced. "It was my fault," he told Shelly when Madeline brought him home to meet her. "I had an affair. The only thing I can say in my defense is that I was twenty-three years old and didn't know any better." He was only twenty-six now.

He talked about his job. "Corporations hire me to help with the climate in their workplaces. Basically it's all about team building and conflict resolution. It involves a lot of brainstorming and strategic planning so employees can learn how to feel safe with each other and work productively together. And of course there's a lot of travel."

Shelly didn't know what to make of him. He was disarmingly forthcoming, self-deprecating in some ways but almost a braggart in others, with what seemed to be a high level of confidence combined with a delight in owning up to his failures. "What a dope I was," he said about his infidelity. "Let's hope it was just immaturity and not some deficiency in my character." To Shelly, it seemed as if his confidence masked some kind of vulnerability, and yet he was personable and likable, and obviously smitten with Madeline.

"What do you think?" Madeline asked her later.

"Well, what do you think?" Shelly asked.

Madeline was defensive. "Obviously I like him, or I wouldn't have brought him over here. What do you not like about him?"

"There's nothing I don't like. I can't say I have a real sense of him yet, but—"

"Really? He's like an open book. It's a good thing, Mom. He's enthusiastic, and that's refreshing. It's a nice balance for me since I get too cautious. Did I tell you he speaks four languages?"

"Four?"

"Fluently. Including some Hebrew—his mother's Jewish. He grew up in Louisville. His dad was an alcoholic and his older brother killed himself when Andy was just thirteen. I think it's pretty miraculous how he's managed to keep his faith in human nature. Frankly, the fact that he's so optimistic makes me happy. It makes me feel safe."

When he was traveling for work, he often called Madeline at night, and she fell asleep with the phone pressed to her ear. He told her about his first marriage and the guilt he felt for betraying his wife with another woman. Madeline told him about her father's death and her mother's loneliness. She talked about a dark desire to visit Devil's Sinkhole, and a feeling that she had abandoned her father to that place. The sheriff had taken her away from there, and she had not seen her father's body when it was lifted out. She had not seen it at all. Sometimes she dreamed that it was still down there. Her last memory of him was his face in the yellow beam of the flashlight, and how he had said, "Nice and slow," and "Madeline, honey? Do this," and how she had pressed her foot on the gas to keep from stalling, shifted from neutral to second, felt the truck lurch.

She married Andy not long after she met him, choosing a honeymoon in Hawaii over a wedding reception in Austin. They spent what little savings they had on a down payment for a small, picturesque two-story house in the quiet old Clarksville neighborhood, not far from Shelly.

The next year, in 1999, they had a baby whom they named Nicholas. When the baby was two, a distraught Andy came home from work one night and confessed to Madeline that he had slept with another woman. He swore he didn't love the woman—he had known her, he said, for years. He didn't know why he had done this and swore he would never do it again. It was clear he believed this promise.

Disillusioned and devastated, Madeline lifted Nicholas out of his bed, put him into the car, and drove to her mother's house, where Shelly put the child into her own bed and sang him back to sleep.

Madeline cried in Shelly's arms as she had not done since her father's death, her tear-stained face pressed into Shelly's neck, her thin shoulders heaving with uncontrolled sobs.

Shelly had difficulty controlling her sense of outrage. Andy had coaxed Madeline out of her grief over Dan's death, and now had shattered that sense of safety that he had given her. The fact that he had done it so carelessly and casually only increased the cruelty. It wasn't lost on Shelly how hypocritical she would be to condemn Andy outright, given the fact of her own past, but she also knew there was a difference between deep love and mere dalliance.

When Andy showed up at Shelly's house after midnight, Madeline opened the door and told him to leave. A few minutes later, the phone rang. "Don't answer it," Madeline told Shelly. It rang and rang, until Madeline unplugged it from the wall.

Andy was at the door again at seven o'clock in the morning, unshowered and unshaven. Shelly was in the kitchen with Nicholas; she answered his knock. "I know Madeline won't see me," he said. "I want to talk to you. I can't believe I've done this to her. I love her, Shelly. And I can't believe I've hurt her this way. Can I please just come in?"

"Andy, she's still asleep—"

"Daddy!" Nicholas yelled with delight, and went running to him.

"Hey, little buddy!" Andy scooped him up in his arms.

"I been sleeping with Nana!" Nicholas told him excitedly. "Having breakfast with Nana!"

"Wonderful!" Andy exclaimed, tousling his hair. To Shelly he said, "I hope you believe me, that I'd never intentionally do anything to—"

"I believe that, Andy. But this isn't the time to talk."

Andy agreed that it wasn't. He took Nicholas on a walk so he wouldn't be too upset that his father was leaving so soon. When he brought Nicholas back, he told Shelly he would go home and wait for Madeline to call. "Tell her I'll do anything."

Madeline came out of her bedroom after he left, and settled Nicholas in front of the television. "What should I do?" she asked Shelly. "He loves me—I know that. But I'm starting to see that it comes from weakness, not strength."

"I wish I knew what to tell you, honey, but it's not clear to me what you should do. I think he's sincere, and I think that matters. And I know he loves you. I understand that you don't trust him now. Whatever you do, think of Nicholas."

They talked throughout the day. Shelly took Nicholas to Baskin-Robbins for ice cream. In the evening, Madeline loaded him into the car and drove back home to Andy.

# 32

# THE LOVELY PAINTING

Shortly before Christmas two years later, on a freezing night in South Texas, Aileen died at the Beeville hospital where Shelly had given birth to Carlotta almost thirty-four years before. Shelly had been sitting beside the hospital bed all day, but she had gone to Aileen's house to sleep, when Aileen began to go very quickly in the middle of the night. Shelly responded to the call from the nurses' station and arrived at the hospital in time to hold the thin little hand and watch the pulse become faint and then still.

Aileen's body was rolled away on a stretcher at daylight, and Shelly returned to the house. She called her mother, who was home nursing her father through a bout of the flu, and broke the news that Aileen had died. Afterward she called Madeline, whose voice grew tight with sadness; she had loved Aileen since she was a small girl hiding out with the portrait she had thought was a fairy godmother in the quiet closet of Aileen's house. She said Andy could take care of Nicholas and that she would start for Beeville right away.

Shelly sat in Aileen's kitchen and looked at the place on the floor where she had stood squeezing oranges onto a juicer when her water had broken and formed a pale pink puddle. She didn't know what to think about Aileen's life or about the sorrows around which she and Aileen had built their love for each other.

After a while she got up and went into Raymond's bedroom, where she had slept those months when she was pregnant with Carlotta. Entering the room, she felt the winter chill. The vents had been shut off. No one came here anymore. For all these years, Aileen had waited for Raymond to return, hoping the phone would ring and his voice would be at the other end, or that he would appear at the door. Her fear that he was dead had evolved, mysteriously, over the decades, into belief that he was alive somewhere, even while the chance of that had faded.

Shelly knew that the portrait was stored in the closet of this sad room. She had not thought of it very often in recent years. She opened the closet door and looked at the outdated clothes—the shirts and slacks, a striped cardigan sweater, moth-eaten. The shoes. Three belts hanging from a nail stuck in the wall. It would all have to be packed up and disposed of, but she felt sad and false-hearted at the thought of tossing out Aileen's son's clothes.

She would need boxes. She had seen a few in the garage, but they were dirty, littered with mouse droppings. Not that it mattered: No one would want the clothes after she boxed them up. She wouldn't be carting them off to Goodwill, she would be hauling them out to the trash.

Turning away from the closet, she saw her face in the mirror over the dresser and stopped. She had been so young when she used to look in this mirror. Now, in 2003, she was fifty-six years old, and her hair was turning gray. She remembered how she had stood on the bed to look at her pregnant belly, and how she had dreamed that Wyatt would walk through the door, and how she had wished he would send her a letter, even though he didn't know where she was. He had remained as missing as Aileen's son, in spite of all her pitiful, young desire. The two of them had been ghost men haunting this room.

The mirror was unframed, oval, beveled around the edges. It hung from a chain. The silvering was spotted, giving a speckled look to Shelly's image. Her jawline had a small sag instead of the plump youthfulness of pregnancy that she had seen in this mirror before. As a girl, she had been pretty enough, and as a woman, the same. She didn't expect to be beautiful. Still, the picture of that youthful girl lingered disconcertingly in the mirror.

She sighed—resigned, exhausted. The bed had sheets and a blanket, but she didn't want to lie down where she had slept when she was pregnant with Carlotta. And she didn't want to crawl back into Aileen's bed where she had been sleeping hours ago when the nurse had called. With Aileen gone forever, Shelly felt like an interloper instead of a guest in the house.

In the kitchen she found plastic lawn bags under the sink and went to Aileen's room to start the tedious job of packing things up. Aileen had told her to take whatever she wanted, to throw things away and give whatever was left to the Methodist church. But when Shelly opened Aileen's closet and looked at the stale clothes and the shelf stuffed with socks and panty hose, she didn't feel up to the effort. She walked back down to Raymond's bedroom and started dragging shirts off the hangers and stuffing shoes into the bags.

There was nothing here to decide about; everything would go. Handling the baseball glove, she wondered briefly if she might give it to Nicholas as a family keepsake. But it was old and cracked, too large for his hand, and she was disturbed by the thought of her grandchild wearing a glove that belonged to a boy who had gone to war and never come home.

When she had finished emptying out the closet, nothing was left except the portrait. She leaned it against the wall, facing her, its frame thick with dust. Roaches had nibbled away at the green paint in one of the upper corners.

She eyed herself in the portrait. "You again." The painting made her think of all the mistakes she had made—how she had slept with somebody else's husband. How she had stood in front of him naked, posing for this portrait, and allowed herself to believe they would not make love. How young and utterly foolish she had been.

At times, she wondered how she would feel if she ever saw him or heard his voice again. Her life had seemed pointless when he had left her—she had needed him that much. But now she had lost her husband, and for Wyatt to drop his voice into that void would be like dropping a penny into the ocean. It wouldn't create so much as a ripple.

She knew all she deserved to know about his present life. He taught in the Art Department at Columbia now. He and Elaine lived in New York but had a summer house in Bar Harbor, Maine, where Wyatt painted. His paintings sold for tens of thousands, sometimes more. He had come to Austin a few times when his work was shown at galleries, but Shelly had never attended the showings. She wasn't so much afraid of what would happen if she saw him, as what wouldn't. A lackadaisical meeting would steal whatever legitimacy there had been to that relationship in the first place. The only excuse they had for what they had done was the strength of their need for each other. It had seemed too powerful to resist. And now—if they resisted it? If it proved to be meager and dismissable, what could she feel about their actions back then?

There was no reason to daydream about something so obviously over. Those memories were still painful. But looking at the painting now, she half-wished she could scrape away the blue smock and let the truth show, reveal her difficult secrets to anyone who wanted to see, and be done with hiding them. That might provide a kind of consolation. She could haul the painting out of the closet and take it home and hang it up on her wall.

Of course, she wouldn't. And there remained the question of what to do with it. She didn't want to linger here in this room, feeling nostalgic over a painting, when Aileen had just died. So she pried open a lawn bag for trash and stuffed the painting in it. She hoped for a sense of finality when she cinched the bag, but instead she felt desolate and depressed, as if she had thrown herself away. Leaning the bag upright against the wall beside other bags filled with shoes and clothing, she sat on the floor and looked at the lumpy outcasts.

Madeline arrived late in the afternoon and found her mother cleaning out drawers in Aileen's bathroom, making piles of bobby pins and old curlers and tossing rancid creams and outdated medications into the trash can. She made a pot of coffee, brought two mugs into the bathroom, and sat with her mother, sorting through cans of hair spray and bottles of old perfumes. Shadows of naked tree limbs rocked back and forth across the windowsill while the women worked, and a feeling of quiet companionship settled.

"There's one thing in the house I'd like to have if you don't want it," Madeline told her mother. "The painting of you that's in the closet."

Shelly resisted the impulse to turn and look at her daughter. She continued to peer into the medicine cabinet. "The painting?"

"The portrait. In the closet in the other bedroom. I used to go in there and look at it when I was little."

Shelly searched an aspirin bottle for an expiration date. "I didn't know you did that. I didn't know you ever saw that painting. What would you do with it if you had it?"

"Hang it on our stair landing. I'm assuming you don't want it, since it's always been in the closet. But if you do . . ."

"I don't."

Madeline went down the hall to look at the painting, but she found the closet empty. "Where is it?" she called, then noticed the bulky shape in one of the lawn bags. The room was cold, and she shivered. Her mother had come to the doorway.

"What were you going to do with it?" Madeline asked her, untying the bag and pulling the painting out. "Tell me you weren't going to throw it away."

"I didn't realize anyone wanted it."

"Why would no one want it?" She settled it back against the wall. "It's beautiful. Just look at it. Who was the artist? It sort of reminds me of Wyatt Calvert's paintings, except they're not usually of people."

"Someone in the UT Art Department painted it. A student."

"Male, or female?"

"He was a guy."

"You posed for it?"

"Only for photographs. I think he painted from those."

"Who was he? It's not signed."

"He was a graduate student."

"Well it's really a lovely painting. I love the smocking on the blouse. The way he did the fabric. It's pretty fantastic."

"You're welcome to it," Shelly said.

"Were you really going to throw it away?"

"I suppose I was."

"Then I just rescued you."

The rest of the day, they worked on funeral arrangements and sorted through Aileen's knickknacks and linens and dishes. At dusk they sat in the kitchen among the boxes and empty drawers and had a glass of wine.

"To our dear, sweet, old Aileen," Madeline said, sadly, raising her glass.

Shelly thought of the painting propped in the empty room at the end of the hall. It would hang in open view on Madeline's stairwell, after all the years in hiding. She was glad it had been saved, glad Madeline was here in the house with her. Looking at her daughter across the table, she raised her glass and felt as if the upward movement lifted something else away from her—a lingering sorrow and sense of loss. For a moment she was at peace here in Aileen's disassembled kitchen, forgetting that her secrets were buried no deeper than a few thin layers of paint.

# 33

# UNPREDICTABLE SHIFTS

Carlotta first met Martin Tipton, shaggy-haired and wet, when he ducked into her rock shop to escape an autumn rainstorm, having ridden his mountain bike up from Terlingua to distribute a stack of newsletters about UFOs to storefronts around town. He stood at the counter of her shop, telling her of a UFO he had seen hovering over the haunted old Chisos Mine when he was seven years old. Soft-spoken for a proselytizer and younger than Carlotta, he had beautiful green eyes. He took an immediate interest in the rocks on display and bought a cheap necklace and a bundle of incense for his girlfriend, and a crystal for himself. The crystal was for good luck in the Terlingua chili cook-off.

He waited out the rainstorm in Carlotta's shop and then went back to Terlingua, where he won the chili cook-off and broke up with his girlfriend.

Then he returned to see Carlotta. Eventually he became her boyfriend and hauled his trailer up to Alpine. Rock and gem sales had moved to the Internet now, and the shop was producing less income than in earlier years. Carlotta had begun to wonder if she would need to close it and find a more reliable way to support herself. To pay the mortgage, she rented out the space where she had lived on the second floor, and moved in with Martin.

He made beautiful love with her: his eyes, luminous as green chrysolite, looked as if they could see right into her soul, even if they never quite managed to do it. Every morning, she stepped from the trailer to see the sun rise over the vast plateau. Martin puttered around in Alpine and grew his marijuana plants in painted Mexican pots and spent a lot of Carlotta's money on his UFO newsletter.

In the summer of 2006, after living with Martin for a year, Carlotta discovered she was accidentally pregnant. She hadn't prepared for this but was immediately and profoundly joyful. She was thirty-six years old and had always believed she would marry and have a family at some unspecified time—always far in the future. She had dreamed of meeting her husband in the same vague, mystical ways that she had dreamed of meeting her biological parents. It would happen. It would be beautiful.

The thought that he would be Martin Tipton had never entered her mind. She had no intention of spending her life with him. When she told him about the pregnancy, he agreed with her that he wasn't ready to marry or have a family. They both thought he should take his trailer and move on.

Carlotta decided to wait and tell her parents about the baby when she had figured out where she would live. She knew her mother had always wanted her to have children someday, but having a baby without a husband, and without a home, and with a business that was barely making a profit, would require logistical planning.

On a sonogram Carlotta saw the tiny, tiny heart in the little body no bigger than a knuckle, pumping and pumping. It was pumping too slowly the next time she saw it. The doctor told her to go home and put her feet up—to get in bed and rest. She understood he believed the baby would die. She got in bed, her energy sapped by the struggle for life inside her. When she returned to see the doctor the following afternoon, he searched for a heartbeat, moving the probe to detect a flicker. But it was simply gone. He wanted to schedule a D & C to scrape her uterus clean, but Carlotta decided to let her body take care of the baby its own way. She drove to her shop with a heavy heart, sat at the counter, and strung glass beads.

Ten days later, in her shop, the painful cramping started. She suffered the pain until the placenta came out, the spongy mass spreading inside the toilet like flattened pizza dough. She fished it out and searched for anything that might resemble a fetus, but she could find no solid matter.

A few days afterward, the tiny thing came out when Carlotta was taking a shower. She felt it slip from her body without any pain at all, and she held it in her hand. It was a small little thing, two inches long, curved like a nautilus shell. It had miniature buds of arms and legs, and she thought she could see the eyes. The umbilical cord looked like a piece of string and fell apart in her fingers. She wrapped the fetus in silk, then drove to a place where she had camped sometimes with Martin, on a creek called Peña Blanca, and buried it there among sparse grasses with a view of the creek and the mountains.

She had so wanted the baby. She could almost feel its presence inside her still. She would never forget how quickly life could slip from her body without any detectable leave-taking. A heart could just stop beating. Life was as tenuous as a flickering flame.

Within a week, Martin had moved away. Since the upper floor of the shop was rented out, Carlotta had no place to go. Too disheartened to tell her parents about the baby, she moved into her old room in her parents' house and tried to take stock of how a woman who loved adventures, and loved water and scuba diving and seeing the world, would come to be hiding out in her childhood bedroom in the dry middle of Texas. The experience of losing a baby made her think of her biological mother. Why had she given Carlotta up? Where was she now, and what would she think of her long-lost daughter? For the first time in years, Carlotta thought perhaps she wanted to find out who this woman was. She had dug up enough rocks to know about sediment. It wasn't as solid as it seemed. It had cracks. Porous areas. You could drop a fossil and break it. There would be ways to find her mother.

At her shop during the day she began to browse websites for information on how to search for adoption records. She looked at links to support groups and "search angels"—experts in facilitating reunions. She also searched for information about artificial insemination. She had seen the umbilical cord, no wider around than a string, disintegrate in her fingers, and had placed her tiny baby in its little dirt hole, and she felt disconnected, more incomplete than ever. Her life was like a dot-to-dot picture without the one or the two. She decided to talk to Shelly and see what she advised, or what she remembered or knew.

Loading a box of merchandise to sell on the Drag, she called Shelly to say she was coming to Austin, locked her shop and drove east with her truck windows down, the radio playing country songs until reception became erratic and the lyrics surged and faded with the rise and fall of the hills. During bursts of clarity and static, she reflected on the mysterious origins of her life. She parked on the side of the road and sat in the bed of her truck to watch the sun behind her hover above the road, as fierce and red as the round carnelian stones that were said to encourage boldness and initiative and self-realization and to banish sorrow. She continued eastward, watching the moon climb in the pale sky and spread its calming light on the flattening landscape.

It was after midnight when she arrived at Shelly's house. Shelly had gone to sleep but had left a welcome note in the kitchen. "Make yourself at home. If you have to set up your table early and I'm not up, help yourself to coffee and I'll pick up some rolls from the bakery and meet you at your table for breakfast. I don't need to be at the office until eleven."

Early the next morning, in a coin toss, Carlotta secured a prime spot in the market on the dead-end stub of the pavement at Twenty-third and the Drag. She set up her table, laying out jewelry and baskets of beaded scarves. The Drag had changed since she had been in school here: an Urban Outfitters now inhabited part of one block, and down the street the old café called Quackenbush's had picked up and left. The market area looked brighter and cleaner than when Carlotta had last seen it, but the tables were sparse this morning, the artisans fanning themselves, their merchandise a hodgepodge of copper rings and leather bracelets, homemade soaps that sweated in the heat, belts and bags hanging from clothes rods. Everything was limp and hot already; only a few of the tables were shaded with canopies. The landmark murals on brick walls flanking the market were a dizzying sea of Texas wildflowers and cityscapes and cartoon figures of Texas heroes and celebrities. In the largest mural, Stephen F. Austin cradled an armload of armadillos.

The UT tower had found its way into all three of the murals, and the actual tower loomed over the red roofs of the campus across the street. The blazing sun was too hot already—the sun no longer the symbol of inspiration that it had seemed the evening before. Now it sapped at her resolve. The only people out at this time of the morning, with students away for the summer, were panhandlers dozing in storefronts along the sidewalk with their dogs.

# 34

# CARLOTTA'S QUESTION

At nine in the morning, Shelly parked at the block where many years ago she had seen Wyatt standing on the sidewalk, holding Nate, while Elaine got something out of the car. The scene had deeply troubled her at the time, but this morning she thought of it only briefly, wondering what Nate Calvert would be like now, at nearly forty years old. With a bag of pastries under her arm and cups of coffee in her hands, she hurried down the sidewalk until she spotted Carlotta, who stood in the bright sunshine at her table at the edge of the market area, demonstrating for a customer the different ways to tie a scarf.

Shelly stopped and watched her for a moment. Carlotta's hair was gathered in a fat braid that glittered orange-red in the sun; her summer dress was loose and had a pattern of airy flowers. She was delightful to look at—tall, like Wyatt, and freckled like Shelly's mother. She turned and saw Shelly and greeted her with open arms. "You're here!"

"I am!" She held up the bag. "They were out of the rolls you like, so I got an assortment."

When the customer had purchased a scarf and moved on, Shelly borrowed a chair from an old man fanning himself over a table of tooled wallets and pulled it to Carlotta's table. She sat beside Carlotta and was taking the pastries out of the bag when Carlotta said, "I need to talk to you about something important. First of all, I broke up with Martin."

"Oh, honey. I'm sorry."

"I was pregnant."

Shelly tried not to let surprise register on her face. She took Carlotta's hand and gave it a comforting squeeze.

"I miscarried. Three weeks ago. I hadn't told Mom and Dad I was pregnant—I was going to do that whenever I could figure out where to live and how to support the baby. But then it just seemed wrong to tell them after it was over. There was no point in it." She shooed a fly from a cinnamon roll. "I wasn't very far along when it happened. That was a blessing. And I've moved back in with Mom and Dad until I can figure out what to do now. It's possible I'll close the shop, as much as I don't want to. It's just not making enough. I could close it and sell things online, but I'm not sure I want to do that. It's the shop I like— not just the merchandise. Anyway, I'll find a job if I close it—I can worry about that when the time comes."

A teenage boy with lip rings and wooden plugs in his earlobes paused to look at a basket of crocheted bracelets. When he was gone, Carlotta said, "Also—and this might be a surprise to you—I was thinking about trying to find my other . . . my . . . biological parents."

Shelly's face flushed hot with a prickling sensation. "Oh?"

"There are a lot of sites on the Internet where you can sign up and they'll help you with the search."

"Have you talked to your mom and dad?" Her eyes swept over the bright murals with their caricatures of Michael Dell holding his computer and Matthew McConaughey running naked with bongo drums, the cartoon towers hulking in the background.

"I just—talking to them about this is going to be hard, you know?" Carlotta paused. "What are your thoughts on artificial insemination?"

"You mean . . . for yourself?"

"I've been reading about it. Mom wouldn't like the idea because the Church doesn't approve, but I'm thirty-six, and I don't know when I'll get married. And if I were to consider artificial insemination, there are things it would be good to know about my biological parents. I can tell by the look on your face you think it's a bad idea."

Across the street, the tower bells had started to chime. They were halfway into chiming eleven o'clock before Shelly was even aware of them, as if the sound had been muted and suddenly turned on. "Would the medical information be all that useful?"

"It depends on what it is. But that isn't the main reason I want to do this—to look for them. I want to know who they are. Nobody ever knows where their life is going, but most people know where it started. For me that's a big blank. So I want to know who my mother is. Short of that, I just want to try to find out. I don't even have to meet her. Even just searching will feel like something. There are a lot of things I wasn't so puzzled about until the miscarriage. You know?" She frowned. Her voice fell. "How could someone give a baby away?"

For a confused moment, Shelly wanted to tell her—to cross the aching distance and connect with the daughter she might have kept and explain all the things she had held back all these years. She wanted to pretend there were no obstacles and to ignore everything but this secret bond and this beautiful girl who had been hers for a few brief days in the hospital.

"When I was miscarrying," Carlotta said, "when the baby was dying, I felt what was happening. I felt it was dying. I was that connected. And maybe my mother felt that way about me. Maybe she's hoping I'll look for her."

"But you need to involve your parents." This seemed like the most imperative thing to Shelly at the moment: She and Carlotta could not be in this alone, no matter how tempting or possible.

"I don't see why they should be involved, and I can't talk to Mom as easily as I talk to you. She and I are close, but we're different. And I'm not sure how she would feel about my looking. We never talk about the adoption. I don't see what's to be gained by talking to her about this. She and Dad have given me everything and been wonderful, so why should I give the impression I feel like something's missing, when nothing is?"

"Because it would be a breach of their trust not to talk to them first."

Carlotta shook her head. "When I was little, I used to think I was special because they chose me. Of course, the reality is that I was only available because someone else wanted to give me away. But Mom and Dad always made me feel like the only thing that mattered was how much they loved me. I'm not going to make them feel like that wasn't enough."

"But it's too big of a thing to do on your own, Carlotta."

"Which is why I'm coming to you. I'm hoping you'll help me with it."

"I'm glad you've come to me, but it's important for you to talk to your parents about it first."

Carlotta rearranged the jewelry spread on the table before her, matching the colors of stones, placing the blues with the greens, the oranges with the reds.

"I'm sorry if my reaction isn't what you expected," Shelly told her.

"But I feel strongly about this. How long are you going to be in Austin?"

"I'm actually driving back tonight. The real reason I came was just to talk to you."

"Could we continue the conversation in Alpine? I have to work this afternoon, but I can drive to Alpine tomorrow for the weekend. And then if you decide to talk to your parents—"

"I'm not going to talk to my parents. I appreciate that you're honest, and I trust your opinion—I always have. But it's *my* past, not yours, that I'm looking into; it's mine. You're welcome to come to Alpine and we can talk all you want, but you're not going to be able to convince me to talk to my parents about all these complicated feelings I have about the adoption."

Carlotta was done with the conversation. For a moment or two, they made small talk to try to dispel a feeling of strain between them. Shelly's response had made Carlotta feel lonely, and empty, and indecisive about the dream that she had set her heart on. And she didn't think Shelly was right. She wouldn't consider taking the chance of hurting her parents, especially when her biological mother—if she were ever even to find her—might not want to be in her life. What would be the benefit?

Finally Shelly gave up trying to act as if there were nothing wrong. She patted Carlotta's hand, said, "I love you; we'll talk through this. I'll come to Alpine." Then she walked to her car, feeling as if her life had just turned over. She pulled her phone from her purse and called Jack's mobile. In front of a shop window with a display of retro clothing—go-go boots and top hats—she closed herself in her car.

"Jack? It's me." She was betraying Carlotta, but didn't feel she had much choice.

"Oh, hey."

"Are you where you can talk?"

"In the bookstore. Front Street."

"Can you go outside?"

"Is Carlotta all right?"

"She's fine. I just need you to be where you can talk."

"One second." A moment later, he said, "Okay. I'm outside. What's up?"

"Carlotta just told me she wants to look for her biological parents." She waited for his response. "Jack? Are you there?"

"I'm here."

"I tried to convince her she needed to talk to you and Delia about it, but she's worried you'll take it wrong and think she feels there's something missing in your relationship. I told her I'm coming to Alpine tomorrow. I hope that's all right. I think she needs to be told the truth."

He was quiet, and then he said, "Of course she does."

"Will you talk to Delia and see if she thinks it's right for me to be there? That should be her call."

"She's going to want you to be here."

Shelly stared at the go-go boots in the window and opened the car door for air. A run-down Mazda covered in bumper stickers pulled into the place beside her, so she closed the door to make room.

"And I'll call Wyatt," Jack said.

Wyatt. How strange—she had not even thought of Wyatt.

# 35

# THE SALT AIR

He had just flown back to Bar Harbor after six months in New York and was hauling bags of art supplies out of the trunk of a taxi, wondering if he should have stayed in New York with Elaine. She had remained behind to attend a party for colleagues in the public-relations firm where she was now working, and she would close the apartment in a few days and follow him here to Bar Harbor.

He had offered to stay and wait for her, but she had wanted the time alone to reflect on things. It was nine months since she had been diagnosed with endometrial cancer, and she was finished with treatment now—the surgery and grueling weeks of radiation and chemotherapy, in which her optimism had been squarely tested. There was still a chance of recurrence, and having endured the treatment, she was now trying to come to terms with the uncertainties in her future.

It was surprising to Wyatt how deeply he feared losing her. Given the length of time he and Elaine had been at odds with each other—the number of times he had actually wished himself to be free of her—he would have expected less torment. They had battled each other so habitually over such a range of marital issues that when Elaine had told him of her diagnosis, and they had found themselves suddenly on the same side, facing the chance that she would die, the sincerity of his affection for her, and the fierceness of her need for him, had come as a shock to them both. He realized he had grown to love Elaine's willfulness, which in the early years had dogged and irritated and frustrated him. Her tenacity and emotional fortitude had appeared in stark relief against her physical weakness during those months of treatment. As a man devoted to seeing things exactly as they were, for whom background and juxtaposition were basic and studied and valued, Wyatt was surprised to see his wife in this new light. She had assumed a stunning radiance in his eyes. He realized how different his marriage might have been had he not continued to be in love with another woman for all these forty years. The marriage had had its problems from the beginning, but his infidelity with Shelly—in spite of the fact that Elaine never knew about it—had depleted its reserves.

He now believed his marriage to Elaine held everything that mattered—even, strangely, his love for Shelly, simply because it had weathered it. The two children he had raised with Elaine—Nate and Maggie—had grown into kind, generous people with children of their own. They had been a constant presence during their mother's illness.

What if, back then, he had left their mother for Shelly? Maggie would not have been born. Nate might have carried some lasting grudge against his father, or a loss of respect—neither of which Wyatt could have tolerated. After all, it wasn't as if Wyatt had any reason to leave their mother other than to chase after his own satisfaction— which it now turned out he had caught up with anyway. He loved Shelly all the more because she had told him to stay with Elaine when he had been too weak to make that decision on his own.

Slamming the trunk, he paid and thanked the driver and turned to look at the farmhouse he and Elaine had renovated many years ago. Down a path streaked with sunlight he could see the barn he had remodeled into a studio, nestled under towering birch and aspens, the tall plate-glass windows reflecting a jewel-like green from the branches.

He looked forward to settling his things into the house and then unpacking his porcelain tray and sable brushes and jars of pigment in the studio. Then he would go for a run and maybe call up friends to meet for dinner.

Breathing the salt air, he looked at the blue sky overhead and wondered if it might be time to retire from teaching at Columbia and move here permanently. Years ago he had craved his time in New York; it had motivated and energized him. But the older he got, the less patience he had with the frantic art scene. He no longer knew, or cared very much, where he ranked as an artist—whether in any objective sense his paintings were better or worse than the others on walls in the upscale galleries. But he liked his work and got paid large sums for even the simple paintings, and because he had made a name for himself he could paint what he pleased. If Elaine were not so attached to

New York, he would move back here year-round and paint in restful surroundings. He loved the weather. The sea.

With a suitcase and a box of books, he made his way into the house and saw in a glance that the renter had left the place a mess, the pillows bunched on one end of the sofa and the rug scooted to one side, giving the room an off-kilter appearance. The air conditioning had been turned off, so the place smelled musty. He went through the rooms, inspecting the disarray, which he decided wasn't extreme enough to complain about, only thoughtless enough to convince him he was past the stage in life when he should be renting the house. He wouldn't have done it this time if the renter had not been a friend of Nate's and been going through a divorce and needed a six-month lease with a landlord who would cut the rate to a nominal fee.

In the kitchen, he inspected the cabinets and drawers. Nothing was where he and Elaine had left it. Boxes of unfamiliar cookies and cereals in the pantry were open and half-consumed. "What is all this stuff?" he grumbled. Discovering a box of granola, he ate a handful and looked for milk in the refrigerator but found only various manhandled chunks of gourmet cheeses sloppily wrapped in plastic.

Maybe he was too set in his ways. When he was young on bright summer days like this, he had felt exhilarated. With Shelly Maddox, he had felt euphoric for two whole years. Even with all his guilt about the love affair and all the devastation that he must have known was coming, he had been happy. Where did that elated feeling go? His self-respect, as glad as he was to have it now, had cost him some of his passion.

But these thoughts were certainly not improving his mood. And he had left his pigments out in the driveway. He should get them into the studio before they overheated. Hopefully, Nate's friend had not been mucking around in the studio after Wyatt had asked him not to go in there.

He was walking out of the house to check on the studio when he heard his cell phone ringing from inside one of the bags piled in the driveway. By the time he got to it, it had quit ringing, but Jack's number was on the screen, so he called him back.

"You called?"

"Yeah. What are you doing?"

"I'm in Bar Harbor. I just got in from New York."

"Is Elaine with you?"

"No, she's coming next week. Why?"

"Is she doing all right?"

"Better every day. What's up?"

"Carlotta wants to look for her biological parents."

Jack had spoken so calmly that for a second Wyatt suspected he hadn't heard right. "What?"

"Just what I said."

"Since when?"

"She told Shelly this an hour ago."

"She told Shelly?"

"That's right. She went to Austin and told Shelly she was planning to look for her biological parents."

"And how did Shelly respond?"

"She told her to talk to Delia and me. Which Carlotta apparently doesn't intend to do."

For a moment Wyatt scrambled in his mind for a way to handle this so that Elaine would not find out about it. He had been lying to her by omission for so many years. But none of his thoughts would settle into anything that made any sense. "How is Delia taking this?"

"She's worried how Carlotta will take it. Also I think she wishes Carlotta had come to her instead of going to Shelly—I think that hurt her a little, though she'll never admit it."

"God, this is unexpected," Wyatt said. "I guess I thought . . . I don't know what I thought."

"You thought we had dodged this bullet."

"I guess I did. Though I knew we probably couldn't forever. What happens now?" What would he tell Nate and Maggie? What would they think of him once they knew? Nate was older than Carlotta, and Maggie younger. It would be obvious when their father had been unfaithful to their mother.

"We'll have to come clean," Jack said. "Delia and Shelly agree. But how we do it partly depends on how you intend to handle this with Elaine."

"After what she's been through this year, I can't imagine how she would take this."

He waited for Jack to comment, but Jack said nothing.

"But it doesn't make sense to let Carlotta go looking, when we know what she'd find." He pictured Elaine, home in New York, gaunt and sickly after the treatments, her hair just growing back in. He tried to think if there was a way to protect her. Of course there would be no way to protect her forever. It would only be another injustice to her if Carlotta were told this crucial information while she herself was kept in the dark.

"Carlotta's driving back here to Alpine tonight, and Shelly's coming tomorrow," Jack said.

"Well, I need to be there," Wyatt told him.

"No you don't."

"Of course I do."

"Look, Delia and I have already talked about this, and even aside from Elaine's situation, we don't think it's a good idea for you to come. It's too many of us for Carlotta to cope with all at once. She's already brought Shelly into it, so that's a given. But there's no reason you need to be here. You can come later."

"I don't think you can possibly know what Carlotta will want or not want. If I'm there, and she doesn't want to talk with me, I'll leave and come back when she does. If you think it's a problem to have me there at the house, I'll stay in the cabin or get a room. But in case Carlotta has something to talk to me about, I'm going to be there. She's your daughter—I know that. But this is not the time for me to act like she's not mine too."

He looked at the house, and at the studio under the tall trees at the end of the path, and at the clear sky. The air smelled salty. The silence on the phone was so profound he could hear waves in the distance washing against the shore.

"And what about Elaine?" Jack finally asked.

"I'll tell her. Everything. When this is over."

# 36

# A MERE MISHAP

Until the moment happened, Madeline's day was like any other summer day. She took Nicholas to soccer practice, dropped him off afterward for a playdate, went by the school to tutor one of her former students who would be starting middle school in the fall but had scored in the range of a third grader on his math aptitude test. She picked Nicholas up and made dinner for Andy, who was on his way home from an out-of-town convention. Her mother called to say she was going to Alpine and would leave town early in the morning and return in a couple of days.

Andy was home in time for dinner. Nicholas, who was seven, wolfed it down, wearing his ball cap. Two of the girls in soccer had been mean to everybody, he said.

It was ten o'clock at night when Madeline glanced up from washing the dishes, saw Andy in the kitchen doorway, and knew at once that something was about to go horribly wrong. She didn't know why she felt this sense of doom. Andy had been home since dinner and not spoken of any problem. Nothing had seemed wrong. The phone had not rung. Nicholas was asleep upstairs. The dog had not barked. What was the telltale sign? Only Andy's hesitation? It was more than a pause. It was the advent of disaster. Madeline battled a childish urge to put her hands over her ears.

"Honey," he said. "There's something I need to tell you."

She put the plate in the sink and reached for a phantom towel to dry her hands, her fingers groping along the slippery countertop. "Something you did?"

His nod was barely perceptible. "Honey, I'm so sorry. I am so incredibly sorry. But really, I swear, it's not as bad as you're thinking."

"At the convention?"

He nodded.

"Do I know her?"

"No. Let me explain what—"

"No."

"I can't explain?"

She shook her head. "No."

"Madeline, it did not go that far."

"Please don't tell me what that means."

"I screwed up, but I didn't—"

"Stop, Andy." The water dripped in the sink; she turned it off. She left her hand on the knob. "Don't even dream of trying to clear your conscience by telling me the details."

"But it wasn't exactly . . . what you're thinking."

"Did it happen at the hotel?"

"Yes."

"Then it's what I'm thinking."

"Honey—"

"Go away."

"It meant *nothing* to me," he said. "I just felt . . . I don't know . . . sorry for her. Her fiancé broke things off, and she was telling me about it, and we went to her room, and . . ."

"One thing led to another," Madeline said.

"But it was nothing like last time. Not even close. Not even *close*."

She thought of Nicholas asleep in his bed upstairs and how this moment was now a part of her life. Nothing would ever erase this moment.

"I am so, so sorry," Andy was saying. "I am so incredibly sorry."

She went upstairs and locked herself in the bathroom, where she sat on the floor and stared bleary-eyed down at the tiles. She stayed there most of the night. Andy spoke to her through the door, but she didn't bother to answer. He told her more than she wanted to know. She felt as trapped in the marriage as she was trapped in the bathroom. How could she stay with this man?

But the thing at stake if she stayed with him would be only her happiness. If she left him, it would be her son's.

Andy was a decent person and a loving father. He was a lousy husband.

In the morning when he went downstairs, Madeline came out of the bathroom and sat on the bed, stunned with grief and exhaustion. She listened over the stair rail to Andy talking with Nicholas about breakfast. Nicholas asked for peanut butter and jelly. She heard them letting the dog out. After a while, Andy returned to the bedroom. When Madeline didn't speak to him, he retreated into the shower. She sat on the bed, listening to the steady hiss of the water. At last she pulled a suitcase out of the closet and started packing her clothes, then went into the bathroom. "I'm taking Nicholas and going to Alpine to be with my mother."

He pushed the shower door partly open, his face flushed from the heat and his head topped with a cap of suds like whipped cream on a sundae. Water ran into his eyes. He squinted at Madeline through the spray. "No, no, no, no . . ." The water pounded his shoulder. "Don't go. I *swear* it won't happen again."

She opened a drawer beside the sink and packed mascara and dental floss and toothpaste.

"I didn't *want* it to happen. It just *happened*, honey. Please. I can't believe you're doing this. When are you coming back? You are— coming back?"

"I'll stay as long as my mom's there. After that, I don't know."

He wiped the water out of his eyes. "Are you going to tell her what happened?"

"I haven't decided that." Of course she would tell her mother.

"Tell her I'm sorry," he said.

She lugged the suitcase down the stairs and found Nicholas in the family room, curled up with his dog on the sofa in front of the television. "Guess what," she said, trying to sound excited. "We're going to Alpine."

He was wearing only his underwear, and his eyes were fixed on SpongeBob.

"Your dad can't go, but you and I can," she told him.

"Dad isn't going?"

"He has to stay here."

"Is Nana going?"

"Yes. She's probably on her way now. Let's hurry, so we can catch up."

"Can't I go to soccer?"

"I thought you didn't like soccer."

"Can Ranger come?"

"Ranger needs to stay with your dad."

The dog was glowering at her. He was a short-haired black-and-white terrier, a troublemaker who murdered squirrels in the yard, dragging them down from the bird feeder by their dangling tails.

"Why can't we bring him?" Nicholas begged, turning his back on SpongeBob.

"Coyotes—remember?" she told him.

"But I'll make him stay in the house. Jack and Delia don't care. I'll take him out on a leash."

"Not this time. Pack your things. We have to leave as soon as we can."

Wheeling her suitcase through the kitchen and out to the dank garage, feeling the muggy, claustrophobic heat settle oppressively on her, she hoisted the suitcase into her old Suburban.

"Are you packing, Nicholas?" she called from the foot of the stairs when she was back in the house.

"Can you help me, Mom?"

"Just bring your things down!"

"Come help me!"

Climbing the stairs, she passed her mother's portrait on the landing and wished she still believed in fairy godmothers.

Nicholas stood in front of his chest of drawers, dunking a flowered coffee mug into the habitat of his pet tadpole and sloppily pouring the murky contents into an oversized Baggie.

"What are you doing?" she asked him.

"Getting Jerry ready to go."

"Oh, baby, we can't take Jerry. It's too much sloshing around. It wouldn't be good for him, honey. You're dribbling water into that drawer."

"But Mom!" he pleaded. He was small for a seven-year-old. His hair was an indiscriminate brown and badly in need of a cut. "I'm getting some of the water out. So it's not going to slosh. I'll hold him in my lap the whole way." Dipping the mug again, he dumped the water into the Baggie.

The habitat was U-shaped—a flimsy plastic receptacle too large for a skinny, fidgety boy to hold in his lap for six hours.

"I'm not worried about the car," Madeline told him. "All the activity wouldn't be good for Jerry. He'll be happier here with your father."

"Tadpoles don't get carsick. He doesn't want to stay here alone in this room. *Please*, Mom? Can't I take him?"

He was already having to leave his dog. And his father.

*"Please?"*

"Oh, sweetie." She looked at him. "Okay. Leave the rest of the water in there with him. And pack his food."

"Thanks, Mom!"

"Get your toothbrush. Pants, T-shirts, socks, shoes. Boots if they still fit. Choose a couple of books." She took the Baggie of fouled water into the hall bathroom and dumped the contents into the toilet.

Ranger had started to bark in Nicholas's room. Madeline heard him jumping against the blinds, clanging them into the window, and went back in and scolded him until he quieted to a growl, his forepaws on the sill and his ears rigidly forward. A squirrel on a branch outside was flicking its tail at him.

She had gone back down to the kitchen, when she heard a thumping sound. She stepped into the hall and saw Nicholas, now wearing his jeans and ball cap, descending the stairs with a stack of video games and equipment, the wires trailing a clump of plugs, his Magic 8 Ball perched on top of the load and secured under his chin.

"You don't need video games in Alpine," she told him.

He halted, looking at her, his body hunched over the mound of equipment. "Dad said I could take them."

"It isn't your dad's decision. Your dad isn't going with us."

"But Mom! There's nothing to *do* there!"

"There's plenty to do. Up. Up."

Turning, he made his way grudgingly up the stairs, Madeline following and holding the cords to keep him from tripping. But when he was in his room, he looked so disappointed. None of it mattered anyway. "Oh, go ahead and take it," she said.

"Thank you, Mom!"

She lifted the pile of equipment, stacking the cords and hand control and video games on top. "I'll put these in the car. Get the basketball out of your closet and get packed. I'll come back up for Jerry."

"Can't I carry him down? I've done it before."

He set his basketball at the top of the stairs and started down behind her. She turned to see him carrying the habitat studiously, his eyes fixed on the tadpole rocking in the shallow water.

Suddenly, from behind him, Ranger charged at the basketball.

Madeline yelled a warning. The ball smacked into the back of Nicholas's knees and knocked him forward into her. She stumbled downward toward the landing, thrusting her arm out to brace herself against the wall. Her palm smacked hard into her mother's portrait, and she lost her balance, tumbling to her knees, the equipment crashing before her, the basketball bouncing beside her. The portrait landed on top of her, and she threw it off with her elbow. Nicholas lay sprawled on the landing beside her. Ranger barked excitedly at the top of the stairs before starting down, moving slowly, his ears upright and cocked forward, his eyes on the little tadpole flopping on the floor amid a scatter of plastic rocks and faux plant life and a yellow plastic bridge.

"No, Ranger!" Madeline shouted. "Bad dog! Sit!"

The dog was mesmerized by the flaps of legs and the slimy flanks paddling uselessly on the floorboards. Diving across the wreckage, Madeline cupped her hand over the tadpole as Ranger suddenly catapulted from the steps above. She scuffled with the dog, pushing him away, the tadpole wriggling in her hand, and then she got to her feet and tried to help Nicholas up.

"My knee is broken," he said, but she could see that he wasn't hurt. He sat on a step to roll up his jeans and look at his knee.

The tadpole squirmed unpleasantly in Madeline's hand. Hurrying down to the kitchen, she filled a glass from the water filter and dropped the tadpole in it, then dried herself with a dish towel and returned to the stairs, where Andy was tending to Nicholas.

"I have a headache," Nicholas said. "The ball hit me in the head."

"It hit you in the legs," Madeline told him. "You're okay."

"Is Jerry okay?" Nicholas asked.

"He's fine. He's in a glass in the kitchen."

"Was Ranger going to eat him?"

"Yes, honey. He was."

Andy went for a mop while Madeline lifted the portrait from the debris and propped it against the wall. Ranger sniffed it and tried to lick it, but she pushed him away. The paint was wet, and Madeline dabbed at it with the end of her T-shirt, glad that it was painted on a hard surface rather than on canvas. Canvas would have torn. The frame had come apart at one corner, but at a glance, the paint still looked okay.

"What exactly happened?" Andy asked her, returning with a sponge mop and a wad of paper towels.

"We fell," Madeline told him.

"It was my fault," Nicholas said ruefully.

"It was Ranger's fault," Madeline said, watching the dog lap at the puddle of water.

Andy mopped while Madeline turned the portrait right side up and looked at it more closely. She noticed a scatter of cracks in the paint that had not been there before. The blouse her mother wore appeared in danger of chipping. Andy gave her some paper towels, and she carefully patted the paint while he and Nicholas loitered about on the stairs, watching her despondently.

"I wish you could go to Alpine with us," Nicholas told his father sadly. "How come you're not going?"

It crossed Madeline's mind that Andy might actually tell him. "Your father needs to work," she said.

The three of them went into the kitchen, where Nicholas stood at the counter, peering at Jerry in a glass. Andy searched the drawer for wire and picture hooks.

"I'm taking the painting to Alpine," Madeline told him. "To get the frame fixed so the board won't warp. There's that frame shop next to Carlotta's store."

"If you take it, your mother will see it and she might be upset."

"My mother was going to throw it away."

"I can take it to a frame shop here," he offered.

But she wouldn't allow him to handle another piece of her life. She didn't want him anywhere near the portrait.

Her momentum was starting to flag. She looked at her husband in front of the junk drawer, his hair uncombed and jutting out on one side of his head. He was better-looking than she was.

"Nicholas," she said wearily. "Let's get you packed."

# 37

# THE ROAD WEST

It was after noon by the time they finally left Austin under a merciless sun. Madeline squinted through her sunglasses. Nicholas stopped fretting over his sloshing tadpole, but became restless from sitting so long, and announced he felt sick to his stomach.

"We'll stop for a Coke," she told him. They stopped more than once. They parked at a roadside rest stop to settle his stomach.

Madeline was miserable, ruminating about Andy and the woman. Nearing the Highway 41 exit to Rocksprings, she felt the familiar panic, as if she might take the turn, and go to Devil's Sinkhole, and despite herself see that terrible place again.

That night was still horribly with her—the blackness of a hole much deeper than God should have made it, the girl dangling from the rope, the boy with bleeding hands, screaming and waving his arms in the blazing headlights, and her father in a makeshift harness going down . . . and down.

Tears rolled out from under her sunglasses, and she shifted the rearview mirror so Nicholas wouldn't notice. She wished she could somehow launch herself beyond that exit without having to look at it. But when she had reached it and sped past, she only felt worse, as if every important part of her life were slipping away—as if she couldn't hold on to a single thing in the world. Her father was gone, and now she was leaving Andy. She wanted to get to her mother, suddenly afraid that her mother, too, would be lost to her.

Why, always, this sense of impending loss? She had felt it so far back she couldn't remember when it began, and in her heart she sensed that it wasn't because of losing her father, but somehow because of her mother. And yet it didn't add up. Her mother had never left her.

There had been the normal squabbles between a mother and daughter, and the burning, buried resentment Madeline felt for Carlotta, but her mother was devoted. There had never been a threat of losing her.

Whenever she glanced to the right she saw her mother's likeness wedged in the passenger side of the front seat. The slant of the green eyes in the painting looked unnatural from this angle.

She decided that Andy was right: Her mother shouldn't see the painting in this condition. She should stash it in the cabin at the Stones' house and leave it there until she could take it to be fixed. She ought to have left it with Andy. How pathetic that she was dragging her blighted fairy godmother along in this flight from her husband.

She kept glancing at the face. The shy pinkish smile was pretty and the eyelashes were so distinctly painted they looked soft to the touch. The intricate smocking of the blue blouse had a sweet, sixties, peasant look, and the perfect shading of the skin, as smooth as a china teacup, was precisely like a youthful complexion. All of it together gave the painting a sensuality that Madeline found vaguely disturbing in a portrait of her mother—however young her mother had been at the time. She still longed for it to be a magical being with a benign and ethereal influence over her life, not a flesh and blood girl who years later would become her mother.

And in the rich brightness of the afternoon sun, she noticed something unusual. Where the light in the painting fell, with the ribbon, over her mother's shoulders and rested in the folds of the blouse, the paint had been applied differently. It was flat in most places, but the hair and the blouse were painted more thickly, with obvious brushstrokes.

"I'm thirsty," Nicholas said from the backseat.

"We'll be somewhere in ten minutes."

In Sonora she stopped at a Chevron station and filled the car at the pump. Nicholas topped a Sprite with a squirt of Big Red at the soda bar. Heading back to the interstate, Madeline looked in the rearview mirror and saw him staring pensively out the window, his arm protectively looped around the tadpole habitat.

"What's on your mind, pumpkin?" she asked him.

He shrugged, slurped from his straw, and stared out of the window, his cap low on his head and his cheeks flushed from the warmth of the low sun. Her heart sank at the thought that his happiness and security were in jeopardy because of what Andy had done.

Past Ozona, along the parched, monotonous miles, tall white wind turbines turned slowly in the cloudless sky. Madeline pulled to the shoulder so Nicholas could pee beside the road. When he was out of the car, she called her mother's cell phone.

"Hey Mom. Are you in Alpine?"

"Hi sweetie. Yes, I'm here."

"Well, this is going to surprise you, but I'm on my way too."

"On your way . . . *here*?"

"Yes."

"To Alpine?"

"Yes."

There was a conspicuous hesitation.

"I'll explain when I get there," Madeline said.

"Honey, I'm not sure this is a good idea."

"For me to be there? Why? Jack and Delia won't mind."

"They have another guest coming. And Carlotta's moved back home. So . . ."

"There's still enough bedrooms," Madeline said.

"Yes. But . . . since they didn't expect you—"

"Mom, they're like family. It's a standing invitation. They've always made that clear."

"I know, honey, but—"

"Carlotta's moved home?"

"She broke up with Martin."

"You sound like you don't want me there."

"Of course I do. It's . . . Is there a problem—a reason you wanted to come?"

Nicholas was getting back in the car, slamming the door.

"Yes, there is," Madeline told her mother.

"Can you tell me what it is?"

"No."

"You mean you can't talk?"

"That's right."

"Because Andy and Nicholas are with you?"

"Just the latter."

"Just Nicholas?"

"Yes."

"And not Andy?"

"No."

"So . . . is there a problem with Andy?"

"That's right."

"Oh, my dear. Well . . . What . . . what can I do?"

"I'll talk to you when I get there. If for some reason there's a problem with my being there, I'll leave." She felt rebuffed and peeved. "Though I can't imagine what that would be." She signaled to pull back onto the road and turned to look at her son. "Are you buckled?" she asked him.

"Yep."

"We're almost to Fort Stockton," she told her mother.

"That close?"

Madeline lowered her voice. "You sound like you don't want me to be there. I don't get this. This is weird. I have a big problem, and you sound like you don't want me." She pulled onto the road and accelerated.

"Of course I want you. Oh honey. Is it . . . the same problem with Andy?"

"Essentially the same. I'll talk to you there."

"Sweet lamb."

From the backseat, Nicholas said, "Are you talking to Nana? Can I talk to her?" Madeline handed the phone over the seat. "I brought my tadpole," Nicholas said excitedly, and then his tone dropped. "Ranger isn't with us, though. Dad's not coming either."

On the last leg of the journey, the sun grew red and large and sat belligerently on the horizon for a long time before sinking onto the road before them and slipping out of sight. Madeline strained her eyes against it, shading them with her hand, and felt an escalating irritation toward the sun until it vanished much too quickly, drawing away its rosy glow and leaving her speeding along an empty road in a vast grayness and feeling a fretful urgency to be somewhere.

# 38

# AN UNINVITED GUEST

When Madeline finally turned the car onto the dirt road that led to Jack and Delia's house, the moon—a quarter full—was rising over Lizard Mountain. The house was silhouetted against the craggy shape in the falling darkness, a few of the windows lighted, and Madeline drove toward it before veering onto the narrower road that led to the cabin a hundred yards away. The road curved around three stunted, graceless willows, and the cabin appeared in a stand of junipers, glowing white in the headlights. Two wicker chairs with cushions faced each other on the porch, and the sight of them there, unoccupied, gave Madeline an empty feeling.

"Why are we at the cabin?" Nicholas asked from the backseat.

"Stay in the car," she told him. "I'm just taking the painting in." She turned the motor off but left the headlights on, their piercing gleam shining back at her from the windowpanes. The sharp smell of the junipers greeted her when she opened the car door. A breeze lifted her spirits slightly. Knowing the cabin was usually left unlocked, she carried the painting to the porch and flipped the lights on as she entered.

The interior was a single room with a closet and a small bathroom, a bed with a quilt, an armchair with flowered upholstery. A coffeepot sat on a table near the bathroom door. Madeline took the painting to the closet and propped it upright under a trio of coat hangers.

"Can I drive?" Nicholas asked when she returned to the car. "Jack let me do it before. And he let me drive the golf cart."

She remembered how her father used to let her drive on these roads when she was Nicholas's age. A heartsick longing overwhelmed her. "Not in the dark," she told Nicholas. "You can unbuckle the seat belt and put your head out the window."

The brushy limbs of junipers scratched noisily over the hood as she put the car in reverse. "Sweetie, don't mention that we stopped at the cabin; I don't want Nana to know the painting got wet. I don't want her to worry about it. We'll take it into town tomorrow to get the frame fixed."

"What did you say?" Nicholas shouted against the rush of air in his face as she drove toward the house.

She repeated herself more loudly.

"What?"

"Get your head back in," she told him, and when he was looking at her through the sheen of the rearview mirror, she said, "Pretend we didn't stop at the cabin." He had taken his cap off, and his windblown hair stood straight up. "Don't say anything about the painting. It isn't a lie."

"Got it," he answered, shoving his head out the window again.

She parked the Suburban next to her mother's car in the gravel driveway. Nicholas shouted out of the window as his grandmother and Jack came out of the house to greet them. "Hi Jack! Hi Nana! I brought Jerry!"

Madeline knew how bad she must look as she got out of the car. Her hair was oily and pulled back in a clip, strands of it hanging in her face. Her mother hugged her tightly, but seemed somehow nervous.

Nicholas scrambled into his grandmother's arms. He dragged the flimsy tadpole container out of the backseat, setting it on the ground in the glow of the buzzing pole light and squatting beside it while Jack peered in and admired Jerry.

"Sorry to show up unexpected," Madeline said. "I hope it's not a problem."

"It's never a problem to have you here," Jack told her. "Delia just put clean sheets on the bed; your room's all ready." He pulled her bags from the back. "Well, Nick, my boy. Shall we take your tadpole in?"

Madeline lingered with her mother. "I don't want to go into it now, but basically Andy's done it again." She shrugged her purse strap over her shoulder. "He felt sorry for some woman who had broken up with her boyfriend. I don't know how far it went."

Shelly put her arm around her, but Madeline said, "Don't do

that—don't act like anything's wrong. I don't want Nicholas to know."

They went inside to the kitchen, where Delia offered Madeline a glass of wine and asked about the drive. She mentioned how dry everything was—how long since it had rained. "Carlotta's doing some things at the shop, but she'll be home shortly. I think your mother told you she's moved home."

"Yes, and Mom said you have a guest coming?"

Delia started unloading the dishwasher. "Jack's cousin, Wyatt."

"Wyatt Calvert?" Madeline looked at her mother. "You didn't tell me it was Wyatt Calvert."

"I only found out he was coming after I got here. I'm sorry, I should have mentioned it right off."

"I can't believe you didn't." She stared at her mother, amazed. "When I called from the road, you just said someone was coming and didn't tell me who it was."

"I was going to tell you when you got here."

"But until I called, you didn't know I was coming. And you know I've always wanted to meet him."

"It was a surprise to everyone that Wyatt was coming," Delia said. "And we love having you here, Madeline, and you're absolutely right that you should meet Wyatt—I imagine he wants to meet you, too. And he's going to stay out in the cabin, so there's no problem with rooms. He often stays there. If you want to get settled, Jack's upstairs with Nicholas."

Madeline and Shelly went upstairs and found Nicholas with Jack in the sitting room. They had opened the sofa bed and cleared a space on the bookshelf for the tadpole, and Jack was helping Nicholas set up his video games.

Madeline went into the bathroom to set her toiletries on a shelf, and Shelly followed her in. It was a small bathroom, the footed tub rigged with a showerhead and enclosed by a curtain. The floor had rotted in patches where people had dripped water when getting out of the tub.

"Can you tell me anything more?" Shelly asked her.

"I honestly can't. He 'almost' slept with her—that's all I know. But I don't want to talk about it right now. And I can't believe Wyatt Calvert is going to be here and you were trying to tell me not to come. Not that I'm in the mood to meet anybody. When does he get here?"

Her mother sat down on the edge of the tub. "Very late tonight, I think. He's flying into Midland, and then it's a three-hour drive. We won't see him tonight—he'll go to the cabin."

"Won't it be strange to meet him, after so long?"

"A little strange, yes. It's been a lot of years." She brushed the question aside. "Sweetie, how do you know what Andy did?"

"Because he told me. He couldn't wait to get it off his chest. In fact, I couldn't get him to shut up."

"Oh, honey. Just like last time."

"Except last time was the first time, and this is the second. There's a big difference. At least I know there weren't any times in between, since he can't keep a secret any better than that." She plopped down on the floor under the towel rack. "I couldn't make him stop talking to me through the bathroom door last night. Telling me all kinds of things I didn't want to hear about. He said the woman reminded him of me. That was supposed to soften the blow. Can you believe he would say that? If it wasn't for Nicholas, I'd divorce him. I swear. Even if I didn't want to. But Nicholas ought to be able to get up every morning in the same house with his dad, you know? He's a good dad. That's the insidious thing." Nicholas was calling from the sitting room. "Will you go see what he wants, Mom?"

"Of course."

When Shelly left, Jack appeared at the open door and saw Madeline sitting under the towel rack. "Are you all right?"

"Yeah."

"You're sure?"

"I'm sure. But can I ask you something personal?"

"I might not answer it, but you're welcome to ask."

"Have you ever had an affair?"

"No."

"That's good."

"Nor would I tell you if I had."

"Oh. Would you tell Delia?"

"Probably not."

The dreaded tears had started again; they distorted her vision. Jack, in his plaid shirt, looked blurry. "Could you hand me some toilet paper?" Madeline asked.

He pulled some from the roll and gave it to her, and she wiped her eyes, bits of the paper clinging to her lashes. She saw white clumps when she blinked. She wanted to wash them off but was too reluctant to move from the floor. It was the first place she had found any comfort all day.

"Is this about Andy?"

She nodded, and blew her nose into the soggy paper. "I don't want Nicholas to pick up on the tension. That's one reason I came here. To get him out of the house."

"He's playing Tarzan. He's fine."

She tossed the damp ball of toilet paper into the wastebasket and got up and rinsed her face in the sink. Her eyes were red, her nose puffy. "I have to get hold of myself. Will you ask Mom to take care of Nicholas so I can go for a walk?"

Heading downstairs and out the front door, she started in the direction of the cabin amid the raucous screeching of insects. She had been making this trek from the house to the cabin since she was a toddler in diapers and the cabin was a shack where Carlotta kept her rock collection on plywood shelves.

She turned the light on and sat in the chair for a minute, then got up and slid the portrait out of the closet to see how the paint was holding up.

Not very well, she surmised in a glance. Some of it seemed to be missing. She leaned the painting against the wall and squatted down for a better perspective. A chip of blue, the size of a pea, had fallen away from the smocking across the bust, revealing a speck of tan-colored board.

How she had always admired this painting, with its eerily animate eyes. The stitching of the blouse was miraculous. The paint had the fragile look of pastel, but with a deeper sheen. The figure appeared so real that Madeline kept expecting it to move.

And yet something was not right. Looking more closely, she realized it wasn't board under the peeling chip, but an underlayer of paint the color of flesh. She dabbed at a crack in the sloughing area and dared to pull a chip away, leaving a spot of brown that gave the disturbing impression of being a bare nipple under the blouse, as if her mother's image had been painted over a nude portrait.

But that idea was absurd. How on earth would her mother have been painted over a nude? Could the artist have been recycling the board?

She turned the bedside lamp on and studied the painting as a whole, rubbing her hazy eyes for better focus. With the light hitting it from the side, the paint's texture was exaggerated, and Madeline noted for the second time that day how the blouse and the strands of hair trailing with the ribbon against the porcelain skin of the neck were painted more thickly. Pulling away another sliver of blue paint, she revealed the pale lines of the outer edge of a puckered scar.

"Oh," she whispered wonderingly. This wasn't some anonymous nude. This was her mother.

She was removing another fragment of blue when she heard a woman's voice calling from outside and quickly shoved the painting back into the closet.

It was Carlotta who came in. She was wearing a sleeveless top and a skirt that sat low on her hips, and her hair dangled in springy curls around her freckled face. "Hey there," she said quietly. "Your mom said I could probably find you here. She said something happened with Andy. So I guess that makes two of us in the same boat. Kind of unsettled. I'm glad you came."

Her thoughts still on the portrait, Madeline could only nod.

"Are you coming back up to the house?" Carlotta asked her. "Do you want me to wait for you?"

"I'll be coming up in a minute. But thanks."

"All right. Well, I'll see you up there."

When Carlotta had gone, Madeline stood with her back pressed hard against the closet door while delicate winged insects flitted weightlessly in the lamplight.

# 39

# A SECOND UNINVITED GUEST

Shelly took a hot shower in the footed tub, put her nightgown on, and got in bed, stuffing the pillows behind her back. She tried to distract herself with magazines, but kept setting them down. A tapestry of a farm scene hung off center over the dresser, so she got up and shoved the dresser over a couple of inches and then centered the rug. Her thoughts kept shifting from the situation with Carlotta to the situation with Madeline. She would not see Wyatt until morning—he would arrive very late tonight and stay in the cabin—but the thought of that meeting scared her. Her past had swung around in front of her, and tomorrow she would be forced to face it with her daughters looking on.

She could not even guess how the day would unfold. Jack and Delia had been planning to talk to Carlotta in the morning, but Madeline's presence would upset those plans. They would have to find time away from Madeline. And then afterward, Madeline would have to be told. And this would be the worst-possible time for her to learn of the role Shelly had played in someone else's marriage and of the ways she had distorted their family life to accommodate so many deceptions.

Eventually, Shelly got up and opened the shutters, slid the window up, and stood breathing the cool air and looking through the fluttering leaves of the cottonwood at the contour of Lizard Mountain.

The moon cast only grudging illumination on the landscape. Lights of far-off houses dotted the dark hills that loomed behind the mountain. Shelly watched them blink. So much of her life had taken place in this lonely west Texas outpost, and yet, even here, she felt a lingering sense of displacement. The last time she had been certain of where she was, and where she was going, was August 1, 1966, when she had started off to buy tampons from the Rexall on the Drag. The life she might have lived, if not for that day, was lost to her. She had headed northwest across the South Mall and been hauled off to the hospital in another direction, her life irreparably changed by the timing of her exit from the math class on that summer day when she was nineteen years old. Charles Whitman had singled her out of hundreds of people crossing the campus, and even now she wondered why he had decided on her. Was it only where she had happened to be on the plaza—like a piece on a chessboard? Had he simply, after shooting the boy who was walking toward her, lifted the barrel an inch or so and found her in his sights? Or was there some more personal reason he had chosen her—the color of her blouse or the way she hesitated before deciding to cross the hedged-in grassy square around the flagpole?

Maybe he had chosen her on nothing more than a random impulse. That was probably the case. But the older she became, the more she wanted to feel that she'd had a hand in the matter—that some action of her own had determined the outcome, that she had plotted her own misguided course. It seemed better than being a luckless victim of fate.

Looking out at the landscape, she recalled how she had seen Dan from this same window the day he hiked out to explore the mountain, and how he had turned and waved and shouted for her to come with him. She tried to picture him now, in the shadows of desert shrub, but his image was as faint and illusive as the tepid light of the moon.

How differently she would do things now if she had the chance. She would go with him to Lizard Mountain. And later, she would stay behind in Austin for Madeline's play on the day Carlotta opened her store, and Dan would never take the road to Devil's Sinkhole.

Of course, all of this was pointless ruminating. Changing into her jeans and T-shirt, she went out into the hall and saw that Jack and Delia's door, on the far side of the stairwell, was open, revealing Jack in his reading chair. Carlotta's door and the door to the sitting room where Nicholas slept were closed, but Madeline's stood wide open, the room dark and empty.

Shelly went downstairs and found Madeline eating yogurt and watching the small television that sat on the countertop, her legs, in sweatpants, propped on the table, her feet bare.

"You can't sleep?" Shelly asked her.

"No."

"What are you watching?"

"*To Catch a Predator.* You won't like it."

On the screen, a tall man in a suit interrogated a dumpy middle-aged man in a gimme cap who was seated, looking frightened, at a table.

"The guy in the hat was planning to have sex with a fourteen-year-old he met online," Madeline said, licking the last of the yogurt from her spoon. "Only she wasn't fourteen. It was a setup."

Shelly searched the pantry for tea bags. "Delia usually has chamomile somewhere, doesn't she?"

"In the canister by the sink."

The man in the cap had started pleading. "I wasn't going to do anything," he said. "I swear. I just came here to talk to her." His bottom lip trembled.

Shelly put a cup of water in the microwave. "If you don't want to talk about this, just let me know. But were things all right with Andy otherwise? Before the convention?"

"They were fine."

The pedophile was weeping and apologizing when Carlotta wandered into the kitchen in her bathrobe. "Oh, I hate this show," she said. "I don't like having to feel sorry for these creeps."

"He wanted to have sex with a fourteen-year-old," Madeline told her. "He brought condoms and a bottle of wine."

"I don't like watching him cry," Carlotta said.

"I do," Madeline told her.

Carlotta took a banana from the fruit bowl on the counter and peeled it as the man in the suit told the pedophile he was free to leave. The pedophile stood up shakily from the table and exited the house into a cluster of police officers who ordered him to the ground and handcuffed him. Shelly was dropping her tea bag into the trash when a car's headlights fanned against the windows.

Carlotta went to look out. "It's Andy's car."

Madeline turned her head. "Andy's car?"

"He drives a Volvo, right? Dark color?"

"Yes."

"Well he's parked under the driveway light."

Madeline swung her legs down off the table. "He's not supposed to be here." She went out into the hall and slammed the screen door as she left the house.

Shelly looked out of the window and saw Madeline approach the car and talk to Andy. "Let's go upstairs and leave them alone," she told Carlotta. But then she heard a cry from Madeline and looked out again to see Ranger, poised in the driveway, his pointed ears erect and his squat body tense.

Madeline shouted at Andy so loudly her words carried through the window, "Why did you let him out?"

"I didn't know he was near the door!" Andy shouted back.

They lunged for the dog, but he scampered out of their reach and ran in a circle within the perimeter of light, his nose to the ground, as if he were in a spotlight on a stage. He paused for only a second before racing off into the dark. Madeline and Andy vanished with him.

Shelly ran outside and down the steps, with Carlotta behind her, just as Ranger dashed once more through the puddle of light and then darted around back of the house. They knew how important it was to catch him. Coyotes had nearly carried him off the previous year when he bolted out of the house one night and charged to the edge of the driveway, barking at them. Nicholas had foolishly run after him and seen a pack of them come out of the dark and grab Ranger, one of them snatching him by his throat and strangling his barks to a horrible gurgle. Only because Delia had driven up just at the right moment and scared off the coyotes by honking and flashing her car lights had the dog been saved. It could happen again, or he could escape to the highway and get lost, which also had happened one year.

"Get a tennis ball!" Madeline yelled from the shadows. "Bounce it under the light! He might come if he sees the ball!"

Carlotta rushed into the house to find one.

"I'll drive to the highway in case he runs in that direction!" Andy shouted. He got in his car and backed it up in a spray of gravel and sped off, calling for Ranger out of the open window.

"Mom, I'm barefoot! I have to get my shoes!" Madeline yelled.

Shelly started quickly around to the back of the house. "Ranger!" she called. "Ranger!" Her slippers picked up dirt through the open toes as she struck out toward the barn. From around the front of the house, Carlotta was calling musically, liltingly, "Ranger? I've got your ball! Come get your ball!" And from a window upstairs, Jack called down, "Shelly? What's going on?"

"Andy came and brought Ranger and he's run off."

"I'll be right down."

Everything was unsettled under the strange reptilian eye of the mountain with its tail stretched on the horizon, but something in the shimmer of moonlight over the open spaces, and the sounds of purring night birds in the brush, and the thought of Ranger leaping erratically through the tall grasses, ecstatic with his freedom, filled Shelly with a sudden excitement, as if trailing along in the dog's wake she was infected with his delirium.

His bark perforated the darkness to the left of the road. He had found an armadillo or some other varmint, and she heard a running skirmish as he attacked it. She yelled for him but didn't want to venture out into the cactus to find him. The tussle ceased in a moment, and Ranger continued barking from a stationary position when the animal must have retreated into a hole. Finally the dog came bouncing out of the grass and charged across the road in front of her.

"He's over here!" Shelly called. He vanished again, then skittered onto the road and raced directly at her. She stooped to grab him as he veered and passed her. "He's coming your way!" she shouted toward the house, turning to follow him.

Madeline and Carlotta came running. "Come get your ball, Ranger; I have your ball!" Carlotta called.

"He's coming your way, Jack!" Madeline yelled.

"He passed me!" Jack's voice came back. "He's going toward the barn now!"

Shelly turned, retracing her steps toward the barn, listening for the dog and scanning the silhouettes of rocks and vegetation, the stalks of century plants swaying stiffly in the breeze. At the barn she paused and listened, leaning for a moment against the fence of the empty paddock where she used to lead Carlotta around on Freckles. It was peaceful here, and the night smelled good. She wished she could stay longer.

Madeline's voice drifted to her. "Mom? We got him!"

She whispered a word of gratitude, relieved for the dog and for Nicholas, who loved him. Leaving the quiet refuge of the empty paddock, she was walking back toward the house when she realized that the voices of Jack and Madeline and Carlotta, coming from the front of the house, were suddenly cordial. A fourth voice wove in and out of the conversation. Andy's? No. She paused.

It was Wyatt's voice.

She stood very still and listened, unable to make out the words. The tenor of his voice, the way it rose and fell, the warm, low, laughter, played tricks on her heart, as if the last forty years had never happened.

And yet they had happened, and they had brought her here—to this place in back of Jack and Delia's house, where she stood in unflattering jeans and an old white T-shirt. Her slippers were dusty. Her toes were gritty. Her hair was still wet from the shower. And Wyatt was just around the corner.

But what did it matter? He was married, and her heart belonged to Dan.

Jack came walking around from the front. "Shelly," he whispered.

"Yes. I know."

"He caught the dog near the cabin."

She smoothed her hair back. "How do I look?"

"Honestly?"

"Honestly."

"Nervous."

"Stay with me," she said.

They walked around to the front. Wyatt was talking to Madeline in the driveway. He held the panting dog under one arm, his other arm around Carlotta. Even from yards away Shelly could see he looked better than she had hoped. He wore jeans and a nice jacket. The years fell away like confetti.

She forced herself to smile.

Why hadn't he lost any hair? Nothing about his appearance was drastically different, except that he looked more authoritative. The last time she had seen him he was twenty-five years old, and now he was in his sixties. Even holding the silly dog, he looked good.

# 40

# THE BLUE BLOUSE

Watching Shelly walk toward him, Wyatt felt like a rush of amphetamines was hitting his system. She was gloriously authentic, her face older and softer, her hair no longer the color of bronze, but tinged with a pliant, silvery gray. She said something banal that washed over him—a greeting of some kind—and hugged him lightly, then patted the dog and mentioned her grandson—that he would be so grateful the dog had been found. "He loves the dog," she said.

"It came running up to me at the cabin when I drove in," Wyatt told her, confused by Madeline's presence here. Carlotta had introduced him to Madeline, so now he knew who she was. But what was she doing in Alpine in the middle of this delicate situation with Carlotta? He took a closer look at her, curious if there was any resemblance to Shelly, or even to Carlotta. He didn't see any. She was petite, with pale skin and dark hair and remarkably long eyelashes.

She took the dog from him. "I've always wanted to meet you," she said.

Carlotta looked from Wyatt to Shelly. "I guess it's been nearly forty years since the two of you have seen each other."

He tried not to stare at Shelly. He was vaguely aware that Madeline was telling him she had seen pictures of his family in the house over the years and had looked at some of his paintings online. She told him he would meet her son in the morning. "His name is Nicholas," she said. While she was talking, a car approached, and she spoke to the driver through the window. "Wyatt Calvert caught him," she said.

The driver put the car in park and got out with the motor running. He was clean-cut and nice-looking. "*The* Wyatt Calvert?" He shook Wyatt's hand. "I've been hearing about you ever since I met

Madeline. I didn't know you were coming. I'm Madeline's husband, Andy. God, I'm glad you rescued the dog. It was my fault he ran off. What good luck that you're here."

Jack mentioned how late it was and remarked that it was an hour later for Wyatt. Shelly said very little. Wyatt tried to catch a better glimpse of her eyes. All these decades he had thought about her, and seeing her under the light in this dusty drive was confounding.

After everyone told Wyatt good night and went into the house, he walked back down to the cabin and carried his bag in from the rental car. Sinking into the chair, he pulled off one of his loafers and sat for a while, trying to reconcile this new image of Shelly with the girl he had known. His knees were stiff and his back hurt from the flight. So many years hunched over his work had been hard on his back and his eyes.

But the sight of Shelly had set his adrenaline running.

He sat for a long while, watching a moth flutter and bump against the lamp. Usually here in Alpine he felt landlocked by the endless terrain, but tonight he welcomed being isolated from his life and his family.

Sitting and holding his shoe, thinking about his affair with Shelly, he hardly knew how to judge the man he had been back then, or the man he was now, with so many burdensome secrets. He had been twenty-three at the beginning of the affair, twenty-five at the end. He would like to think he couldn't be tempted to have an affair again, but the knowledge that he was capable of so much lying had humbled him.

Finally he got up and shoved the window open, admitting a small breeze. The screen captured the interior light in the crosshatch of gray wire and muddied his view. Clumps of vegetation in the gloom outside looked like loitering, misshapen humans. He opened the cabinet over the microwave in search of snacks of any kind, but it was empty. The bed had only one pillow, so he opened the closet to look for another, but the shelf over the hanging rod was bare. He was starting to close the door when he noticed the painting.

It was shoved in sideways, settled flat to the wall. He pulled it out and looked at it. "There you are," he whispered. In this odd way, she had come to visit him. He felt a sudden sexual urge at seeing her quiet smile and the way the ribbon spilled over her pale shoulder. He stared into her eyes. He had come to Alpine expecting to see her as a woman nearly sixty years old, and found himself confronting the face of the girl she had been so long ago.

He noted the frame had come loose at one corner. Studying the face, he saw how little justice he had done to it. He had failed to capture the subtleties in the expression and neglected her sense of buried energy, applying his paint too thickly on the initial layers—too heavy-handed with highlights—and making the surface pasty and dull compared to what he could paint now. And then he had added the final burden of clothing. The piece was hackneyed and prosaic. He examined the features, lingering in her abstract presence as he had not been able to linger in her presence in the driveway. Searching along the sweep of the satin ribbon and the soft strands of hair, then over an area that he slowly came to realize had been damaged by water, his gaze came to rest at last on the small, taut, pinkish nipple revealed by the flaking chips of the blue blouse.

# 41

# PROMISES, PROMISES

In boxer shorts, Andy paced the room, asking for forgiveness and promising never to be unfaithful again. He offered to return to Austin and see a therapist and suggested his encounter in the hotel room was actually a step in the right direction because he had not made love with the woman. Madeline stared at him, wondering how he could think this partial resistance would be of any comfort. It was the wanting, the *almost*, that hurt her.

"That's great, Andy," she said. "And since you're being honest, I should probably tell you that our neighbor Bob came over when he caught his son smoking weed, and I let him kiss me because I felt so bad for him. Nothing else happened."

Andy's face dropped. "You really let him kiss you?"

"Of course not."

"Did he try?"

"No, Andy."

"Thank God. You scared me. Look, I'll do whatever you ask."

"Then put your fucking pants on; you look ridiculous."

"No, really, I'll do whatever you ask."

"I'm asking you not to feel tempted by women."

He would be a liar if he agreed to this, and one of the problems with Andy was that he was never a liar.

Madeline hugged her knees. "I don't want this marriage anymore."

"You mean—" He stopped at the foot of the bed.

"Yes, I might mean that."

But she didn't. She couldn't.

"Because of *this*? Because of *her*?"

He was disarmingly good at regret.

"How could you do this to Nicholas?" she demanded.

"I don't *know*. I don't *know*."

Turning the light out and pulling the covers up, she ceased responding to him. Long after he had stopped talking and thrown himself onto the sofa and fallen asleep with an arm flopped over the edge, Madeline lay awake in the dark, alert to his breathing. She ached at the thought of his body next to another woman's. The thought of this seductive woman made her think of her mother's portrait, and she tried to imagine her mother posing naked. The idea bothered her more than it should. How strange that the portrait had hung in her own stairwell like a sensual alter ego of her mother, watching her go up and down the stairs all day. She wondered what other things she might not know about her mother. Andy's behavior hurt her more, but it confused her less.

She would need to get the portrait out of the cabin. Wyatt Calvert probably wouldn't notice it or mention it, but she should get it back in her car. She couldn't take it to the frame shop by Carlotta's store now that the scarred breast was showing. Instead, she would have to haul it back to Austin, its journey here as futile as hers and ending where it had started.

# 42

# THE MAGIC 8 BALL

Wyatt awoke to bright sunlight through the screened windows at six-thirty in the morning. He showered and dressed and walked to the house, and in the kitchen found a small boy who looked about six or seven years old: Madeline's son, he supposed. The boy sat at the kitchen table, wearing only pajama bottoms and slurping cornflakes out of a spoon. He made low humming noises and swung his legs energetically as he ate. The dog from last night's escapade sat expectantly at his feet, but jumped up and greeted Wyatt by pawing at his knees. Wyatt scratched his ears, and the dog resumed his vigil beside the table.

"He wants my cornflakes," the boy said with his mouth full, holding the spoon awkwardly.

"You must be Nicholas."

He nodded. His hair hung shaggily around his face, and his chest heaved with tuneless humming. A Magic 8 Ball perched on the table beside the bowl.

"Is Jack around?" Wyatt asked.

"He went to buy coffee," the boy said.

"Do you know where?"

Nicholas shrugged, staring into his cornflakes and focusing on the spoon as he plunged it into the overfilled bowl.

"How long ago did he leave?"

"When I was pouring my cereal."

Wyatt examined the coffeemaker and found it filled with water but without coffee in the filter. Jack hadn't gone for a cup of coffee; he had gone for a bag.

"My daddy got here last night," Nicholas said.

"Yes, I met him last night."

"I have a tadpole upstairs. Do you want to go see him?"

"I do. But I'd like to see him later. Right now, I'm looking for Jack. Is everyone else still sleeping?"

"Yesterday he fell on the stairs, and Ranger tried to get him."

"I'm glad he escaped."

"Mom saved him."

"Your mom is a hero, then."

Nicholas seemed to contemplate this idea. "She's still asleep," he said. "She's in the bed. There wasn't room in the bed for Daddy. He's on the couch."

"Oh. I'll see you later, okay? I'm going to look for Jack."

Nicholas nodded. "Don't let Ranger go outside. He runs away. We have to take him out on a leash. One time the coyotes got him."

Wyatt walked back to the cabin and got in his rental car. He figured the two grocery stores in Alpine weren't open this early and that Jack had gone to Amigos, the closest convenience store. He turned off the dirt road onto a potholed road bordered by an assortment of small houses—shingle and brick and stucco. Shadows of tall agave plants and Spanish daggers lay in stark stripes across the pavement. Cactus and century plants stood in the yards amid lawn furniture and a clutter of ornaments. He was about to turn onto the highway, but then saw Jack's old blue Honda approaching from town, so he pulled off to the shoulder and got out to wait.

Jack made the turn and stopped in the road.

"Pull over," Wyatt told him. Wyatt got in with him, his knees crammed up to the dash. Under his feet cassette tapes by B.B. King and Asleep at the Wheel littered the floorboard.

"What's the plan?" Wyatt asked.

"Originally it was to talk to Carlotta this morning. But then Madeline and Andy showed up uninvited. They're having a marital crisis. Madeline came here to be with her mom, and then Andy got here just a little before you did." He tapped the wheel impatiently with his thumb. "I haven't had coffee yet. I'm about to go make some."

"Okay. But why is the portrait in the cabin?"

"What portrait?"

"The one I did of Shelly."

"It's not."

"Yes it is. In the closet. It's damaged."

"Then maybe Madeline brought it."

"I thought Shelly might have brought it."

"Shelly gave it to Madeline years ago."

Wyatt considered that. "Anyway, the top layer of paint is chipping."

"What do you mean?"

"Over the breast," Wyatt said.

"You mean, you can see—"

"You might say."

"I don't have a clue what that's about," Jack said. "This place is a minefield. I don't know where to step."

A raven landed aggressively in the road, chasing away a sparrow that was pecking at the pavement. "Am I invited for coffee?" Wyatt asked.

"Come on," Jack said irritably.

"Why are you so disgruntled?"

"Because this is a hell of a mess. We have to take care of this with Carlotta, and there are too many people in the house."

Wyatt got back in his rental car, gave Jack's Honda a head start to let the dust settle, and then followed, the sun glinting off the hood, the pitched roof of the house at the end of the road before him.

Jack was making the coffee when Wyatt walked into the kitchen. Nicholas wasn't there, but the Magic 8 Ball sat beside the bowl of soggy cornflakes. On the television a CNN newscaster reported on recent American casualties in Iraq, and Jack picked up the control and muted the sound. "Too many guys getting killed in this stupid war."

Wyatt watched the silent broadcast while coffee dribbled into the pot. He pulled the pot out prematurely and poured himself a cup, wiping the spill with a sodden sponge. "You think there's any chance Madeline and her husband might leave, so we can go back to plan A?"

"Why don't you ask the 8 Ball." Jack lifted a skillet down from a rack over the stove. "Do you want any eggs?"

"Yeah."

"Scrambled?"

"Yeah." Wyatt sat at the table and drank his coffee. He picked up the 8-Ball. "I'm sorry about all this. Is this going to go okay?"

"No, it's not going to 'go okay,'" Jack said, cracking an egg and dumping it in the skillet. "It's going to stir up a lot of painful information. At the very least, a lot of people are going to be confused. I doubt anyone's life is going to be ruined, but let me tell you, this won't just 'go okay.'"

"I was asking the 8 Ball," Wyatt said.

He turned the ball over and gave it two shakes. Staring into the small window of murky liquid, he waited for the answer to surface. Slowly the message *CANNOT PREDICT NOW* bobbed up.

Wyatt shook the ball again, and *BETTER NOT TELL YOU NOW* appeared in the window. He shook it again, and *YOU MAY RELY ON IT* floated sideways before righting itself.

"That's more like it," he said.

Nicholas came in from the hall in his pajama bottoms, the dog behind him. "That's my 8 Ball."

"It wouldn't give me a straight answer," Wyatt told him.

"You always have to shake it again before it gives you the right answer," Nicholas said. "Do you want to see my tadpole now?"

"Later, when everyone's up."

"We can be quiet," Nicholas told him.

Dutifully, Wyatt got up from the table. "Hold the eggs," he told Jack. Slipping his shoes off, conscious of the loud jangle of tags on the dog's collar, he followed the dog and Nicholas up the stairs. Nicholas forgot to be quiet and skittered into the sitting room, and Wyatt hoped Shelly wouldn't appear from one of the doorways. Having shown up at the house last night, unexpected, with the dog, he didn't want to be caught creeping sock-footed upstairs.

"His name is Jerry," Nicholas said too loudly. "I got a certificate, and we had to order him. He came in the mail."

The room was cluttered with wires draped from the television to a game machine on the floor at the foot of the sofa bed. Nicholas pulled a plastic water-filled container off a bookshelf and set it carefully on the floor. He knelt, looking inside it. "Sometimes it's hard to see him. He sleeps under the bridge. It's not a real bridge. Nothing can really go over it." He poked his finger into the water. "There he is. He's sleeping."

Leaning down, Wyatt set his hands on his knees, and staring into the water saw the creature bob, belly-up, to the surface and float there inanimately, like the buoyant device in the Magic 8 Ball.

"Nicholas?" he said quietly.

The dog crowded in. Nicholas pushed him away, trying to right the tadpole with his finger. "He needs to wake up," he said, then tilted his head back and raised his eyes to Wyatt. His unwashed hair was musty and warm. Wyatt settled a hand on his thin shoulder. He felt the hard bones, the strong pulse in the neck, and watched the boy lower his head again and stare at the tadpole floating over the yellow bridge. "Is he all right?" Nicholas asked. "Is he dead?"

"I think he is dead," Wyatt said as gently as he could. "Should I get your mother?"

The boy continued to stare at the drifting body, its legs outspread, its belly exposed to the air.

"Do you want me to get your mother?"

Nicholas reached in slowly and scooped the tadpole into his palm, water dribbling through his fingers. Cupping his hand, he brought it to his chest. His bottom lip curled down, and his eyes squinted closed. A whimper turned to a cry. He got to his feet. Holding his fist to his chest, he walked in a small circle, his body hunched at the shoulders. Finally he leaned over and let out a high-pitched wail, the tears dropping out of his eyes and a stream of spittle falling as slowly as a spun web from his mouth to the floor.

# 43

# A SEARCH PARTY

Shelly was brushing her teeth when she heard the wailing. She pulled her bathrobe on, flung her door open, and ran to the next room, where she found Nicholas on the far side of the sofa bed, clutching something and weeping, while Andy, in boxer shorts, pleaded with him to surrender the object he held. Madeline knelt at Nicholas's side, saying, "Oh honey, sweet boy, I'm so, so sorry," the thin strap of her sleep-shirt dangling off her shoulder. Beside Andy stood Wyatt. He turned to look at Shelly.

The scene baffled her: her half-clothed daughter and son-in-law and her weeping grandson alongside Wyatt Calvert, whom she had once loved so profoundly that she had wished herself dead.

"His tadpole died," Wyatt told her.

"It's my fault!" Nicholas howled. "It's because he sloshed around!"

"It isn't your fault, honey," Madeline reassured him.

Shelly waded through the clutter to wrap Nicholas in her arms. "Sweetheart, your mother's right; you didn't do anything wrong."

"But he sloshed around! I shouldn't have brought him with me! I wish I had left him at home! I wish I hadn't come here!" He buried his head against her, his bony ribs pressed into her breast.

Andy said, "Take a deep breath, son. Get hold of yourself—you can do that," and finally Nicholas opened his hand and let his father take the lifeless tadpole. "I want to bury him in a jar with water," he sniffed. "Will Nana pick it?"

"Of course, sweetie. A perfect one." Leaving the room to go downstairs for a jar, she saw Carlotta looking out of her bedroom door.

"Is that Nicholas crying?"

"His tadpole died."

In the kitchen Shelly found Jack scrambling eggs, and told him about the tadpole. She selected an olive jar from the cabinet, rummaged for a lid, and then walked out to the porch to settle her mind. The sun was spreading warmth over the floorboards. A rusty windmill turned slowly in the distance. Madeline came outside to stand beside her.

"I blame Andy for this," Madeline said.

She blamed him for a lot more, too. The ruin of the portrait—everything—their whole lives seemed to be coming apart because of what Andy had done. The best Madeline could do for now was manage the pieces.

She would start by getting the portrait out of the cabin and back in her car. So while Andy and Nicholas dug the tadpole's grave at the base of the big cottonwood tree outside Shelly's bedroom window, Madeline borrowed a sheet from the utility room and drove down to the cabin. She took Ranger along to be sure he didn't escape from the house and run off again. Wyatt was still at the house, so she let herself into the cabin without knocking, took the portrait out of the closet, hauled it outside, and shoved it upright into the Suburban, pushing Ranger back when he tried to jump out. She slung the sheet over the portrait.

She had driven only a few yards back toward the house when a draft of air swept in. Glancing back, she saw Ranger with his forepaws on the window button, sniffing the wind. Before she could react, he leaped out. She braked and flung her door open, but the dog was already running. He didn't look back when she called. She drove to the house, slammed the car into park, and ran around back to the cottonwood where Andy and Nicholas, on their knees, were digging the hole with spades.

"Ranger's out again!" she shouted at them.

Andy wiped his forehead. "Which way did he go?"

"That way." She waved.

Andy tossed the spade and looked disgusted.

"You're the one who brought him!" Madeline yelled. "Go look for him on the highway. Ask Mom to look. Nicholas, come with me."

Nicholas climbed into the front seat. He called Ranger from the window while they drove around the property and through the neighborhood across the road. Several times they heard barking in the distance but couldn't place where it came from, and it ceased when Madeline turned the motor off to listen.

"What if we never find him?" Nicholas asked her.

"We'll find him. He has tags."

In the neighborhood they stopped and asked a small boy on a tricycle if he had seen the dog, but he hadn't. They talked to a girl who was petting a tethered horse by a rusty water trough and to a woman watering plants on a porch. "*No, mi hijo*," the woman told Nicholas, shaking her head.

"First Jerry and now Ranger," Nicholas said mournfully as he climbed back into the car.

They returned to the house, where they found Andy, Jack, and Delia in the kitchen.

"I've been everywhere," Andy explained.

"Where's Mom?" Madeline asked.

"With Carlotta in the truck. Wyatt's driving around too."

"Get a drink," Madeline told Nicholas. "Fill up a water bottle. We'll be better off on foot. We'll take a tennis ball with us."

Delia was describing the dog over the telephone to a neighbor. "He's white with black patches. His ears are erect."

"He's more black, with white patches," Madeline corrected her. "With brown on his nose."

"No one would notice the brown," Andy said. "Just say he's a rat terrier."

Madeline added, "Like a fox terrier, but with short hair and a different-shaped head."

Delia said into the phone, "He's the size of a small poodle."

Andy said he would take the golf cart and search the back of the property.

At one o'clock in the afternoon, trudging a mile from the house near a dump of rusting cars, toting Nicholas's water bottle and a tennis ball, Madeline had begun to think they would never see the troublesome dog again, when he appeared on the trail before them, trotting in their direction.

"There he is!" Nicholas yelled.

The dog sat down on the trail. His face had an unfamiliar expression, his top lip curled in a freakish smile. Nicholas ran to him and tried to pick him up, but then turned and shouted, "Mom! There's something sticking out of his nose!"

"Probably cactus," Madeline said, and went to examine him while Nicholas squatted and held the collar. Ranger panted, flicking saliva and jerking his head. Madeline was trying to hold his head still when something pricked her fingers and the dog yelped, slinging his head and tugging to get away. Needlelike spikes protruded out of his nose. "It's not cactus," Madeline said. "It's porcupine quills."

"Will he die?" Nicholas cried. "Is he going to die?"

"No, honey. Jack and Delia will know how to get these out."

"But he can't close his mouth!"

Dropping the ball and the water bottles, Madeline carried the dog while Nicholas trotted beside her. By the time they reached the driveway she was sticky with sweat and dog saliva, her arms itching from Ranger's hair.

She set the dog on the kitchen floor in front of Jack and Delia. He didn't move, just panted and rolled his eyes. Delia gave him a bowl of water, but he didn't attempt to drink. Pacing around the bowl, he whined, rubbing his snout on the floor and scraping it with his forepaws.

Jack left and returned with a pair of pliers. "Will it hurt him?" Nicholas asked.

"He won't like it," Jack admitted.

Ranger moved in circles. When Jack set him up on the table, he started to tremble. "Madeline, hold him still. Nicholas, help your mom. Talk to Ranger so he'll stay calm."

Nicholas couldn't stand the sound of the whimpering and put his hands over his ears. "Stay calm," he told the dog. "Stay calm."

Delia took the pliers and put on reading glasses, Jack tucked Ranger under his arm, and Madeline clamped her hands tightly around the dog's head, flattening down his ears. Ranger rolled his eyes around, watching the pliers and tossing his head whenever they touched a quill.

"I'm afraid I'm crushing his skull," Madeline said, wrestling to keep her grip.

Ranger nipped at the pliers, darting his snout like a snapping turtle at Delia. He growled and stiffened his legs, trying to shove away from the table. Madeline wrapped a dish towel under his chin and over his eyes and ears. Blindly, he flung his head, lunging and nipping ferociously when he sensed the pliers in front of his face. In rapid, successive jabs, Delia extracted a few quills, laying them out on the table.

"He bit me," she said, pulling her hand away.

"He's fast," Jack said.

Nicholas had started to cry. "It's hurting him!" He looked at the quills on the table. "Two of these are whiskers! You're pulling out his whiskers! Let him go!"

Jack took over the pliers, but he was less efficient than Delia. "We need Carlotta or Wyatt. Someone with manual dexterity."

When Carlotta and Shelly came in, Madeline said "Porcupine" before they had even asked. "We can't get the quills out."

"Maybe Wyatt and I can do it," Carlotta said. "He's on his way in."

"Ever pulled porcupine quills?" Jack said when Wyatt walked in.

Wyatt enlisted Nicholas. "Where's your dog happiest—inside or out?"

"Out," Nicholas told him.

"And who does he trust the most?"

"Me."

"So if you hold him in your lap, he might relax."

"Maybe not," Nicholas said. "He's pretty upset."

"Give it a try. Take him outside and sit with him in your lap at the top of the porch steps, and Carlotta and I can sit on a lower step so we can see what we're doing."

Nicholas gathered the dog in his arms and carried him outside and sat where he had been told. The dog was docile but thrust his tongue from the pain of the quills and made coughing sounds.

Madeline and Shelly stood at the far end of the porch. "Where's Andy?" Shelly asked.

"I guess driving around in the golf cart."

"You haven't called him to say we found him?"

"No."

"Oh, honey," Shelly said.

Madeline was unhappy to be so angry and disillusioned and yet to suspect that she still loved Andy. She feared she might forgive him and use Nicholas for the excuse. Why hadn't she fallen for someone like Jack, or Wyatt? They seemed to be faithful husbands.

Carlotta looked up from the step. "Bad news. I think I see quills in the back of his tongue." Wyatt wrestled the dog's mouth open so she could look farther in. "Yep. In the back of his throat," she said. "I'll have to call Emmett Johnson. He's a mobile veterinarian and can probably come pretty fast."

She went inside to make the call. Shelly went in and made sandwiches, which everyone ate on the porch steps. Madeline sat in the swing. She noticed that Wyatt seemed to look at her mother attentively as he talked and ate his sandwich and that her mother always seemed to be looking off in the other direction.

# 44

# EMMETT JOHNSON, MOBILE VETERINARIAN

Madeline was with Nicholas in the swing, holding the dog, when a large white truck rolled to a stop in the speckled light under the trees, EMMETT JOHNSON and a phone number painted in red on its side. A man got out and lifted a tackle box from a hatch in the rear, and as he came toward them, Madeline realized she had met him years ago, when she was fourteen or fifteen and he had come to see Carlotta. Most of Carlotta's friends had never paid any attention to Madeline because she was so much younger, but he had sat with her on this very porch and talked about his A&M classes in immunology and pharmacology. She had not seen him since then, but the encounter came back to her now as she watched him climb the steps in his dusty work boots, his eyes on Ranger.

"Well, the dog did get into it," he said. He paused when he looked at Madeline. "Hey, I know you."

"I think we met when I was about fifteen," she said.

"Must have been about then. We had a conversation right here on the porch." His build was stocky and solid; he had blue eyes and sandy blond hair cut very short.

"Yes, we did." She smiled at him. "This is my son, Nicholas."

"Well, Nicholas, let's take a look at your dog." He leaned to examine Ranger, who growled, showing his teeth, his lips like a pincushion, the quills sticking out.

"What's his name?"

"Ranger," Nicholas said.

"Is Ranger a pretty good dog?"

"Yeah."

"He's a tough dog, too," Emmett said, sitting down beside Nicholas for a closer look. "Can you hold him still while I give him a shot? It's going to put him to sleep for a while so we can get these quills out. Otherwise he's going to take a chunk out of my hand."

Nicholas locked his arms around Ranger while Emmett Johnson got a syringe and needle out of the tackle box, inserted fluid from a vial, and injected it into the dog's foreleg.

Carlotta came out and greeted Emmett and turned the ceiling fans on, creating a lazy breeze. Ranger began to look loopy and closed his eyes. "He's all right," Emmett assured Nicholas, moving a tall plant stand into the light and settling Ranger, stomach down, on top of it. "Here's our operating table." He looked into the dog's mouth. "Okay, Nicholas. Hold him steady. My son usually helps me out, but he's not here, so you're my guy. To get these out, I'm going to have to give some pretty strong yanks, and that's going to tug at your dog's head and jerk him a little. You hold him still."

"Could he have swallowed any quills?" Madeline asked.

"If he did, they'll go the usual way. It's the ones he didn't swallow we have to worry about. Nicholas, you look concerned. If you put your fingers here, you can feel his heartbeat. See? He's all right."

Nicholas felt the heartbeat, then took hold of Ranger's head again while Emmett propped the jaw open with a metal device and used surgical scissors to snip the ends of the largest quills inside the mouth.

Delia pushed open the screen door. "Emmett. Hello. Turkey or ham on a sandwich?"

"Turkey sounds great. Thank you, Mrs. Stone."

"Coke?"

"Do you have any Diet Coke?"

"Diet Dr Pepper."

"That'd be great."

Delia went into the house, and Emmett probed inside the dog's mouth, clipping quills and pulling them out by the blunt ends with a pair of small forceps. He paused to look at Nicholas. "If you need a break, I bet your mom would fill in."

Nicholas went inside, and Madeline took his place, her head so close to Emmett's chest she could smell his sweat.

Angling the dog's head in the sunlight, Emmett studied the floppy tongue. From the way he leaned down, Madeline saw the perspiration in the small wrinkles on the back of his neck. "If he had a bigger mouth, I could get in here better," he said. "No need to hold him that tight. He's not going to go anywhere. I just don't want him to flop over."

"So you said you have a son?"

"Two girls, one boy." He pulled the rubbery lips back and examined the gums. "You might want to get these teeth cleaned at some point. The good news is, I think we've got all the quills." A cell phone rang, and he pulled it out of his pocket. "Emmett here." He listened. "I could get there in . . . oh, fifteen, maybe thirty minutes. I'm at the Stones'." He paused again, flicking his eyes toward Madeline and continuing to look at her while he talked. "Naw, it's not a problem. I'm out and about anyway." He closed the phone and put it back in his pocket. "Friend of mine got drunk and banged his horse up trying to get him into a trailer."

"Oh."

"I guess Nicholas's dad is around here somewhere?"

"Somewhere. Are you always this busy on Saturdays?"

"Pretty much always on call. I like the work, and there seems to be plenty of it. Must be the charmed life I've been living." He ran his thumb over Ranger's chin, checking for hidden quills, and looked in the dog's ears and between his toes. "And my good luck."

"Your good luck?"

"You bet. My wife walked out on me two years ago, and if I were an unlucky man, that would have been for no reason at all."

Madeline was trying to figure out what this meant, when Carlotta came to the doorway and told Emmett his sandwich was ready. "You want me to bring it out?"

"I'm afraid I'll need a rain check on the sandwich. I got a call from Gus Reeves, and he needs some help with his horse."

"I'll wrap it up for you," Carlotta told him.

"You planning to be at the rodeo tonight?" he asked her.

"You know my opinion about rodeos." She went inside for his sandwich.

"So there's a rodeo tonight?" Madeline said.

"The Big Bend Ranch Rodeo."

"Are you going?"

"Wouldn't miss it. Actually, I don't have that option. They have to have a vet there, and Alpine's only got two of us. It's my turn." He chewed his bottom lip and settled his eyes directly on hers. "I bet Nicholas would like it."

"That's true. It might cheer him up."

"Oh, look here," Emmett said. "Somebody's coming around." Ranger's paws had started to twitch.

"Is that a breeze, or just the fans?" Madeline asked.

"That's a breeze. We're supposed to have wind coming."

"Do you think it might bring any rain?"

Emmett shook his head. "No. Not likely. Just dust."

# 45

# THE TADPOLE'S FUNERAL

When Andy had returned, and he and Nicholas had gone back to digging the tadpole's grave, Jack and Wyatt retreated to the cozy library alcove of the parlor where Jack kept his collection of history books. "I found this one at McMurtry's place in Archer City for twenty-five dollars," Jack said, taking down an old clothbound volume called *The Men Who Found America* and handing it to Wyatt. "It's a kids' book, but I couldn't resist, because look at the cover. And this one . . . it's new. You should read it. It's a biography of Hopper and has a lot of background on the paintings. I thought of you while I was reading it."

Watching Jack pluck one volume after another from the shelves, speak a line or two about each, and then push it back in its place, Wyatt toyed with the idea of putting a stop to the small talk about books and asking Jack how he was really doing—how he was handling his concerns about Carlotta. They were certainly concerns the two of them shared.

But the mechanical way Jack kept pulling out one book and then another, offering some terse comment about it and then placing it back on the shelf, was evidence enough that he was not in a mood for hashing over a thorny situation that both of them already understood. It reminded Wyatt of the evening at Brackenridge Hospital all those years back, when Jack had told him, while deflecting any discussion or pity, the exact nature of his gunshot wound.

Jack had rarely even spoken of that injury since then, in spite of the glaring fact that it had changed his life in untold ways. If not for the injury, he and Delia probably would have had three or four kids of their own instead of adopting Carlotta. They might have stayed in

Austin or moved to San Antonio to be closer to Delia's large family, with all her nieces and nephews. But Jack never mentioned any of those things that might have happened differently, and Wyatt never asked about them, knowing that the intimacy between them depended on letting Jack keep his thoughts to himself. This didn't prevent Wyatt from knowing instinctively what those thoughts were, but it often stopped him—as it did now—from bringing them up.

He was about to say a few optimistic words of encouragement about the situation with Carlotta, but Nicholas burst into the room, shouting, "It's time for Jerry's funeral!" He held a dirty spade at his side, and looked happy and excited. "Me and my dad finished digging the grave! My dad said not everybody would want to come, but I told him everybody would! We need to leave Ranger inside, though." Ranger, to Wyatt's knowledge, was still shivering under the kitchen table from the aftereffects of the anesthesia. "See you in a minute!" Nicholas turned and ran upstairs to alert the others.

And then Andy appeared at the door, looking apologetic. "Sorry about this. I hope you don't mind. I think Nicholas wants everyone out there. Apparently, I'm officiating."

————

The grave was under Shelly's bedroom window, between the wide trunk of the towering cottonwood and the rattling compressor of an air conditioner. It was a foot across and deep enough for the olive jar that contained the tadpole to sit in upright. Wyatt made an effort to stare down at the hole instead of across at Shelly, who was facing him from the far side, the hump of Lizard Mountain rising off the sunny landscape behind her. He scanned the company around the grave while Andy recited a prayer of some kind in Hebrew. Jack, he noticed, looked impatient and had started to sweat in the heat. Madeline's bra strap fell from under her skimpy tank top. Nicholas stood so close to the grave the tips of his tennis shoes hung over the edge, but he seemed over his grief. Delia's flip-flops and cutoffs looked too young for her. She was older now. They were all older now. Carlotta, he thought, looked upset about something—obviously not the tadpole. Something else. She had a frown on her face as she stared down at the grave. Was she starting to suspect that his visit was more than a casual drop-in?

He doubted that anyone understood what Andy was saying in

Hebrew—he certainly didn't. Andy was a patient father to take his son's loss so seriously, but to Wyatt he looked like he was enjoying the role a little too much.

Wyatt stole another glance at Shelly, who stood with her arms folded, the injured arm concealed by her blouse. Watching her there like this, memories poured over him and he felt a wave of tenderness, recalling how she had loved Roger Miller's songs and how she would sing along with the Temptations to "My Girl." He had halfway hoped that seeing her after all these years, in a new light and with the advantage of hindsight, he would notice things that would have doomed their chances after all.

But there was nothing like that. He still loved everything about her. He loved the way she looked, the way she stood there, her soft and plain way of speaking her mind. For most of his life now, every painting he had made, in ways he couldn't even describe, had been for Shelly. As he'd worked, he had wondered what she might think of the finished painting she would likely never see. No matter how he had made peace with Elaine, no matter how much he loved Elaine, Shelly remained a painful sacrifice.

He knew he should stop looking at her if he intended to get through the weekend without falling in love all over again. Forty years, and he had finally managed to tolerate the memories with less discomfort. But now here she was—the mountain behind her, the sunlight filtering down and dancing on her shoulders, the rising wind tugging at her hair, every moment revealing a new Shelly he would have to get over.

Wyatt wasn't the only person in the gathering whose thoughts were not with the dead tadpole. Everyone at the grave was lost in private thoughts. Shelly's were a patchwork of worries as she stared down at the splintered roots and considered how everything that had happened in the last twenty hours had made it nearly impossible to reveal the truth to Carlotta. The unexpected arrivals of Madeline and Nicholas, and then Andy, and then the death of the tadpole, and the runaway dog—it had all created so much confusion. If Madeline were to follow through on her plan to take Nicholas to the rodeo tonight, and if Andy were to go along, then there would be a chance to talk to Carlotta. But it was an imperfect chance, and Carlotta deserved a more thoughtful introduction to the truth than one slotted to match the timing of a rodeo. And of course Madeline would need to be told afterward.

Shelly avoided looking at Wyatt, Jack, and Delia—worried to meet their eyes. The unwieldy truth hung between the four of them as they stood over the tiny, ridiculous grave. She looked instead at Madeline, who was obviously chafing at Andy's voice, and at Carlotta, who appeared especially pensive.

Madeline's eyes were only on Andy. She resented his stage management of this funeral, and thought how her own father would have taken her off to bury the tadpole in private. Nobody knew the Hebrew words Andy was saying, or cared what they meant. He was indulging Nicholas more than she thought was healthy—trying to excuse himself as a weak husband by being an overly decent father. Nicholas couldn't be getting much out of this ceremonial mishmash. And he was no longer grief-stricken.

She moved in closer and placed a hand on his shoulder. Small as he was for seven, he seemed to be growing so quickly. She remembered when he was four years old and had pointed to the telephone wires and power lines on their street and asked what they were used for. She had tried to explain electricity and how sound could travel through wires, but had realized from his disappointed expression that this wasn't the kind of answer he had wanted. "What did you think the wires were for?" she asked him.

"For the birds to sit on," he told her. How touching and sad it was that he had believed people were good enough to set up all those wires just so the birds could rest.

Across from Madeline, Carlotta was in a somber mood, reflecting on the small grave she had dug not long ago beside the little creek called the Peña Blanca. She looked at sweet little Nicholas, and thought how lucky he was to have a father who would take so much care to bury the tadpole, and how strangely nice it was here under the shade of the tree, with everyone gathered around like family.

# 46

# A FAMILY OUTING

By dinnertime, Madeline was sure something apart from her marriage was wrong in the house. Nothing was going the way it usually did. The dinner was store-bought lasagna Delia had dug from the back of the freezer, and no one bothered to sit at the table, but ate alone as they got hungry, standing up in the kitchen or taking their plates out to the porch.

She sat at the bottom of the stairs to eat her portion, puzzling over the situation. Nicholas stood at the top of the stairs and complained that his boots didn't fit. Andy appeared beside him in a cowboy hat and a pair of boots he had borrowed from Jack. The hat was too small for his head, and he looked ridiculous, like he was wearing a costume.

They took Madeline's Suburban to the rodeo. She insisted on driving. She didn't want to surrender control of anything in her life. She turned the radio off, not wanting to listen to sappy songs.

The highway into town became the main road through it, running alongside the railroad tracks, past the bus station and the post office and the feed store. Just beyond a building supply and the Dairy Queen, Madeline pulled into a gas station and waited while Andy and Nicholas went inside. Andy came out with two bottles of Guinness and opened one by shoving the mouth into the door-lock mechanism.

"You know you're not supposed to drink in a moving vehicle," Madeline told him.

"The rodeo's just down the road."

"I don't want to drive if you're drinking in the car."

"I'll drive."

"Not while you're drinking."

"Okay, I'll just hold it then."

"It's an open-container law."

He looked at her.

"Complain to the Department of Public Safety," she told him.

He pressed the cap onto the bottle. "Bottle's no longer open." He was irritated now. She could tell he'd had enough of her anger. She'd about had enough of it, too, but wasn't ready to let it go.

Nicholas came out of the store with bags of Cheetos and Corn Nuts and got in the car. The parking lot was busy with people heading to the rodeo, a line of vehicles at the pump. Waiting to pull out, Madeline was stuck behind two pickups. Nicholas said, "Mom? There's something the matter." She turned and saw he was on his knees, peering over the backseat. He had pulled the sheet off the painting.

"Put the sheet back on, honey," she told him.

"But, Mom? Is that Nana's . . .'"

"Cover it up, honey."

"Does she have clothes on?"

"Yes, she has clothes on. Put the sheet back."

"What's he talking about?" Andy asked.

"The painting."

"You've left it in the car the whole time? The heat's going to ruin it."

"The water ruined it."

"Why's he asking if she has clothes on?"

Nicholas said, "Because she doesn't have any on."

Madeline spoke under her breath to Andy, "Just let it drop. Some of the paint has chipped." But he had already swung the door open and joined Nicholas in the back. "Holy moly," he said, looking over the seat at the painting in the very back.

"Goddamn it, Andy," Madeline said. "Cover it back up."

"Mom! You're cussing!"

Andy slid back into the front beside her. "Wow. What do you think is the deal?"

"Hell if I know!"

"You're cussing again, Mom!" Nicholas said.

Andy looked at her from under the too-small cowboy hat. "It's okay. So your mom posed nude. It was the sixties."

"We don't know if she posed nude!"

" 'Signs point to yes,' " he quoted the 8 Ball.

"Would you shut up? God. Why won't these people pull out?"

"Because there's a lot of traffic," Andy said, and added, "I think it's sort of cool if she posed nude."

"Can we not talk about this, please? With Nicholas?"

"I already saw it, Mom," Nicholas said.

"When did you notice it?" Andy asked her.

"Last night. After I got here."

"Why didn't you tell me?"

She glared at him.

Nicholas said, "Are we ever going to get out of this gas station?"

When they finally pulled out, Andy changed the subject by telling Nicholas about the rodeo. "These aren't rodeo people," he said over the seat. "These are cowboys who work on real ranches. When they ride the bucking broncos, they'll be using real saddles, not specialty saddles, and the money from the rodeo will help out cowboys who have been hurt, or whose kids are sick or want to go to college."

What a phony he was, Madeline thought. He knew nothing about rodeos. He had learned all this from a website an hour ago.

Passing the saddle shop at the edge of town, they drove bumper to bumper in a line of trailers and pickups, the lights of the rodeo forming a dusty halo in the darkening sky before them and obliterating the stars. Teenage boys roughhoused in the bed of the truck in front of them, scuffling over a T-shirt. A sign at the rodeo exit announced no alcohol would be permitted, but Madeline decided she would drink a beer after she parked.

Andy was telling Nicholas about calf roping. She pictured him lecturing to perfectly functional corporate employees on how to relate in the workplace. It was hard to believe, looking at him in that hat squeezed on his head, that people took him seriously about anything.

At the clogged entrance to the parking lot the woman selling tickets had a bouffant of bleached hair. "Adults are eight dollars," she said. "Kids are free. Park where you want." She flagged them through when Madeline paid. Madeline circled slowly among buses and campers, dodging pedestrians and a man with gray pigtails on horseback. Finally she parked near the livestock pens. A train rattled along the nearby tracks, close enough to shake the Suburban and drown out the sound of Nicholas crunching on Corn Nuts. When it had passed, a steady, nervous lowing of cattle settled over the silence.

"I want to sit here and drink a beer," Madeline said. "You all go in."

"We'll wait for you," Andy told her. He got out of the car with

Nicholas, and they stood together peering through the rungs of a metal fence at a skittish horse pacing around in a cramped pen. Madeline sat in the car drinking, smelling damp manure and dusty hay through the open windows. She could hear the shouting of the announcer from inside the covered arena, "Get on up behind him, boys! Stick to him! Stick to him!"

Andy walked over and spoke to her. "Why don't you just talk to your mom and be honest. Tell her the portrait got wet and some of the paint is cracking and you're wondering—"

"Please don't tell me what to say to my mom."

He returned to the fence and scooped a handful of hay from the ground and offered it to the horse. Beside him, Nicholas squinted from blowing dust and the lights of vehicles circling the parking lot.

"Why are you feeding that horse?" Madeline shouted through the window. Andy turned and stared at her blankly. "It's not your horse," she told him, and he dropped the hay on the ground.

She was starting to feel like a bully.

What if it wasn't his fault that he was inclined to be unfaithful? He was possibly like the species of voles she had read about in a magazine. They were different from prairie voles. Male prairie voles were monogamous, and these others were not. Prairie voles had hormones that addicted them to their mates.

But marriage was not an addiction. Marriage was a commitment.

Still, whatever Andy had done was over. He wasn't doing it now. Now he was only offering hay to the horse again.

"It's not your horse!" she shouted.

"Okay, *okay.*"

Could he not even keep any boundaries with a *horse*? She yanked the rubber band out of her ponytail and twisted it back in.

Andy and Nicholas stroked the horse's nose through the rungs of the fence.

The metallic voice continued to rumble from the arena: "You are on the money, boys! Goodness gracious! That's a fifty-three point twenty-two! You are *on* it!"

A thin boy in a ball cap with riding gear draped over his shoulder jogged past Madeline's window. His hurry, and the jangling gear, and the ball cap, the reins flapping shattered her thoughts with a sudden memory of the boy at Devil's Sinkhole running toward the car. The memory flew at her, spinning her into a panic, as if she were once again heading down the white caliche road toward the nightmare at the sinkhole. She was wrestling with her dread when Andy came to the window.

"Are you ready to go in?" he asked.

"I need a minute more. Go on and take Nicholas."

"Honey? Are you okay?"

"Yeah." She didn't want to ever confide in Andy again. "Go on in."

She watched the two of them disappear among the vehicles. A dry wind gusted through the Suburban, carrying cattle sounds and the whinny of horses. Madeline rolled the window up, finished the rest of the beer, got the other beer from the back, and drank it, too. Mildly intoxicated, she found her way through slatted shadows of livestock pens, past an on-call ambulance parked near the rear of the bucking chutes, and into the arena.

The lights and chaotic atmosphere helped to dispel her dark thoughts, and she began to think about Emmett Johnson and wonder if she would see him. The announcer's voice thundered down from the booth, "And now for the Escamilla brothers—world-famous *charros* here from Mexico to amaze us with their rope tricks!"

She spotted Andy and Nicholas buying burritos at a booth and climbed into the stands with them as they ate. Mariachi music played over the speakers while the *charros*, in sombreros and studded leggings, performed horseback stunts and lariat feats. A cowgirl riding an Appaloosa galloped across from the pens, the horse's hooves churning up dirt and the girl's braid flapping against her back.

Scanning the arena, Madeline finally saw Emmett standing near a banner for McCoy's Building Supply. He wore jeans and the same work boots he had worn earlier, but now with a western shirt and a cowboy hat. She waved at him, and moments later he appeared next to her and squatted down on a step, a boy just older than Nicholas standing behind him.

Emmett introduced the boy as his son, Clay, and Madeline introduced Andy.

"Thank you so much for the help with Ranger," Andy told Emmett, standing to shake his hand. "You really saved the day."

"Not any problem at all. How's he doing?"

"Fine, I think. Thanks to you. I'm just glad you were able to get there."

Clay bounced in his boots, his hands in his back pockets, his hat brim resting on his ears. He had the same solid build as his father.

In the arena, two mounted cowboys in matching plaid shirts were trying to rope a steer with a number placarded on its back. "Hang it on him!" a woman sitting behind Madeline shouted. "Come on, Skinny! Stay with him. Get in closer! Hang it on him!"

When the steer was roped and on the ground, Nicholas asked, "What are they putting on that cow's head?"

"Chalk mark," Clay told him.

The stands erupted into applause. "That's a thirty-seven point nineteen!" the announcer shouted. "Headed, heeled, and caught! That'll do! That'll do!"

An elderly man with a large belt buckle tapped Emmett on the shoulder, and they talked of a colt with a leg ailment that Emmett had cared for. When the man was gone, Emmett invited Nicholas to participate in the boot scramble. "It's a kids' event coming up," he explained. "Clay's going to be in it. You can come down with him if you want to."

"Can I, Mom?"

"I'll keep an eye on him," Emmett said.

When they'd been gone for a minute, Madeline got up to follow them down.

"Where are you going?" Andy asked. "We can see better from up here."

"I want to go check on him."

"He's right there with the other kids." Andy pointed. "He's fine. You won't be able to see as well from down there."

"I'd just rather be there." She made her way down to where Emmett stood at the rail, jammed between other parents and onlookers.

"Hi there," he said when Madeline squeezed in beside him. "I was hoping you'd come down."

They watched the jostling kids bunched like motherless calves in the arena. Nicholas and Clay were hopping around on one boot each, waiting to start the scramble, having tossed their other boots into the pile mounding up in the center.

"Your husband seems like a nice guy," Emmett said. He was crowded close; she could feel the heat of his body.

"We're not getting along right now," she told him. "He fooled around with someone a few nights ago. I have no idea why I'm telling you this. Maybe because I just drank two beers in the car."

Emmett patted her shoulder, his hand resting there for a moment, and she wondered if Andy noticed this from where he sat in the stands. She didn't care if he did.

They watched the arena. "So what's going to happen?" she asked.

He gave her an overlong glance, his gaze resting on her mouth and then traveling down a little. "I can't say I know."

"I mean in the boot scramble."

"Oh, that." He smiled and turned to look at the boys. "They'll run out there and scramble around for their boots."

# 47

# SORTING STONES

Spread before Carlotta on the hardwood floor of her childhood bed-room was a collection of tin cans filled with gemstones. She plucked the stones from the tins, pairing those of similar size to make into ear-rings, searching out compatible colors for necklaces. The icy feel of the gems in her fingers was soothing and familiar. She wore an embroi-dered Mexican dress, once bright red but now faded and threadbare from having been used as a cover-up for her swimsuit on dive boats. Stacked throughout the room were boxes of merchandise for the shop and suitcases from the trailer home where she had lived with Martin. Rock hunting tools lay piled in a corner—work gloves, hammer and chisel and shims, a bucket of dusty agates shaped like biscuits, their surfaces sparkling with quartz and clusters of black that looked like lumps of caviar. There was a cool and earthy smell of polished stones and a faint scent of perfumed candles.

For fifteen years she had cut and polished and strung together all these beautiful shiny pieces of earth. She wasn't sure what she would do with her life if she closed the shop. She loved the sparkling objects and smell of incense and the decorative peacock feathers. She could make more profit by selling over the Internet, but probably not enough, and certainly not enough if her dream of raising a child were to come true. And she didn't really want to spend her days wrapping mer-chandise in bubble packing and shipping it off to customers she had never met.

She should re-envision her life completely and start fresh. This would require a lot of planning, and she wasn't sure how to take the first step. There were so many things she would need to do. She would close the shop and get a job—which might require a move. And then she would have to find a doctor who would guide her through the process of having a child on her own. She didn't suppose there were many of those in Alpine. Also—and this weighed heavily on her mind—she was thirty-six years old. She did not have so much time.

Hearing a sound at the door, she looked up and saw her mother and father standing there together. "Can we come in?"

"Of course."

Her mother moved a pile of clothes to sit in the chair. She put her hands on her knees. Her father sat on a wooden chest at the foot of the bed.

"Shelly told us you would like to find your biological parents," Delia said.

"She wasn't supposed to tell you that."

"I know she wasn't, love. There's a reason she did."

"I can't imagine what reason. I didn't want . . ."

"Shelly is your biological mother," Delia said. "And Wyatt is your biological father."

For a second, Carlotta had no emotional reaction at all. She had the vague sense that something was not true. It occurred to her, fleetingly, that this was a trick of some kind to keep her from looking for those other parents. Perhaps those parents were cruel and destructive, perhaps jailed for some heinous crime, and her mother and father and Shelly and Wyatt had made up this story to protect her from the truth.

Except this was not the kind of thing they would do. Her parents had never lied to her.

"That doesn't make sense," she said. Either she had been lied to her whole life, or she was being lied to now.

"Should we start at the beginning?" her mother asked her very gently, very quietly and solicitously. "And tell you everything?"

Carlotta looked at her father. He cleared his throat. "It's true, angel."

"Listen with an open heart," her mother said softly. "It was hard for me, too, in the beginning, to accept these things that I'm about to tell you. You have to remember we wouldn't have you if none of this had ever happened. I don't want you to blame Wyatt and Shelly. Does this make any sense to you?" Delia's hands were shaking.

Carlotta whispered, "Yes," but it did not. She tried to listen closely as her mother spoke, but the halting sentences washed over her. The affair Shelly and Wyatt had was very, very sad, and nearly destroyed them both, her mother said. "They loved each other very much. Their lives were bound together by what happened that day on the mall, in ways only two people who share that experience can possibly understand. And I know they loved each other. And when Shelly found out she was pregnant, they stopped seeing each other. They never saw each other again until last night."

Carlotta pictured Shelly and Wyatt there in the driveway last night, talking to each other as if none of this had happened—as if the only relevant thing at the moment was that Wyatt had caught the dog. "It's extraordinary," she whispered, looking at her parents, her fingers plucking at the little pool of turquoise pebbles she had left in her lap, as if the familiar feel of such tiny trinkets could restore a whole lifetime that suddenly seemed to have gone missing. "I don't know what to say . . . or think. I feel like it's wonderful, in some terrible way."

"She didn't want to give you up for adoption," Delia went on. "But she was young and couldn't support herself or give you what she thought would be a happy childhood, and her parents advised her that this would be the best thing for you. I'm not sure that she would have given you up if it weren't to us. She was broken up that day in the hospital when we came to get you. When we saw her in the lobby . . . you can't imagine . . ." Jack reached over and put his hand on his wife's knee.

Carlotta remembered the day she had gone to the hospital in Beeville, how she had walked into the plain little lobby in the small, flat town, and had not even gone to the desk to ask any questions, having not been ready for answers.

And now the answers had come to her, right here in her own bedroom: She had known her biological parents all her life. This was astounding. They were not the fantasy parents she had imagined; they did not live in obscure, far-off places and walk around in indistinct bodies and wonder, or not wonder, what had ever become of her. Those fantasy people were as lost to her now as the unformed baby buried beside the creek, their features never seen. And her biological parents were people she already knew. She admired them both. They each had a daughter who had worn her hand-me-down clothes. Shelly was her closest confidante. Wyatt's talent was breathtaking. He painted pictures of stones so realistic Carlotta could tell exactly what those stones would feel like in her hands.

"I've never seen anyone suffer like Shelly suffered that day in

Beeville," her mother was saying. "If you could know the way she cried. She thought she was losing you forever. And later, when she wanted to be part of your life, your dad and I thought it couldn't be wrong, since obviously she loved you so much."

"So you worked it out together?"

"I guess we've worked it out together for thirty-six years. Shelly wanted it to work out, more than anything else in the world."

"But did you want it, too?"

A look of sadness came over Delia's face, but was instantly gone. "I felt she would only add good things to your life, and I think she has."

"But what about your life, Mom? I can see this was hard for you. And I think I confided in her too often. Did you feel like I was turning to her too much? I never would have done that if I'd known."

"It would have been too selfish for me to care about that," Delia said. "If you could have seen her, and how she cried when she thought she had lost you, then you would know why I couldn't hold it against her that she loved you. And I'm happy with how it's turned out."

"Are you?"

"Yes. I'm just . . ." She faltered then.

"What, Mom?'

The tears came spilling out. "Yes, I envied her some. Because you had so much in common with her. And I always thought . . . I always thought that if you found out . . . if you asked . . . and we told you"—she shook her head as if to shake her feelings off—"then you might love her even more. But if you don't go on loving her like you always have, then I haven't done my job as your mother."

"Oh Mom, Mom . . ." Carlotta got up, dropping the stones from her lap, and threw her arms around Delia. She squeezed herself into the chair with her mother and held her close. "I shouldn't have gone to Shelly. I should have come to you! And to you, Dad! It was just because I didn't want to hurt you! I feel . . . so confused about her now. And you say if my feelings about her change, then somehow you've failed as a mother! You're the best mother I could have had! I can't believe she would put you through this. She gave me up, and then wanted to have me back. I can't sort it all out."

"You don't have to sort it out now, except to know she only wanted the best for you," Jack said.

"But I have to know what to say to her. And . . . what am I going to say to Wyatt?"

"If you don't want to talk to them right now . . . tonight . . . tomorrow, that's all right. They just wanted to be here in case you do."

"Are they downstairs?"

"Shelly is. She's in the kitchen. And Wyatt's out in the cabin. But honey, they realize you might not want to talk."

Carlotta felt as if she had been dropped into a different life. Nothing was as it should be. The people she had planned to look for were already here, as if she had found them and brought them home and now they were already part of the family, all in a few minutes. "And to think I sometimes worried that my biological mother might not want to meet me."

She didn't know what to do next. She felt she should prepare herself to talk to Shelly and Wyatt. She should change her clothes . . . do something . . . at least think something through. "I'll come down in a minute," she promised. "I just need a minute alone. I need to think about what to say."

When her parents had left the room, the strangest thought came to Carlotta: She owed her life to a sniper. All those years ago, someone had gone up in the tower of the University of Texas and for some unknowable reason had started shooting people. And now here Carlotta was. If Wyatt and her father hadn't rushed onto the plaza to help Shelly, she herself wouldn't exist.

What was she supposed to feel for Wyatt and Shelly now, other than what she had felt for them all her life? How strange to live with a mystery and then to have it resolved and have nothing about the resolution change anything. There were times in the past when she had felt like an imposter or amnesiac here in Alpine—as if she was meant to be living somewhere entirely different, with different parents, and only by fortune had ended up here with Jack and Delia. And now it appeared she had always belonged here; that this was the way it was meant to be, and these were the people—all of them—who were meant to be in her life. There was nobody on the outside she was supposed to bring in. They were all here, and always had been.

She understood everything her parents had just told her, and yet, as she thought about it, she partly resented her parents, too. Collectively with Shelly and Wyatt, they had misled her. She felt conspired against and duped, having worried over questions any one of these four people whom she had trusted could have answered.

Still, Wyatt and Shelly had never abandoned her. No one had ever given her up for good. Her whole life, she had imagined her mother handing her over to Jack and Delia and disappearing somewhere. And now, as it turned out, no one had disappeared. She didn't know whether she was relieved or angry—and if she was angry, whom she was angry with.

She took off her faded dress and put on jeans and a clean blouse. Placing the sorted rocks into small plastic bags, she dropped the rest of them into the cans, hearing the little clinking, plunking sounds— agate and lapis, spiderwebbed turquoise, and blue angelite. As she pressed the lids back on, she had the sorrowful feeling that she had lost Jack and Delia as parents instead of finding Shelly and Wyatt. As if she were suddenly orphaned.

Pulling open the shutters, she looked at the night sky over the curved road that led down to the cabin. She had always loved the darkness from this window. She loved the crystal stars. But the moon had troubled her, and she recalled how as a child she had wondered about its far side—the side she couldn't see. It had reminded her of all the unseen places on earth her parents might be. It had been like a luminous stone, a shiny Mexican jelly opal, taunting her with its distance, filling her with sadness and pointless wishing for something she couldn't have, or something she didn't know.

And yet now it was the milky moonlight that gave her a glimpse of Wyatt making his way up the road from the cabin. Carlotta studied him. He was tall, although he appeared smaller with the moon angled above him. He walked against the wind. He didn't look left or right, but walked with purpose. An eddy of dust swirled on the road before him. Carlotta watched him climb the slope of the narrow road in the wide landscape under the clear sky.

# 48

# WAITING FOR CARLOTTA

Shelly had washed the dishes, turned the kitchen television on and then off, walked outside and paced around in the windy driveway, only to come back in to sit at the kitchen table with the lights off and listen anxiously for any noise on the stairs.

What she heard was the squeak of the screen door in the front hall, and then Wyatt came in.

"It's breezy out there," he said.

"Yes."

"Nothing yet?"

"They're still upstairs."

"Did you have any dinner?"

"No. Did you?"

"Lasagna." He opened the refrigerator, the bright interior light throwing his shadow backward across the planks of the floor. "I'll make you something."

"There's no possible way I could eat."

"How about tuna salad? There's some here. And fruit salad."

"No thanks."

"Have you eaten at all today?"

"A sandwich."

"I could make you a milk shake."

"I really don't want anything."

"Then how about just a glass of wine?"

"I don't drink anymore."

He looked at her. "Ever?"

"I was drinking too much after Dan died, so I gave it up. Now and then I have a glass of wine, but tonight isn't the night."

He served himself a bowl of ice cream and carried it to the table. Watching the way he held the spoon reminded her of watching him paint. His presence still felt strongly illicit.

"How are you?" he asked.

"I'm not sure if I'm more worried about Carlotta or Madeline."

"How are *you*, Shelly?"

She shook her head. "Scared to death of what they'll think of me after tonight. And still ashamed . . . on a number of levels . . . I guess. Which seems unnecessary after all these years, but it's the case. I'm not sure I'll be able to look anyone in the eye."

"You can look me in the eye."

She did so for a second, but the intensity of her feelings unnerved her, and she looked away.

"And you can probably look Ranger in the eye," he said. "His behavior is worse than yours ever was."

She laughed.

"I feel I can look Ranger in the eye myself," he added.

Her laughter slid away, and she touched his hand on the table. "Not that it matters . . . with things as they are. But I have missed you."

He took hold of her hand. The light from the chandelier in the hall shone in his eyes, partly obscuring her in the shadows as he watched her, her shirt wrinkled, the cuffs unbuttoned. Her hair had fallen into her face, reminding him of the windy day at Port Aransas and how she had watched the sandpipers dart in and out of the water and leave their teasing prints in the sand.

For forty years, he had dreamed of her, and now he marveled at the subtle changes. Her eyelids sagged a little, and her mouth dropped at the corners, ever so slightly. But she was beautifully familiar. Age had softened, not coarsened her. The small dip in her clavicle created a shadowed hollow. "For what it's worth," he said, "when I left you that day in Lockhart, at your parents' house, I didn't believe it was over. Not that I held out real hope, but . . . I've never believed it was over."

"It was over," she said gently. "If it hadn't been, I couldn't have married Dan."

"Of course." That was as it should be. But her statement saddened him, because he would have liked to believe she had always belonged to him in some way. With her truthfulness, she had taken herself back.

She let go of his hand reluctantly and they spoke in low voices about their lives, their children, how generous and good Jack and Delia had been. They talked about Elaine's cancer and how strong the marriage had become in spite of everything, and how agonized Wyatt was at the thought of telling Elaine the truth now. Shelly told him how much she missed Dan, and Wyatt asked her if she thought she would ever remarry. She said she didn't think so. "But I've stopped ever trying to predict anything," she said. They shared memories and talked about the choices they had made and not made, and Shelly thought of how Wyatt had rescued her, only to break her heart, and how the rain had tumbled out of the sky when she sat in the station wagon and told him she was pregnant. She remembered how in Lockhart he had turned and left her. "After you were gone, sometimes I felt like I had made the whole thing up. The way it ended so suddenly, without even a phone call after that . . . It didn't just take away what we had; it took away what we'd been through."

He wanted to stand and pull her into his arms. "You have no idea how many times I had my hand on the phone," he said, and she pictured herself, pregnant, watching *Petticoat Junction* and *The Newlywed Game* on Aileen's couch and wishing the phone would ring.

But those memories were a world she didn't want to return to. Madeline and Carlotta were what mattered now, and she longed for Carlotta to come downstairs so the waiting would be over.

"She'll get through this," Wyatt assured her. "She's like you. She's resilient."

"She's never let things upset her too much," Shelly said. "She gets pensive and restless, but she tends to see the bright side. Honestly, I'm most worried about Madeline. She's especially vulnerable right now because of the problems with Andy. Carlotta will have gained something from tonight, even if it's just answers, and Madeline will have lost faith in me at the exact time she needs somebody to trust. Before Dan's death she was jealous of my relationship with Carlotta, and Dan thought we should tell her the truth. We were going to talk with Jack and Delia about it, and then see if Jack would talk to you. But then after what happened, I just couldn't do that to her. I guess you know that the reason we were coming to Alpine that weekend was the opening of Carlotta's store."

Wyatt nodded.

"Madeline hasn't forgotten that."

"You couldn't have known what would happen, Shelly."

"I've had that conversation with myself—plenty of times. It never sinks in totally. Anyway, that's too painful to talk about right now. I should be telling you what a spectacular teacher Madeline is. She teaches fourth grade, and the kids love her. She's dogmatic in the way she imposes order, but they flock around her."

Wyatt listened while she continued to talk about Madeline. "There's something I'm curious about," he said. "Why you gave her the portrait."

"How did you know I gave it to her?"

"I asked Jack why it was in the closet out at the cabin and he said Madeline must have brought it."

"It's in the cabin?"

"It was last night. When I looked again this afternoon, it wasn't."

"That doesn't make any sense. I can't see why she would bring it with her."

"I noticed it was damaged."

"Damaged?"

She apparently hadn't known this, so he was sorry he had mentioned it. "Not badly. Some of the paint looks like it got slightly damp. It can be fixed."

"What does it look like?"

"Just some of the paint has a little damage. It's not serious."

"Damage, where? Which part?"

"Some of the paint that was less stable."

"But which part?"

"The part that was added," he finally said.

It dawned on her. "The blouse?"

"Just part of it."

"How much of it?"

"Not a lot."

"Can you see—what's underneath it?"

"No, not unless you were really looking."

"Madeline *would* be looking." Agitated, she got up and walked to the refrigerator and began searching the shelves.

"What are you looking for?"

She didn't know. "Something to drink." The refrigerator was crowded. She removed a jug of milk that blocked her view and set it on the floor, then removed a plastic container of cherry tomatoes, a bag of miniature carrots. She was looking into the back, but all she could see in her mind was the portrait.

Wyatt stood up. "Shelly?" She let the door swing closed, sweeping away the interior light, and then was aware that the yellow light from the hallway had shifted and blinked away. Turning, she saw Carlotta in the doorway, her curls an orange halo.

She stood for a moment without saying anything. No one said a word. Then, haltingly, Carlotta said, "Mom and Dad told me. It's a little bit of a shock. I want you to know I'm happy, but . . . it's kind of hard to think of you as my parents . . . because you've both always been someone else to me. It's not like I'm starting from scratch to get to know you."

Shelly forgot the portrait, and Madeline, and Wyatt, and all the events of the day, and almost all the events of four decades. They vanished, leaving only Carlotta, silhouetted by the light.

Shelly managed to say, "If there's anything you would like to ask . . . something you want us to explain—"

Carlotta said, a little flatly, "So you were in love, and you were pregnant, and Wyatt was married. And you believed it was best to give me up."

"I hoped it was best. I wasn't sure what I believed."

Carlotta fell quiet, looking at her, and then said, "Then why don't we start with Beeville."

The jug of milk was still at Shelly's feet. The cherry tomatoes. Wyatt stood by the table. "I went to Beeville to stay with my mother's aunt, Aileen."

"So no one would know about me?"

"Yes."

"And you gave birth to me there in the hospital?"

"Yes."

Carlotta turned to Wyatt. "And you saw me . . . later?"

"When you were a month old. I was living in Provincetown. I came to stay with your parents in Austin."

She blinked. She looked at Shelly again. "When I was born, did you hold me?"

The memory came to her—the little pink bundle that the nurse had carried away. "Yes."

"You held me?"

"I held you. For a few days."

"Oh," Carlotta whispered.

The memories were too clear for Shelly—the blue, blue eyes, and delicate ears, the fierce grip of the little hands, the round clock on the wall stealing the hours by seconds.

"And Mom and Dad came to get me?"

She recalled how she had run in her gown through the lobby, even the useless breast dripping milk. Delia had worn a green dress. Delia had embraced her, so that both of them at once were holding the baby. She remembered the red coat her mother had brought her, and getting into the station wagon, and how she had wanted to scream and open the door and throw herself out into the street. She put her hands to her eyes and squeezed her eyes shut to stop the flood of tears and all the grief from coming. She felt her chest heave. "I wasn't supposed to love you," she cried.

# 49

# THE END OF THE RODEO

The announcer's voice echoed loudly through the arena: "She's a fighter! We got ourselves a fighter! Get aholt of her tail!"

Wedged between Nicholas and Emmett, Madeline stood in the crowd at the rail, watching a man on a piebald horse lean back in his saddle and tug hard at a rope with a horned cow at the other end, the noise and hammer of hooves shaking the rail under Madeline's palms. The man was trying to stop the cow before she slammed into the bucking chutes. Three cowboys on foot chased after her, while George Strait's "Amarillo by Morning" blared from the loudspeakers and wind tugged at the tin roof.

Nicholas stood on the middle rung of the rail, having retrieved his boot from the scramble and now wearing both boots again. Clay, on the far side of his father, leaned out toward the arena, watching the heifer buck and strain at the rope.

Emmett said, "Not my favorite event. Kind of hard on man and beast."

The rider dismounted, digging his boot heels into the dirt as the cow hauled him forward. The running cowboys closed in and trapped the cow between them, securing her in a headlock. Two of them twisted her head while the third grabbed hold of her tail but was kicked away by her hind leg. Finally they managed to tug the rope off and hold the cow in place for long enough to get a bottle under her udder and a few squirts of milk. The skinniest ran with the bottle to a circle drawn in the dirt, and the audience cheered.

Clay leaned over to Nicholas. "Want to go look at the broncos?"

"Can I?" Nicholas asked his mother.

"He'll be fine if he's with Clay," Emmett assured her.

"Okay," she said. "Go tell your father where you'll be, and ask him to keep an eye on you."

She turned around and watched him climb into the stands and talk to Andy. In a minute, Andy came down. "I'm going to go with him to look at the broncos. Don't you want to come?"

"I think Clay's going to show you where they are," she said. "And I want to watch this milking event. I'll find you in a minute."

Andy hesitated.

"Follow me," Clay said. "This way."

Nicholas hurried behind him, and Andy followed, glancing back at Madeline and Emmett.

Another team positioned themselves in the arena while a handler opened a gate and a black cow burst through. The cow pitched and moved in circles when she was roped, plunging toward the rail. Emmett took hold of Madeline's arm and pulled her back just as the cow crashed into the rail in front of them. One of the cowboys had hold of the tail; another had hold of the rope. Two others tried to drag her head to the ground, but she charged at them and they fled. She wheeled around to confront them, planting her hooves, and swayed her head from side to side, puffing her nostrils. The cowboy still holding the rope approached and pulled her head to the ground while another ran up, shoved the bottle under her udder, and started to milk her.

But the cow sank to her knees.

"Gotta milk her standing up!" the announcer shouted. "Get her up! It's a rule! Get her goin'! Get her movin'!"

The heaviest of the four team members took hold of her horns and attempted to pull her up as the cow rolled onto her side. The others shoved at her, one of them flapping his hat at her face, but she showed no more life than a boulder. The cowboys stood shaking their heads. The shortest one turned and shrugged his shoulders at the announcer.

"We got a mishap, ladies and gentlemen," the announcer said. "That cow is not movin'. Emmett? Emmett Johnson? Are you out there?"

Emmett was already climbing over the rail. Madeline watched him stride into the arena and kneel to examine the cow. She saw him say something to one of the cowboys, who turned and shouted to the announcer, "She's breathin'! She'll probably come to!"

"Did you hear that, ladies and gentlemen? She is not movin', but she is not dead. Maybe she got a little overexcited. Knocked herself out on the rail."

Emmett looked over toward Madeline just as the cow lifted her head, her horn striking hard across Emmett's brow and knocking his hat off. He stood and stumbled aside, pressing his palm to the wound as the cow rose sluggishly and trotted away.

The announcer said, "Ladies and gentlemen, we have got another mishap. The cow's fine, but Emmett's took a pretty good lick in the head. We sure hope he's all right."

Several people gathered around Emmett. Madeline wondered if she should climb down into the arena and offer to help him. She looked around for Clay, but he had disappeared with Nicholas and Andy. An ambulance pulled in through a gate and two EMTs—a man and a woman—jumped out. The woman dabbed at Emmett's forehead, trying to staunch the bleeding, but he took the gauze from her, pressed it to the wound, gave a cursory wave to the announcer, and started up the ramp from the arena.

"He's all right," the announcer said. "Just a little bang to the head."

Emmett looked at Madeline as he headed toward the exit, the front of his shirt bloody. The female EMT trailed behind, insisting he give her a better look at the wound. When he stopped and pulled the gauze away, the blood ran down his face, and Madeline hurried over to see if she could help. "Get that ambulance out of here," she heard him tell the EMT.

"This could be a serious head injury," the woman said.

"It is not a serious head injury." He sounded peeved and disgusted. "It's a cut on my eyebrow. I just need to change my shirt."

"We should put a butterfly on it at least," she insisted.

"Then give me the butterfly." He put his hand out.

"We should clean the wound first."

"I can do that in my truck. Just give me the butterfly, Alice."

Reluctantly, she dug a bandage out of her medical case and handed it over to Emmett.

Madeline followed Emmett outside, where a hard wind blew dust around the parked vehicles and agitated the penned animals. Horses paced and whinnied, and cattle bawled, jamming themselves together. The lights in the parking area had turned a lurid red in the blowing dust.

Emmett turned and waited for her.

"Are you all right?" she asked, raising her voice over the wind.

"Hell of a stupid thing to do," he said irritably.

"How deep do you think it is?" she asked.

"Not deep. Of all the goddamn things. Come with me to my truck." He peeled the bandage out of its wrapper, shoving it on his forehead as he walked.

"You can't put it on like that," she told him. "You need some antibiotic ointment."

"I just need to stop this bleeding. Shit."

"Are you light-headed?"

"No." He stopped walking. "But where the hell is my truck?" He squinted at the rows of school campers and jacked-up pickups. "This way."

The grit irritated her eyes. She could taste it. It stung her skin.

"I felt that cow move," he said. "I don't know why the hell I didn't get out of the way. I just . . ." He shook his head. "I think I was looking at you." He turned and looked at her briefly again, the bandage plastered across his brow soaked with blood already.

"How long is this dust going to last?" she asked him.

"Awhile."

At the truck, he opened one of the hinged doors of the vet box in the bed and pulled out a Ziploc bag of first-aid supplies. Yanking the bandage off his forehead, he got behind the wheel and looked at himself in the rearview mirror, dabbing at the cut. Madeline climbed in on the passenger side, relieved to close herself away from the wind. She tried to help Emmett, but he wouldn't allow her to look at the wound up close.

"I'm not going to hear the end of this," he grumbled. "Not in Alpine. I'll be a laughingstock." Pressing a wad of gauze over the cut, he started taping it down. "There's a clean shirt, back in the box. Would you mind getting it for me?" He was having trouble making the tape stick over the dust. "It's in the front compartment on top of the refrigerator."

She got out, shielding her eyes. Her hair had come loose from the ponytail. It whipped around her face. When she lifted the lid of the vet box a light came on, shining on ropes and halters that hung from hooks, a jumble of buckets and tubes, a pair of rubber boots, and a small refrigerator. Taped on the underside of the lid, beside Emmett's medical license, was a Gary Larson cartoon about a veterinarian and a handwritten note that said, "Mel owes fifty dollars." An astringent medicinal smell was strong in spite of the wind.

Madeline grabbed a T-shirt from a stack and got back in the truck and gave it to Emmett. He already had the bloody one off and was rolling it up and stuffing it under the seat. She tried not to stare at his naked chest as he pulled the clean shirt on.

"Now all I need is my hat," he said. "Damn it, where's that?"

"It fell off in the arena. Do you want me to go look for it?"

"Somebody'll get it for me." He settled back against the door, and she saw that his eye was discolored and starting to swell. "Just stay with me for a minute. Talk to me. Would you?" Reaching across the seat, he took hold of her hand and rubbed his calloused thumb over her knuckles. They sat for a minute like that. She knew she should pull her hand away and fight the wind to go back inside, but then she would never have this illicit excitement again. The best she would be able to do was patch up a problematic relationship with her unfaithful husband.

"What do you want to talk about?" she asked him.

"How's the dog doing?"

"We already talked about that."

"How are you doing, yourself?" he asked.

"Fine. Hating this wind. Wishing I hadn't told you about Andy fooling around."

"You ought to forgive him for that," Emmett remarked. "Everyone screws up sooner or later. One way or another."

"I haven't," she said.

"Oh?" He looked amused.

Not yet, she hadn't. She studied his bandaged forehead in the darkness. "Does that hurt?"

"Like the dickens."

She twined her fingers into his hand and felt heedless, closed in the truck this way, with the wind hurling dust at the windows. Maybe Emmett was right: No one was perfect. People were meant to muddle their way through marriage.

Emmett slid his thumb back and forth over her knuckles while she stared at the dashboard and listened to the rumbling approach of another train. She wiped at the dust on her face and tried to gather the courage to move close enough to put her hand on Emmett's leg. The silence between them had started to feel demanding. She almost spoke, but didn't. Emmett's gaze suddenly shifted away from her face, and she turned and saw Andy knocking on her window, looking in from the brown haze, holding the cowboy hat beside his head to shield his face from the blowing dust.

Emmett released her hand, and Madeline opened the door slightly. "Hey, hi," she shouted over the piercing wail of the train's whistle.

"Hi," Andy shouted back.

"What's up?" she asked as the whistle faded, replaced by the din of the train moving along the tracks and the loud moaning of the wind.

"I was looking for you." He had a puzzled expression.

"Where's Nicholas? I thought you were watching him."

"He's with Clay. The lariat guys said they'd keep an eye on him. I saw you leave—"

"Emmett needed to change his shirt. Did you see what happened?"

"I did." He looked at Emmett suspiciously. "Are you all right?" he yelled to him over the noise.

"I am now."

Madeline climbed out of the truck. "I'm going to go find Nicholas," she told Emmett. "I'll see you inside."

But she wasn't sure if she would see him inside. Before closing the door of the truck she looked at him, the bandage stuck to his head. She suddenly hoped she would never see him again.

Andy tried to use his hat to screen her from the wind as they walked toward the arena. "What were you doing?" he asked over the train's departing shriek.

"I helped him put on a bandage."

"Is anything wrong?" He had to yell to be heard.

"No."

"You were gone a long time. You were helping him out?"

She shrugged and kept walking.

Inside, teams of men were wrestling calves to the ground and pulling boxer shorts onto their hind legs. Andy and Madeline found Nicholas coming back from the bucking chutes. "We need to go," Madeline told him.

He started to argue with her, but the announcer's voice thundered over the loudspeakers: "Ladies and gentlemen, we have got a dust storm coming our way. The National Weather Service just issued a high wind warning. As much as we hate to disappoint all you folks who have come out to support our cowboys, we're going to have to shut down. We got a lot of animals to secure in this situation. You're welcome to stay here if you want to, but as you can see, we are not exactly airtight. I think it's time for all of us to head home."

People started to rise from the stands and file toward the exits. Andy helped Nicholas pull his shirt collar up over his mouth.

"Drive slow," the announcer said. "You old folks with breathing trouble like me keep your mouths shut and covered. Not a easy task when you like to talk, I know."

Tucking Nicholas between them, Madeline and Andy made their way with the crowds. People moved in groups, burying their faces into the backs of strangers for protection from the flying dust as they sought their cars. Vehicles in the parking lot appeared and vanished in heavy squalls. The lights overhead were dim orbs.

By the time they reached the Suburban, Nicholas was sputtering and near tears, complaining about the dirt in his eyes and saying he couldn't breathe. Madeline gave the keys to Andy and hurried Nicholas into the backseat. She climbed into the passenger seat and dug from under it a half-consumed bottle of water she had bought on the drive from Austin. Pouring it into her palms, she dabbed at Nicholas's eyes from over the seat. "Don't rub!" she told him.

"You're making it worse!" he wailed. "I can't see!"

The traffic moved slowly, bumper-to-bumper. The headlights of oncoming traffic looked as red as taillights, and it was hard to see the road and make out which way cars were moving. For half an hour, they crept along. The grimy air was so thick in some places their headlights seemed to be shining into a hill of dirt. Nicholas, in the backseat, exaggerated his cough. Madeline told him to stop it. Her cell phone rang.

"Honey?" It was her mom. "Are you all right?"

"We're on the way home."

"You're driving home?"

"Of course we're driving."

"Where are you?"

"Not sure. I can't see much past the road."

"Oh sweetie, you should pull over."

Madeline heard Jack's voice in the background and some discussion between him and her mother. "Jack says if you can't see the road, you should pull over," her mother finally said.

"We're at a snail's pace, Mom. There's a lot of traffic. Nobody's pulling over."

"Oh honey, be careful." She had more discussion with Jack. "Jack says if you have to pull over, you need to turn your lights off so they won't confuse other traffic about where the road is. And set your parking brake."

"Mom, we're not pulling over. We're following the other cars."

It was as if they were traveling on a planet far from earth, the particles of a hostile landscape blown by terrific winds. Closed in here with Andy and Nicholas, and with the portrait of her mother in the back, she couldn't believe she had sat in Emmett Johnson's truck and held his hand. How sad and pathetic. How desperate to try to cheer herself up like that, to sit in a truck outside a rodeo with a man she barely knew. There was a vast difference between the intimacy she longed for and the clumsy, meaningless circumstance in which she had put herself. She didn't feel wrong to have treated Andy this way—his betrayal had been much worse. But she didn't feel like the person she had thought she was.

When Andy pulled into the drive, the lights inside the house looked gloomy. Madeline put her arm around Nicholas and ran with him to the porch, Andy running behind them. Shelly flung the door open for them. Breathing hard, coughing, Madeline saw herself in the mirror over the hall table. The dust covering her was darker than her skin and lighter than her hair, so that she looked monochromatic, with only her eyes retaining their usual color. "That was the weirdest drive!" she said. "Look at us."

She expected her mother to be relieved to see them, but instead Shelly looked somber. "I'm so glad you're home safely."

"Is something wrong?" Madeline asked.

Nicholas stood on tiptoe to see as much of himself as possible in the mirror. "Look how white my teeth are!" He grinned at himself. "And look at my eyes!"

"Mom?" Madeline asked. "Where is everybody? Is everyone okay?"

"Yes, everyone's okay. But I need to talk with you."

Andy said, "Upstairs, son. Into the shower."

"But look at my eyes!"

Andy ushered him upstairs.

"Do you want to rinse your face off, first, honey?" Shelly asked Madeline.

"No, I just want to know what's wrong."

"We can talk in the parlor."

It was dark in there. Her mother sat down in a high-backed chair.

Madeline flipped the switch by the door, flooding the room with light.

"If you don't mind, leave it off," Shelly said. "It seems so bright."

In the instant before the room went dark, Shelly saw Madeline with striking clarity: her hand on the switch, her dusty, darkened face, her perplexed look. She fought the urge to stand and warn her out of the room and away from this moment of truth.

Then Madeline turned the light off.

"Sit down," Shelly said.

She sat on a sofa across from Shelly.

"There's something I have to tell you." Shelly spoke slowly and plainly, her voice not quite her own. She wanted to set out the pieces of information in a systematic way that Madeline could take in. "It is not bad news. But it will be a shock to you." She took a deep breath. "Carlotta is your half sister. She is my daughter. Wyatt Calvert is her father. Jack and Delia adopted her because they could not have children and because Wyatt and I were having an affair at the time. This was in the sixties." She waited.

Madeline did not speak.

"Before I married your father, I told him everything."

Madeline stood up and turned toward the door. Then she sat back down.

"Jack and Delia have told Carlotta everything tonight. She had wanted to look for her biological parents, and we couldn't let her go through that, knowing what we knew." The wind beat on the windows in powerful gusts. "Are you all right, honey?" She couldn't see Madeline's expression in the dark.

"No."

"I know this is confusing."

"I don't understand any of it."

"Tell me what you need to know."

"What I need to know?" She was dazed.

"Yes."

"I need to know why you're telling me this now. Why haven't I known it?"

"There are a lot of reasons, honey. Your father and I were going to tell you—we were planning to. But then after his death, I felt like you had been through too much. I felt like it would only be another adjustment that would be hard for you."

"But I was sixteen then. What about the years before?"

"Understand, we couldn't tell you without telling Carlotta."

"And why couldn't you tell Carlotta?"

"That question is so complicated. First of all, there wasn't a time when it seemed like she would be better off knowing. There wasn't a time when she said she wanted to know. And Wyatt has a family that doesn't know any of this. You can imagine what effect this could have on them."

"So I was sort of the last consideration?"

"It's not like that."

"*How* is it not like that? You couldn't tell me because of Carlotta. You couldn't tell her because of Wyatt and his family. And all that other stuff you said. I feel like I don't know you. I have a sister you didn't tell me about."

"Please try to see how complicated this is. You're making it sound very simple, and it's not simple."

"But all you had to do was ask me not to tell."

"I know it seems that way, but when should I have done that? It would have been a burden for you when you were little—to have to carry a secret like that. And impossible during that period after your father's death—you weren't up to coping with this then. And then when you were older, the relationships had evolved into something else. There was no reason to bring all this out in the open. Carlotta wasn't asking to know who her parents were, and the possible consequences for Wyatt's family—"

"I don't care about Wyatt's family! What about *our* family?"

"Our family was fine, sweetie. There was no risk to our family."

"You made Daddy lie to me."

"He never lied to you. It was important to both of us never to lie to you."

"Did Granny and Grampa know?"

"They knew everything at the time it happened."

"So they knew, too?" She stood up and paced to the end of the room and back. "I feel like I've lived in a stage set all my life! Like you set everything up and let me playact my whole life!"

She walked out, stood in the hall, and didn't know where to go. In the mirror, she saw herself—her skin the color of rusty ash. She wanted to leave the house, but the wind had imprisoned her here. She started up the stairs but felt dizzy and sat down halfway up. She didn't know who to turn to. What had just happened? She thought she heard Delia in the kitchen, but she didn't want to talk to Delia or Jack. They had deceived her the same as her mother had. The most painful thought was that her father had, too. He had known all along. She had told him she was jealous of Carlotta, and he had taken her to Devil's Sinkhole to try to make her feel better. He could have just explained the truth to her instead. Why hadn't he? If he had, he wouldn't be dead.

She tried to think it through, asking herself if she honestly would have been better off knowing about Carlotta. At what age would she have wanted to know? Six? Seven? Seventeen? Twenty-seven? She was not sure. She was not sure of anything except that everyone had lied to her.

Her mother had followed her out of the parlor and now stood at the foot of the stairs, pleading with her. "I know you're angry, but please, let's keep talking."

"I can't imagine what we would say. I don't even know if I can believe anything you say."

"I haven't lied to you, Madeline. There were things I didn't tell you, but I wasn't lying."

"It's all starting to make sense. The portrait. Who painted it?"

She heard the drop in her mother's voice. "He did. Wyatt did."

"So that was part of it? The portrait that's been hanging in my home? Now I see why you wanted me to forgive Andy. His mistakes are nothing compared to yours."

Pulling herself to her feet, she turned away from her mother and climbed the stairs and found Andy in the bedroom. He turned to her when she came in. The dirty cowboy hat was on the bedpost. "Even my pockets are full of dust!" he said. "Look at this!" He turned a pocket inside out.

"Where's Nicholas?" she asked.

"He's in the shower."

"Mom and Wyatt Calvert had an affair in college and Carlotta is their child."

"What?"

"They had an affair and Carlotta is their child."

"You're making this up."

"No." She didn't know what response she wanted from Andy. Not comfort. "My husband is a cheater, and my mother is a liar. Some family." She left the room, crossed the hall, and knocked on Carlotta's door.

"Mom told me," she said when Carlotta opened the door.

"Oh, Madeline, look how dusty you are! Come in. You can use my bathroom and rinse off."

"No thanks."

"I was just sitting here thinking about everything. Come in."

Madeline went in but did not sit down. "It's inconceivable," she said. "I wonder if they would ever have told you if you hadn't decided to look for them. Didn't it ever occur to them that you might want to know who they were?"

"Honestly, I'm not sure I did want to know. I've been going over this all night, and I'm just now figuring it out. It would have been confusing to know this when I was younger. It's confusing enough now."

"Mom has basically lied to us her whole life," Madeline said.

"Yes, and so have my parents. I'm still getting used to it. But if you think about it, what choice did they really have?"

"Honesty. That choice."

"True," Carlotta said. "But at a huge cost to Wyatt's family."

"Yes—the way it was handled makes perfect sense for Wyatt and his family, as long as you think his wife deserves to be lied to. But I feel conspired against. Why are you being so pious about it?"

Carlotta was taken by surprise. "I don't mean to be pious. I resent some of this the same as you do. But it would have been strange for us to know we were sisters when we were little."

"What about when we *weren't* little? Mom could have told me the truth when I was grown! I would have understood."

"And you would have kept it from me? And lied to me like our parents did?"

Madeline didn't answer.

"And then I would be finding out just now that you had known all along," Carlotta said. "And that wouldn't seem right. And if you and I had both known, then whenever I was around Wyatt's kids, I would have had to lie to them. It would have been hard to keep that secret—to know they were my half brother and sister and not tell them. The way it is, at least we've all been happy, and we all had good childhoods; the only people hurt by all this are our parents. It seems to me like this is their difficulty, not ours. They protected us from it, and I don't think we should make them feel bad about that."

"And I would agree with you," Madeline said, "if I hadn't spent so much time trying to figure out why my mother wanted to spend so much time with *you*."

The words clanged in her ears even as she said them, but she didn't try to retract them. She didn't feel like herself, or even know who she was anymore. Even her memories seemed invalid.

"I see how that must have felt," Carlotta said. She took a small step toward Madeline and started saying something about the importance of forgiveness. But Madeline walked out.

From the dim lighting at the top of the stairs, she looked down at the twinkling chandelier. Andy came out of the bedroom, but she rebuffed him. "Just take care of Nicholas; get him to sleep," she told him.

She was out of options, even about where to stand or sit. She didn't want to go to her mother's empty room; her mother might come up, and she didn't want to talk to her mother. She didn't want to be with Andy or Carlotta. She couldn't deal with Nicholas just now. She didn't want to go downstairs and face her mother in the parlor or Jack and Delia in the kitchen.

She went to the small window that overlooked the driveway and stood with her hands clasped, staring at the panes as if she could actually see through all the dust.

# 50

# "ONE KISS?"

Alone in the cabin, Wyatt listened to something knock around on the roof and watched a juniper branch wag back and forth outside the window. Dust like this was new to him. It was coming in under the door, seeping in around the window and collecting on the sill. He had the impression that if he stayed here for enough time, it would bury the cabin.

He was anxious to know how things were going for Shelly up at the house. When he felt he had waited long enough, he buttoned an extra shirt over the one he was wearing and tied a T-shirt around his face to breathe through. Leaning into the howling wind, he had to keep his eyes closed most of the way. He kept his bearings only by looking through a squint every so often to locate the brown glow of the light over the driveway. The house itself faded and reappeared in clouds of gusting dust.

Jack and Delia were in the kitchen watching the weather report with Ranger at their feet when Wyatt stumbled inside, shaking the dust off his clothes. He pulled the T-shirt down from his mouth, took off the extra button-down and hung it over the back of a chair. "What's the report?"

"More dust," Jack said.

"Blowing forty miles an hour and picking up," Delia added.

"I mean on Shelly. Where is she?"

"Across the hall," Jack said.

"Is Madeline with her?"

"No. They talked—very briefly, I might add—and Madeline went upstairs."

"So it didn't go well?"

"Apparently not. Shelly's still in there. I have the impression nobody wants to see anybody."

Wyatt drank a glass of water to wash out his throat and walked across to the parlor, where he found Shelly sitting alone in the dark. He sat across from her. Dust had begun to hiss at the windows, making a shushing sound.

"That bad?" he asked.

"Pretty bad."

"Madeline's upstairs?"

"Yes."

"What about Carlotta?"

"Upstairs."

"Have they talked?"

"I don't know. I don't see any point in going up there now. It'll just set Madeline off. I'm going to stay here in case she comes back down and wants to talk."

The abrasive *shhhh* at the window surged and faded. Wyatt wished he could ease Shelly's mind, but they had outgrown false assurances long ago.

"You're planning to leave tomorrow?" she asked him.

"Yes. For New York. To talk to Elaine."

A banging sound came from the porch, and Wyatt got up to look out. In the muddy sheen of the porch light, he saw Jack hauling the wicker chairs in. A cushion blew over the railing.

They listened to Jack drag the chairs into the front hall, and heard Delia talk with him about latching shutters, then heard both of them go upstairs.

Wyatt closed the drapes to keep the dust out, but something began pounding against the house. When he looked out again, he saw the porch swing blowing sideways, the end of it beating the wall like a medieval flail. "It's the swing hitting the house. I'll be back in a minute."

She followed him out of the parlor. It would be easier to face the wind than her thoughts of Madeline.

"What are you doing?" Wyatt asked her.

"Going out to help you."

She stepped outside behind him. The wind nearly swept her off her feet. It seemed malign, volitional, but at least it was a physical force that she could fight against. It pelted her with blistering dust and sand and seemed to be trying to tear the hair out of her scalp. It threw leaves into her face and filled her lungs with dust as thick as smoke from a toxic fire. She yanked her collar up over her mouth. She could see nothing beyond the porch.

Steadying herself against the wall, she looked at Wyatt, the wind hitting him from the side and flattening his hair to his head. He took hold of her arm and together they made their way to the swing, where they wrestled with the hooks but couldn't detach them from the chains. "I have an idea," Shelly shouted. "Hang on to the swing for a second."

Her hands on the wall for balance, she struggled her way inside and dragged out one of the wicker chairs Jack had piled in the hall. Wyatt flipped it onto its side and wedged it tightly under the swing, jamming the legs against the wall so nothing was free to blow. They were fighting their way back into the house when Shelly saw two orbs of light appear in the driveway.

"Was that a car?" she asked, pushing the door closed and then peering out from the window beside it. "Who would be driving up now?"

They waited, watching from the window. In a minute a man appeared out of the dust, staggering up the porch steps, his hand pressed hard on top of his cowboy hat to keep it from blowing off.

"It's that veterinarian," Wyatt said. "Carlotta's friend."

Shelly opened the door partway, trying to keep the wind out. The man grinned at her and stomped the dirt from his boots. "Is Madeline here?"

"You came to see Madeline?"

"If I can. And check on the dog."

She studied him through the crack in the door, confounded. Clearly there was something the matter with him, to have driven out here in a dust storm. "Madeline's involved in some things right now . . . but . . . if you'd like to come in . . ." She felt she had to invite him.

He shook his head and kept smiling. It occurred to her he was drunk. His forehead seemed to be bandaged under the hat. Shelly was still looking at him and trying to figure out what he wanted, when Madeline came down the stairs.

"The veterinarian's here to see you."

Madeline paused a moment, her hand on the newel post. Then she walked past Shelly and pulled the door wide open, stepping outside so quickly that all Shelly saw was the wind catching the back of her hair before the door slammed shut.

Outside, the wind smacked Madeline hard in the face. She squinted at Emmett, a dusty, hulking shape on the porch. "What are you doing here?" she shouted, furious that he had followed her. "What is the matter with you?"

"Pretending to check on the dog."

"Are you drunk? We're having a family crisis. You have to leave!"

He continued to grin insipidly, as impervious to the whistling wind as a concrete statue. "Come out to my truck."

"No!" The dust was making her cough.

"One kiss?"

"Are you crazy?"

The door opened and Andy came out. He was showered and wearing clean shorts and a T-shirt and holding a washcloth over his mouth and nose.

"I'm talking to Emmett alone!" Madeline shouted above the tumultuous din of the wind.

"I want to talk to him for a minute!" Andy told her. Turning to Emmett, he shouted, "Look, I happen to like you just fine! But it's fairly obvious you're hitting on my wife!"

"Okay," Emmett said.

"All right then!"

"All right then," Emmett repeated, and turned to Madeline.

"Go!" she told him.

"Okay, I'll head out," Emmett said, and turned and made his way down the steps and was swallowed up by the dust.

Madeline opened the door, and the wind shoved her inside. Her eyes stung. She coughed. She barely looked at her mother and Wyatt there in the hall. She caught a glimpse of herself in the mirror: filthy. She shouted at Andy, who was behind her. "What gives you the right? What gives you the fucking right?"

"Nothing. I'm sorry. I know."

On her way up the stairs, she shouted back over her shoulder, "I was already making him go!"

Upstairs she went into Nicholas's room and stood over the sofa bed and looked at her sleeping son in a patch of light from the hallway. He had tangled himself in the sheets. The pillow half-covered his head. His breathing was loud, his mouth open.

Tears rolled down her grimy cheeks. She could taste them mixed with the dust. She took hold of Nicholas's hand and sat on the lumpy sofa bed and studied his little fingers through her muddy tears. His nails were dirty and needed trimming. She looked at the tadpole's habitat sitting upright on the floor, empty now of water. The plastic plants and yellow bridge were missing. She felt around in the sheets and found them nestled close to Nicholas's chest, and picked up the yellow bridge and turned it about in her hands, rubbing her thumb over the pattern of cobblestones imprinted in the plastic.

# 51

# THE FIERCE WIND

"He's been flirting with Madeline." Andy paused to explain to Wyatt and Shelly before following his wife upstairs. "It was decent of him to leave. And really decent of her to tell him to. I wouldn't have blamed her if she hadn't." He wiped his arms with the washcloth. "And by the way, she told me about . . . you know. You two. And I want you to know I don't think less of you for it. Of course it would be unreasonable if I did, given the mess I'm in. But . . . for what it's worth. I admire you for doing the right thing in the end."

Wyatt said, "Admiration might be a bit of a stretch."

"If I can influence her at all, I'll try to get her to come around," Andy said. "And Shelly?"

"Yes?"

"I'm sorry for what I did to hurt her."

When Andy had gone upstairs, Wyatt stood looking at Shelly under the light of the chandelier. It was hard enough with thousands of miles and forty years between them, but close to her, he couldn't help but love her. Even loving Elaine as he did, he felt his resolve slipping. He wanted to take Shelly's hand and lead her into the parlor and kiss her dusty face and hair and forget the mistakes he had learned from, and make them all over again. He knew he would never forgive himself if he betrayed Elaine's trust once more, but he also knew how the world could disappear when he was alone with Shelly.

There were voices from upstairs: Delia talking with Andy. Then Delia started down. "Andy told me Emmett was here," she said. "It doesn't surprise me. He has a problem with alcohol."

"I hope we didn't just turn him loose on the road, drunk," Shelly said. There was no way now to get him back.

"Not a lot of sober people out there for him to run into," Wyatt said.

Shelly went into the bathroom to splash the dirt from her face, and Wyatt followed Delia into the kitchen, where she filled cups with water and put them into the microwave. The dog got up and lapped from the water bowl, then sniffed around and tried to squeeze under the oven.

"His tennis ball's under there," Delia said.

Wyatt watched the dog twist sideways and pump its legs until only its rump was visible. "Does he ever get stuck under there?"

"He has." She dropped a tea bag into a cup and handed it to Wyatt. He took a sip, then got down on his hands and knees and peered under the oven, where he spotted the filthy ball beside a Roach Motel. Delia gave him a broom so he could sweep it out. It rolled out sluggishly, dragging a wad of cobwebs and debris. Ranger dived at it, grabbing it in his mouth as Wyatt got to his feet, dusted his hands off, and sat back in the chair.

He thought he was done with the dog, but Ranger dropped the ball in front of him and stared at him expectantly, cocking his head from side to side until Wyatt gave the ball a small kick with the toe of his shoe. The dog grabbed it again and brought it back.

"There's something I have to tell you," Delia said. "Elaine knew about Shelly. I told her."

Wyatt stared at her.

"She asked."

"She asked?"

"Yes."

"She asked what?"

"If you were having an affair. She saw you in your office, looking at pictures of Shelly."

"My God."

"I couldn't lie to her," Delia said. "You were distraught over the pictures, and she saw that."

He knew when it had happened: after he found out Shelly was pregnant and he had known he would lose her. He had wept over the photographs that he had taken for the portrait. "She never told me."

"I know."

He couldn't believe it. He was dumbfounded. "Why didn't you tell me?"

"Because she asked me not to. And Wyatt? She knows about Carlotta. When you came to me, with Jack, and told me Shelly was pregnant, and Jack said he wanted to adopt the baby, I knew this would be the closest he could ever come to having a child of his own. But I didn't know how Elaine would feel, since she knew about you and Shelly. So I talked to her about it."

He stared at her. "What did you tell her? What did you say?"

"I told her Shelly was pregnant and you were the father."

"And she said—"

"To take the baby."

"She said to—"

"Take the baby."

"She's been coming here, knowing Carlotta was . . ."

"Yours. Yes."

"And never talked to me about it?"

"She felt the conversation would never end if she started talking to you about it. She believed . . . Well I think she believed your marriage wouldn't survive that conversation—that once the door was opened, you might . . . go through."

Certain things Elaine had said were coming back to him now—things she had hinted at. Her buried anger for many years. How the marriage was not the same after the move to Provincetown. It occurred to him that maybe the move to Provincetown had been Elaine's idea and not her parents'. Maybe she'd simply been trying to get him out of Austin for the sake of their marriage and for Nate. And maybe, as things had turned out, it was best that she had.

He was trying to cobble together his thoughts, when the room went suddenly dark.

For a stunned moment, they were silent. Then Delia said, "The electricity went out."

"I noticed."

"If I can find matches, I'll light the stove. It won't light without electricity."

He heard her rummaging near the stove. The wind rattled the window. "Can you look in those drawers over there by the table?" she asked him.

He felt around for the knobs.

Shelly's voice came from the doorway. "Wyatt? Delia?"

"We're here," Wyatt said. "Looking for matches."

"For the stove," Delia said. "To light a burner. Oh, here they are."

She struck the match, and a circle of blue flame ignited. The three of them could see each other's faces now.

"A tree probably fell on the power lines," Delia said.

Jack came down the stairs with a flashlight. "Everyone okay here?"

"Fine," Wyatt said. "Why didn't you tell me Elaine knew?"

"Knew what?" Jack switched off the flashlight, his features going vague in the faint blue glow of the stove. "Honey, do we have any more D batteries, in case these run out?" he asked Delia.

"About Shelly. And Carlotta," Wyatt said.

"What?"

"Why didn't you tell me Elaine knew?"

"She didn't."

"Yes," Delia said. "I told her."

Shelly said, "She knew?"

Delia raised her arms and shoved her palms at the air as if pushing everyone away from her.

Jack said, "Honey, my God."

Madeline and Andy appeared at the door. The dirt was still on Madeline's face, disconcerting in the scant and eerie light. She looked like a feral creature with eyes too big for the tiny face, her hair matted and wild. In a voice seething with anger, she said, "Wyatt's wife knew?"

The dog continued to stare at the ball. He pounced at it and picked it up in his mouth and plopped it back toward Wyatt, then barked at Wyatt to kick it.

Delia said, "Madeline, dear, would you take the dog?" But Madeline didn't budge. She seemed to be waiting for everyone to admit to something, though there was nothing left for anyone to confess.

"Maybe we should all sit down and talk everything through," Andy said. "This is just an idea, but it seems like there are a lot of secrets, and nobody's got any bad intentions, and we could look at everything with an eye of tolerance."

"Oh for God's sake, Andy," Madeline snapped.

Shelly said, "Madeline, please."

"Please what? Behave? You're the moral authority, Mom? Do you have any idea what you put Wyatt's wife through? I can fill you in, if you're wondering."

Wyatt said, "Leave my wife out of this, can we?"

Madeline turned on him. "I don't know, can we?" She could see they were all gawking at her.

"Are you all in the kitchen?" Carlotta called softly, coming down the stairs. She appeared at the door in her nightgown, holding a lighted candle that emitted the scent of sandalwood. "Has anyone checked the breakers?" she asked.

"Come on in," Madeline said. "We're all just learning more news. Wyatt's wife has always known about you."

A silence fell as the cruelty of the words registered on everyone. In the fluttering candlelight, Carlotta's eyes sought Delia's.

"Yes, sweetheart," Delia said. "She's always known, and it hasn't made any difference in her feelings toward you."

Madeline said, "I don't think any of you could know about her feelings."

"You're making this about you," Carlotta said quietly to Madeline, but there was an edge to her voice. "It isn't."

Andy said, "Unfortunately, she has a reason to be feeling especially bad about infidelity right now."

"Shut up!" Madeline yelled. The volume of her own voice shocked her. She had lost control. She felt a rising rage toward her mother for the deceit, toward Andy, toward Carlotta. "All of you! I hate all of you! Nobody's trustworthy but my dad, and he's *dead* because of all of you!" She turned her furious face to Carlotta. "If not for *you* and *your shop*, he would still be alive!"

Carlotta took a step back, and the sudden look of pain on her face, lit by the candle, was something Shelly could not bear.

"Madeline, leave this room, right now," Shelly said. "Carlotta's shop had nothing to do with anything."

"Oh? Then why were we all coming to Alpine that night? The night he had to distract me from being jealous by taking me to Devil's Sinkhole."

Delia said, "I won't listen to this anymore," and started for the door.

"You're all liars!" Madeline screamed.

Shelly moved toward her, reaching out, but Madeline pushed her away, shouting, "Don't touch me!"

Ranger picked up his tennis ball and followed Delia toward the door, wagging his nub of a tail.

Madeline grabbed the flashlight from Jack's hand. She ran past Delia and the dog, into the dark hall and out of the front door into the punishing wind.

Shelly followed her, plunging into the wind's fury. Gravel flew at her ankles and dust clotted her eyes. She felt as if she was choking. She had no idea where Madeline was going or what she intended; she followed the beam of the flashlight. It shone on the path, the cars, the wild limbs of a tree. It settled on the Suburban. The rear door swung open, the interior light blinked on, and Madeline dragged something out of the back. It was cloaked in a white sheet, and she tore this away and released it to the wind. The flashlight brushed a swath of light across what she now held. When Shelly saw what it was, she stopped running.

Madeline ran with the painting to the edge of the driveway and set it down at the base of a tree. Holding it firmly against the pull of the wind, she shone the flashlight on it. Then she shoved her foot against the portrait. Viciously, she kicked it. She did this again and again. Shelly watched as if she were seeing an execution.

Andy came running and tried to save the painting, crying out, "Stop! Madeline! Stop!" over the scream of the wind. He tried to pull it from her grasp, but she clung to the wooden frame, shone the light at the face, and shoved her heel at the face again.

The green eyes splintered on the board. The cracked blue paint revealed the breast. The ribbon dangled in the hair. The pale smile split in two.

Andy tried to hold Madeline, but she struggled away from him and ran with the painting across the drive, and stopped and aimed the flashlight's beam at it once again. The face was caved in. All that was left was the broken frame holding the pieces together.

She almost allowed the wind to sweep the painting away then, but her hands would not let go. She lost her bearings, and turned in a circle, unable to see where she was. The only light to orient by was the one she was holding. "Mom?" she screamed. "Mom?"

She heard her mother answering. Andy, from the darkness, flung his arms around her. A voice was crying something over and over again, and Madeline realized she had been hearing this voice for some time. Pulling away from Andy, she ran toward the crying, still clutching the painting, shining the light. Through the dust, the beam revealed the porch steps and the railing, and then the porch itself, and at the door a small boy in pajamas, coughing on dust, screaming for his mother, kicking his legs, trying to run to her while Jack, his arms locked around him, held him back.

# 52

# MOONLIGHT VISIT

Even after the wind had slackened, and Jack had disposed of the portrait, and after Madeline, without a word to anyone, turning her back on Shelly, had taken Nicholas upstairs and curled herself around him on the sofa bed in the dark, and the others had gone to their rooms, and Wyatt had gone to the cabin, the awful scene continued repeating itself in Shelly's mind in pictures as reckless and fragmented as if they had been snatched away by the wind. The house was unnaturally quiet with the electricity still out—nothing ticking or humming, only the walls settling and the wind worrying around the corners. Dust was everywhere. It covered the floors, the furniture, the quilt on Shelly's bed. Shelly lay in the bed, looking at dusty shadows and dusty, slatted moonlight tossing over the walls. She wanted to go to Madeline and try to make things right again, and wanted, against her better judgment and convictions, to go to Wyatt for solace.

She was ashamed of her daughter. It was understandable that Madeline believed her mother was not the person she had pretended to be. But this could not excuse the bitter things she had said to Carlotta. She had been pitiless. Destroying the painting was one matter, and Madeline's own loss. But blaming Carlotta for Dan's death was spiteful and beneath her.

Shelly ached to forget the look on Carlotta's face when Madeline had spat those words at her—how the candle Carlotta held had thrown the light upward over her features. She thought of sweet Nicholas, and of the tadpole buried under the cottonwood tree whose branches waved shadows through the shutters, and of Carlotta's lost, unborn baby.

She might never see Wyatt again after tomorrow. She would manage the years ahead in the same way she had managed the last forty, but she was not sure how she would manage to say goodbye. If only she could carry her suitcase out to her car right now and drive home without a last look to haunt her memory, instead of lying here staring at shadows.

But she couldn't possibly leave Madeline here, in such painful distress. And she didn't want the sight of Wyatt walking to the cabin in the moonlight, as she had last seen him, with his back to her and the dying wind kicking up meager eddies of dust in the road, to be the final one. Already she was feeling the old compulsive need for him, and she knew from the past how hard it would be to outlive that feeling. Those moments on the South Mall had imprinted in her mind the idea that she needed Wyatt in order to survive, and while she had managed to prove long ago that she could endure without him, the impression was still there, as deep as ever.

She needed to gain something from this difficult reunion—even if only an ending she could live with.

Her thoughts moved from Madeline to Wyatt and back again, and to Carlotta and Jack and Delia, and always back to Madeline, until finally sleep began to come over her in dark shapes drifting like slow waves across her mind. In that near sleep, she imagined her body was whole again, her breast perfectly round, her arm moving with ease. She recalled Carlotta's birth and the nurse who had referred to labor as "going over." She had said Shelly was "going over."

A noise at the window startled her and she sat up, thinking the wind had knocked something against the panes. She got up and went to the window and pulled the shutters open.

An owl—staring at her, his enormous face only a foot away. She took a step back. He was perched on the branch of the cottonwood tree, the dusty leaves shimmering around him. The wind pulled ragged pieces out of the clouds, and the moon appeared and disappeared, but the owl was still. His eyes were like black glass, the feathers blossoming out around them in patterns that looked as soft as fur and rippled in the air. His head was round, and his unblinking eyes were directly level with hers.

Shelly stared back, mesmerized, her gown loose around her. The owl slid his head to the side and back in a smooth and fluid movement, keeping his gaze on her, and blinked once, a slow blink, as if to acknowledge her. His beak was curved and yellow, his feathers striped and spotted. His claws curled around the deep grooves in the bark. He gazed at Shelly as if he had some pressing reason to be here.

How had he made that thudding noise against the window? Had he knocked a mouse against the panes? There was no mouse in his claws. Had he whacked the window with his wing? For a long time, she looked at him. He swiveled his head around in a languid movement, as if turning to look behind him at the dark land and Lizard Mountain. Then he fixed his eyes on Shelly again, thrusting his broad face next to the panes. He made no move to indicate he would ever fly away, and eventually Shelly reached out and carefully closed the shutters, counted slowly to ten, and opened them again, expecting to see the owl. But he was gone.

She peered from the window, through the broad leaves and across the stretch of land that Dan had walked the day he went to explore the mountain. She remembered how he had turned, waved his arms, and called for her to come with him.

Needing to see his face, she latched the shutters, lit a candle Carlotta had given her, and went out into the hall, where she found the row of Jack's college annuals pressed between bookends Carlotta had once cut from a crystalline geode. Taking the annual for 1966, she returned to her bed. She set the candle on the table and turned the pages, struck by the clean-cut men in black-rimmed glasses, the girls with flipped hair. Dan's face was in a row of faces; he was a junior that year, six years before she had met him. He looked friendly and clean-shaven. His hair was shorter than when she had known him.

She turned to Jack's class picture, and Wyatt's, and then to the memorial page in the front, where the names of students and faculty killed by Charles Whitman were printed on the pale and grainy sky above a flag at half-mast. She thought of how that boy had lifted his hand as if to wave before he fell, and how the girl who lay beside the steps had moved her legs languidly, up and down at the knees, and how Jack had run toward the boy who lay on the ground in the surfer shirt, and then fallen when the bullet struck him, and dragged himself up, and moved like an inchworm.

She turned to the class picture of Charles Whitman, with his crew cut and his bland young face. She had seen this picture before, and others of him in magazines—family photos and wedding photos. Forty years was plenty of time to come across even the things you didn't care to look at. She recalled a picture of him sitting on a stone wall, another of him asleep with his dog. He had posed with his beautiful wife at the Alamo two weeks before murdering her. She remembered a snapshot of the note he had left with his mother's body, saying how sorry he was to have killed her, and a graphic picture of him lying dead in a corner of the tower deck, his face pocked with buckshot.

Intending to wait the night out, hoping the candle would last awhile, she continued turning the pages.

# 53

# THE UP END OF THE SEESAW

Madeline was too despondent to shower or bathe. Gritty with dust, she lay on the sofa bed, her arms wrapped tightly around Nicholas, her tears dripping into the back of his hair. Her ankle bled from kicking the painting; she had tied a dishrag around it. It was two o'clock in the morning. Her only consolation was the locked door. Nicholas sweated in his sleep; she felt the heat of his body and the rise and fall of his small chest as she lay against him and remembered the hateful accusations she had made toward Carlotta, and how she had broken the portrait, kicking it into pieces—shocking to her the moment she did it and even more so now. She had shoved her heel into the face with a powerful cracking sound.

What was left, now? What had she not ruined? How unfair to have blamed Carlotta for what happened at the sinkhole when she knew in her heart that she was the one at fault. Her father had gone to that place to distract her from her petulance and self-doubt and to jog her out of self-pity. And now she had tried to shift the blame because of that same persistent self-pity. If only Carlotta had been outraged to learn who her parents were and how they had deceived her, then she and Madeline would have been on the same side. But Carlotta had been gracious. She had chosen the side with her parents and Shelly and Wyatt, leaving Madeline teetering like a lone figure on the up end of a seesaw.

How had she become this person who could say such things as she had said to her mother and Carlotta? She wanted to go home. She wanted the world to have no one in it except herself and her son.

Her foot had begun to throb. She could feel its pulse and the hard pounding of her heart. She dragged herself away from Nicholas's damp warmth and ventured into the hall and to her mother's door. It was cracked open, revealing a light from inside. Peering in, she saw her mother sitting in bed, looking at a large book in the yellow glow of a candle, her hair loose to her shoulders, her crooked arm revealed by the sleeveless nightgown. She looked sad, tired. But in the candlelight, with her hair down, she looked almost young.

Madeline opened the door and went in and sat down on the foot of the bed. "I shouldn't have ruined the painting or said those things to Carlotta," she said.

"It was a lot for you to take in today." She spoke softly, but did not sound entirely forgiving. She looked at Madeline's foot in the rag. "Have you put anything on the cuts?"

"No."

"You need some ointment."

Madeline shrugged. "What are you reading? Is that a UT annual?"

"Yes."

"Why?"

"I couldn't sleep. Sweetheart?"

"Look, I know I behaved badly," Madeline said. "I'm thinking about leaving and driving back tonight. Andy can bring Nicholas home tomorrow."

"You shouldn't be on the road. You're too exhausted."

"I don't want to be here tomorrow when everyone gets up. I especially don't want see Wyatt Calvert. You've put his family in front of ours all these years."

"No. That's one thing I've never done. Our family was never threatened. I was honest with your dad, and I'm being honest with you. I know you think it's late for that, but what is this really about, Madeline? If it's about your jealousy of Carlotta, I wish you'd be bigger than that. You can, if you decide to be. You can get up in the morning and apologize to Carlotta and drive home. I'm sorry I wasn't able to tell you about my past before now, but nobody's ever wronged you. You don't have to live with my past—I do. And in case you're wondering, I love you more than I love anyone else in the world, and that includes Carlotta."

Madeline stood up. She hesitated. Then she said, "I'm going to get my things together and start back. I'll leave Andy a note and tell him to bring Nicholas whenever they're ready to come."

The spark of alarm in her mother's eyes was a meager victory.

Then Shelly flung the covers back and got out of the bed. "If you're going, I'm going."

"What do you mean?"

"I'm going to take you. You're not going to get on the road like this. You haven't slept in two nights. Get your things together, and I'll say goodbye to Wyatt. I'll meet you in the driveway in twenty minutes."

"We both have cars here," Madeline said.

"Cars are the least of our problems. I'll leave mine."

# 54

# A NIGHT SKY

Branches littered the dark yard; piles of dust and sand lay against tree trunks and the tires of the cars. The wind had dropped to a breeze, and Shelly walked the road to the cabin, listening to coyotes chattering far away, their voices carrying with strange clarity through the empty spaces. The land looked blanched and colorless under the dust. Eyes glowed from the brush. A small bird flew from a century plant. Shelly walked in the wheel ruts. Searching the night sky, she saw no sign of the owl.

She rounded the scraggly willow trees and saw the rental car nosed up under the junipers. She didn't at first see Wyatt sitting at the top of the three small steps of the porch, his elbows on his knees. She stopped walking when she saw him. "Hey," she whispered.

"Hey."

"Not sleeping?"

"No. Come sit down."

She sat beside him, the moonlight fanning over the low terrain before them, and car lights crawling on the far-off highway. Stars salted the sky all the way to the ground.

"Madeline's leaving," she said. "So I'm going to take her."

"Now?"

"Yes."

"Ah." He took a moment with that. "Shelly?"

"Don't say anything I won't be able to forget," she told him.

And he said nothing. She remembered how helpless she had been lying in her puddle of blood on the South Mall—how Wyatt had looked running toward her in his wildly colored shirt. Slanted from her point of view. How he had saved her, and painted the portrait that now was in pieces, stuffed in the trash, and how he had made love to her, and left her.

And here they sat, on these narrow steps, at this age.

"When are you leaving?" she asked.

"Early. I have a flight from Midland at noon."

"To New York?"

He nodded. "Through Dallas."

"And then to see your kids?"

"Yes."

"Will you see Jack and Delia before you go?"

"Yes."

"Will you explain to them that I've left because I don't want Madeline driving when she's so miserable and tired?"

"Of course. She's still very angry?"

"Very."

"I like her," he said. "In spite of how she feels about me." He laughed quietly, and the sound was a relief to Shelly. "She had nerve to do what she did to that portrait."

"Yes she did."

"She'll get over this," he said.

"Hopefully, she will. I'm the only mother she has."

"Yes, and she obviously needs you."

"Will you tell Jack and Delia how much I love them for all they've done?"

"They know, but I'll tell them."

"Tell them I'll call them later. And I'm sorry to have hurt Elaine, Wyatt. I'm sorry about a lot of things."

"We both are," he said solemnly. "But I doubt either of us would undo any of them."

"No. Who would ever undo Carlotta?"

"She is wonderful, isn't she?" he said.

"And she's forgiving," Shelly said. "We're certainly an imperfect set of parents to have found. Fortunately Carlotta has never minded imperfection."

"No."

"Reality's fine with her. Do you remember the painting you showed me that first day when I went to your office—the very small painting of the apple on the windowsill?"

"All I seem to remember about that day is you."

"The apple was bruised, and the windowsill was peeling. And you had painted it all exactly—with all the flaws, just like you painted me with the scars. Looking at that painting made me feel so comfortable. And Carlotta has your tolerance for what's not quite right or perfect. I remember a fish in the pond Jack used to have in back of the house. It was missing part of its tail, and Carlotta thought it was the prettiest one." She smiled to herself, thinking about Carlotta. "We did all right by Carlotta in the long run, didn't we?"

"More than all right, in the long run."

They sat a little longer, surrounded by the vast world filled with faraway things—the pinprick stars, the fracas of crickets and cicadas, and the occasional distant headlights of cars. Shelly had once said to Wyatt, as he shielded her behind the base of the flagpole, "Don't go. Don't leave me." She did not say this now, though she wanted to. Instead she turned to him and touched his face, and said, "Don't get up." Then she forced herself to her feet and walked around the side of the cabin and slowly up the road.

# 55

# THE WAY HOME

Madeline washed the grime from her face by flashlight, sponged herself with a washcloth, put on clean clothes, wrote a note for Andy, and whispered to Nicholas that his dad would bring him home tomorrow and she would see him when they got there. She wore a slipper on her injured foot and carried a satchel and a needlepoint pillow that featured a longhorn grazing on green grass.

Her mother was already in the Suburban, the motor running, the wipers sweeping the dust from the windshield, when Madeline tossed the satchel and pillow into the backseat and climbed in after them. "I'll get this back to Delia later," she said about the pillow. "Mind if I sleep?"

"That's the plan," Shelly told her. With a glance at the empty porch and the dark house and the road down to the cabin, and then at her daughter curled on the backseat with her head cocked stiffly against the pillow, Shelly started out. The road and the land were so blanketed in dust it was hard to tell one from the other. She turned onto the potholed street bordered by houses, and then onto the smoother Highway 67 through town, skirting fallen tree limbs and debris. Streetlights were out; crews were working. She picked up speed on the desolate part of 67 and then headed toward the endless stretch of Interstate 10.

Madeline, in the backseat, kept her eyes closed, not wanting to talk about anything that had happened tonight. For a long time, she said nothing. Shelly pulled into a truck stop on the interstate, and though Madeline was aware of the bright light shining down on her face, she did not open her eyes. She heard the nozzle clank into the car and the gas flow into the tank, but did not so much as shift her head on the pillow. On the road again, she managed almost to fall asleep, but her thoughts kept jolting her awake. She thought up arguments against

Andy and her mother for the ways that she had been wronged. But after a while she began to realize that all this struggling would probably only lead her to the same place she could get to much sooner by simply accepting that what was done was over.

"The stupid thing is, I still love Andy, and I don't want to leave him," she finally said, her eyes still closed.

"I don't find that stupid," Shelly said.

"But I'm afraid he'll do it again. I don't want to live my whole life knowing that my fears might come true, and just hoping for them not to."

Shelly didn't answer for a moment before saying, "But that's what most of us do. And if they do come true, we survive and then walk down the middle of whatever road we choose then."

In the slow passage of moments, blinking her eyes open, watching the moon slide down in the window, Madeline imagined what her life would be like without Andy. Eventually she sat up and looked at the apparition of her face on the dark window.

They had been driving for a long time through a vast, empty stretch when she saw they were approaching the turnoff toward Rocksprings and the sinkhole. The headlights caught the outline of a sign far ahead at the side of the road, and Madeline said, "There it is."

"What?"

"The turnoff." As they came closer, the sign began to come into focus. Madeline said, very quietly, "Maybe we should go there. Maybe we should see it."

A light-headed feeling came over Shelly. She slowed and pulled to the shoulder and stopped in front of the sign, which said 41, 1 MILE. For a moment, she and Madeline sat in silence, the headlights shining brightly on the green sign and the darkness around it, and then Shelly turned to look at Madeline. "You want to go there—now?"

"Do you?"

Shelly thought of the pictures she had seen in the book at the library—the aerial photograph of that enormous oblong stain on the landscape, and the diagram of the interior, and the picture taken from deep within, with the camera lens aimed up. Devil's Sinkhole was to her the most evil and horrifying place on the face of the earth. She couldn't imagine looking down into that monstrous cavern where Dan had fallen. And yet, she always had imagined it.

"In the dark?" she said. "When you're exhausted?"

Madeline's eyes glistened in the dim light. "My emotions are so saturated right now nothing could hurt me. I feel like I could face it now. I feel like maybe this is the only time I ever could."

"And you think you need to face it?"

"Don't you need to?"

She didn't want Madeline to go there. She didn't want to go there herself. But turning to look again at the sign in front of her, she felt the gravitational pull—for herself and for Madeline too. It was palpable. She tried to wish it away, but couldn't. She got out of the car and leaned against the hood, looking in the direction of the sinkhole at nothing but a dark wash of grass and cedars. When she got back in the car, she centered her hands on the wheel. "Do you know the way?"

Madeline got in the front seat. "I can find it."

Shelly pulled onto the highway. She exited onto 41 and drove for a long time on the flat road before Madeline guided her onto a small road of white caliche that glimmered bright in the headlights. Cedar grew dense on either side, brushing the sides of the car, an ever-narrowing tunnel. Past a gate, the cedars retreated from the road, and the road unfolded, white in the harsh glare, and the scooped moon sat almost on the horizon.

"Stop," Madeline said.

Shelly braked slowly, and Madeline sat staring down the road as if waiting for someone.

"What is it?" Shelly whispered.

"This is where we saw the boy."

"Here?"

Madeline thought of asking her mother to turn back. But they had come this far, and the gate had been open, and the past was just in front of her. "Running at us, down this road," she said. "Yelling that his girlfriend was down the hole." The frantic voice came back to her, the leather harness dangling, the bleeding hands, and the ball cap with a logo for Detroit Deisel. "Dad told him to get in the car."

"Do you want to turn back?"

Madeline shook her head. "No," she whispered.

Shelly eased forward. The pastureland on either side was rocky and level here, dotted with scrub oak and catclaw and prickly pear. A jackrabbit blinded by the headlights darted along before the car, swerving from side to side of the road until Shelly flicked the lights off and let it escape into the dark. A mile farther on, Madeline said, "I think we're close to it." Then she said, "Veer off here."

"There's no road here."

"But veer off."

Slowly, Shelly did so.

"Now, stop here."

When the car had come to a stop Madeline reached over and turned the motor off, and they sat in silence, looking at the brush lit by the headlights. "It's in front of us."

Shelly couldn't see it. She stepped out of the car. Katydids chirped in the grass. The headlights shone through tall grasses and clusters of prickly pear and then abruptly dropped off into the hole. Beyond the hole, the faint gray light of morning etched the trees on the horizon.

Madeline took a flashlight out of the glove compartment and got out to stand beside her mother. In her memory, she saw the old white pickup gleaming in the moonlight, its back end sagging, lopsided, over the edge of the cavernous pit. She had forgotten until this second that the girl in the hole had been calling for help when they arrived. The sudden recollection of that beseeching cry was so strong and unexpected she felt as if she was hearing it again. "Listen."

"What do you hear?"

"Something."

"In the grass?"

"No."

It came from the hole—a distant, echoing supplication, as if the sound had lingered there in the dark chasm for all these years and was now circling up from the depths with the rank smell of bat guano, and drifting into the open spaces over the rocky pasture.

Was the noise only a memory? Or was it the sound of bat pups calling for their mothers? The place was unchanged from that night. Time seemed not to have happened. The invisible sun lay below the horizon in the same way now as then, but with the promise of rising instead of sinking. It had the same measured timing, the same obstinate blindness to what was happening on the face of the earth. Even the air was the same as that night—dry and breathless. The same invisible creatures moved stealthily in the brush.

Madeline shone the flashlight at the hole and walked toward it, limping slightly from her injured foot. She stopped at the edge. Painting the beam along the sharp rim of the limestone, she found the scratch marks and gashes made by the underside of the truck, and steadied the light on them. "Here." She looked at her mother. "This is where he fell."

For a long moment, Shelly didn't move. She stared at the blemished edge of the dark pit. And then she walked to Madeline and stood beside her. Madeline aimed the light down into the hole, but the beam faded to nothing. "He knew the rope was frayed even before he hooked onto it."

She remembered how the boy had paced at the edge, yanking his ball cap on and off and yelling down to the girl who twirled like a tiny acrobat on the rope. The swallows had circled and dived, the bats had begun to chatter, the girl's voice had seemed to vibrate with the sound, the dark had become darker, and her father had gone down while she had tried to hold on to him with the light. The dank smell of the guano brought it all back clearly. Even now, she had the desperate feeling that she must do something to call her father back.

He had come up out of the dark like an apparition, the girl in her tangle of rope hanging below him. He had almost been close enough for Madeline to touch him. He had tied the girl to the strap with his bent fingers, cut her loose from him, and condemned himself to the frayed rope that scraped at the rim.

"He told me to drive the truck. He said to be sure the brake was set, so I wouldn't roll backward. He said not to use first gear—it was too close to reverse. He said to use second. I knew it would make the truck jerk, but he said it didn't matter. He said to give it plenty of gas and let the clutch out slowly. And that's what I did. He said it was the only chance to save her." She wrapped her arms around herself and rocked her body back and forth as if she could soothe herself like a child. "He knew the girl would live and he wouldn't," she said, her tears beginning to flow. "He did. He knew." His choice to save the girl had carved a path through time to this dark, quiet morning, this long, lingering moment between a mother and daughter beside an abyss in a pastureland in the middle of nowhere.

Shelly pictured how he had fallen—the exhaust from the tailpipe sputtering into his face, the rocks tumbling around him. The rush of air. "What did he say before he went down?"

"I tried to stop him—"

"But what did he say?"

"He said 'I have to.'" Madeline bent over, tears flying from her face and twinkling in the headlights.

"He believed the rope would hold," Shelly said.

"No. He wanted to save the girl. He knew it might not hold. And I knew. I had to know. Didn't I? I couldn't have stopped him from going in—no one could have stopped him. But I didn't *have* to drive the truck. I didn't *have* to—" She threw her head back. "He was here because of me! It was my fault! It was *all my fault!*" She stumbled away from her mother. "He took the truck to town for help—"

"Who did?"

"The boy—"

"Afterward?"

"Afterward."

"And where were you?"

"Here."

"With the girl?"

"The boy took the girl."

"Here, by yourself?"

"With Daddy."

"But—" And suddenly Shelly understood how it had ended—how Madeline had kept watch over the hole, in the dark, alone, screaming into it for her father until she no longer expected an answer but kept shouting into the echo of her own voice because there was nothing else she could do, and because she needed to drown out the unbearable silence.

Madeline plucked a rock from the ground and threw it into the cavern, crying, "Goddamn hole!" She fell to her knees at the edge where her father had fallen, crying into her hands. Shelly held on to her, coaxing her back from the rim, and they sank to the ground together, Madeline weeping, clinging to her mother in the prickly grass. The gray light became tinged with blue, and Shelly was suddenly aware of something fluttering around them, and realized that the bats were coming in. Madeline raised her face at the sound of their wings beating the air, and cried in terrible sobs as they descended, only a few at first and then thousands sinking into the cavern.

On the rough ground with their arms around each other, Shelly and Madeline saw the world come into view. The eastern sky turned orange, the light expanded rapidly, and the sun lifted hurriedly, as if pulled up by a string, flooding the pasture with color. The light did not flood into the hole, but they saw it reach the rim—the scarred shelf of limestone where Dan had fallen—and slide downward to the ledges where the swallows nested.

# 56

# THE OYSTER SHELL

When Carlotta woke the next morning, it was to a dusty but sunny room and to the astounding knowledge of all that had happened not only the night before but during her whole lifetime, and even before that, when Shelly and Wyatt fell in love. It filled her with wonder that so many lives were blended with hers, all flowing in and out of one another like the colors in a piece of tumbled bloodstone.

From downstairs, there were voices. A door closed. The dog barked once. Carlotta pulled her robe on and went downstairs, where she saw Ranger waiting at the screen door with the obvious hope of escape. Shooing him out of the way with her foot, she went out onto the porch and found her father drinking coffee and reading a newspaper while Andy stood at the railing, remarking on the litter in the yard. Nicholas, in his pajama bottoms, was swinging so high in the porch swing that the chains rattled.

"Look how high I can make it go!" he told her, shoving off hard, his hair rising and flopping.

"That is amazing," she said. "I had no idea it would go that high."

Her father looked at her over his reading glasses, and she knew, because she knew him so well, that he was ready for the guests to leave. He wanted his porch back, dusty though it was.

Andy said, "Good morning!"

"Good morning. I take it we have electricity. I'm going to get some coffee. Does anyone need a refill?"

"No thanks," Jack said.

Nicholas dragged his feet to stop the swing, and followed her inside.

"Where's your mom and Nana?" she asked him.

"They're gone," he told her. "My mom left a note for my dad. They went home, and we're going home too. We have to go home because my mom is there, and she's going to feel bad about kicking the painting of Nana. Can I have some cereal?"

"Sure."

She set out a bowl and a spoon and a box of cornflakes.

"The other man is gone too," he said.

"The other man?"

"The tall one."

"You mean Wyatt?"

"Yeah. He went."

"This morning?"

"He came to talk to us on the porch and said goodbye. He told your dad he was going to call you."

"Okay. Has my mom been down?"

"No." He dumped the cornflakes into the bowl, and she helped him pick up the stray ones, then poured the milk for him.

"Can we look for some colored rocks to put on top of Jerry's grave?" he asked her.

"Of course. I have a lot we can choose from up in my room."

"Maybe we need a big one with Jerry's name," he suggested.

"Jerry was little. Little stones will be better."

She sat at the table with him and drank her coffee while he ate his cereal; then they went together up to her room and looked through canisters and boxes. "This one would be good," she said, holding up a jagged piece of blue chrysocolla. "It creates tranquility and serenity. And this rose quartz represents unconditional love, which is the kind you had for Jerry, because you loved him no matter what."

"Even when he was dead," Nicholas said.

"Even then," she agreed. "And this green dioptase is quite rare and expensive. We won't put it on the grave, but you can have it, because it heals sadness, especially in children. If you feel sad about Jerry, hold it next to your heart."

He took it and turned it about in his hands and pressed it against his bare chest.

"And this is black obsidian for protection," she said. "So we should put it on the grave to protect it. Also this malachite, for friendship, since Jerry was your good friend."

In search of a special piece of water-polished seer stone, she opened a box of her personal items, each carefully wrapped in a sheet of brightly colored tissue paper. Unfolding piece after piece, she unexpectedly came across the fossilized oyster she had found when she was thirteen, on the school trip to Big Bend. She removed it from the paper and marveled at it, remembering how it had looked embedded in the canyon wall and recalling the imagined scenes of how she would present it, someday, to her mysterious mother, on a lovely beach or by a campfire. A small feeling of loss came over her, as gentle as the morning breeze floating through the window. She had so looked forward to meeting her mother, and it was disappointing that the meeting had already come and gone, and so long ago that she couldn't even remember.

But there were other things to look forward to—a new job, in a new place, after she closed the shop. Maybe a diving trip at the end of the summer if she could afford it. And possibly even a baby in the future.

She showed the fossil to Nicholas—how the top could lift off and fit perfectly back together, and then she wrapped it again in the tissue paper, and put it back in the box.

Perhaps some day she would give it to Delia.

"Now let's put these on the grave," she said, gathering up the stones they had selected.

# 57

# FROM THE TOWER

On a cold day in early January, eighteen months later, Shelly walked into the new art museum on the UT campus, climbed the steps to the gallery, and stood in front of a long row of Wyatt's paintings that were perfectly spaced and beautifully showcased, few of them bigger than twelve by twelve inches, their titles tacked alongside them.

The painting titled *1966* was the first in the row. It looked uncomfortably small on the enormous wall, depicting the tower with off-kilter windows frozen forever in a scene that looked to Shelly surprisingly innocuous now—an afterthought to a moment long over. Maybe it was the magnitude of the surrounding white space, or the relative smallness of the painting itself, about ten inches square, but for some reason Shelly did not feel the same pang of emotion, or recognition, that she had felt when she came across this image years ago in the book of tempera paintings at the top of Jack and Delia's stairs.

She stood before it a while now, listening to a young couple remark to each other on the clarity and tonality and choice of palette, and then moved on, walking the length of the wall and looking at Wyatt's other paintings. She tried to see into the depths and decipher all the pale layers of color, but as always, she was stopped by the picture—the obvious whole. People, buildings, trees. Wet leaves and porous stone. They hung in front of her, as detailed as her own life, the thin layers of paint blended as inextricably as days that were over, adhered to one another as tenuously as flakes of pastry dough. The shades were lost in one another. They eradicated each other.

She was nearing the end of the wall, only a few paintings left to see, when a complex image confounded her. It was much larger than the others and depicted a window divided into panes—six across and four down—that reflected leafy branches and blue sky, and some distance away the middle portion of what Shelly came to realize was the tower, with its ascending rows of windows. The image was so perfect that if it were larger it might be mistaken for an actual window, though the viewer would be uncertain, because of how perfectly the reflections were painted onto the glass, whether the perspective was from the outside, looking in, or the other way around. Shelly was studying this conundrum when something startled her, and she took a step back.

A man's face—in the window. Looking out. Ghostly features. Insubstantial as glass, obscured by the sheen of reflected leaves. A look of horror more vivid than the features themselves, in conspicuous eyes.

She looked at the title. The print was stark next to the complicated layering of the image—the reflections on the window, the shimmering glass itself, divided into panes, and the face behind it. *A Window.*

She knew this window. She knew its shape, more wide than tall, and how it was bordered with white stone. It was the center window on the third floor of the English building, overlooking the plaza of the South Mall.

Was it possible? Had Wyatt seen the face in the window, just as she had? Was it Dan's face? Wyatt could not have known that—not then, and not afterward. She had not told him about Dan's confession of how he had looked down from that window, a bystander, as Wyatt and Jack lifted Shelly from the hot cement of the plaza. There had been no reason to share with Wyatt what Dan was most ashamed of. If he had seen Dan in the window that day, he could not have surmised the significance to any of their lives.

And yet here the face was, ambiguous, all but obliterated by sky and trees and the tower across the way with its many windows having reflections of their own, but looking out with eyes that seemed to grasp the full pathos of everything happening beyond the panes of glass.

Could Wyatt, with Shelly in his arms, have looked up at that window at the same time Dan was looking down, and recognized in the distant impression a presence that would linger there, in spirit, long after the moment had ended? Dan had once said that he felt as if, in marrying Shelly, he had won the princess without slaying the dragon.

In the end, at Devil's Sinkhole, he had finally slain it. His words to Madeline before he lowered himself over the edge—"I have to"—were proof enough of that.

Everything now in Shelly's life had come from that moment when

Dan looked down from the window, and Wyatt looked up. Carlotta came from that moment. Dan's regrets, and his atonement. Madeline's loss of her father. All of it was set in motion at that exact moment that now confronted her from the painting.

She studied the painting a while longer, trying to figure out what to do with the emotions it evoked, and finally she went downstairs and left the building. Rain and sleet were forecast, but she saw no sign of them yet; the day was brisk and sunny. It was nearly four, and shadows stretched in rows like ladder rungs from the small trees trying to get a roothold around the massive new building. She heard traffic from Martin Luther King Boulevard—Nineteenth Street, as she had known it— but this area of stone archways and winter grass and rows of small trees was mostly shielded from noise. Shelly was aware of the tower off to the north, invisible from where she stood, hidden by the many rooflines of tall campus buildings. The tower had been on her mind in one way or another for most of her lifetime, but over the years it had lost its sinister stare. If she could see it from where she now stood, the clock would look like any other immense clock, the shattered glass replaced long ago, the observation deck enclosed with a wire fence. Even the tower's looming height would be less impressive in the clear, gusting winter air.

As she looked in that direction, wrestling with the feelings the painting had stirred up, it came to Shelly suddenly what she would do. She would go up there.

Buttoning her coat, walking purposefully, she turned left on Twenty-first Street, and then turned again at the fountain with the bronze horsemen and winged rider, the wind blowing a cold spray into her face. She walked past Benedict Hall, where she had studied imaginary numbers that day.

How confused she had been about those numbers. She recalled now the parting words of the teacher as he had dismissed the class, a quotation from some famous mathematician about perfection—that a person would achieve it not when there was nothing left to add, but when there was nothing left to take away. It had proved to be true enough in her own life: She had never come anywhere near perfection, but had come close to a rightness with herself, through her losses.

She had walked out of Benedict Hall on her way to the plaza, an average girl from Lockhart, with flipped hair, wearing Dr. Scholl's wooden sandals and a pencil skirt too tight and a cotton blouse dotted with tiny flowers. Other people were coming and going now, in sweatpants and hoodies; it was winter break and the campus was quieter than usual but still imparted that sense of life and youthful expectation. It was, Shelly realized, a Monday.

Up the walkway, under the bare trees, surrounded by the cawing of grackles, she headed for the plaza. Under the bronze statue of Woodrow Wilson, she climbed the steps and started across, remembering the boy with the transistor radio, and the tinny sound of the song. Emblazoned on the front of the main building before her was the Bible verse YE SHALL KNOW THE TRUTH AND THE TRUTH SHALL MAKE YOU FREE. Long ago, she had found these words too abstruse—easy enough to dismiss in spite of their size on the building. She would like to think of them now as relevant to Carlotta, and Madeline, and all the secrets revealed and truths exposed, but the words still seemed to her useless and too high-minded to capture anything real about life. The truth did not set you free; it bound you to your life. It bound you to the people you loved.

Looking up at the tower, she paused for a moment. It was a pompous, ugly piece of architecture, in her opinion, with those tall vertical rows of windows. The security fence around the observation deck made the top seem cluttered, and the huge columns that housed the bell tower looked like a stunted version of the Parthenon in Athens. The building was pretentious and unappealing. And it still frightened her a little.

But she approached it, pausing only briefly at the patch of pebbled cement where she had bled, and wondering if there might be a remnant or stain—any sign at all that she had been there. Of course there was no indication. The pebbles that had blistered her face were cold now. The shadows sloped away from the bright main building before her. She turned and looked at the English building, but saw no one looking back at her from the windows.

Climbing the steps of the main building, she entered through the heavy doors and asked a girl who sat with a pile of books on the elegant, curved stairway if she happened to know the procedure for going up in the tower.

"You have to buy a ticket over at the Student Union," the girl told her. "It's a tour."

Shelly walked down the hall with its checkered tiles and hanging light fixtures and the marble drinking fountains, and left from the west entrance. She crossed the service drive and entered the Student Union through the doors that she and Wyatt had walked out of that day after their chance meeting and meal at the Chuckwagon—which, she noticed, was gone now, replaced by a different cafeteria and a cluster of fast-food restaurants.

At the information desk she was told there were still openings for the four o'clock tour. Tickets were six dollars, and she would have to check her bag. For an extra dollar, she could rent a locker. "You'll have to hurry," the student at the desk told her as she paid him. "The others have already gone over to meet the guides at the elevators." He gave her a key to a locker. "You can't take anything up."

Shoving her bag into the locker, she retraced her steps to the main building and joined the dozen or so people waiting with a campus policeman in front of the alcove to the elevators.

The crowd of visitors was eclectic, all of them bundled in heavy coats, the youngest a chubby boy about Nicholas's age, who wore a puffy parka and a ski cap and had rolled his tour brochure into a cylinder that he was using as a monocular, holding it to his eye and aiming it at places on the walls and ceiling.

Shelly couldn't help but picture Whitman on his journey through the building that day. It was well known how it had all happened. He had been in the building many times before and had often gone up to the observation deck. Once, he had even visited the school psychiatrist in this very building for help with his disturbing hostility and because he had abused his wife and feared he would do it again. But on that day of the massacre, he didn't intend to be merciful. He pushed his dolly, bearing a footlocker from his marine days, onto one of the two elevators. He was dressed in janitor coveralls, and no one asked him what was in the footlocker. It was filled with guns and ammunition and enough supplies for an extended siege: canned foods, an alarm clock. Among a lot of other things, he had a jar of honey, some deodorant, cans of Sego diet drink, toilet paper, and sweet rolls.

The tour guides today were two female students who greeted the little group and collected tickets while the campus policeman, an elderly man, escorted everyone through the metal detector and into one of the elevators. No one said much as they crowded in, the boy staring up at the floor numbers with his monocular. The elevator was halfway to the top when a man who stood at the back inquired, "I guess you'll tell us about Whitman?" The policeman didn't turn, but one of the guides, an Asian girl, answered. "If you have questions I'll try to answer them," she told him, "but we don't usually talk about him as part of the tour."

On the twenty-seventh floor, the elevator stopped and opened before a metal door that the officer, jangling a large key ring, unlocked. He admitted the group and led them around a corner and up a half flight of narrow concrete stairs, their shoes echoing loudly. Shelly imagined Whitman lugging the heavy dolly up these stairs.

At the top, another steel-meshed door, obviously not in place when Whitman was here, blocked the way. The officer unlocked it and escorted the gathering up several more flights to a third barrier door, this one opening into a room painted entirely gray—the ceiling, floors, and walls all the same gray shade, but glaringly bright from the sunlight through the banks of windows. A female officer greeted them here.

The group ambled around this small reception area, gazing out of the windows and waiting to be admitted onto the deck. Shelly remembered reading how Charles Whitman had clubbed and shot the receptionist here and dragged her behind a sofa and left her for dead. He had fired a sawed-off shotgun into a family of tourists coming in from the stairs, shooting repeatedly as they tumbled backward. All of this he had done while Shelly had puzzled about imaginary numbers and left her classroom in Benedict, stopping in the bathroom. She had walked out of Benedict Hall about the time that Charles Whitman had tied a white band around his head and stepped out onto the heat of the observation deck, jamming the door behind him with his rented dolly.

Here in the gray room now, the Asian girl said nothing about Whitman or about the subsequent tower suicides that had caused the administration to close the deck for twenty-five years until security measures were installed. She talked about the architect, Paul Philippe Cret, and how he had managed to create a cohesive look to the campus with the modified Spanish style of the red tile roofs. He had studied architecture, she said, in Paris.

The boy drifted away from the gathering, looking from the windows with his paper monocular.

"Does everyone here know how many bells are enough to make a carillon?" the Asian girl inquired.

No one did. "The bells above us are known as the Knicker Carillon," she said. "It's comprised of fifty-six bells, which makes it the largest carillon in the state. Tom Anderson is the current carillonneur. He plays once a day, three days a week, as a hobby. He's been doing this since the fifties. You might have heard him on rainy days playing

'Raindrops Keep Falling on My Head,' or 'Let It Snow,' when it snows. What do you think he plays during finals?"

No one ventured a guess. "I don't know," a man said.

"The Death March," she told him.

Shelly looked around at the few pieces of furniture and wondered if the sofa was in the same place as the one that Whitman had dragged the dying receptionist behind. A young couple had walked in off the deck after he finished stashing the body, having changed their minds about waiting ten minutes longer outside to hear the noon bells ring. They saw Whitman standing over the sofa, holding two rifles, and assumed he had come to shoot pigeons. They spoke to him, and he asked how they were, and they walked over the trail of blood, the girl presuming that it was varnish he had wiped onto the floor and warning her companion not to step in it. They had walked down the stairs to the elevator on the twenty-seventh floor just before the family about to be massacred had walked up.

It was frighteningly random—who lived and who died.

"We'll go outside now," the Asian girl said. "Tara and I will be happy to answer questions while you look around the deck."

"Can you see the turtle pond from up here?" the boy's mother inquired. She was a burly woman, wearing baggy trousers, a purple ski jacket, and a ski cap with a tassel. "The one that honors the people Whitman shot?"

"It's hard to see the Tower Garden from up here because it's so close to the building," the girl answered. "If you remind me when we're out there, I'll point out where it is. It's over on the north side. We're coming out on the south side."

Shelly had never seen the Tower Garden with its turtle ponds. She had known of the dedication a few years back because of the controversy over whether the university should create a memorial. Some people had felt it would only be a reminder of the infamous Charles Whitman, who ought to be forgotten. Shelly's emotions about the subject were too mixed to be opinions, and she didn't feel them strongly. She had avoided the debate as well as the garden.

Now she filed out onto the observation deck with the others. The cold wind hit her. She clasped her arms around herself and flung her hair back, taking in the view.

The scene astounded her, it was so vast. She ventured to the wall—a thick limestone parapet about four feet high. A protective steel lattice extending from the top and curving high up over her head made her feel as if she were standing in a birdcage. Directly below was the South Mall plaza, flanked by the two flagpoles in their grassy squares bordered by hedges—the U.S. flag on the right, in its circular concrete base behind which Wyatt had shielded her that day, and the Texas flag on the left, tossing erratically in the wind. The plaza itself was a flat expanse of beige stone with stairs leading down to the tree-lined walkways of the mall.

She was probably standing where Whitman had stood when he saw her. She could all but see herself back then: Up the walkway she had come toward the tower, up the steps, onto the plaza. She had hesitated, deciding whether to cut through the small opening in the knee-high hedge and across the grassy square. She had seen the boy approach her. He had lifted his hand to wave and then had fallen. And Charles Whitman had settled his scope on her as she had stared at the dying boy. She had dropped to the hot pavement of the plaza even before she heard the blast of the gun.

And now here she was, forty-one years and five months later, and Charles Whitman was gone. The frigid wind roared around her. The wall was as high as her chest; she leaned into it to watch the pedestrians—tiny figures with long shadows—make their way across the plaza. A girl mounted the steps and hurried across in the same direction Shelly had gone that day, cutting through the hedge and over the square of grass, just as Shelly had meant to. Looking out toward the far end of the mall, past the trees bordered by buildings roofed in terra-cotta, out beyond the fountain, along a perfect axis, Shelly could see the dome of the Texas capitol in the distance. How clear and open the vista was, compared to the sliver of vision she had seen through her squinted eyes that day, framed by her bloody arm: a view of the shoes of the man lying at the top of the steps, the soles pointing upward like the ears of a rabbit.

She swept her eyes over the skyline of tall buildings and cranes. To the left was the roof of the new Blanton Museum, which she had just walked from, and the art building, where Wyatt had painted her portrait, and the stadium, and farther off, Brackenridge Hospital. The hospital was now a sprawling series of structures built next to the site of the old one, which she and Jack had been taken to after the shooting and where years later she had brought Madeline into the world. It engulfed the location of the Planned Parenthood Clinic, long since demolished, where Shelly had gone for the pregnancy test, wearing the fake wedding ring.

She had been so devastated to learn that she was pregnant. It was different for Carlotta now, pregnant on purpose, unmarried, the father unknown to her, and everyone happy about it. The baby was due in a month. Carlotta had sold her shop and everything in it to pay for the sperm donation and the fertility drugs, and now was living with Jack and Delia indefinitely; they had offered to help her raise the child. Even being Catholic, Delia had accepted the situation, saying she had always wanted to have more children around. Carlotta would work part-time with a jewelry maker in Marfa and leave the baby—boy or girl, Carlotta had refused to find out—with Delia during the day. It was a good arrangement, if a little confining for Carlotta, who had loved the freedom to travel. Shelly couldn't help but wonder what her own life would have been had she been offered this kind of support from her parents all those years ago.

Her parents were in their eighties now, her father suffering from arthritis and no longer able to drive. It was strange for Shelly to see how easily they had accepted Carlotta when they finally met her a year ago. They had welcomed her into their home and proudly told their friends and neighbors she was their granddaughter, almost as if it had been Shelly's idea to give the baby up for adoption back then.

She looked at the place where Jack had fallen in the grass, and the wall he had been lifted over, and the red roof of the English building beyond the wall. In the falling light, she smelled rain, though the sky was cloudless, a winter blue, washed with a yellow smudge low to the west. The windows of the English building reflected the blanched light, and she thought of Dan standing there at the large center window on the third floor.

She missed him constantly. It was a shame for Nicholas not to have known him.

She wished she could see as far off as the river—the boat dock where she had met Dan. But the city was in the way. She was searching in that direction when the sudden pealing of bells broke out behind her. Wheeling around, she saw the clock face, so close that it filled her vision, just in front of her, slightly above her head. Pressing her hands up over her ears to block the thunderous chimes from the bell tower above it, she stared at the Roman numerals and the ornate golden arms.

It wasn't until the ringing had stopped that she looked for the pock-marks made by the bullets. She had heard they were still here, embedded into the stone walls around the clock, evidence of the Austin police, the DPS, county deputies, and civilians—students with deer rifles—firing up at Charles Whitman. They had shot at him from the ground and the rooftops with every kind of gun they could get their hands on, such a free-for-all that when the police had finally made their way into the tower and onto the deck, their lives had been endangered. The ground fire had been useful until then, pinning Whitman down and preventing him from standing up to take aim as he had done in the beginning when he killed so many people so quickly. It had forced him to shoot through the rainspouts at the base of the thick parapet, and whenever he shoved a barrel through, it was met with a volley.

Shelly stepped forward and placed her fingers into a few of the indentations in the walls. But she couldn't distinguish the bullet holes from natural holes in the rock; it all seemed scratched and dented. She turned to look at the rainspouts—narrow rectangular openings cut at even intervals—and tried to imagine Whitman crawling from one to another, firing and reloading, grabbing ammunition from his footlocker and moving from side to side of the tower, his radio tuned to the live broadcast with the urgent warnings for people to stay away from the campus. But try as she did, she couldn't really picture him there. All she saw were the floor tiles striped by the shadows of the security fence curving high over her head.

She had seen enough of this side of the tower, and would walk the full deck, she decided, one time around, and then be finished with this place.

On the east side, she found the Asian guide pointing out campus buildings below and shouting out their names over the roar of the wind for the tourists gathered around her. Shelly paused to listen, but she already knew the buildings: There was nothing up here she needed to see or wanted to find. It wasn't as if she had come up here to settle her thoughts about anything—especially Charles Whitman. He was a seething, selfish boy who had lost control, and thinking about him depressed her.

She walked around to the north side and saw a bank of black clouds advancing, carrying the electric smell of rain. The burly woman tried to hoist her chubby son up high enough to peer down over the wall at the turtle ponds in the Tower Garden directly below; she had planted her foot against the wall as a purchase. Looping his arms over the wall, the boy complained above the whistling of the wind that he couldn't see the ponds.

Shelly imagined all that had happened so quickly—within seconds—along this wall, the two police officers coming around this very corner and firing a pistol and shotgun at Whitman as he crouched in the opposite corner, his radio blaring the news about his actions. He had just fired a round up at the small airplane circling in the summer sky, manned with a passenger trying to shoot him, and she thought of how he must have felt victorious watching the plane's departure. But on the south deck, a civilian—a floor manager of the university's co-op, who had made his way, with the police, up into the tower and onto the deck—accidentally fired a gun into the west wall, causing Whitman to swing his aim in that direction, to the southwest corner, just as the two policeman came from the northeast and shot him.

Shelly walked over and stood on the red tiles and the white grout where he had died. The clouds were closing in on the building now, erasing the pattern of shadows.

But low in the western sky over the hill country, the rosy rays of the sun persisted. Storefronts on the Drag were dull and puny under the red sky. The street market was closing. Figures struggled against the wind, folding a canopy away. And off to the south, the sky was blue and the sun still bright.

She completed the square of the deck, returning to the south side and looking down once more at the places where she and Jack had fallen when the bullets hit them. She remembered lying there and playing dead, but couldn't clearly remember the pain—not because she had somehow risen above it by standing way up here, but because she wasn't that girl any longer.

Others were starting to go inside. The woman and her son came around the corner, their clothing billowing in the wind, the boy still clutching his paper monocular and talking about turtles. "They're reptiles," he told his mother. "They molt."

This was something Nicholas would have preoccupied himself with—molting turtles—and Shelly had to smile.

It occurred to her that everything she had needed to see up here just happened to be down there.

Turning to look at the face of the huge clock, she saw that the bells were about to ring.

# ACKNOWLEDGMENTS

Apparently I'm in the habit of thanking such a plethora of people in my acknowledgments that occasionally I've received messages through my website from someone asking, as tactfully as possible, why they had just seen their name in one of my books. Did they know me? Had they helped me in some way? A couple of times I had to admit I didn't have a clue.

It's probably a little inflated to have lengthy acknowledgments in a novel, and looking at the list I've scribbled in the seven years it's taken me to cobble together Shelly's story, I see some people I'm pretty sure will be puzzled to find themselves mentioned. But I'm going to acknowledge them anyway, because I appreciate the help they gave me—even if some of us might have forgotten over the years exactly what that was.

And then there are those I'd be terribly remiss not to thank. First and foremost of these, as always, is my friend Steve Harrigan, who tolerantly read several drafts and suggested major editorial changes that sometimes altered the entire focus of the story—always for the better. If not for his judgment and astute comments I'd probably still be trying to make this book worthy of print.

Jeff Long—writer, climber, photographer, and generous long-time friend—advised me at great length about the scene at Devil's Sinkhole. Without him, the poor stranded girl would still be dangling from the rope. When he read the final draft and discovered I had rescued the girl using only one Jumar—an impossible feat even for a courageous character like Dan Hadley—he told me how to rig a second one, in the nick of time, out of a shoelace and a piece of tow strap.

Timothy McBride, a brilliant poet and my favorite unmet friend, meticulously combed through the manuscript, as did my sister Noel Crook—there's nothing luckier for a novelist than a sibling who's a poet.

Caryn Carlson, Marco Uribe, and my mom, Eleanor Butt Crook, were immensely helpful in the early stages when I was defining characters and trying to figure out what the book was really about.

Pam Colloff set the stage for the story when I read in *Texas Monthly* her chilling account of Charles Whitman's 1966 killing spree. She generously put me in touch with a number of people who had been wounded or otherwise affected by the shootings and who were nice enough to talk with me and share their experiences. Among these I'm especially grateful to Cliff Drummond, Devereau M. (Matlin) Huffman, and Shelton Williams.

In his excellent book *A Sniper in the Tower*, Gary Lavergne provided a definitive account of that day and the events leading up to it. He was patient enough to spend a great deal of time walking me through the campus and explaining what had happened.

Several of my friends who attended UT in the sixties were a constant source of information, most especially Tracy Curtis, Michael Gillette, Kirk Wilson, and Sally Wittliff. Margaret Berry was a willing and reliable source on the university's history.

Alex Garcia initially and later Phil Schirmer graciously shared with me their knowledge and their passion for egg tempera. As Shelly's portrait began to appear in the story, Phil spent a lot of time on the phone and over e-mail answering my idiotic art-related questions. If there are mistakes, they are all unquestionably mine.

Anne Kay, Pat Moore, Carolyn Chamberlain, Rosemary Soladine, and Jean Henry at Marywood, formerly Home of the Holy Infancy, were helpful in sharing the history of adoption laws and practices in Texas. Joye Blankenship shared personal knowledge that helped in major ways to shape the story.

Colonel Alan C. Huffines was a supportive source on the Vietnam War, and although I used only a small fraction of the information he gave me, all of it was essential to my understanding of Jack Stone.

Scott McGehee of my hometown of San Marcos took time to explain how he and others escaped the 1970 floodwaters at Aquarena by shoving out the skylight of the restaurant, and how they rescued stranded people from the roof by swimming for the glass-bottomed boats. In the effort to keep Shelly's story on track I abbreviated the scene, but I'm still sorry to have left out so much thrilling detail.

David Keller was my go-to for all things Alpine: desert hippies, volcanic dikes, What's the best tall tree to put my owl in? And are the Marfa Lights honestly real? Many thanks to my dear old friend Dan Flores for introducing me to him. David Marion Wilkinson, Steve Griffis, and D. J. Stout were also fountains of knowledge about Alpine. Thanks likewise to Chachi Hawkins, Mike Perry, and Monty Kimball for the information about the Big Bend Ranch Rodeo, to my friend Kenneth Groesbeck of Camp Verde for his brainstorming about rodeos in general, to the Maverick Inn for their hospitality, and to the lovely staff at Hotel Limpia in Fort Davis, who made my family and me feel so welcome. Ben Toro of Moonlight Gemstones in Marfa was a great source on the intricacies of crafting bolo ties, jewelry, and belt buckles from local stones, though we met only by e-mail and he would not, now, know me from Adam.

For the scene at Devil's Sinkhole, Geary Schindel, chief technical officer of the Edwards Aquifer Authority in San Antonio, told me everything I needed to know about the cave and the mechanics of hauling a lifeless body up from the depths. Joe Herring described in detail what the morgue in the basement of the old Sid Peterson hospital in Kerrvile looked like in the early 1990s, and Bill Pennington explained what takes place in a morgue when someone has died in a violent accident such as Dan Hadley's.

I'm grateful to my friend Nelwyn Moore for her information about Beeville in the 1960s, to my old high school buddy Mark Williams for his veterinary advice about porcupine quills, to my brother Bill Crook for helping me yank quills from my own dog and for sharing his knowledge on too many topics to list, to Carol-Lynn Meissner, who let me poke around in her vet box, to Lillian MacDonald and Guadalupe Uvilla, and to Carlos Cigarroa, John Merritt, Joseph Quintanilla, Sheri Boyd, and Paul Salo for various bits and pieces of information that they may or may not remember having given me.

Gail Hochman—loyal friend and agent extraordinaire—is a blessing to any book and all writers lucky enough to find themselves in her care. Gail's passionate devotion to her writers is as persistent as that of a mother dolphin pushing her loved ones to the surface for air. Thank you, dear Gail!

Sarah Crichton at Farrar, Straus and Giroux has an uncanny way of working magic on books. I'm forever and deeply thankful to her for embracing my manuscript with her signature enthusiasm, for editing with such insight and meticulous care, and for making everything so much fun. Every single person I've been lucky enough to come into contact with at FSG has been pure joy to work with—all rock stars, in my opinion.

Last but most important, my husband, Marc Lewis, and my kids, Joseph and Lizzie, not only put up with my writing career and kept me company on several ill-conceived research trips, such as the hellish Amtrak ride from Austin to Alpine while I was on crutches with a broken ankle, but also taught me, in so many beautiful ways, what it means to be a wife and mother—which, after all, is what this book is about.

## A NOTE ABOUT THE AUTHOR

Elizabeth Crook is the author of three previous novels. Her most recent, *The Night Journal*, won a Spur Award from Western Writers of America and a WILLA Literary Award from Women Writing the West. She has written for magazines and periodicals, including *Texas Monthly* and the *Southwestern Historical Quarterly*. She lives in Austin with her family.